IN THE SHADOW OF THE STORM

Also by Anna Belfrage

Praise for The Graham Saga

"A brilliantly enjoyable read" *HNS Reviews*

"This is a series that will take both your heart
and your head to places both light and dark, disheartening
and uplifting, fantastic and frightening,
but all utterly unforgettable" *WTF are you reading*

"Anna writes deep, emotional historical novels, adding the
fantastical element of the time slip and a "what if?" scenario,
and creates for us a world in which to be lost in on rainy days
and weekend reading fests."
Oh for the Hook of a Book

"It seems Belfrage cannot put a foot wrong.
Long may she continue to give us installments
in this truly wonderful series." *Kincavel's Korner*

"Like I always say in these reviews, if you haven't read this
series, go do it!" *So Many books, so little time*

"An admirably ambitious series" *The Bookseller*

Further to excellent reviews, The Graham Saga has been
awarded multiple B.R.A.G. Medallions, five HNS Editor's
Choice, has been shortlisted for the HNS Indie Book of the
Year in 2014, and won the HNS Indie Book of the Year in
2015.

ANNA
BELFRAGE

In the
SHADOW
of the
STORM

Matador
9 Priory Business Park,
Wistow Road, Kibworth Beauchamp,
Leicestershire. LE8 0RX
Tel: (+44) 116 279 2299
Email: books@troubador.co.uk
Web: www.troubador.co.uk/matador

ISBN 978 1785893 506 (pb)
ISBN 978 9198334 402 (eb)

British Library Cataloguing in Publication Data.
A catalogue record for this book is available from the British Library.

Typeset in 11pt Bembo by Troubador Publishing Ltd, Leicester, UK

Matador is an imprint of Troubador Publishing Ltd

This book is dedicated to Mr Ian Mortimer, who writes non-fiction in such an engaging way it not only inspires to fiction, but also reads like fiction

Chapter 1

"Will she do?" The voice came from somewhere over Kit's head.

"Do? She will have to, won't she?"

With a series of grunts, the men carrying her deposited her in a cart. Kit made as if to protest. A large hand gripped her by the neck, tilted her head, and held something to her mouth. No. No more. She spat like a cornered cat, to no avail. Her mouth was forced open; sweet wine was poured, obliging her to swallow. And then there was nothing but a spinning darkness. Nothing at all.

When next she came to, a wrinkled face was peering down at her.

"Remarkable," the old woman said. "Absolutely remarkable."

Kit shrank back. Her heart leapt erratically in her chest, her gaze flitting from one side to the other in this unfamiliar chamber, taking in tapestries and painted walls, streaks of sunlight from the open shutters. Where was she? All she had were vague recollections of days on a cart, being jolted this way and that. Days in which strong fingers pinched her nose closed until she was forced to open her mouth and swallow the unctuously sweet concoction that submerged her in darkness.

"Not so remarkable when one considers that they have the same father," someone else said drily. A pair of light blue eyes studied Kit dispassionately. The eyes sat in a narrow face, a nose like a knife blade separating the two halves. A wimple in pristine linen and a veil in what Kit supposed to be silk framed a face that would have looked better on a man than on a woman – harsh, aloof and with an expression which reminded her of old John back home when he'd cornered a rat.

"M…m' lady," Kit stuttered. She tried to sit up but was pushed down again.

"Oh, no. You will not move until we have reached an agreement."

"Agreement?" Kit pulled at her hands, noting with a burst of panic that she was tied to the bed – a simple thing, consisting of a rough wooden frame and a straw mattress.

"We are in a quandary," the lady with the blue eyes said. For an instant, she pressed her lips together. "Stupid, wilful child!"

"Me?" Kit's head hurt, a constant thudding behind her eyes. What had happened to her?

There was a barking sound which Kit took for laughter.

"You, little one, will be anything but wilful. If you are…" The lady made a swift motion across her throat with her hand. Kit cowered. What did they want with her, these two old crones? The older of the women patted her hand.

"It will be none too bad." From the homespun material of her clothes and the coarse linen of her veil, Kit concluded that she was not a lady but a servant.

"Where am I?" Kit asked.

"Where you are doesn't matter. It is what you are that is important." The lady gave her an icy smile. "You are a soon-to-be bride. At noon, you will wed Adam de Guirande."

Kit did not know what to say. She didn't like the look in the lady's eyes, and for some reason she suspected that should she refuse to comply, she would end up dead in the latrine pit – the lady had that sort of air to her.

"Who are you?" she asked.

"Me?" The lady cackled. "Why, I am the bride's mother, Lady Cecily de Monmouth."

Kit wanted to protest. Her mother was Alaïs Coucy – dead since two months back. Grief tore at her, and she turned her face towards the wall, not wanting these strangers to see the tears welling in her eyes.

"I know all about your whore of a mother," Lady Cecily said. "My husband's great love, no less." She sounded bitter. "But at least his bastard will come in handy."

Kit tugged at her bindings. "I am no bastard!"

"What lies has little Alaïs told you? That your father is dead? That he abandoned her to pursue a religious vocation?"

Kit flushed. "My father—"

"Is my husband, Thomas de Monmouth. My husband, you hear?"

"But…" Kit slumped back against the thin pillow. For most of her eighteen years, she'd heard her mother's sad story: how two young lovers fled their irate parents, exchanged their vows before a priest and hoped for an eternity together – except that her father had died of a fever. She didn't understand. Life as she knew it was caving in on top of her – all at the say-so of this unknown woman. "You lie," she tried.

"I most certainly do not," Lady Cecily said.

Kit closed her eyes to avoid that penetrating light blue gaze. She suspected the lady was telling the truth: every question Kit had ever asked about her father had been met with an evasion, or the sad tale of star-crossed lovers as trotted out by her mother. When she'd taken her questions to John or to Mall, they had looked discomfited and referred to her mother.

A hand on her shoulder shook her – hard. "No time for all that now. Those dolts I sent to abduct you took their time getting you here, and we have urgent matters at hand. First and foremost, your impending wedding. Mabel, call for a bath – the child is revoltingly dirty."

"No." Kit raised her chin and stared Lady Cecily in the eye, summoning what little courage she had. "I'll not wed on your say-so."

"No? Oh, I think yes." Lady Cecily's eyes were of a sudden far too close, filled with such menace Kit flinched. "If you don't, I will have you thrown out of Tresaints and publicly branded a bastard."

"Tresaints? It's my home."

"It was deeded to your mother for life. And she is quite, quite dead, isn't she?" Lady Cecily smirked. "You have nowhere to go, little…Kit, is it? But here you'll respond to the full version of the name you share with your sister, Katherine."

A sister? Kit gaped.

Lady Cecily smiled wickedly. "What? You didn't know you had a trueborn half-sister? A girl who looks just like you?" She laughed as she straightened up to her full height. "So, what will it be? Destitution or marriage?"

Kit wanted to say destitution. She wanted to snarl and spit in Lady Cecily's face – accuse her of abduction, even – but she knew it would be futile. Women like Lady Cecily had power and wealth on their side. Kit had nothing. She swallowed a sob.

"If you say no, I will evict every single one of the tenants as well," Lady Cecily said, effectively nailing down the lid on what felt very much like a coffin.

"And if I say yes?"

"If you say yes, your father will include Tresaints in your dowry."

Kit was trapped. She knew it; Lady Cecily knew it. She acquiesced with a single nod.

Lady Cecily patted her cheek. "Good girl."

"Why?" Kit asked Mabel once they were alone. She rubbed at her wrists, at her ankles, and studied herself with dismay. Lady Cecily was right; she was covered in grime, and from the state of her kirtle, she'd been sleeping in it for days.

"Hmm?" Mabel gave her a vague smile, motioning for her to stand up.

"Why do they need me to marry this Adam?"

"Ah well, my lamb decided not to." Mabel chuckled, relieving Kit of one garment after the other.

"Your lamb?" Kit bit back on a snort.

"Your namesake, little Katherine." Mabel sighed. "That one has no sense of self-preservation."

There was a knock on the door, and Mabel hurriedly wrapped a sheet round Kit. Moments later, the room filled with men carrying a tub and a stream of water boys, bringing bucket after bucket of water. A young woman dressed like a nun entered the room with a basket of dried herbs. Lavender and rosemary were thrown into the steaming water, linen towels were piled on a stool, and just like that the room was empty – well, except for Mabel, who rose, went over to bolt the door, and then beckoned Kit towards the bath.

"Get in," Mabel said.

Kit remained where she was, gaze fixed on what little she could see of the autumn landscape through one of the two narrow windows. One of the shutters hung awry, she noted, creaking slightly as it moved in the wind.

"What is the matter with you?" the old woman complained. "Has an earwig or two crawled in through your ears and made you deaf?"

"That would have been unfortunate – and unusual," Kit muttered. Reluctantly, she dropped the sheet and clambered into the tub, her mind whirring as she attempted to find a way out of her predicament. This couldn't be happening to her! Only days ago, she'd been safe and content at Tresaints, mistress – or so she assumed – of the little manor that had been the only home she'd ever known. Maybe it was a nightmare. Yes, dearest Mother Mary, please make all of this a dream, a terrible, terrible dream, starting back when Mama died. Kit drew in a deep breath and held it, willing back the tears that stung her eyelids.

Mabel began scrubbing her back and Kit sat hunched, taking in her surroundings. Her gaze drifted over to the huge four-poster bed, enclosed by heavy bed-hangings in a dusty green. Other than the pallet to which she'd been tied, there was a chest, a table with a chipped earthenware mug containing a drooping bouquet of Michaelmas daisies, and two silver candlesticks, set on either side of a miniature Madonna.

She made big eyes at the carpet that covered the thick wooden boards – the only carpet she'd ever seen before was a small, precious square of vibrant reds and blues that her mother kept hanging on the wall in her solar. Her mother…Kit's throat ached with the effort not to cry.

"Why?" she asked.

"Why what? Lean back, so I can wash your hair." Mabel's hands busied themselves with undoing Kit's braids. "Such beautiful hair, m' lady, as dark red as your sister's – and just as thick. Well, Sir Thomas can't deny you, that's for sure, and—"

Kit's main concern was not her hair. "Why does Katherine not—" Kit spluttered as Mabel upended a bucket of water over her head. "Is he that terrible, this bridegroom of hers?" She

5

shivered. She was going to marry a man she didn't know – had never heard of – and every part of her baulked at the thought.

"Not really. But Katherine had her sights set higher, foolish girl that she is." Mabel exhaled. "And now God knows where she is." She lathered Kit's hair, hands softening into a gentle massage that had Kit groaning. Not since her mother's death had anyone touched her like this. Her throat clogged with tears. Her mother had lied to her. If what Lady Cecily said was the truth, all of Kit's life was built on a lie – and now her future was to be built on a new one. She forced her attention back to the elusive Katherine.

"She's gone?"

"The little minx," the old woman said, laughing softly. "She took the only way out."

"What did she do?"

"She refused to agree to the match with Sir Adam, and when Lady Cecily threatened her with the switch, our Katherine ran away. As I hear it, she is well on her way to Spain by now." Mabel clucked at this sad state of affairs. "Stole most of her mother's baubles."

"Spain?" A place Kit had only heard of, as exotic as the Holy Land or the wilds of the Barbary kingdoms. "She is travelling on her own?" Kit felt a rush of admiration for this unknown sister.

"Not any longer." Mabel clamped her mouth shut. "The silly lamb has found another suitor – just to properly shame her father. A titled man, no mere knight." She gestured for Kit to get out of the tub.

"Oh." Kit stood, arms over her head as Mabel patted her dry. "But why not tell Adam his bride has fled?"

"Katherine's wedding to Adam de Guirande is a boon from Baron Mortimer. It comes with other boons, such as a place in his household for Lady Cecily's firstborn, Richard, and more power and land for Sir Thomas."

Baron Mortimer? No one living in the Welsh Marches could have avoided hearing of the magnificent baron, even if Kit had never seen him – but then she'd seen nothing beyond Tresaints, except for the odd visit to Worcester and the annual excursion to visit Alaïs' uncle. She frowned: Lady Cecily's revelations went a long way towards explaining her mother's self-imposed isolation, but she had never questioned her mother's decisions – not until recently, when Tresaints had become too small, too boring. Why had Mama never told her the truth? How could she have gone to her grave without ensuring Kit knew? A surge of anger rose through her, crested and broke, converting into yet another wave of grief. Alaïs was gone.

"She must be very important for Lord Mortimer to arrange her wedding," she said.

Mabel's mouth twisted into a little smirk. "Oh yes, very important – to Lord Mortimer." She sighed. "It does not matter. Katherine is gone, but fortunately we have you to fill her place." She tilted her head. "No one will ever see the difference, you're that alike. Not alike enough to fool the family, but the others, yes. Well, maybe not Lord Mortimer – not if he gets close enough."

Kit was afflicted by yet another case of the shivers. "I can't do this." This had to be a grievous sin, to impersonate someone else and marry a man under false pretences.

"Oh yes, you can. I will not have my dear lord and his lady wife shamed by their daughter on her wedding day."

"I'm not their daughter! And I'm not about to marry a stranger."

Two eyes as hard as black pebbles bore into her. "You're his daughter – it suffices with one look at you to see that: same cornflower eyes, same hair. You *will* honour the contracts. If not, Lady Cecily will have you whipped until you bleed, and then she'll throw you out to fend for yourself. How long would you survive out there, do you think? You, a pampered young woman with no skills, nothing but her looks? You'd end up on your back in the stews within a week."

Kit swallowed. There was no way out. Mabel was right: if she didn't go through with this, she'd be left at the mercy of whoever came along, as would the tenants of Tresaints. "I'll do it," she whispered.

"Good." Mabel beamed at her and gestured for her to sit so that she could comb her hair. "How is everyone at Tresaints?"

Kit craned her head back. "You know Tresaints?"

"Bless your little heart, of course I do! I was born there. Besides, Sir Thomas grew up there, and I've been with him since he was three weeks old." She smiled. "Is my brother John holding up?"

Kit smiled. "Old but hale."

"Old? I'll have you know he's younger than I am."

Kit found it wise not to comment further on this. Instead, she answered Mabel's questions, and her heart lightened as they spoke of her home, the little manor nestled into an undulating landscape that to the south rose towards the Malvern Hills. She only had to close her eyes and she was there. The hornbeam hedge that bordered the lane was beginning to show patches of autumn brown, the old oak that stood closest to the house had begun to shed leaves, while the vines that clambered over the crumbling gateposts burned a bright, fiery red. From the kitchens came the scent of baking bread, and to the side of the manor house proper was the little chapel, her mother's favourite place in the world. Kit sighed. Home. When would she see it again?

A sharp rap to her head brought her back to the present. "I asked how old you are."

"Eighteen," Kit said.

Mabel looked her up and down. "You don't look that old. Are you untouched?"

"Mabel!" Kit threw the hag an incensed look.

"Just asking. If Adam de Guirande does not find his bride a virgin, there will be hell to pay."

"He will." Her stomach cramped, her eyes filling with tears.

"Shhh." Mabel gave her an awkward hug. "Don't cry – it will not help, will it? Besides, do you not see something good coming from all this? You'd never have found a husband on your own, would you?"

Kit threw her a heated look. "Robert—"

"Robert Fitzhugh? Down in Worcester?" Mabel laughed. "He'd never have married a destitute orphan." She gave Kit a little shake. "This is for the best – and Tresaints remains with you."

The room filled with people. A sea of light veils, of dresses in rich colours contrasting with white linen chemises and wimples. Lady Cecily sauntered in, followed by two girls carrying armfuls of colourful fabrics. Kit was urged to stand, and women chattered and laughed as they dressed her. Someone stuck a goblet of sweetened wine in her hand.

"Drink," said Lady Cecily. "It will steady your nerves." Beady blue eyes ensured Kit swallowed every drop before Lady Cecily turned away to talk to one of the other women. The wine tasted a bit odd, overly sweet.

"Poppy wine," Mabel said. "Your lady mother wants to ensure you're at your most docile today, my Katherine." She grinned, topped up the goblet and had Kit drink it all.

"I'm Kit," she slurred, but obediently downed yet another goblet of the sweetish wine. It made her agreeably relaxed, blurring the surroundings into dreamy fuzziness.

"You're Katherine de Monmouth," Mabel corrected sternly. She lowered her voice. "Over there is your sister Alicia, and you have three brothers called Richard, Thomas and Roger. Richard is Lord Mortimer's squire and your father is Sir Thomas de Monmouth, loyal vassal to Roger, Baron Mortimer, as is your future husband."

"I can't remember all that!" Kit said.

"You'd best try." Mabel patted Kit on the shoulder. "But today all you have to remember is that we are celebrating. Baron Mortimer has achieved what he set out to do, those dastardly Despensers are forever banished, and so we will make merry. And what better cause for celebration than a wedding – your wedding? Remember, all you have to do is to smile and look content. No one expects more of a bride."

Chapter 2

Adam de Guirande approached his impending nuptials with as much enthusiasm as a lamb about to be led to slaughter. Had it not been for the dowry, further enlarged by Lord Mortimer's generous gift, he would have refused the honour, all too aware of the fact that most men viewed his intended wife as used goods. He'd only met Katherine briefly, but rumour had her spending a lot of time alone with Lord Roger – especially during the past winter, when their baron had resided for several consecutive weeks at Wigmore – and Adam knew better than most just how carnal a man Lord Roger could be. Not for him the refined love of troubadours and chansons – no, Roger Mortimer preferred his pleasures in the flesh, so to speak.

Adam stood to the side, flanked by his brothers, and watched as the bride came out of the great hall. Surrounded by a flock of women, she made her way carefully down the stairs, supported by her lady mother on one side. A gossamer-thin veil covered her hair, but a sudden gust of wind lifted the material and Adam caught a glimpse of locks the colour of chestnuts. She wore her hair loose, a statement of her virginity. It made Adam swallow back a rush of bile. He was not looking forward to the bedding, had no notion how he would react should he not find her a virgin. He laughed, converting the sound to a cough. He knew she wasn't a virgin – his brother Guy had maliciously told him one sordid tale after the other, starring Mortimer and Katherine de Monmouth.

Walking some paces to the side of the bride was Lady Joan, Lord Roger's wife, and when she saw Adam she smiled, prompting him to bow in return. He had a great fondness for Lady Joan, a most gentle and noble lady who had more than once accompanied her husband on his campaigns, taking mud, bloodied men and dismembered corpses in her stride. This time, though, she had remained in the Marches, bringing the womenfolk to join them only when Lord Roger had concluded his recent matter with the king – and the rapacious Despensers.

Adam's gaze strayed, beyond the walls that encircled Stratfield Mortimer, to the tents that housed most of the Mortimer men. Disciplined and experienced, Lord Roger's men-at-arms had cut a swathe of destruction through Despenser land, meeting almost no resistance as they marched from Glamorgan through the Earl of Arundel's land. To do such was to invite future retribution, in particular when the Despensers – both father and son – were the king's favourites. Adam sighed. Fortunately, at present the Despensers were no longer in this realm of England, the king having been forced at sword-point to banish them.

The bridal party was halfway across the bailey when Lord Roger appeared, making his way towards it. Adam stiffened; did his liege lord intend to humiliate him on his wedding day by doing something inappropriate, indirectly marking Adam's intended bride as his? Mortimer said something in passing to his wife, his hand grazing hers, before approaching the bride. Katherine gave him a vacant look, as if she'd never seen the man before. To Adam's amusement, Lord Roger looked irritated. He gripped Katherine's hand and lifted it to his mouth in greeting, and she retracted her hand as if scalded. Mortimer's dark eyes bored into Katherine. She stared straight through him, mouth slightly open.

As his bride progressed towards him, it struck Adam she was moving unsteadily. Her eyes were bright and wide, her mouth was somewhat wet, and her cheeks were flushed.

"Milk of the poppy," William whispered beside him. Adam nodded in agreement. His brother was right – the bride appeared drugged. Mayhap this wedding was as unappetising to her as it was to him. The thought made him frown. He was uncomfortable with wedding a woman who might not want him – ever. He surreptitiously studied her waistline. Might she come to his bed already with child? She didn't look as if she was carrying, if anything she looked confused, blue eyes sliding from one person to the other as if she had no idea who they might be.

"I don't recall her being that tall," Adam muttered to his brothers. Or as shapely – the cut of her kirtle displayed a generous curve of hips, a trim waist. She lifted her hand to her cheek to brush at a strand of hair, and her fingers trembled. For an instant, her eyes met his, and Adam felt as if she'd sucked all the air out of his lungs.

William laughed. "She's a pretty girl."

More than pretty. His bride-to-be was striking, Adam thought, studying her as she continued towards the chapel.

"Oh yes! Pretty enough to catch Mortimer's eye," Guy snickered. Adam clouted his youngest brother over the head. But she was undoubtedly comely, if somewhat flat over the chest.

"It doesn't help much," he said with some bitterness. "I don't like used goods – especially not my women."

"Not much choice," William said. "Besides, she'll make you wealthy – her dowry doubles your land." He eyed his future sister-in-law. "She looks healthy enough. I dare say she'll give you a nursery full of heirs."

Adam shrugged. He bowed in the direction of Lord Roger, who inclined his head in greeting before striding off to join the bride's father. "I don't like it," he muttered. "Mortimer is playing with fire, and if he burns, so do we all."

"He won!" Guy laughed in his ear.

"He did?" Adam shook his head. "For now, maybe."

"The king pardoned him, did he not?" William said. "The deed is not yet a fortnight old, and already you fear it may not hold."

"It won't. The king will have no compunction in declaring his pardon null and void – he will claim coercion, that he had no choice, not with our lord's men camped outside London." Adam shifted on his feet. As one of Mortimer's most trusted captains, Adam had seen more than his fair share of the recent action, and he had been among Lord Roger's men at the recent meetings with the king. Tall and handsome, Edward II had swept into Westminster Hall, every inch a reigning monarch when in fact there was not a man present who didn't know it was Hugh Despenser who did the actual ruling.

Edward Plantagenet had developed such a fondness for his favourite that there were whispers of unnatural behaviour, of nights in which the king and Despenser did more than just share a bed. Adam found it hard to believe those rumours – the king had sired several handsome children – but King Edward had been close to tears when he exiled his favourite, and from the look he had thrown the assembled lords, Adam had concluded that the king intended to get his own back – somehow. It made his scalp itch with premonition.

"He had the right of it, I think," William said, nodding in the direction of Lord Roger. "The king should not have allowed the Despensers to ride roughshod over laws and customs in their never-ending hunger for more riches. If greed ever has a face, it will look mightily like Hugh the younger." He spat. "And it was downright foolish of the king to give the Despensers Mortimer land."

Adam smiled cynically. "He's the king, William. He does as he pleases."

"Wise kings don't," William retorted, scratching at his tonsured head. "Nor are great kings ruled by their favourites."

"Great kings don't have any favourites," Adam said. "They don't need them."

William shoved him. "Go on." He gestured at the bridal party, now come to a standstill by the chapel doors. He slapped his brother on the back. "And don't look like a man about to witness his own hanging."

Adam scowled at him, tweaked his scarlet silk tunic into place and made his way towards his waiting bride.

Somewhere halfway through the lavish feast, the effect of the poppy wine started to wane. Kit sat back in her chair and gawked. The hall was thronged with people, the floors were covered with strewn flowers, and dogs slunk from one table to the other. She fingered the heavy fabric of her gown. A deep, rich green, it was adorned by a wide girdle and embroidered flowers, and when she raised a hand to her head she could feel some sort of circlet on her hair.

"Here." Someone poured wine into her cup and she

downed it in a gulp. Aagh! It was too sweet and full of spices. With an effort she stopped herself spitting it out, not wanting to attract undue attention. The man sitting at her side turned towards her and smiled briefly, a guarded look in his eyes. She had no notion of who he was, but had a vague recollection of standing beside him some hours back at the door of a chapel. At the door of a chapel? Kit hiccupped; this man was her new husband – not that she had any memory of anything beyond walking up to stand beside him.

She dared a quick peek from under her lashes, met his appraising look and ducked her head. Her husband! Kit knotted her fingers into the fabric of her skirts.

From somewhere to her right came loud laughter, and the man – her husband, dear God, she had a husband, a man she'd sworn to honour and obey under false pretences – joined in.

"Look," he said, and she followed his finger to where a jester was prancing about in motley. There was more laughter, at the further end of the hall a fight broke out, and right in front of her danced a girl, accompanied by two musicians.

She felt as if she was drowning. So many unknown people, so much noise, and beside her a man she was now tied to for life. She felt an urge to run, to flee before it was too late. Kit rose, and the man rose as well, his thick fair hair gleaming when it caught the candlelight.

"I…" She sat back down again, giving him a tremulous smile. He just looked at her. "Wine?" she asked. Her husband – Adam – snapped his fingers, and a child rushed over, a heavy pitcher in his hands.

"Not too much, I prefer my bride conscious on our wedding night." There was an edge to his voice that made Kit quail. He smiled, yet another smile that came nowhere close to touching his eyes. Kit licked her lips; her husband was clearly as unhappy about having to marry her as Kit had been at the notion of marrying him.

"It's not my fault," she muttered.

"How do you mean, my lady?"

"It wasn't me who forced you to marry me, my lord."

He sat back, looking surprised – and amused. "There's not

a man alive who could force me to wed you," he said after some moments of silence.

"How fortunate – for you." She emptied her cup, waved it at the wine-boy. "Not everyone has a choice."

"It is done." He regarded her intently. "It is up to us to make it work – or not."

"Yes, my lord." She drank some more, false courage collecting in a burning heat in her belly.

Adam held out his hand. She placed hers in his, and it was warm and strong, closing over hers. He ran a finger down her wrist and she shivered. When he rose, she accompanied him to the dance floor. A graceful dancer, despite his size, he twirled her through the complex steps of the ronde, now leading her to join the line of other dancers, now swinging her in the air until she was breathless and rosy, laughing despite herself.

The music changed, and the people rose to stamp and clap, and there was her husband again, and he had her firmly by the waist as he led her through the crowd. His hold was strong, his face was set, and not once did he look at her as he hastened her along dim passages. Up some stairs, and she was surrounded by women who chattered and laughed while they undressed her, and Kit wanted them to leave but her tongue had gone numb with too much wine. Minutes later she was led stark naked towards the bed that dominated the small room.

There were candles everywhere, filling the room with the scent of beeswax and golden light. Kit wanted to hide, not to be exposed, but instead more candles were lit, and the fire in the hearth was coaxed into renewed vigour, adding tones of ruddy red to the soft glow of the candles.

The women settled her in the bed, her hair was arranged to lie over the pillows, and the door crashed open. Kit half sat up before recalling that she was naked. The man from the table – her husband – was standing on the threshold, in only his shirt and with an entourage of loud, laughing men. He – Adam, she reminded herself – stood half a head taller than most of them, and succeeded in looking unperturbed despite his state of undress. They led him over to the bed, his shirt was pulled off him, and the room erupted with catcalls and encouraging remarks.

Dearest Father in heaven! Suddenly Kit realised this was happening for real. He was in the bed, faces smiled down at them and she squeezed her eyes shut, but she could still hear them, all the people in the room. The priest intoned one last blessing, and the spectators cheered and laughed. Finally, the sounds of laughter and song drifted away. They were alone, and Kit had no idea what to do, lying beside this stranger.

His hands. Warm and firm, they skimmed her breasts, her hips. She lay rigid at first, but as he continued his tactile exploration, she softened, turning towards him. No one had ever touched her like this, and she was torn between shame and unfamiliar anticipation, her skin heating under his hands. Was she supposed to touch him as well? He was on his side, regarding her through narrowed eyes, and she felt intimidated by the assessing look in them, so she remained silent and passive, allowing this stranger – her husband, she reminded herself, her lord and master from this day forward – free access to her naked body.

A hand between her thighs, nudging them apart, and she felt mortified at the surge of pleasure she experienced when he combed his fingers through her curls, explored her privates. Her legs widened of their own volition, all of her melting under his expert fondling.

"Best get it over with," he said, and just like that he was on her. She panicked and tried to heave him off, but it was too late, he held her down, and with a grunt he pushed himself inside.

"Aah!" She couldn't stifle the gasp. He froze, staring down at her. She heard him mutter something, he pushed again, and Kit could feel something give. She turned her head to the side and bit back on a sob, lying perfectly still as he finished.

There was utter silence – no, not quite. Kit could hear the sound of her heart, of his breathing, but she herself was holding her breath in a determined attempt not to cry – that would be one humiliation too many on this terrible day. He lifted himself off her and rolled out of bed in one fluid moment, cursing under his breath. Kit curled together: he was displeased.

Adam went to the nearby table, sloshed wine into a goblet and drank deeply before passing it to her.

"I hadn't expected to find you a virgin," he said, eyes the colour of pewter raking her body up and down.

"What do you mean, my lord?"

"Don't give me that." He reclaimed the cup and leaned against one of the bedposts. "Do you think I don't know about you and Lord Roger?" Not only was he tall, he was big, a thick, fair fuzz covering his chest, the hair darkening closer to his groin.

"Lord who?" Kit's head ached.

"Mortimer," he clarified with an edge to his voice. "Our lord and master."

"I have no notion what you are referring to, my lord," Kit said.

He regarded her over the rim of the goblet.

"I don't!" she insisted – which was, after all, the truth.

His eyes flickered over to the bloody smear on the sheets. "Did it hurt?"

The sudden change in subject made her blink. "Yes. You were rough and uncaring." She pulled the sheet up, covering herself.

He flushed. "I thought—" He broke off, cleared his throat. "Lord Mortimer has been most generous to you – to us. Three manors as a wedding gift, and I thought these lands were intended to compensate for your lost maidenhead."

Lord Mortimer? What had that silly Katherine played at? "Well, you were wrong," Kit replied tartly. Her husband frowned at her and in one swift movement he pulled the bedclothes off her, leaving her feeling very naked under his gaze.

"Enough of Mortimer. It seems I have amends to make to my virgin bride." He gave her a tight smile, leaning forward to touch one of her breasts. "Small but pretty." She crossed her arms over her chest. He laughed, gripped her wrists and lifted her arms over her head, one large hand holding both her wrists

17

while the other yet again brushed at her breasts. "They'll grow bigger with time," he said, pinching one of her nipples gently.

"They will?" She looked down her own body.

"A woman grows rounder with each child, everyone knows that."

Children! Kit struggled, trying to sit up. How could she give this man children, and not tell him the truth? She had to—

"Lie still, woman," he said, tightening his hold on her wrists. "I am but exploring what is mine to have." He met her eyes, a smile twitching at the corners of his mouth. Kit licked her lips. She couldn't quite find the courage to tell him he had the wrong bride in his bed. Instead, she wondered what had given him the scar that ran like a thin white line from his left temple down to his jaw. Strong fingers touched her belly, moved downwards, and all the while he held her eyes.

She jolted when he rubbed his thumb over her cleft, when he slid a finger into the wetness he had left behind the first time round. She shouldn't like this, she thought fuzzily – to take too much pleasure in the joining with a man was sinful. But she did like it, and besides, he was her husband, and as such he had the right to her body, whenever he wanted it. Her hips moved in time with his fingers, making him smile.

He bent his head and nibbled her neck. She inhaled loudly. No, she shouldn't be enjoying his touch – but she did. Holy Mother forgive her, but she did! His mouth on hers, at first a brushing of lips, no more, but it had her heart racing. A forceful tongue demanding entrance, and she yielded gladly, pinned into place by the grip on her hands and his weight on her body.

Her husband: he was her husband and she could not deny him – did not want to deny him, not now, when he was gentle and kind, when his warm breath tickled her skin. Those fingers… she lifted her pelvis towards them, wanting to deepen the contact. A laugh rumbled through his chest, a strong thigh wedged itself between her legs. Obligingly, she made way for him.

He stared her in the eyes when he entered her, inch by careful inch. She felt stretched and sore at first, but when his fingers caressed her flank, grazed her breast, she relaxed. He held her gaze as he began to move. Her breath hitched. Heat raced up her skin, flew through her loins to where they were joined. He took his time, and Kit had never experienced quite so many sensations at the same time, had never imagined her blood could heat like it did. A wave of something akin to red-hot pleasure surged through her, scorching her. Coherent thought escaped her; she just was, her body shattering into a myriad of little pieces. She could swear he smiled before he let himself go.

They lay silent afterwards, him still on top of her. She caressed his back, fingers travelling over ridges and scars. He grunted and shifted to lie beside her instead. In a matter of seconds, he was fast asleep, but Kit lay wide awake. Only when this new husband of hers rolled towards her, draped an arm over her and mumbled, "Sleep, wife" did she drift off.

It was close to dawn when she got out of bed.

"Where are you going?" he said, opening an eye.

"I…" Her bladder was about to burst.

"The garderobe is yonder," he said, pointing at one of the walls. "Come back when you're done."

Moments later, Kit was urged down onto her back, her husband's weight and size holding her in place. But this big man was possessed of gentle hands and fingers that knew just how to touch her, of lips that left damp impressions on her neck and breasts. Not a man to hurry through his pleasures – her pleasures – she thought when he kneed her legs apart. Oh, no – Adam de Guirande took his time, those silver eyes of his never leaving hers. Neither was he a man who would ask permission before he bedded his wife – that was made eminently clear, no matter how considerate and accomplished a lover he was. But that was how things were ordained: the man demanded, the wife acquiesced. Kit gave herself up to the moment, to the feeling of skin against skin, to the burning heat he awoke within her. With a shudder he came, then collapsed on top of her.

"With luck you'll be with child within a fortnight," he said as he rolled off.

What? Her hand fluttered down to her belly.

"Good breeding stock, the lot of you," he added with a yawn. "Very good."

Chapter 3

When Kit woke some hours later, she was alone – for an instant, before Mabel bustled into the room, followed by two maids.

"All right then?" she asked, gesturing for one of the girls to hand Kit a steaming earthenware mug.

"Alive, at least," Kit replied, seeing no reason to tell the old crone she'd actually enjoyed some parts – a few parts – of yesterday's events. She sipped at the hot cider. One of the maids opened the shutters, and an icy blast of wind flew through the room. A bowl of water was set down, Mabel clucked happily at the sight of the stained sheets, bundled them into the arms of one of the maids and shooed them all out, before having Kit sit down on a stool while she brushed her hair.

"Ow," Kit protested when Mabel began braiding it – tight. "I never wear it like that."

"Now you do," Mabel snorted. "Married women don't go about with their hair undone – as you well know."

Kit made an acquiescing sound. Her mother had always kept her head covered, saying that all well-bred women knew better than to display their crowning glory to the world. Kit grimaced: unlike her mother, she had a thick tumble of hair that protested loudly at being so constrained. Her scalp hurt by the time Mabel was done.

"When can I go back home?" she asked, adjusting the sheer veil Mabel handed her.

"Home? Your home is wherever your husband is. For now you stay here."

"And if I don't want to?"

"What you want matters not at all. It is what your husband wants that is important." Mabel rapped her over the head with the brush. "Silly child! Has your mother not taught you anything at all? You belong to your husband – your lands belong to him, your clothes, your servants – they are all his, as is your body. If you don't please him, or if, God help us, you do not conceive, he may punish you as he sees fit, even put you away."

"Put me away?" Kit's hand fluttered up to her mouth. And what would he do when he discovered he'd been duped into marrying the wrong Katherine?

"He may decide you'd make a better nun than wife – not that it happens often, but it does happen."

Kit fell silent.

Mabel nodded seriously. "Best keep it in mind: a wife does as her husband bids – or bears the consequences." She sighed. "And Adam de Guirande has every reason to be distrustful of his young wife."

"He does? I have not done anything!"

"But Katherine has." Mabel frowned. "Witless girl, always simpering at Lord Mortimer, so convinced she could play the man."

"So it is true? Katherine bedded with Mortimer?"

"I don't know. But it does seem probable, tempting little wench that she could be when she set her heart on something. One of Lady Joan's maids stumbled upon them in a compromising situation." Mabel looked away. "My poor little lamb, where may she be now?" She cleared her throat. "Well, we will never know, will we?"

As Kit dressed, Mabel regaled her with a summary of the latest political events, insisting that Adam de Guirande would expect his wife to be well informed. Not that Kit was entirely unaware of the upheaval that had swept England in this the year of Our Lord 1321, but she gaped all the same.

Lord Roger Mortimer was a recently pardoned rebel, the king – Edward II, according to Mabel a pale and disappointing copy of his illustrious father – preferred his favourites, such as the Despensers, to real men of worth like Mortimer, and Kit's newly acquired husband was bound by oath to side with Mortimer. Bound by much more than oath, she gathered as Mabel told her briefly about Adam's life, from destitute son to a good-for-nothing drunk, to a young man with lands to his name – and all of it as bequests from Mortimer.

"Kings generally win," Kit said, interrupting Mabel halfway through yet another adoring description of the marvellous baron.

"Let us hope that this time he doesn't – and that he is wise enough not to invite the Despensers back." Mabel pulled the blue kirtle over Kit's head and helped her do up the laces. "Stay away from Lord Mortimer," Mabel said as she ushered Kit out of the room. "You don't want to set all those tongues wagging again."

"It's your precious Katherine who cavorted with him, not me."

"Now you're her, so best start working on repairing your reputation." Mabel grinned, showing off a set of yellowed teeth. "You can start by winning your husband's heart – or at least his loins."

"Why would I want to do that?" But she smiled, recalling the weight of his body, the gentleness of his touch. Given her situation, she might as well follow Mabel's advice, if nothing else because it would make her life easier to have a happy husband than an unhappy one. The idea of an angry Adam was intimidating.

Kit broke her fast on honeyed wafers and a mug of heated ale. Beside her, Mabel kept up a running commentary as to who was who, and Kit's head ached with the effort of attempting to remember all the names and faces. No sooner had she finished her ale than Mabel dragged her off to the small chapel, there to attend mass with the household. It was crammed and dark, filled with people who reeked and fidgeted, very different from the services back home in Tresaints, in a chapel that shimmered with light.

Kit staggered out from mass and clutched Mabel's arm. "It is wrong!" she hissed. "I have to tell him the truth." Guilt bowed her back; it dried up her mouth.

"You can't! Not now, not after the bedding. In the eyes of Our Lord, you are his true wife.

"The wrong wife," Kit moaned. "I must—"

"No." Mabel cut her off and dragged her back into the

chapel, all the way to the altar. "Swear that you will not. Swear it on the cross, on the Virgin and the saints. You must not tell him – ever." Her voice shook. "Lord Mortimer would be mightily aggrieved, and my dear lord would pay dearly for the subterfuge enacted by his wife."

"But what if he finds out?" Kit said. "What then?"

"We will cross that bridge if we must." Mabel gestured towards the altar. "Swear." Her hands sank with surprising force into Kit's arms, forcing her to her knees. Kit did as she was told.

The events of the last few days, combined with the emotional turmoil that inhabited her, left Kit quite exhausted, and even more so when she stepped outside into the huge yard. Stratfield Mortimer was crammed with people, appearing to Kit's eyes like a cross between a castle and a huge manor. There seemed to be men everywhere, leading horses, carrying armloads of weapons, loading carts. Most of the men wore nondescript tunics in muted brown homespun, but quite a few sported eye-catching creations in green, with the right shoulder and sleeve a contrasting yellow. Mortimer men, Kit concluded, squinting at the heraldic badge that decorated their chests.

A young man came striding towards them, hand raised in a wave. "Brother Richard," Mabel whispered just before the man enfolded Kit in a hug.

"And how is my favourite sister today?" he asked. There was an edge to his voice and he took a step back to study her.

"Seeing as you only have two, that's no major distinction, is it?" Mabel said, making Richard laugh. Kit gave him a shy smile, shocked at seeing so many of her features in this male face. The same eyes, the same mouth – even similar ears, somewhat overlarge. Richard's hair was much brighter than hers, but harshly cropped. His hands were large and calloused, his dark blue surcoat adorned with the pattern of bright blues and yellows that Kit recognised as the Mortimer arms. By his side hung a massive sword.

"My lady mother was right – the resemblance is uncanny." He gave her a wary look. "This must all be very confusing to you." He frowned. "Was he kind?"

"Kind enough," Kit replied, touched that he should care. She had yet to see her husband, and kept on throwing discreet glances this way and that in the hope of catching a glimpse of him. From the stables came a series of loud thumps, a horse shrieking in anger – or fear. Richard turned towards the commotion, frowning.

"That dratted horse," he muttered. "He'll be the death of someone one day." A large bay was led out, eyes rolling, nostrils flaring. It stamped and snorted, hind legs flying whenever anyone got too close. It was a handsome horse, even with bared teeth and ears laid flat against its head. The coat glistened in the September sun, each leg decorated with a white half-sock. A wide chest, a powerful neck, and a rump that bunched with coiled muscles.

"Lord Mortimer's horse?" Kit asked, mesmerised by the stallion.

"My lord has more sense than that," Richard said. "No, my dear, that's Adam's horse." As if on cue, Adam appeared, advancing slowly on the horse. Keeping his voice low, he spoke continuously to the horse – not, Kit noted with some surprise, in French, but in English. The stallion shivered, hooves moving restlessly over the cobbles. Its neck relaxed, the ears rose, and by the time Adam placed a hand on its neck, the stallion was no longer fighting the stable boys. He was standing still.

"Beautiful horse." Kit came over to stand beside Adam. "Spanish stock?"

"Aye, but keep your distance," Adam warned. "He bites."

"Not me, he doesn't." The horse's head snaked out, but Kit was too fast. "Oh, no you don't." She took a firm grip of the horse's nose. It snorted and rolled its eyes, but Kit just laughed, crooning softly as she rubbed the horse's broad forehead. "What's his name?"

"Goliath." Adam looked from her to the horse, at present standing quite still under Kit's hands. "I was told you don't like horses."

"You seem to be hearing a lot about me that isn't true." She gave him a look from under her lashes. His mouth twitched. "One should never believe hearsay," she added. "Much better to verify the facts oneself."

He laughed softly, standing close enough that she could feel the warmth of his body. "Is that so?" he said.

"It is. And some things one should verify repeatedly." She stepped close enough to whisper in his ear, feeling very daring. "Every night." It pleased her to see the light in his eyes.

She was called away from her husband by Mabel, who told her to make haste, as her lady mother was leaving and Kit was expected to help with the packing.

"Leaving?" Kit hurried after Mabel. Not that she cared.

"Sir Thomas must stay, of course, but Lady Cecily returns home to the Marches to manage the estate."

"And you?" Kit gripped Mabel's arm. "Will you stay?"

Mabel flashed her a grin. "I'm your nurse, and I aim to be raising your children as well, my lady, so aye, I'm staying."

Kit exhaled with relief – navigating these uncharted waters with no one to help her would be a daunting challenge.

The room was turned upside down. Kit came to a halt, surveying the bevy of maids who were packing everything into various chests. The feather bed, the hangings, the bedclothes and the various smaller items of furniture were all carefully stowed away, as were Lady Cecily's silver candlesticks and little statue of the Virgin. Lady Cecily sat in the middle of the room, sharp eyes on the girls who were handling her household goods, and at the sight of Kit she gave a satisfied smile – looking verily like a replete wolf – and beckoned her to approach.

"You look well," Lady Cecily said. "I take it your wedding night left you none the worse, then?"

Kit shrugged, not sure what to say.

Lady Cecily raised her brows. "And was the groom satisfied?"

"I think so." Kit looked away.

Lady Cecily chuckled. "Keep it that way, my girl." She gave Kit a considering look. "Make sure you keep Mortimer happy as well."

Kit couldn't believe her ears. "What are you saying, my lady?"

"Oh, don't be so obtuse, child! Baron Mortimer wouldn't be the first lord to enjoy his underlings' wives," Lady Cecily said, adjusting her wimple. "It might bring Adam more lands, more power, to do as our baron wishes."

Kit gave Lady Cecily a venomous look. Keeping Mortimer sweet would also line the lady's coffers. "I'm Adam's wife, not a whore to be pimped out. Besides, I don't think he wants me to."

"No?" Lady Cecily fiddled with her veil. "And must he know everything?" She gave Kit a look. "You must remember where your loyalties lie. Family first, Katherine, always family first." She clapped her hands together, told everyone to make further haste, and with a fleeting smile left the room.

"My own mother," Kit said to Mabel some while later, watching as the chests were carried out of the room. "Well, not my own mother, but all the same, and she's telling me to bed with my husband's lord?" She set her teeth. "I will not do it." And as to Lord Mortimer, should he ever try anything, Kit would scream like a flayed cat.

"It's the way of the world, lass," Mabel sighed. She gave Kit a look. "But it is to your credit that you are upset."

Lady Cecily and her youngest children left amidst a lot of loud noise. A litter for the lady herself, two carts and a dozen or so of men-at arms set off just before noon, with an assortment of servants following in their wake. No sooner had the party left than everyone made for the hall and the waiting midday meal, Mabel hurrying Kit along.

The large hall filled with retainers, and Kit quickly gathered that there was an invisible pecking order. The high table was reserved for Lord Mortimer, his immediate adult family and such men as he would choose to place there. Kit noticed with interest that quite a few of the men wore the flowing robes of senior churchmen, and when she asked, Mabel nodded, saying that the man sitting closest to their lord was the Bishop of Hereford, Alan of Orleton, and a good Mortimer man he was. The tables closest were for the Mortimer's trusted captains, his younger children and their nurses and an assortment of wives.

"You sit with your lord." Mabel shoved Kit in the direction of Adam before darting off to find a seat in the further end of the hall, where servants and men-at-arms sat cheek to jowl. Voices rose in laughter, people babbled in French and in what Kit recognised as Welsh.

After the long, confusing meal, Kit succeeded in sneaking off to her room – their room, she amended, noting that the small space was cluttered with Adam's belongings, most of them spilling from a large chest. In contrast, her few garments were hanging neatly from the clothes pole, tucked away in an alcove just beyond the bed and half-hidden behind a length of linen suspended from the roof.

She sank down on the bed and cradled her head in her hands. How was she to cope in this unfamiliar role? How was she to keep up the subterfuge that she was someone she wasn't? She'd spent most of dinner shoving the food around on her trencher while she watched the others eat. Spicy roasts, bread that was warm from the ovens, cheeses and wines, frumenty studded with raisin and almonds, miniature pies – she'd never seen such a selection of food before, accustomed to the plain fare and quiet peace of meals at Tresaints. Her stomach grumbled, unhappy with her for not having fed it more, but Kit had spent most of the meal struggling with her conscience. What she was doing was wrong, and things were not helped by Adam's courteous behaviour at dinner, or by the way his eyes had lingered on her. Sweetest Virgin, what was she to do?

Kit rose and wandered over to Adam's chest. Tunics lay thrown together; she saw the coloured leather of a boot, the heavy buckle of a belt. She picked up a long length of hose, found its pair and rolled them together. The tunics were shaken, inspected and folded, with Kit caressing the fine silks of his two supertunics. There was a deep blue woollen tunic that must fall down to his knees, a number of linen braies and three long linen shirts. She held one to her nose, capturing a faint remnant of his scent. Her husband…despite the unorthodox aspects of their union, she couldn't quite suppress a little shiver. Just the thought of him had her privates contracting, heat flaring between her legs. Lust, she chided herself, this is mere lust.

"My squire can do that."

She whirled, finding her husband by the door.

"I don't mind," she said. This was something she felt comfortable doing, with the added benefit of being out of sight of all the people who thronged the castle.

She folded a thick cloak, knelt to tuck it in, and heard him crossing the floor towards her. His boots squeaked, and a leg clad in thick hose appeared in her field of vision. She placed a hand on his leg. He inhaled when she moved her hand upwards.

"What are you doing?"

Her cheeks heated at her daring. Would he find her too forward? "Exploring my husband," she said, caressing the narrow patch of bare skin she found on his upper thighs. The hose-points were tied to the rougher fabric of the linen braies, and Kit counted two ties as her fingers traced their way round his leg. She suppressed a nervous titter. She had never inspected a man's undergarments before. His hand clasped hers, arresting it, through the fabric of his tunic.

"My turn today, my lord." She looked up at him, still kneeling at his feet. His face was flushed, those grey eyes of his inscrutable.

Adam gestured with his head. "The door – it's unbolted." He sounded hoarse, breathless even.

Kit lurched to her feet, nearly stumbling until he caught her, holding her close. Stubble gilded his cheeks, straight, fair lashes framed his eyes, and a lock of dishevelled hair fell across his brow. His lips grazed her ear, her jaw. She breathed through her mouth, eyes closed. His lips on hers, a strong hand at her waist manoeuvring her backwards, to the door. The bolt screeched into place. He pressed her against the door and she moaned into his mouth. Adam tore away, gasping for breath. His hands under her skirts, masses of fabric wedged between them, making it impossible to get him really close.

"Bed," she said, tugging at his belt.

"Here," he panted, "now!" He lifted her, entered her, and

she clung to him, helpless in his arms, incapable of doing anything but taking what he gave her.

"God's blood!" he exclaimed afterwards, leaning his forehead against hers. Her pulse was painfully loud in her head, her legs wobbly. Kit released her hold on his tunic, tried to straighten up.

"Indeed." The bed. She stumbled towards it, needing to lie down, to rest. The bed creaked with his weight when he joined her. Supple fingers loosened her veil and braids, travelled further down to the lacings at the side of her kirtle. Garment by garment he stripped her, before undressing himself and lying down beside her.

"It seems that in this we are well suited, my lady," he murmured. His eyes were dark and soft, his hand gentle as it caressed her cheek. "A good start," he added, leaning over to place the lightest of kisses on her mouth. Hesitantly, she raised her hands to cup his face.

"A very good start," she agreed. He laughed, took her hand and placed it on his chest.

"All yours," he said. "Explore me to your heart's content, my lady."

Chapter 4

In general, by the time Kit was up, Stratfield Mortimer and its surrounding tent camp was seething with industry. Long before mandatory morning mass, the smiths had the forge going, women scurried back and forth with heavy baskets, and small children rushed around, carrying or fetching. Some were far too small for such hard work, Kit reflected, watching a girl of about six lugging a basket almost as big as herself, full of soiled linen.

Baron Mortimer's children, in comparison, were clean and well-dressed, the eldest already a married man – even if his bride still lived with her mother, being only eight or so – and the youngest bar the baby a little girl with a special fondness for her father, an emotion that was reciprocated, to judge from how Mortimer would smile at little Beatrice, now and then lifting her up in his arms and swinging her back and forth until she shrieked with laughter.

"A most loving father, is our lord," Mabel commented, sounding proud. "A hard but fair ruler," she continued. "Even the Irish found him so."

"Ah." Kit did not care about the Irish's opinion of Mortimer. Now and then, she'd catch him glancing her way, and whenever she did, she'd contrive to look elsewhere, turn away.

By now, she had her immediate family down pat: her purported mother had given birth to ten children, of which five had survived infancy. That sounded very sad, and she felt a rush of compassion for cool, elegant lady Cecily – most momentary, given the lady's recent behaviour.

Of her siblings, Kit knew little; Alicia and the youngest, Roger, were with their mother, while Thomas was serving as a page to the Earl of Hereford and therefore as yet an unknown young man. Richard she saw plenty of, but generally only at a distance, as he seemed to consider it his role in life to follow his lord like a constant shadow.

The single member that truly interested her was her father, Sir Thomas, a man with a distinctive mop of curly hair, the same rich, dark red colour as her own. An able captain but an even better organiser, he served Mortimer as chief provider, ensuring there were horses and food, weapons and money. From being a small lord with no more than a couple of manors under his name, Sir Thomas was now sufficiently wealthy to walk about in surcoats made of rich velvet and edged with fur, his hose in silk and his feet encased in elegant, embroidered footwear made of the finest Spanish leather. Kit watched him from afar, and had upon a couple of occasions caught him doing the same, but so far the man had not approached her.

Apart from William, Adam's priest brother who served as a clerk, Kit had never seen so many gaudily dressed men. Not, perhaps, so surprising, as male company at Tresaints had been restricted to the odd visit from their elderly neighbour, Stephen d'Aube, and the servants. Guy de Guirande, her rather dashing if loutish brother-in-law, sported the most extraordinary creations, and at first Kit assumed him to be exceedingly rich, until Mabel pointed out that the young man was mixing and matching, sleeves of various colours combined with only the one surcoat of silk.

Most dashing of all was Lord Mortimer, his fingers decorated with gold rings, heavy golden collars adorning his chest. Around him hovered a bevy of men, almost as richly dressed, while his wife tended to opt for a somewhat more neutral exterior, even if Kit had no doubt that her gowns in soft green, her cotehardies and kirtles, were all made of the finest of fabrics. She wouldn't really know, having as yet had only one close encounter with Lady Joan, at which she'd felt dissected by cool blue eyes, regarding her with little warmth.

Her own husband opted for more sober colours, and even if Kit quickly gathered this was due to lack of means rather than a preference for dark blue and brown, she much preferred him that way, finding the male peacocks that surrounded her risible. Besides, in Kit's opinion Adam was the comeliest of the lot, sticking out like a sore thumb with his fair hair among the much darker Mortimers. As per Mabel, this was due to the Welsh blood that coursed through Mortimer veins, while Adam came from mixed stock, his father an impoverished knight of Norman descent, his mother of ancient Saxon blood.

Kit rarely saw her husband during the mornings, except for a brief glimpse at mass. At dinnertime, he was often invited to sit with Mortimer and his men, and Kit would feel disappointed at having her husband hogged by his lord – and even more so for being so pointedly excluded, never invited to join the circle of women around Lady Joan. But William was good company, and Guy could be entertaining, even if he mostly spent the mealtimes glowering at the men closest to Mortimer, resentment at not being included oozing out of every pore.

"He is one impoverished knight among many," William said with a shrug when she cautiously raised the subject of Guy. Kit was surprised by his callousness.

"But why is he poor, when Adam—"

"Adam is not much richer," William interrupted. He gave her a quizzical look. "Surely you know that? I thought that was why you were so disinclined to wed him."

"Disinclined?" Kit smiled at Adam's broad back.

"It is your dowry that raises him from minor lord to somewhat less minor lord," William said with a laugh.

Kit made a sound that she hoped conveyed that she already knew all this. "And Guy?"

"No one is about to arrange a marriage for him. Adam is one of Lord Roger's most trusted men. Guy has so far never distinguished himself at other sports than brawling and whoring."

"You don't like him much, do you?"

"Not much, no." William sighed. "He's my brother, but he thrives on discord, and is intensely jealous of everyone, primarily Adam."

"How jealous?" Kit asked, regarding her youngest brother-in-law in a new light.

"Too jealous," William replied grimly. "But then, it isn't

always easy to be the runt, and even less so when you're not part of the original litter."

"He's not your brother?" Kit eyed the swarthy youngest de Guirande brother. Where both Adam and William were fair and light-eyed, Guy was all dark hair, dark eyes. The only thing the three men had in common was their height.

"Not by blood." William shrugged. "But he bears our name, and our father took him as his own."

In the afternoon, Adam would frequently come to find her, and they'd take a walk, or visit the kennels, or loiter in the garden – hours spent discovering each other. Mostly, they'd go riding, Kit relishing this opportunity to escape the constant press of people.

"Why won't you let me ride him?" Kit asked, like she always did, eyeing Goliath's gleaming hide with envy.

"He is too much of a horse for a woman." Adam frowned. "This is no mild-mannered palfrey, this is a warhorse."

"He has four legs and a tender mouth. He's a horse, just like any other horse." She rode her mare closer. "I reckon I'd have him dancing for me in less than an hour." Despite her own fear of horses, Alaïs had insisted Kit be taught to ride, and she'd been astride her first horse before the age of four.

"Well, we will never know, will we?" Adam set his heels to the stallion and charged off, holding him back to wait for her by the nearby stream. Around them, soft hills flowed in undulating waves towards a distant, unseen sea, an autumn sun painting the slopes in every nuance of green and brown possible.

"Is it me or the horse you're most concerned about?" she teased once she'd caught up.

"The horse, of course. He's worth his weight in gold, and especially on the battlefield." Adam stroked the arched neck.

"And I'm not," she said.

He gave her a considering look. "Not your entire weight, no," he said, laughing out loud when she stuck her tongue out. He rode close enough to grip her reins, drawing them both to a halt. "But I don't want you to come to any harm either." He leaned towards her and placed his lips on her cheek, then waited until she turned her face towards him to kiss her again, this time on her lips. "So stay away from him, or I'll have you belted."

"Belted?" she murmured.

"I'll do it myself," he promised, his mouth moving against hers. "In bed."

"Careful. You're making it sound tempting." She bit his lip. Without knowing quite how, she was suddenly sitting in front of him, making Goliath snort and throw with his head.

"Naughty wench," he scolded, "I told you to stay well away from my temperamental stallion, and then where do I find you? Astride him!"

"I didn't—"

"Shush. Consider instead what the consequences will be." His voice quivered with laughter. The horse took a couple of stiff-legged jumps. Kit was transferred back to her own mount and rode back, her cheeks heating as her husband told her exactly what he intended to do to her once he had her in the privacy of their bedchamber.

"You look well, daughter. All this fresh air seems to become you."

Kit whirled. Sir Thomas was standing some feet away, regarding her intently.

Kit handed the reins of the palfrey to one of the stable lads. "I enjoy riding, my lord. My mother insisted I be taught to do so."

He smiled, but to her consternation the smile wobbled, his eyes filling with tears. "Your mother," he sighed. "My Alaïs."

"Yes, my mother, your mistress – or whore, to use Lady Cecily's words."

"Alaïs was no whore." Sir Thomas looked away. "A *mesalliance*, an impossibility, and yet she was my single love."

"A single love you never visited," Kit said harshly.

"A single love I could not visit – not unless I wanted to risk both her life and yours." His face twisted into a scowl. "Cecily would have had no compunction in having you assassinated. She hated Alaïs and her hold on my heart."

To Kit's surprise, Sir Thomas enfolded her in an embrace. "I am so glad that I at last get to meet you." He tugged at a wisp of her hair. "My daughter, in the flesh." He cupped her face, studying it intently. "Mabel is right, you are uncannily similar to our Katherine – but here…" he touched her nose, "…and here…" he tweaked her chin, "I see Alaïs shining through."

Kit disengaged herself and retreated a couple of steps. Having a father was something that would take getting used to.

Sir Thomas threw a quick look at Adam, who was talking to William. "Have you resigned yourself, then?" he said in an undertone. Kit wasn't quite sure what he meant. "To the marriage," he clarified.

"Too late to do anything about that now," she replied, and Sir Thomas looked quite stricken.

"I…" he began, licking his lips. "My lady wife was quite insistent this would be for the best."

"She was?" Kit pursed her mouth. Horrible, manipulative woman, saving the interests of her own family at the expense of her husband's love child. All in all, that particular aspect of things was probably a further boon to Lady Cecily. "Maybe it is." She sank her eyes into him. "As long as Lord Mortimer doesn't expect me to…err…meet his demands. My lord husband would be most displeased – and besides, I don't want to."

"No, no, of course not." Sir Thomas' cheeks acquired a ruddy hue. "Our lord is an honourable man. He would never force a woman."

"My lady mother would expect you to do whatever is required to keep Lord Roger happy."

Kit jumped at the voice, turning to face a scowling Richard. He looked from his father to Kit and back again. "You owe us as much, she says, as without her, you'd be begging – or worse – for your livelihood."

"Richard!" Sir Thomas glared at his son. "This is your sister, and you will treat her with courtesy – always."

"My sister?" Richard looked at Kit. "She's not my—"

"Oh, yes she is! She is my daughter – a most beloved daughter whom I have never had the opportunity to treat as I should. But because of your mother's interference – without my collusion, I might add – my girl is now openly a part of my family. Our family."

Richard looked about to protest.

"Not one more word," Sir Thomas warned. "And best keep in mind that Mortimer would not like it if he found out he'd been tricked. It might cost you more than you gained."

Richard studied Kit in silence. Finally, he shrugged. "One sister is more or less like the other. It's not as if I spent much time with Katherine anyway."

"Did he mean it, do you think?" Kit asked Mabel later, having recounted the entire incident.

Mabel sighed. "Richard and Katherine were never close, but he is very fond of his mother. It is in his interest to not expose you, but do not expect him to come quickly to loving you."

"Oh." Kit picked at a thread that had come unravelled on her sleeve. "Will he ever?"

"Does it matter?" Mabel asked. Kit considered this for some time.

"No, not really." But it did.

Mabel smiled and patted her arm. "You have other people, m' lady. People like me, your father and your husband."

"You?" Kit gave Mabel a shy smile.

"Most certainly me. Sir Thomas would not forgive me if I did not take care of his precious girl."

"Precious?" Kit shook her head. "Not precious enough for him to visit my mother."

"Precious enough that he stayed away. Precious enough that he had Father Luke installed as your chaplain. Precious enough that he has a collection of small likenesses of you and your mother, drawn by Luke and sent to him."

"Oh." Kit chose not to continue this discussion, confused by how it made her feel.

According to Kit, the best moment of the day was when Adam was finally excused from his lord's presence and could retire

36

with her to their chamber. The little room looked its best in the dark, several wax candles spreading a golden light that was further enhanced by the fire in the hearth. Apart from the bed and a couple of chests, the room contained nothing more than some stools and a table – the pallet bed intended for Adam's squire had taken up permanent residence in the antechamber, even if Lionel complained loudly about how cold it was, sleeping so far from a fire.

On the table stood a board of draughts, a worn set that Adam admitted to having made himself when he was a boy. It reminded Kit of her mother. Alaïs had been a keen draughts player, showing no mercy towards her adversary. Kit sighed, arrested by a sudden, vivid recollection of her mother, laughing as she transferred yet another of Kit's pieces off the board.

"Coming?" Adam's voice interrupted her reverie. He was already in bed, clothes thrown in a heap on the floor. He watched her avidly as she undressed, making her reflect on the fact that she had never been this naked with another human being before. No one had gawked at her quite as appreciatively as Adam did. No one had beckoned her towards him quite as possessively. It made her smile, to see herself reflected in his eyes and know, without a doubt, that she belonged to him just as much as he belonged to her. Until she remembered that he thought her someone else.

Chapter 5

After three weeks at Stratfield Mortimer, Mortimer decided to move on. It took close to two days to make the necessary preparations, two days in which Adam spent every waking minute overseeing his men. Finally, at dawn on the third day, the men-at-arms marched off in good order, a field of bright green tunics that set a steady north-westerly pace. After the men came the carts, carrying tents and cooking utensils and weapons and food. Very much food, Adam sighed, counting the stacked barrels containing everything from dried peas to salted herring.

They arrived in Oxford two days later, the men silent and tired after long days on their feet. But when Lord Roger promised them ale and wine they cheered up, sufficiently re-energised to set up tents and dig privy ditches. Adam ensured his men were comfortable and hurried off to find his wife.

Lord Roger's house in Oxford was much smaller than the sprawling estate in Stratfield Mortimer. Accordingly, accommodation was cramped, and Adam had been allotted a room right under the eaves, small and dark. Katherine regarded the space in silence.

"How do you think they got the bed in?" she asked, taking the single step necessary to reach it.

"In bits and pieces," Adam laughed. He sidled by his chest and sat down on the narrow bed. It groaned under his weight, and when Katherine sat down beside him, it sagged.

"Very comfortable." Her nose wrinkled as she studied the linen, the dusty bed-hangings. "And here was I thinking you were one of Lord Mortimer's most valued captains."

"I am." He bristled. "But accommodation is handed out according to rank – you know that."

"Ah. So where will I find my lord father?"

Was she baiting him, indirectly reminding him that she was more high-born than he was? "I'm sure you will find him – and should you prefer his accommodations to these, Sir Thomas can arrange for a pallet bed." He stalked out, ignoring her voice telling him to wait.

After vespers and supper – a hasty affair, surprisingly sparse – Adam watched his wife leave the hall with the other women. She threw him a look over her shoulder, brows pulled together into a slight frown. He had been rude towards her throughout the meal, still smarting from her veiled insult as to his lower rank. Except, of course, that she had seemed genuinely bemused, those eyes of her darkening with hurt. And when he'd shrugged off the hand she had placed on his arm, pointedly turning his back on her, he had heard her inhale. Moments later, there'd been the rustle of heavy wool, and without a word she'd glided off.

Now, as she hesitated by the door, he gave her a lopsided smile. He was rewarded with the slightest of nods in return. He raised his brows and lifted his head upwards, mouthing a "later". Katherine blushed and ducked her head.

"And is your wife meeting with your approval?" Lord Roger sounded amused, eyes darting from Katherine's receding back to Adam.

"Yes," Adam replied, having no intention of discussing this further, not with him.

Lord Roger's eyes sparkled with laughter, but he chose not to comment further, leading the way to the large table at which several men were waiting.

It was over three weeks since Adam had wed Katherine, and it seemed to him an inordinate amount of time had been spent in bed with her – long, leisurely hours in which he showed her just what he liked. What she liked, he didn't need her to tell him, it sufficed to study her reaction, from the way her skin flared in red patches to the way her pupils dilated. It made him smile, to visualise her in their bed.

A clap to the shoulder recalled him abruptly to the present, and he bowed to Lord Chirk, Mortimer's uncle, before taking his seat at the lower end of the table. The talk was of war – unfortunately. With September shifting into October, the king had decided to go to Canterbury on a pilgrimage. Mortimer's spies knew otherwise: the king planned to meet Hugh Despenser on the Isle of Thanet, and just the name of his hated adversary had Lord Roger grinding his teeth.

"He gave his oath!" Lord Roger slammed down his goblet. "What sort of a king goes back on his oath?"

"He's weak," Lord Chirk said. "Not like his father. And so he needs these sycophants, these fawning dogs that whisper advice in his ear and bite whoever he wants bitten."

"Like me," Lord Roger said bitterly, throwing himself into a chair. "Not yet three years ago, I was his most trusted baron, and now look at me! Driven to take up arms against my king – my king!" He waved his cup and Richard rushed over to fill it. "Will Lancaster stand with us, do you think?" he asked, directing himself to his uncle.

"He has as much to lose as you do," Lord Chirk said.

"That's not an answer to my question."

"That's all the answer you'll get, lad – at least for now."

Mortimer nodded, looking morose. "Well, for now we plan and prepare – and hope the king does nothing rash." With that, Lord Roger turned the subject to provisioning his forces.

Adam's attention wandered. His lord was striding back and forth before the fire, the skirts of his embroidered surcoat swirling with each step he took. Rich and powerful, Lord Roger was also an attractive man, and Adam felt a surge of anger rising through him at the thought of this man – his lord – making free with his Katherine. Not that he'd noted any indication of untoward affection between them, and this despite him studying them intently. Katherine had, as far as he could make out, not exchanged a single word with Lord Roger since their wedding, and although now and then Adam had caught Lord Roger looking at his wife, it had been no more than the look Mortimer would give any attractive woman. And yet…Guy's descriptions had been far too vivid for Adam to totally erase them from his mind.

Once the meeting was over, Adam left the hall, but was called back by Richard, who hurried towards him.

"Gloomy matters," Richard said. Adam just looked at him. Richard de Monmouth was as yet not knighted, a young man untried in battle but very committed to his lord. According to Guy, it was not a coincidence that Richard had been chosen to be Roger's squire – the lad had been raised so high because of his sister. Hellfire! Adam had to stop recalling every poisoned word his youngest brother had told him. As per William, Guy was jealous, and so Adam had best take everything he had to say with a huge pinch of salt. Maybe William was right – Adam hoped he was – but it wasn't only Guy, was it?

"He's very fond of Katherine," Richard said casually, a malicious twinkle in his eyes. What? Adam came to an abrupt halt. Richard backed away, hands raised. "I'm just saying," he whined. "Lord Roger has a fondness for her."

"She's my wife," Adam snarled. "No one touches my wife."

"If Lord Roger wants to, he will. He could even have the qu—" Richard broke off, looking aghast.

"What?" God help them all! Could Lord Roger really have done something as foolish as playing court to the queen?

"Nothing," Richard muttered. He eyed Adam from under lashes as thick as Katherine's. "What our lord wants, he takes."

Adam turned on his heels and strode off.

He couldn't help it. Through the following days, he watched his wife as a hawk, following her as discreetly as possible as she went about the household. But watch as he might, he saw nothing that merited this black jealousy, this heavy weight that seemed to make him choke whenever he considered the notion that there might be some truth in all that gossip, and maybe his Katherine had writhed in Lord Roger's arms just as she did in his. Fancies, he tried, but this spectre lived in his head and coloured his imaginations, making him short-tempered in general, but in particular with his wife.

"What ails you?" Kit scowled at her husband.

"Nothing." He sidestepped her and exited the room,

calling for Lionel. Kit sank down to sit on the stool. The man was enervating at times, and these last few days his temper had deteriorated to the point of him being constantly rude. No matter what she did, he found fault in it. Either her veil was not properly draped, or her hair had escaped from its braid, or her cloak had to be pulled close. Should she smile and laugh at any other man he would frown at her, yelling at her in private that she should be more modest. Besides, he was drinking too much, and last night had been quite unpleasant before he had left the room, slamming the door in his wake.

She didn't understand. The warm and tender lover had morphed into a surly brute, rebuffing her advances and making her feel like a fool for starting to care for him. Care for him? She was falling in love with him, and now look how he treated her!

Kit went to find Mabel, hoping to find a supportive audience. Instead, Mabel shrugged and told her men were inexplicable at times, and maybe it was all this talk of renewed war that had Adam walking about like a thundercloud.

"Or," she added, "maybe he fears that Lord Mortimer will try to woo you back – now that you've had some weeks of marital bliss."

"Woo me back? He's never had me! Besides, wouldn't that be a terrible thing to do? Not only am I married, but his wife is here." Lady Joan was something of an enigma to Kit. Where her husband was loud and commanding, Lady Joan was unassuming and mild – but she ran her household with a steel hand. At times, Kit caught Lady Joan looking askance at her, and it made her skin crawl to have this noblewoman regard her as if she were a flea she would gladly like to squash. "Shouldn't he be faithful to her?"

Mabel laughed, long and hard. "Make no mistake, m' lady, our lord loves his wife – and she loves him. But a man like that needs more than she can give. He burns from within, he does, while Lady Joan…well, she is all cool smiles and soft hands. She knows he can't help himself – and she also knows he always comes back to her." She laughed some more. "It is Lady Joan that arranged for your wedding. Lord Mortimer had no choice but to agree, and now that you're wed, he should keep his distance."

"Should?" So far, Mortimer had behaved impeccably. Kit hoped things would remain that way.

"Katherine was a wild thing," Mabel said, her voice softening. "I'm not sure he got his fill of her."

"How unfortunate – for him. He's not getting anything from me," Kit told her.

It must have been God's idea of a jest, that on this day of all days, Kit ran into Lord Mortimer. Days of mild October rain had transformed into windy, sunny days, and Kit enjoyed spending time outdoors – preferably as far away as possible from her sullen husband. The Oxford house consisted mostly of utilitarian outdoor space, but in one secluded corner, there was a small bower, and even this late in the year there were roses, small white roses that reminded Kit of home. Her mother had spent hours on her roses, filling her solar with freshly cut flowers for as long as they bloomed. At present, Kit was mostly angry with Alaïs, but sitting in a ray of October sun she was overcome with grief. She rested her head against the sun-warmed wall behind her and closed her eyes, her head filling with memories of her mother.

"Are you planning on avoiding me forever?"

The voice made Kit start, and she sat up, pulling the heavy cloak closer.

"My lord," she said, when Mortimer stepped out from the shadows. He smiled, a slight stretching of the lips that didn't reach his eyes. Kit got to her feet.

Mortimer reclined against the wall, crossed his arms over his chest and regarded her. The deep green of his surcoat contrasted with the shimmering golden silk of the tunic he wore beneath, both colours serving to highlight his chiselled features and dark, hooded eyes. He was an attractive man, Roger Mortimer, from his close-cropped dark hair to the ease with which he carried himself. Not so much tall as powerful, he exuded authority, in everything from how he raised his brows to how he gestured with his beautiful hands. Kit estimated him to be somewhere between thirty and forty, a man in his prime, a man confident in his own strengths and accustomed to having things his way.

"Are you that content with your new husband that you have forgotten your noble lover?" he said in a teasing tone, but he wasn't amused, she could see that in how he tensed his jaw. "The man who dowered you so adequately for that lost maidenhead?" He raised a finger and crooked it, beckoning her towards him.

Kit shook her head. "I'm a married woman now." She made for the gate, but he was fast: three long strides and he had her cornered, his body hindering her from leaving. "Besides, your wife is here." She shrank away from him.

"That hasn't stopped you before," Mortimer said, reaching out to touch her cheek.

"Which was wrong of me," she replied, slapping his hand away.

That made him laugh. "We but dallied, you and I – some moments of bed-sport, no more. My lady wife knows better than to accord such things more importance than they merit. So, am I to take it my wild Kate has turned a new leaf?" He gripped her chin, holding her still. A strong thumb caressed her cheek.

"Your wild Kate no longer exists," she retorted. At least not here.

He studied her. "Hmm. You do look different somehow. Is it Mabel putting the fear of God in you?"

"No." She tried to yank free of his hold. "Release me, my lord."

"Lady de Guirande forgets her place," he said coldly. "She also forgets my generous wedding gift."

"Lady de Guirande is no whore to be paid in land. She is a married woman, and must do as her conscience bids her."

He relaxed his hold, looking amused. "Conscience? And what would little Katherine know about conscience?" His other hand slid down her hip, and he was standing far too close, close enough that she could feel the outline of his body pressing against hers.

"More than you think." She leaned away from him. "If you don't let go, my lord, I'll stamp on your foot."

"Try." He laughed. So she did. Mortimer muffled an oath

44

and Kit fled, nearly colliding with her husband when she turned the corner. He looked at her, looked at Mortimer, who was hobbling off in the other direction. Adam raised a brow.

"Don't ask," Kit said, "but I think it hurt."

Adam had no notion of what he had witnessed. A virtuous wife beating off an unwanted admirer? A lovers' tiff? He followed Katherine out of sight, gnawing his lip. When he ran into Lord Roger some time later, he was still hobbling, but at Adam's question Mortimer waved him off, saying he had been trod on while trying to soothe a recalcitrant mare. The choice of words did not go down well with Adam. He spent the afternoon in sword practice, working until his arms felt like lead, and still the anger bubbled through him.

Supper was a rowdy affair, but Adam sat silent throughout, brusquely brushing off Katherine's every attempt at conversation. Instead, he nursed his wine, calling for Lionel to refill his goblet over and over again.

No sooner were they in their chamber than he pushed his wife back against the wall, handling her roughly. He was drunk, unsteady on his feet, and when she shoved at him, telling him to stop, something snapped.

"I'm your husband!" He flung her into the bed. "You will not deny me."

He was far too hard-handed and uncaring, fuelled by drink and anger, by the derision he saw in the eyes of the men in the household. She cried and struggled, telling him to stop, to let her go. At one point, she raked his face, and he rose on his arm and slapped her hard, twice, and told her to lie still.

When he woke in the morning she was gone. Adam groaned, trying to recall just what had happened. His head hurt, his cheek hurt, and when he finally stumbled out of bed he found a series of scratches decorating his face and his chest. He had no recollection of her nails on his skin, but swallowed in shame at the thought of just how afraid she must have been to have marked him like this.

He found her in the bower. She'd been weeping, and at his appearance she wiped at her cheeks, turning away from him.

Not quickly enough for him not to see the puffy discolouration under her eye, and his innards coiled themselves in tight knots. He had never laid hands on a woman before, considered it cowardly to do so, and now he himself was one such craven creature, taming his wife with his fists. And for what? Because he'd seen her with Lord Roger, her flushed, him hobbling away.

He went over to stand before her. "I'm sorry."

"It's your right to discipline your wife," she said in a thread of a voice. It made him squirm. She raised her eyes to him, red and swollen with tears. "But I do think I deserve to know why."

Had she stabbed him, it would not have hurt more. He sank to her knees before her. "Forgive me, I was drunk."

"I noticed." She sighed. He put a hand on her arm and she flinched.

"It will never happen again," he promised. "I have never raised my hand to a woman before, and—"

"Is that supposed to make me feel better?" she asked. "That I am fortunate enough to be the first woman you've pummelled?"

He winced at her words. It hadn't been quite that bad, had it? But her bruised face, and the way she held her hands, so tightly clasped in her lap, told him otherwise. "I will make it up to you."

"Really?" She stood up. "And how do you propose to do that, my lord?"

Chapter 6

The next few days were terrible. Kit avoided Adam as much as she could, but come night he would appear in their miniature bedchamber, a quiet man that tried to touch her, love her. She retaliated by lying like a dead fish, and invariably sometime during the night he would give up and stomp out of the bedroom.

She didn't understand. First some weeks of marital joy, then those days with an increasingly sullen man who had exploded. Mabel clucked when she told her this, and expressed the opinion that there were others to blame.

"Chief amongst them your own brother," she sighed.

"He's not my brother," Kit retorted automatically – even if he was. Leaving aside the fact that she suspected Richard resented her, she didn't like him much, finding him obsequious to the point of being ridiculous in Lord Mortimer's presence.

"All the same," Mabel continued, "young Richard has his position on account of our baron's infatuation with Katherine, and I dare say he's made a comment or two to Sir Adam, reminding him that what Mortimer wants, he should also get.'"

"Me?"

"You," Mabel agreed. "It can't be easy for Sir Adam," she said, glancing at Kit. "He owes it all to Lord Mortimer – every shirt on his back, every horse in his stable, every square foot of his land – and now also his wife."

"Not my doing, is it?" Kit muttered. "Besides, shouldn't he trust me?"

Mabel gave her a long look, making Kit's cheeks heat as she considered the secret she hadn't shared with Adam – wasn't allowed to share with Adam.

"It's not easy to trust, when so many whisper otherwise," Mabel said. "And many do, enjoying your lord's obvious discomfort. Besides, Richard has a point: what our lord wants, he usually gets." Mabel frowned down at her embroidery.

"Not me – ever."

Mabel patted her hand and suggested she concentrate on her sewing instead.

A few hours later, Kit was standing on the outskirts of Oxford, her eyes lost in the fog-shrouded meadows that bordered the Thames.

"Beautiful, isn't it?" William smiled at her as he came to stand beside her. He was rather out of breath, cheeks bright red. His habit was looking the worse for wear, and his tonsure could do with some soap and a razor, but he smelled of herbs and beeswax rather than the normal male odour of sweat and unwashed clothes.

"Very." She drew her cloak closed and reclined against an oak. To her right, a group of men were engaged in practice, attacking each other with swords and lances. One of the men stuck out, his fair hair lifting in the autumn wind, and Kit was overcome with an urge to run her fingers through it. "Does he always ride around with an army?"

"Mmm? Oh, you mean our baron. No, of course he doesn't. But these are uncertain times, and as I hear it, Lord Roger is thinking of sending Adam back to the Marches to find him more men. You should go with him when he does."

"We're not talking much at present," she muttered, swallowing down on a gasp when Adam was struck over the shield by one of his men. He staggered back for some paces but recovered quickly, retaliating with several swipes.

"No, I know. He told me what he'd done, and I have never seen him so ashamed." William smiled when he caught sight of his brother, yelling his men along in the mock battle. "It's difficult to be as beholden as he is to his lord. Which was why he agreed to the wedding – an opportunity to do Lord Roger a favour and balance the slate somewhat." He glanced at Kit. "I don't think he considered the possibility that he might develop feelings for this new wife of his."

"And has he?" She tried to keep herself from looking at

her husband, but her gaze was drawn to him, her lips quivering into a little smile when he roared in triumph at having won.

"Oh yes, which is why every time our Guy makes an insinuating comment along the lines of sharing a mount with Lord Roger, he dies inside. And it isn't only Guy." William scuffed at the ground, sending a scattering of gravel flying. "Jealousy is a dangerous emotion." He turned and smiled at her. "And so is love."

Kit felt her skin heat. "You think he loves me?"

"Do you need to ask?"

"He hit me!" Slapped would be more correct, and she'd left her own marks on him, but all the same…

"And every time he sees you, he drowns in shame." William straightened up. "It would help if you could find it in you to forgive him." With that, he was off.

Kit remained where she was, eyes locked on the distinctive shape of Adam de Guirande.

Following these two rather elucidating conversations, Kit decided to establish some sort of peace with her husband. She studied him from a distance for the rest of the day, noting just how drawn and tense he looked, and that evening she sat down beside him for supper and placed her hand lightly on his arm.

"My lord," she said with a little smile, having to pitch her voice louder than normal to carry over the surrounding din. Supper this evening was a lavish affair, with dish after dish carried in, from roasted fowls to boar and venison, jellied eels and pies of all sorts and shapes. Dogs circled the tables, serving maids ran back and forth with empty platters, with full platters, pages served wine and at the head table, the men were engaged in a heated conversation.

"Speaking to me again?" He sounded gruff, but took the edge off the rebuke by placing his hand on top of hers.

"Not if you don't want me to."

"I do, of course I do." Adam drew in a deep breath. "I am so sorry, Katherine. I don't know what—" He bit off, looking at the table. "I was jealous."

"I know – even if you had no cause to be."

His grey eyes flashed up to meet hers.

"You don't." She gave his forearm a little shake. "If you ever hit me again, I'll never forgive you. Never."

"I won't," he said hastily. "I swear on the Virgin and all the saints that I will never raise my hand in anger at you again." Adam tried a smile. "Although that doesn't preclude me being angry at you."

"At me? I'm the best wife around, Sir Adam." Kit brushed her hand over his unruly hair. "Well, your only wife as well, I hope." He looked so scandalised she had to laugh, assuring him she was jesting.

They concentrated on their food, with Kit making small talk about this and that. Adam made adequate sounds now and then, but seemed distracted, his gaze stuck on Mortimer who was sitting at the head table, surrounded by family. Belatedly, Kit noticed the hall was like a buzzing hive, everyone's attention focused on Mortimer and the grizzled bear of a man who went for his uncle, Lord Chirk.

"What's the matter?"

"Haven't you heard?" Adam tore off a chunk of bread and dipped it in meat juices. "It's the king. He's threatening to send an armed force to punish Lady Badlesmere."

"Lady Badlesmere?"

"Kin by marriage to our lord – but you already know that."

Kit nodded that she did, recollecting that the eldest Mortimer son was wed to a Badlesmere daughter. "What did the lady do?"

"Lady Badlesmere refused the queen entry to Leeds Castle," Adam went on. "Not, perhaps, the most polite course of action, but the lady says she was motivated by fear, what with not knowing who rules what in this country."

"And the queen?"

"Most irate." Adam chuckled. "Have you ever met her?"

"No. Have you?"

"Aye, a couple of times. Now that is one fine lady, our queen. Tough as old boots and far more worldly-wise than her husband. Born to rule, she is – pity she's a woman."

Kit made an irritated little sound, which made Adam smile.

"Women make bad leaders," he said. "They are first and foremost mothers and wives, and as such are too concerned with the safety of their loved ones to be sufficiently ruthless." Adam wiped his knife clean and sat back.

"They say the queen is beautiful," Kit said.

Adam raised his goblet to her and drank. "Not like you." That made her laugh, and he laughed with her, before saying that Queen Isabella was indeed very beautiful. "Very beautiful," he repeated, looking thoughtfully at Baron Mortimer. "But this matter with Lady Badlesmere is nothing but an irritant – rumour has it that the king has invited the Despensers to come back, and while so far neither Hugh the elder nor the younger has chosen to do so, it is but a matter of time."

"And then what?"

"Then it's war."

"War?" Kit's throat clogged with fear, not for herself, but for him. She tightened her hold on his arm, and he patted her hand, but she could see in his eyes he was also afraid – and resigned to do as he was commanded to do.

The hall was cleared after supper, with only Lord Mortimer and his closest companions remaining behind. The wives were invited as well, and at Mortimer's command, wine was brought in – lots of wine.

"If the king brings the Despensers back, we have no choice," Mortimer said.

"To rebel is to risk everything." Lord Chirk grinned at Mortimer, who grinned back. Now and then, Mortimer attempted to catch Kit's eyes, but every time she ignored him, concentrating on her goblet, her clothes, her hands – anything, really, that allowed her to avoid the knowing look in those dark eyes.

"To not rebel is to risk everything," Lord Mortimer said. "The way things are going, that little arse-licker Hugh Despenser plans on celebrating Christmas in Wigmore Castle very soon."

There were grunts of agreement, men shifting in their seats. Lady Joan went over to stand beside her husband.

"The king is weak," she said. "Surely you can reach an accord with him?"

"Not so weak now as he was some months back," Adam said in an undertone to Kit. "The king's forces grow stronger every day, the former so strong alliance among the rebel barons is unravelling at disconcerting speed, and with the Earl of Lancaster retiring to the north, all opposition is now led by Baron Mortimer and the Earl of Hereford."

Mortimer shook his head at his wife. "Like we did last time? How long did it take him to break his promise and invite those damned Despensers back, eh?" Mortimer threw a bone to the dogs. "They haven't forgiven us – they will never forgive us for the death of their ancestor."

"It was them that were the rebels then," Mortimer's uncle said. "Old Hugh Despenser that was, deserved to die as he did."

"By my grandfather's hand." Mortimer looked at the older man. "Your father's hand."

"Best thing he did, if you ask me." The old man grinned. "Almost as good as when I delivered Llewellyn's head to King Edward."

"My lord, is it true you still have Simon de Montfort's head in your treasury?" Richard asked.

Mortimer laughed. "Of course we do. Care to see it?"

"Not really," Richard mumbled. "Shouldn't…well, shouldn't it have been laid to rest by now?"

"Simon de Montfort was a rebellious baron!" Mortimer shouted. "His head was cut off at the battle of Evesham. Rebels deserve no rest." Utter silence greeted this outburst. With a curse, Roger Mortimer stood and swept out of the room.

"To rise in open rebellion is madness," Adam muttered, directing himself to Sir Thomas, who had joined them.

"And you think our lord doesn't know that? Did you not just hear how aware he is of what he is risking? But what choice does he have?" Sir Thomas said, just as low. "Those Despensers will bring him down anyway. That smirking Hugh Despenser will take every opportunity to humiliate Lord Roger as much as possible – retribution for the destruction Lord Roger wreaked on his lands this past spring."

"Aye. But to take the field against the king…" Adam licked his lips. "Our royal master will alienate all nobles in time. Why not wait until then?"

"Because time is running out," Thomas said. "As we speak, you can rest assured that the Despensers are planning major mischief, all of it directed at our lord. The moment they set foot on English soil, they will direct all their efforts towards destroying Baron Mortimer, the only man brave enough to speak up against their iniquities." He leaned even closer, lowering his voice to the point where Kit could barely make out what he was saying. "It is said he has swayed the queen." He winked. "The poor lady has had a bellyful of the Despensers, and when her royal husband chose to invite them back, she, apparently, has chosen to cast her lot in with Lord Roger."

"She can do very little," Adam said morosely. "A lady, brave and intelligent, but what armies does she command? What men does she have at her disposal? None, my lord."

"One should never underestimate a woman," Sir Thomas said. "To do so can come at great cost." The man spoke from experience, Kit thought snidely, suppressing a little smile. Not that there was anything remotely amusing about the situation, and from the faces of the assembled men, things could quickly go from bad to worse. She glanced at Adam, her throat closing up as she imagined him wounded – or dead.

They didn't talk as they left the hall, making for their little room. He took her hand when they entered the dark stairwell, holding her steady up the stairs. At the door, he hesitated. She opened it and walked backwards into the room, leading him with her. She stood on her toes to place her lips on his, brushing at his hair. He exhaled, his warm breath tickling her face. Arms round her waist lifted her close, he buried his face in her neck and she tugged her fingers through his hair.

Her kirtle, her shift – she was naked beneath him, above him. Her hands grabbed at his buttocks, his waist, she gasped his name, arched her back. Her man, her husband, and she was painfully aware that their time together might be brutally cut short by events none of them could control. Her man…

53

she touched him everywhere, she kissed and fondled, and he shuddered and groaned, calling her name as he let himself go.

They'd forgotten to close the shutters, and neither of them felt inclined to leave their nest of quilts and tangled limbs to do so afterwards. Instead, they lay very close together, she held safe in the curve of his body. Kit fell asleep like that, cocooned in the arms of the man she was beginning to love.

Chapter 7

Things began to unravel a fortnight later, when Mabel came rushing to find her.

"Sweet Lord," she gasped, holding a hand to her side. "Dearest Lord, but this was not supposed to happen!"

"What?" Kit helped Mabel to sit.

"Katherine!" Mabel flapped her hands. "She's here!"

"Here?" Kit's innards flipped.

"Well, here as in England, not here as in *here*." Mabel shook her head. Speaking so fast Kit could barely comprehend what she was saying, Mabel informed her that a rider had come for Sir Thomas, carrying news from his wife. "Stupid, impetuous child that she is, she left her Spanish grandee on account of a tiff, and came home." She snorted. "Expecting a fatted calf, no less, and instead she discovered that her place had been usurped – by you." Mabel sniffed. "She is not happy, I gather."

Kit's heart had been travelling up and down her throat throughout this speech. "She can't do anything, can she?"

"Do?" Mabel cast Kit a weary look. "Not in the sense that you're the one who's wed to Adam de Guirande, but Katherine could very well storm in here and ruin it all – out of spite."

Kit rose. "I will have to tell him." She twisted her hands together.

"And what will he do when he finds out that he's been deceived?"

"I don't know! But I must tell him before he hears it from someone else." Kit drew herself up straight. "I am still me, am I not? It is with me he spends his nights. That I'm not the real Katherine de Monmouth shouldn't matter, should it?"

"Ah, child." Mabel gave her such a sad look that Kit's insides wilted. "First things first: your father and brother are on their way."

Sir Thomas was the colour of a tub of lard. "Why is she doing this to me?" he moaned. "First, the silly goose loses her maidenhead with Lord Roger, and then, once we've negotiated a solution to that problem, she runs off with that unsavoury Spaniard Guzmán, and now, God help me, when everything is back in place, she chooses to return!"

"I don't see the problem," Richard said.

"The problem?" Sir Thomas' voice shook. "The problem, dear Richard, is that there are two Katherines where there should be only one!"

"So send her away." Richard pointed at Kit. "Katherine takes her place, and Adam will never know."

Mabel muttered something along the lines that she didn't think Lord Adam was quite that gullible.

"You can't send me away." Kit glared at her half-brother. "I am Adam's wife. You'll have to send her away – if she comes."

"If she comes," Sir Thomas muttered. "Of course she'll come." He tugged at his tunic. "I am right tempted to have Lady Cecily handle this. She got us in this mess by insisting the wedding had to go ahead – she can sort it."

"Father, I still don't see why you are so upset. As I said, the solution is easy: send your bastard off."

The slap echoed round the room. "If you ever – ever – refer to my daughter by that word again, I will disown you," Sir Thomas snarled. Richard staggered back, holding a hand to his flaming cheek.

"I'm not leaving," Kit repeated.

"Give her Tresaints, Father," Richard said. "Pay her off, and she'll leave."

"I can't give her Tresaints," Sir Thomas retorted. "It's part of her dowry."

"And I just said, I'm not leaving."

"Oh dear," Richard said. "So the changeling has fallen in love with the knight? How sweet." His blue eyes sent bolts of ice at her. "And do you think he has as well? Are you so foolish to believe Adam de Guirande has any feelings for you?"

"I know he does." Kit raised her chin.

Richard laughed. "As I said, he wouldn't even notice if Katherine took your place. In fact, he might prefer it."

Kit felt physical pain at his words; little stabbing sensations that made it difficult to remain upright, when all she wanted was to curl herself around the pain. "He does," she repeated.

"And that doesn't matter. You must leave to make way for my sister."

"No!" Kit looked from Sir Thomas to Mabel to Richard. "I will not. Never."

"Never what?" Adam asked from the door. "What is this about?"

"Dear God," Kit muttered. She took a deep breath. "We must talk," she said, ignoring Sir Thomas' loud protests. It took all the courage she had to look Adam in the eyes. "Alone."

The coming hour was beyond any doubt the worst in her life. From an initial wary stance, her every word had Adam subtly retreating from her, the concerned look in his eyes hardening into something she could only interpret as dislike.

"You lied to me," he said once she'd finished. "All of you lied to me – your father, your damned brother, but most of all you. You!"

"I had no choice – I had to."

"There is always a choice! You could have told me – no, you should have told me!"

"I should," she agreed meekly. "But at first I didn't dare to, and then I didn't know how, and Mabel made me swear on the Virgin that I wouldn't, and…" She was weeping openly now, seeing him through the haze of her tears. "Lady Cecily forced me," she sobbed. "She said she'd throw me out of my home if I didn't comply."

"That's no excuse," he snarled.

"It is if you don't have anything – or anyone." She dragged her sleeve over her eyes and nose.

"And when you've loved me, when you've kissed me and held me, has that also been a lie? A consequence of having nothing in this world?"

"No! How can you think that?" Kit reached for him but he pushed her away.

"What am I to think?" he said bitterly. "You've lied to me all the time."

"I didn't want to," she whispered. "But I was so afraid that if I told you the truth, you would no longer care for me."

"And do you think I care for you now?"

"I…" She hung her head. "I've never been as happy as I've been these weeks as your wife. But I suppose saying it now doesn't help, does it?"

There was an endless silence. Kit hugged herself and leaned against the wall to steady herself. She had to ask. "If Katherine…" She cleared her throat. "If she comes, is it her you want as your wife?"

"I don't know her!" he spat. "But at least she is someone – you are a nobody."

If he had sunk a hand into her chest and torn out her heart, it would not have hurt more. Kit reeled, gripped at the wall and dragged in breath after breath of ragged air.

He shouldn't have said that. Katherine – no, Kit, she called herself – had gone the colour of bleached linen, eyes huge pools of hurt in her pinched face. But he was too angry, too humiliated, to properly care, taking quite some pleasure in how she huddled together as if cradling her broken self. She slid down, sitting with her legs extended before her, and he could see how she shivered. She looked broken somehow, like a child's doll snapped in two, and one part of him wanted to crouch down beside her and kiss her well again, while the other wanted to kick her, make her scream with the pain he was feeling. She hadn't even told him her real name, going by Katherine when she had always been known as Kit. Had it all been a farce? Was she skilled enough to deceive him with her body and eyes? He thought not, but he didn't know – would never know.

So without a word, he left her, closing his eyes at the sound of wordless despair that she emitted when he slammed the door behind him. He needed to think. He had to somehow keep his blood from boiling over and think this through dispassionately. And as to her...well, he would punish her with his distance.

He sorely wanted to talk to someone about it, but Lord Roger was out of the question. Adam shuddered at the potential repercussions on Sir Thomas, but also on Katherine – Kit. Kit. He tasted the name carefully. It suited her somehow – much more than Katherine did. His second choice of confidante was William, but it stuck in his craw to admit to his brother that he'd been presented with a false bride. At least she'd come virgin to his bed, he thought darkly, not, from what Kit had told him, something Katherine de Monmouth would have done.

With no one to talk to, Adam opted for ale. And more ale.

Mabel found Kit staring vacantly straight ahead, so tired she couldn't quite make the effort required to get up from the floor and make it to the bed. Mabel spent most of the first hour berating her for having told Adam, after which she sighed, said matters were now out of their hands, and helped Kit clean herself up. She gave her a posset laced with milk of poppy and tucked her in, urging her to sleep.

She dreamed. She cried and half-woke, she dreamed some more. At one point, she was certain there was someone in the room, watching her, and she half sat up in bed.

"Adam?" she said. No answer, and she succumbed to more dreams, more tears.

When she woke properly, it was dawn, and she dragged herself out of bed. Kit dressed, decided to brave the outside world, and went looking for her husband. He wasn't to be found, and when she asked, people just shook their heads.

"He's avoiding me," she said to Mabel in a half-whisper. They were kneeling in church, surrounded by women.

"Not so surprising is it?" Mabel whispered back.

"What will he do?" Kit hissed. "Will he..." She swallowed. "Will he put me aside?"

"Shush!" Mabel frowned at her. "I dare say he cares too much for you to let that happen."

"He might care just as much for Katherine," she muttered.

"More fool him," Mabel said, taking her hand and giving it a little squeeze.

Over the coming week she came to regret her honesty over and over again. Whenever Adam saw her, he detoured, and after a couple of days trying to cross his way, make him see her, Kit gave up, avoiding him as much as he avoided her. She took her meals in their room, she spent her mornings embroidering on her own or with Mabel, but when she stepped outside the first thing she did was look for him, a spurt of hope rushing through her when she saw him, quickly converting to dejection when he invariably turned away.

"What ails you?" The voice tickled her ear, making Kit start. She whirled, coming face to face with William.

"Oh, it's you," she said.

His mouth twitched. "Yes, it's me, your brother-in-law." He stood beside her, reclining against the wall behind them, and tilted his face up towards the autumn sun. "What is wrong? My brother walks about with a face as if he'd been disembowelled, his fair wife droops like a wilting rose. What have we here? A lovers' quarrel?"

Kit hitched her shoulders. "It is between Adam and I."

William exhaled. "Everyone knows you've been sleeping alone, while your husband spends his evenings – and nights – with his men and their wenches."

"Their wenches?" There was a complement of gaudily dressed women who now and then graced the hall, making it very clear just how they earned their living. But the idea of Adam spending time with one of them instead of her...no; ludicrous. It made her eyes sting, and she ducked her head, not wanting William to see, but a strong hand gripped her chin and forced her to raise her face and meet his eyes.

"You care for him." He sounded surprised. "The low-born knave, as you so rudely referred to him some months back, has won your affections."

"What if I do? He, apparently, prefers the little whores."

"And why is that?"

Because he thinks I'm false, she thought, but as she stood

there, her eyes full of unshed tears, it dawned on her that was not it at all. Or maybe it was, to some extent, but the real reason why he'd been avoiding her was that she'd hurt him deeply, that her admissions made him question the sincerity of her feelings.

"He doesn't believe I care for him," she said out loud.

"Why not?" William asked.

"I gave him reason to doubt me," she whispered.

"Ah." He regarded her in silence for some moments. "Well then maybe you should tell him that you do," he suggested. "Before he drowns himself in ale and leaves me one beloved brother short."

"That I do what?"

"Love him."

Kit shrugged. "It's too late." But silently she prayed it wasn't, that Adam would come to understand she'd had no choice.

"It's never too late. But it takes courage to tell someone they hold your heart, when you don't know if you hold theirs." William gave her a gentle smile. "He cares for you too. Why else would the man be as irascible as a wounded bear?" He jerked his head in the direction of where Adam was coming out of the stables. "Go on."

Kit hung back. William placed a hand at her elbow and pushed her forward. Kit swallowed, smoothed her skirts and set off towards her husband. Unfortunately, the moment he saw her, Adam spun on his toes and rushed off, leaving Kit feeling even more abandoned than before.

Chapter 8

"I shouldn't have told him." Kit had taken to starting each new day with this statement, immediately followed by, "But I had no choice. If Katherine comes…" After eight days in constant apprehension at the potential arrival of Katherine, Kit was walking about on her toenails – and beginning to hope her unknown double had chosen to set sail for France or Ireland.

"One day at the time," Mabel said this day, as she had done all the previous days. She frowned. "If it was her intention to set out for Oxford, she should have been here by now." Mabel patted Kit's hand. "Maybe her lady mother succeeded in deterring her." Her tone belied the statement, and from what little Kit knew of Katherine de Monmouth, she seemed a stubborn creature, who thrived on setting things on end. Like Kit's marriage. She set her jaw. It was best not to think about it and make plans for a new life, one that did not include Adam de Guirande. The thought left her weak-kneed, but Kit could see no other way – she couldn't stay here and submit herself to the eviscerating experience of having Adam reject her.

"I must leave," she therefore said to Mabel.

"You can't leave," Mabel objected. "It would be noted if Adam de Guirande's wife left."

"By everyone but him," Kit said bitterly.

Mabel shook her head. "He watches you more than you think, m' lady."

That sent a burst of hope through Kit's veins, but when next she saw Adam he pointedly turned away, and the dejection that suffused her was worse than before. It hurt to hope. It hurt to be rejected. Kit decided that no matter Mabel's objections, it was time to leave, even if she had no idea where to go, no one to whom she could turn.

That same afternoon, Sir Thomas came rushing to her rooms. "Come, now!" Despite his rich attire, Sir Thomas looked dishevelled, no silk surcoat in the world – however fur-lined – being able to eclipse the horror in his face. Kit followed him, running at indecent haste down stairs and through passages, with Mabel puffing like an overweight sow behind her.

They reached the outer courtyard, and Sir Thomas made for the main gate, one hand holding his hat in place atop his head. It was cold, a thick fog clinging to them as they walked. Kit regretted not having taken her cloak, and even more so when she found Adam standing beside Richard, waiting for them. A hood would have allowed her to hide herself from him, but now his eyes dug into hers, and she had no option but to stare back, noting with some satisfaction that he looked as tired as she felt.

Sir Thomas hurried them through the narrow streets of Oxford, leading them towards St Giles and the nearby inn. An inn? Kit's heart began to thud. Were they planning to dispose of her collectively, set her on a cart bound for London and have her carried off?

Just before they reached their destination, Sir Thomas pulled Kit to a stop. In one swift movement he unclasped his cloak and draped it round her shoulders, pulling up the hood around her head.

"Best you remain unseen." He placed a hand on her back, propelling her through the busy inn of the yard, into the dark main hall, up some narrow stairs, down others, and when they came to a stop they were standing in the secluded garden.

Not a cart – a litter. Kit gripped Mabel's arm, incapable of uttering a word. They had abducted her out of her life, used her to seal their bargain with Baron Mortimer, given her in marriage to a man who no longer wanted her, and now they would ensure she disappeared.

"At least let me take my belongings with me," she said. Adam turned to look at her, brows pulled into a frown.

"Her belongings?" he asked, studying first the litter, then Sir Thomas. "Is my wife making a journey I know nothing about?"

"Don't be a fool!" Sir Thomas was visibly shaking.

"But why the litter?" Richard asked.

"Why the litter, he asks." Sir Thomas rolled his eyes, blew his nose in his sleeves and motioned for one of his men to approach. "The innkeeper is in my service," he explained.

Adam's brows rose.

"Yes, Adam, in my service – on behalf of our lord." Sir Thomas cleared his throat. "So when this…this…"

"Litter," Richard supplied, giving his father a concerned look.

Sir Thomas nodded. "When it arrived earlier today, he took one look inside and sent for me."

"Inside?" Richard moved towards the litter, his gloved hand gripping the richly decorated hangings.

"God have mercy on us," Sir Thomas moaned, just as Richard pulled back the heavy wool. A hand fell out. White, immobile, mercifully still attached to the rest of the body, it hung suspended an inch or so from the ground.

"Christ our Saviour," Richard exclaimed.

Mabel moaned. "No," she whispered, "no, please not this."

"Sir Adam de Guirande," Sir Thomas said, bowing formally, "may I present my other daughter, Katherine de Monmouth?" His voice broke.

What? Kit's gaze flew to the corpse. A young woman, lying on her back with wide-open eyes. Blue eyes, Kit noted through her increasing panic. Mabel was weeping, her gnarled hand moving over the white face to close the eyes. Richard had sunk down into a crouch, his face in his hands. Sir Thomas stared straight ahead, blinking repeatedly. Only Adam seemed unaffected, studying the dead woman dispassionately.

Kit stepped away, not quite sure what to do. She was glad that Katherine de Monmouth was dead. The insight shocked her, and she crossed herself, muttering a prayer for forgiveness.

"How?" Adam asked.

Sir Thomas made a helpless gesture. "Look closer," he croaked.

Kit sidled closer, peering into the dim interior of the litter. There was a lingering scent of almonds, and Katherine's mouth was coated with minuscule white crumbs.

"Sweetmeats," Kit murmured, more to herself than anyone else. An entire little casket of almond confections, she corrected herself, staring down at miniature unicorns and dragons. There was a scrap of parchment attached to the casket, neatly sealed and addressed to Richard.

"Poison," Mabel whispered, her gaze glued to the casket. Kit gave her a confused look: had someone intended for Richard to eat these and die? Her brother had paled to the point of looking as dead as the corpse, his fingers shaking when he tore the seal on the parchment.

"Yes," Sir Thomas said. "Poison. And we all know where that casket comes from."

Kit didn't, and at present she was more fascinated by the dead girl's face than the exquisitely carved rosewood casket. Her sister – and so alike they could have been twins.

"She looks just like me," she said in an undertone to Mabel. Not low enough, apparently, because Adam glanced at her before looking at poor dead Katherine de Monmouth.

"The likeness is remarkable," he said. "Unfortunately, only one of them is dead."

Kit gasped. She raised her arm and slapped him, hard enough to send him staggering backwards. Without a further word, she left.

"That was uncalled for," Sir Thomas said coldly, one hand restraining his son from pursuing Katherine – no, Kit. "Whatever you may think of her, maybe you should keep in mind that she is as much – if not more – a victim of all this as you are."

Adam touched his tingling face, wanting to trap the impression of her hand on his skin. "My apologies," he said. "And my condolences."

"It's not me you need to apologise to!"

No, Adam knew that. But he had no words with which to talk to Kit – at least not yet. His innards tightened with shame as he recalled the look on her face when he'd more or less told her he wished her dead. Besides, it wasn't true. Days without her proximity had driven home just how much he cared for her, needed her.

"She is already considering leaving you, m'lord," Mabel said. The old woman was scowling at him. "Comments like that will just strengthen her resolve to do so."

"She's my wife," he replied. "She stays."

Mabel snorted. "Begging your pardon, m' lord, but why should my lady bide by your wishes when you so clearly demonstrate you would rather be rid of her – for good?" She glared at him once more, bade Sir Thomas farewell and hurried after her mistress.

Adam shifted on his feet. He was fast reaching a point where he had to talk to someone, before the anger inside him destroyed whatever hope he had of contentment in his marriage. With a sigh, he returned his attention to the devastated father beside him.

"You said you recognised the casket," he said, more to break the mute silence with which Sir Thomas was regarding his daughter.

"It belongs to my lady mother," Richard replied, eyeing the dark wood with distaste. "She always keeps it in her room, filled with one treat or the other. Mostly honey cakes." He looked quite stricken, the parchment reduced to a tight wad in his hand.

"Ah." Adam gnawed his lip. "Are you saying Lady Cecily poisoned her own daughter?" It sounded preposterous.

Sir Thomas gave him a tired look. "I truly don't know. But I would beg you not to pursue this further. I will have her buried as Katherine Coucy and give out that she died of the tertian fever, and from this moment on there is only one Katherine de Monmouth – your wife. It would be best if we never told anyone the truth in this sordid matter – for us, for you and for Kit." He straightened up. "At least it sorts the irregularities of your marriage."

"It does?" Adam gave him a chilly look. "I think not." It still rankled, still tore, that the de Monmouths had played him like a pawn, replacing the errant daughter with the lookalike bastard get of Sir Thomas.

"Damn it, man! Are you telling me you don't want her?"

"I'm telling you I don't know."

"Best make up your mind soon, Sir Adam. Before that wife of yours wilts away or flees." The words came from Richard, the insolent pup regarding him steadily from under dark brows.

"Ah. So you care for her now?" Adam asked sarcastically.

Richard flushed. "I am willing to try. I owe her as much after what my mother has put her through." His hand tightened on the scrap of parchment. He regarded Adam steadily. "She had no choice. My mother excels at making people leap through hoops, and I can only imagine what she threatened her with."

It was Adam's turn to flush. But he said nothing more, beyond promising Sir Thomas he would do as he bid and not speak more of this matter. But there was a little something gnawing at his mind, a small warning bell telling him that maybe the casket had been opened by the wrong Katherine – why else had that note been addressed to Richard, why else was Richard staring at the casket as if it were a nest of vipers? He cast the dead girl one last look, and for a moment he imagined it was his Katherine he was seeing. A ringlet of dark red hair floated in a sudden breeze. Adam crossed himself and prayed.

By the time Mabel reached Kit's room, she had finished packing.

"But you can't, m' lady!" Mabel bleated, clinging to Kit's hand. "Where will you go?"

"Anywhere is preferable to here." Kit pulled free. "I will remember you always in my prayers," she said with a tremulous smile.

"No, m' lady, please don't go!"

"So I should stay, hoping a man who wants me dead might reconsider?" Kit shook her head. "I would die a slow death every day, Mabel." She straightened up. "I do believe I deserve more than that, and if nothing else I can enter a convent."

Mabel just looked at her. Kit's shoulders slumped. Who was she fooling? She had no desire to become a nun.

"I'll go back to Tresaints," she said. "Tell Adam that is all I want from him: my manor." She pressed a hand to her belly. That, and the child she was now certain was growing inside of her. Mabel followed her hand with her eyes and raised her brows in a wordless question. Kit blushed. "I will not tell him. I will not have him take me back on account of his child. You understand, don't you?"

Mabel shook her head and gripped at Kit's skirts.

"I have to know he cares for me, for Kit." She gave a short bark of laughter. "But we both know he doesn't – he demonstrated that today." She kissed Mabel, disentangled herself from her hands and slipped down the stairs.

Once she was in the stable, she had one of the stable boys saddle her horse and went to find the captain of the guard.

"I require an escort," she said.

"An escort?" The captain looked her up and down." And why is that, my lady?"

"My mother," Kit lied. "She is ailing and I must go to her."

"Ah." The captain nodded. "I can give you two men."

"Thank you." Kit threw a nervous look over her shoulder. Was that Adam she'd glimpsed, entering the courtyard? She was torn between wanting him to see her leave – and stop her – and slipping away unnoticed, so that she wouldn't have to see him leaning back against a wall, watching her depart without trying to hinder her.

She was already astride, nudging her horse towards the gate, when someone caught hold of her reins.

"Get off. Now." Eyes as cold as ice stared up at her. Kit swallowed.

"Why should I? It is best for both of us if we part."

"I am not asking your opinion, wife, I am telling you to dismount. Either you do it yourself, or I will drag you off the mount."

Kit set her mouth and shook her head.

"Woman!" he hissed. "Do as I say. Now." His eyes flamed, one large hand gripping her thigh. It was the first time in over a week that he had touched her.

Kit slid off her mare, landing lightly on her feet. He loomed over her.

"What were you thinking of? The country is alive with brigands."

"Which would serve your purpose perfectly, my lord," she retorted. "After all, I might end up dead."

A wave of fiery red rushed up his face. "I did not mean that," he said gruffly.

"No? It sounded most sincere, my lord."

He gave her a long look. "Go back inside," he said, before turning to leave.

That same evening, a messenger boy stumbled into the chapel halfway through vespers.

"My lord," he gasped, collapsing at Mortimer's feet. "My lady…" He stuttered, and had to inhale a couple of times.

"What is it, lad?" Mortimer frowned. "It must be dire news indeed that you interrupt us at our prayers."

"Leeds Castle is under siege," the boy said. "Lord Pembroke has surrounded the castle, by orders of the king."

"What?" A potbellied man with small dark eyes rose to his feet. "My wife, attacked by the king? We must ride to her aid!" Lord Badlesmere himself, Kit assumed, thinking the man looked about to collapse in a seizure.

"My lord." Lady Joan placed a hand on Lord Badlesmere's arm. "We must think this through. And you know that your wife is quite safe: the king would never harm a woman – or her children. That would be unchivalrous."

Lord Badlesmere brushed off her hand. "My wife, my children!" He turned to face Mortimer. "We have to help them."

"The king does not make war on women," Lady Joan repeated.

"You think not? Is that not precisely what he is doing?" Lord Badlesmere yelled. "A small garrison facing the men of Pembroke. We must—" He tore at his hair. "My wife, your daughter-in-law," he said, pointing at Roger. "We have no choice."

Lord Mortimer frowned. "One always has a choice, Badlesmere."

"Not this time! Not with my wife in peril."

"My lord," Lady Joan tried again, "no man of honour makes war on a woman."

"And therein lies the problem, does it not?" Lord Badlesmere spat on the floor. "Our king may have many qualities, but honour isn't one of them."

A deep silence greeted this remark. Kit tried to catch Adam's eyes, but his attention was riveted on his lord.

Mortimer swept his closest men with his eyes. "The hall. Now."

Kit sneaked in with Lady Joan and her women, but retreated to stand to the side. Lord Badlesmere was pacing up and down like a caged wolf, now and then stopping to stare in the direction of the south-east, a vacant look settling over his face. Kit had no doubts that the man genuinely feared for his wife, and although Lady Joan kept repeating that women of noble birth were always treated with courtesy, Kit could see from the set look of Adam's and Lord Mortimer's faces, and from the way Sir Thomas averted his face from Lord Badlesmere's pleading looks, that the men were not quite as convinced as Lady Joan was that Lady Badlesmere would not come to harm. For an instant, Kit caught Adam looking at her with an expression of concern, and hope flared hot and wild within her until he saw her looking at him and turned away.

After an endless hour of arguments and discussions, Mortimer held up his hand. "We ride to Kent."

Lord Badlesmere sagged in relief. A babble of noise ensured, but it sufficed with Lord Mortimer raising his brows for the men to fall silent. In a curt voice he issued orders that had men sprinting off in all directions, until it was only the women, Adam and some of Lady Joan's household men in the room.

"You return to Wigmore," Mortimer told Lady Joan. "The womenfolk go with you." Kit couldn't quite suppress a gasp at the thought, causing Adam to hastily look her way. "And you, Adam – you ride with them," Mortimer said, and Kit could have kissed the man. Not so Adam, who launched himself into heated protests, insisting he served his lord better on the field than as an escort.

"I'm not asking you." Lord Mortimer's voice was cold. "I'm commanding you." The rebuke had Adam flushing. Mortimer's voice softened. "I need you to bring up more men, as many as you can. See them armoured and horsed, have them provisioned and ready to go within the month."

Adam nodded, still looking sullen.

Mortimer's brows pulled together. "It has begun, and I have no choice, cornered by my convictions, by my liege's false promises." With an effort, he shook himself. "We have work to do." He clapped his hands and all dispersed – all but Lady Joan.

As Kit exited the room, she saw Lady Joan hurry over to her husband who enfolded her in a long, silent embrace.

Chapter 9

The women left at dawn two days later. Adam sat his horse and waited while Lord Roger and his wife made their farewells. For once, Lady Joan's composure cracked, her mouth trembling when she gave her husband yet another farewell smile. And then she disappeared into the protective darkness of the litter, no doubt there to shed the tears she would never permit herself to shed before others than her husband. Mortimer looked careworn, and just as the litter swung into momentum he strode across the yard, ducking his upper body into the litter. He re-emerged with his hair rumpled, and Adam could swear there was a glimmer of a tear in his lord's eyes.

Adam rode Goliath over to Lord Roger. "I will see her safe."

"I know you will." Lord Roger smiled slightly at Adam. "And maybe you should take care of your own wife as well – it seems to me you have been neglecting her of late."

"She's coming with us, isn't she?" Adam turned Goliath and spurred him away, while from under his lashes he studied Kit, already mounted on her palfrey. As always, she was riding astride, and he noted with satisfaction that she'd arranged her skirts so as to ensure her legs were properly covered. His gaze lingered on the contour of her thighs, a flare of desire rushing through him before he wrenched his gaze away. She was looking unusually pale, fearful even, and it struck him that he should probably offer her some reassurance, but he was still too angry with her, so instead he took the lead, assuming she would ride along as well as she could.

With him rode his brothers, William capably handling his large roan gelding, while Guy was astride an ugly beast of a horse, with, in Adam's opinion, the temper of an aggravated wild boar. Still, there was no denying Guy was a skilled horseman, bending the beast to his will.

"One could think your wife has contracted the pox," William commented once they were on their way.

"Hmm?" Adam injected his voice with disinterest.

"How long is it since you've spoken to her?" William asked.

"I bid her a good morrow just now," Adam replied.

"Aye, because you had no choice. And it wasn't directed at her, it was directed at all of the women." Guy spat to the side. "Nursemaids," he muttered. "Others ride off to fight, we're sent home with the women and our lord's treasures."

"So why? William asked.

"Why what?" Adam gave him an irritated look.

"Why aren't you speaking to her, or spending time with her? Not even your nights, as I hear it."

"Where I spend my nights is my own business."

"And where she spends her nights? Her days? Is that not your business?" William sounded reproving, and Adam squirmed.

"It is definitely not your business," Adam snapped, but couldn't stop himself from casting a look down the line, looking for the distinctive, willowy shape of his wife.

With the exception of yesterday's events, lately she'd been hiding – from him, but also from all those prying eyes that followed her, and him, wherever they went, voices hushed as they gossiped about what could possibly be the reason for Sir Adam's avoidance of his wife. He knew what they assumed, could see it in how some of the men smirked, while others threw him pitying looks. Her fault, he seethed, but was immediately ashamed. How could it be her fault that people tattled nonsense behind her back?

"So what did she do?" Guy asked, a bright gleam in his eyes. "Fondle our baron?"

"No!" Adam was sorely tempted to hit him. "She has not dishonoured herself – or me – in any way."

"No, she did that before the wedding," Guy snickered, his amused expression changing to one of fear when Adam charged him, gripped him by his tunic and threw him off his horse.

"Don't you ever talk about my lady wife like that," Adam snarled, riding Goliath in circles round Guy. "And for all your rumour-mongering, I can assure you she came a maid to our wedding bed."

"Adam." William frowned at him. "Not something the entire world needs to know, is it?" He jerked his head in the direction of the closest men-at-arms, who were regarding the brothers with interest. Adam felt his face heat.

"Why not?" he said. "It's the truth."

"So why the manors?" Guy sneered, getting to his feet. "Why would Mortimer be so generous to you?"

Adam opened his mouth to reply, but William beat him to it.

"Our lord holds our brother in high esteem." He smiled down at Guy. "Is that so strange, given Adam's devotion to him? More than half his life, Adam has served him."

Guy mounted his horse. "Not everyone is fortunate enough to be found beaten to a pulp by a generous lord."

"Not every boy of twelve is brave enough to shield his stepmother and his brothers from his father's drunken fists," William bit back. "And it has benefited you as well, has it not? Had it not been for Adam, you'd have been scouring floors in the armoury. Instead, here you are – a knight."

"A poor knight!" Guy snarled, set heels to his horse and galloped off.

"Thank you," Adam said.

"For what? Trying to talk some sense into his addled head?" William shook his head. "Not much use. Our Guy is quite convinced that had you not existed, he would have been a landed knight, instead of being nothing but a glorified man-at-arms."

"Lord Roger would never have given him any manors."

William grinned. "No, our lord is a good judge of character. But Guy prefers to ignore his own failings." His grin broadened. "I should probably raise the issue at his next confession and have him do long penance for it. Envy is a capital sin."

"Are you Guy's confessor?" Adam would never dream

of burdening his brother with his sins. Besides, it would be uncomfortable to give his younger brother such insight in his soul.

"Guy doesn't do much confessing," William said grimly, "but when he does, he now and then comes to me – hoping for a kinder ear, I suspect."

"Fool," Adam snorted.

"So what has she done, our sweet Katherine, to so aggrieve you?" William asked, reverting to the original subject.

Adam shrugged, his gaze straying yet again in the direction of his wife. "It is between her and I."

"Strange, that is what she said as well. But whatever it is, it is festering into something poisonous," William warned.

"I know," Adam said softly. Any further discussion he effectively put a stop to by riding off to talk to Richard de Burgh, one of Lady Joan's knights.

Kit had hoped the ride to Wigmore would allow for some opportunity to talk to Adam, but was soon to find her husband was as skilled at evading her in a group of forty people as he had been in Oxford. If she rode her palfrey up through the line, Goliath was suddenly trotting the other way. When they halted to eat, she threw him a hopeful look, thinking that it would be discourteous of him not to sit beside her, but instead he waited on Lady Joan, who seemed to enjoy his attention.

The first night they stayed in an inn just outside Woodstock, and it was a noisy, rowdy affair to settle their large party in an establishment boasting only four private rooms. Lady Joan and her women – among whom Kit was suddenly included – shared one room, Adam and his brothers shared another and the other two rooms were shared between the other knights and retainers. This left most of the men-at-arms bedding down in the hall – together with the four girls who'd ridden with them from Oxford. Kit had made big eyes when she realised they were coming with them, but Mabel had drily informed her that rarely would one find a company of soldiers without a complement of trollops.

"Trollops?"

Mabel rolled her eyes. "What else can one call them? Those wenches make their living on their back and with their legs in the air."

"Oh," Kit said, watching the girls fawn on the men – and especially on her big, handsome husband, who laughed at them and drank with them, seemingly oblivious to Kit's presence in the hall. Except that he wasn't – she was quite convinced he knew exactly where she was and what she was seeing. When he gave one of the whores a loud, smacking kiss on the cheek, Kit stood so abruptly her stool fell to the floor with a clatter. Adam turned towards the sound and she glared at him. He raised a shoulder and returned his attention to his female companion.

"Bastard," she muttered as she passed him – loud enough for him to hear.

It was a relief when four days later they arrived at Wigmore. For the last few hours they'd ridden through undulating terrain, large expanses of moors interspersed with glades of trees still holding on to a sparse covering of fading leaves. This was land similar to that which surrounded Tresaints, and Kit had spent the day as far away from the rest of the party as she could, thinking of home while now and then urging her horse into a gallop. For some moments, those bursts of speed made her forget her heartache, her uncaring husband, but inevitably someone would come riding after her and tell her to return to the group. Never Adam, always one of his minions, but at least she had the pleasure of seeing his eyes on her as she rode past him, her hair come undone in the wind, her cheeks stinging with the cold.

The moment Lady Joan's litter was set down in the outer bailey, people poured out from the adjoining buildings. The Mortimer children were swept into welcoming arms, servants bowed almost to the ground as they greeted their mistress, and a bevy of stable boys appeared out of nowhere to take care of the horses. Gone was the French Kit understood, replaced by the somewhat harsher sounds of Welsh. Even Lady Joan spoke Welsh, and Kit had no idea what to do when someone approached her and said something she took to be a greeting.

She smiled vaguely, and luckily Mabel interceded, saying something that made the young woman laugh and wink before speeding away.

"Oh, dear," Kit murmured to Mabel. "It seems I must start learning Welsh."

"You don't speak it at all?" To judge from Mabel's tone, this was borderline incomprehensible.

"No." Kit frowned at her. "My mother had me tutored in Latin, not Welsh."

"No matter." Mabel gripped her by the elbow. "We start your lessons tomorrow."

As to the castle itself, Kit gawked. She'd heard of Wigmore, but the awed descriptions were nothing compared to the reality of the Mortimer castle, a magnificent display of power and wealth.

"Big, isn't it?" Mabel commented from beside her. Kit could only nod, and once she'd been allotted a room – to be correct, Adam had been allotted a room, which his wife was assumed to share with him – she allowed Mabel to take her on an exploratory walk.

They trudged up and down steep slopes and even steeper stairs, walked along the walls and in general admired the new additions Baron Mortimer had made to his ancestral home. Mabel displayed the newly refurbished great hall, for all the world as if she herself was the owner, pointing at the huge tapestries that decorated the walls while confiding that they came from France.

The original castle, including an ancient keep and thick stone walls, lay enclosed by a new curtain wall, creating a huge outer bailey. There were stables and storage sheds, kennels and mews, and quarters for the men-at-arms. There was scaffolding rising towards the sky, there were masons and carpenters, horses and dogs, and repeatedly Kit had to sidestep or come to a halt to avoid barging into people rushing back and forth.

Kit ended up on the curtain wall, just where it was at its highest, behind the old keep. Mabel retreated indoors, muttering that only a fool would stay out longer than necessary in the cold autumn wind. Kit shrugged, promised to be back in time for vespers and reverted to studying the landscape below her. To the west lay an endless expanse of green, but closer to the castle huddled a collection of houses, a small cobbled square and a church.

She leaned forward over the parapet, glimpsing the rocky ground below – very far below. She leaned even further, her left foot lifting for a moment off the ground. A hand on her shoulder yanked her roughly backwards.

"What—" She broke off at the sight of Adam.

"Lean over like that and you may end up dead," he said.

"As if you would care."

He didn't reply, regarding her intently. She couldn't read the look in his eyes, but his crossed arms didn't exactly invite her in.

"Adam…" she tried, extending her hand towards him.

"Go inside." He cut her off, gesturing with his head.

"But—"

"Now, wife." With that he wheeled, making his way nimbly down the sloping wall-walk. Kit decided to stay where she was, hoping he would come and fetch her. The shadows lengthened, vespers came and went, and still she stood, hoping. He didn't come.

Chapter 10

During the first five days or so at Wigmore, Adam studied Kit from afar. His heart had nearly stopped when he'd seen her leaning out over the parapet, but since then he hadn't spoken to her, even if he couldn't stop himself looking at her whenever she crossed his field of vision.

She'd become pale, shrinking into herself in a way that made him want to hurry over to her and hold her, but he couldn't, so he instead he watched over her, a protective shadow that kept his distance. His body twitched with need for her, but in the pit of his stomach an angry voice wailed that she'd played him like a gullible fool, and so he spent his evenings with men and ale, with the odd kiss from a wench or two, trying to drown out the memories of her in his arms.

Come night, he'd take the stairs to their room and enter it silently. The bed was an inviting blob of linen bedclothes and quilts, the room empty of all but her, a lonely shape curled on her side. He'd stand for a while regarding her, wishing the anger in him would abate, allowing him to approach her. Once he heard her cry in her sleep, and on another occasion he could swear it was his name she said out loud, clutching the pillow in her arms to her chest. Some nights, he'd linger, watching her as she slept. Others, he would steal away as quietly as he had come.

"She isn't at fault," Mabel said one day, startling him as he exited the privy. The old woman must have been lying in wait for him.

"She lied, pretending to be someone she wasn't."

"As she's tried to tell you on a number of occasions, she was given no choice. If she didn't comply—"

"Yes, yes," Adam interrupted. "She'd be out on her ear, left to fend for herself."

Mabel twisted her hands together. "It was worse than that, my lord. If it had been only her, I do believe she would have refused. But Lady Cecily threatened to evict all her people, every single one of Tresaints' tenants."

Kit hadn't told him that. All the same, Adam smoothed his face into a disinterested mask and made as if to leave. Mabel took hold of his sleeve.

"She's hurting and you are being needlessly cruel, m' lord. How much longer must she be punished for a wrong not of her doing?"

"I don't know." He twisted loose.

Mabel ducked under his arm and came to stand in front of him, hands on her hips. "I hear that you're riding off tomorrow, to muster your men."

Adam nodded.

"Take her with you," Mabel said. "Talk to her – that much she deserves."

Adam kicked at a broken helmet on his way to the stable. It sailed upwards and crashed back down with a resounding bang. A nearby dog cowered at his approach, and Adam cursed it out of his way. He wanted to be alone, to think, and the best place for that was in Goliath's stall – only a fool with a death wish would approach his testy horse. It soothed him, to work his way over the stallion's broad back, polishing the already gleaming hide. As he worked, he mulled over what Mabel had said, and even though he at present had no notion of what to say to Katherine – Kit – he reluctantly conceded that Mabel was right: it was time to talk.

It took him some time to find her. Only after a long search did he spot her, a solitary shape in the walled garden. It shouldn't have surprised him, as his wife had a fondness for herbal borders and roses, but now, well into November, it was cold, the occasional rays of sun doing nothing to dissipate the damp chill of the afternoon.

She was sitting with her hands held open in her lap, her gaze on the patch of ivy that adorned the facing wall. As he watched, she placed her arms around herself and rocked, an inarticulate, low sound emanating from her. He stepped into the garden, and a twig snapped under his foot. Katherine – Kit

– whipped round. At the sight of him, her shoulders slumped and she turned away, scrubbing at her cheeks.

"You'd best go and pack," he said in a curt voice. "We'll be leaving on the morrow."

"Leaving?" She bit her lip. "Going where?" Her voice shook.

"To Toot Castle." He frowned. "Where did you think we were going?"

"I don't know – to a nunnery where you could leave me?"

That made him scowl. Did she truly think him such a callous man? "Why were you weeping?" he asked, pleased by how his question made her flush and look away. Did she think he wouldn't notice, and her with her face lined with tear-tracks?

"Why?" She kept her back to him. "Maybe it's because my husband – the only person I have in my life – punishes me with his silence, or maybe it's because he prefers to spend his night with the whores instead of with me."

"I do no such thing!"

"That's not what I hear. Besides, I saw you with them, remember? All laughter and smiles for them, nothing but scowls and silence for me." She inhaled, studying her hands. "How do you think that feels, to be so totally ignored – abandoned, even?"

"I told you I had to think," he said, in a voice loaded with ice. "Alone. And as to the wenches, I may spend the evenings with them, but I've spent my nights alone."

"So you say," she muttered, throwing him a look from under her lashes. "It would be somewhat absurd if you were the one committing adultery, seeing as it is not so long ago you struck me, believing me to be faithless."

Her barb stung. "You were! Everyone knew—"

"Not me! Never me!"

"Katherine was."

"I'm not Katherine!" Her voice soared into a falsetto. "I am Kit, forced to wed you under false pretences. I never asked for this to happen, I…" She turned her back on him. Her shoulders sagged, and he took a step towards her, wanting to wipe away her

81

dejection. "I am Kit," she repeated, sounding tired and sad, "and I have only ever bedded with one man – you." She stood to go, but he blocked her way. "Excuse me, my lord, I have packing to do."

"We leave at dawn." He stepped aside to let her pass. A strand of dark red hair floated free from under her veil, and he was tempted to reach for it, use it to reel her in. But he didn't.

She stood for an instant, looking up at him, and he could see the longing in her eyes. Her tongue darted out, wetting her lips. Adam exhaled. His hand moved towards her, but he'd left it too late – she had already turned on her heel, speeding away like a doe in flight.

"Why bring me along if he has no intention of talking to me?" Kit demanded in an undertone the next morning, riding her palfrey as close as she could to Mabel's stout donkey.

"We've only been on our way for half a morning," Mabel said.

"Yes, and he is busy elsewhere," Kit replied, eyeing the woman who was riding beside Adam.

"Not his choice – she latched on to us when she heard we were riding her way."

"He doesn't seem to mind, does he?" Kit eyed the little whore – although Mabel had told her that this Jeanine was more of a courtesan, an expensive luxury a man like Adam could not hope to afford beyond a single night – with dislike. But it wasn't so much Jeanine's simpering female presence she resented; it was the way her husband was laughing with her.

Finally, Kit had had enough. She spurred her mare into a trot and came up alongside Adam, who looked surprised to see her there.

"If you have to pass time with sluts, do it out of my sight."

"I do as I please," Adam said, "and should you take umbrage, dear wife, I suggest you ride far enough down the line that you don't need to see us."

In that moment, Kit hated him. The little whore giggled. Kit gave her a long, hard look, pleased that the stupid girl at least had the decency to squirm.

"You're like a randy tom, devouring her with your eyes," she said coldly. That was not entirely correct. Adam had mostly talked to the buxom Jeanine.

"Randy tom?" Adam's nostrils flared.

"Look at you! Any moment now you'll kiss her – and she's begging for it, aren't you, little Jeanine?" Kit stood in her stirrups and glared at the woman. "You lay one finger on my husband, and I'll kick your teeth in, just so you know."

"I'll talk with whom I please," Adam said, "and should I kiss her, what is it to you?"

Kit looked at him. "That way, is it? If so, maybe it would serve us both better if I take Mortimer up on his amorous offers."

Jeanine giggled – the wits of an addled hen, that one – Adam scowled. Kit drove her horse around, set heels to it and made off back the way they'd come. She hated him, she hated it here, and she yelled the horse on, making it gallop wildly over the muddy, rutted road.

He caught up with her, leaned over to take a firm grip of her reins, and brought them to a halt.

"What are you playing at?"

"Me?" She yanked her reins free. "What do you care, my lord?" Angry tears scalded her cheeks, and she was so tired of all this. She turned her horse and set off at a trot.

Once again he caught up. "I am talking to you."

"Pardon me for not being adequately grateful, my lord. Do you want me to fall off my horse and grovel at your feet because you deign to speak to me, your lowly wife?"

"Don't be ridiculous," he growled. "And I'll not have you ride off like that again." He set his hand on her sleeve, she shook it off.

"Why not? I am but following your command and ensuring that you and your unsavoury trollop are safely out of my sight."

"My what? How dare you insult me, insinuating I'd be interested in bedding that well-used piece of female flesh?"

"How chivalric," she muttered. "Jeanine would like hearing you refer to her that way. Besides, what am I to think? You've been riding beside her for the last hour, eyes stuck on that over-large pouty mouth of hers."

Adam gave her an exasperated look. "She doesn't have a pouty mouth."

"No?" Kit formed her mouth into an exaggerated spout. "If you ask me, she looks like a duck."

"A duck?" His mouth twitched.

"Without the feathers." She slid him a look, met eyes of an intense grey.

"A naked duck," he said, and now he was smiling, the first smile he'd given her in weeks. "It makes her rather unattractive, to think of her like that."

"Not if you like ducks," Kit said.

"I don't." He looked away. "And what of the amorous baron?"

"Lord Mortimer is most certainly not a duck," Kit replied. "He's more like a prowling fox." She clucked the mare into a canter.

"A fox that had best stay well away from my henhouse," Adam said.

"Why? Because you care for the hen or because you begrudge the fox?"

Adam gave her a level look. "It is my hen." With that, he urged Goliath into a gallop, making for the head of the column.

Kit smiled to herself. Should the fox come prowling, this hen would peck him where it truly hurt.

Chapter 11

The inn was small, smoky and crowded. To Kit's annoyance, this put paid to any reunion scene – not that she was all that certain any such scene was in the making, because even if Adam had talked to her now and then during the long ride, he had shown no inclination to pick up on her banter, or her seductive looks.

So here she was, stuck in a small room with Mabel and that hateful Jeanine, while her husband bedded down with Lionel and William, three to a bed. The men-at-arms found somewhere to sleep in the stables, and frankly, after half an hour listening to Jeanine sing the praises of Baron Mortimer – mostly with rather sly looks in Kit's direction – Kit wouldn't have minded sleeping in the stables instead.

"Don't be silly," Mabel snapped when Kit shared this with her. "To sleep in the straw is to sleep with rats and other vermin."

"To sleep here is to share a bed with a woman of no morals," Kit replied, not bothering to lower her voice.

"The pot calling the skillet black, as I hear it," Jeanine said through a yawn. "It's not me that has sampled forbidden fruit while pretending to remain a virtuous virgin."

"Me neither," Kit bit back. "You must have me confused with someone else."

"Your double?" Jeanine snickered, turning over on her side. Her bottom pushed against Kit on one side, while on the other Mabel's knee was digging into her spine. "Besides," Jeanine continued. "I do what I do to survive." Her voice acquired a bitter tone. "No marriages to landed knights await me."

"Try Guy," Kit suggested. A match made in heaven, in her opinion.

"I said landed," Jeanine replied. "Guy de Guirande is poorer than I am."

It was impossible to sleep beyond daybreak. Kit sat up in bed, relieved to find it empty of Jeanine, and padded over to the shuttered window, peeking through the slats at the bustle below. Horses, men, dogs and cattle – an escaped pig, a gaggle of geese and the innkeeper himself, a dry stick of a man who looked ineffectual, but from the way the other men eyed the staff he was carrying, Kit concluded he was more than capable of defending what was his.

"Where's Jeanine?" Kit said, turning to Mabel.

"Need you ask? Conducting business, I'd warrant. She slipped out just before dawn, and her in nothing but her shift."

Kit threw a look at the men in the yard. They didn't look rich enough to pay for Jeanine's services, but maybe there was a lordling or two tucked away in the hall downstairs.

"Do you think we will find our way through this?" she asked out of the blue. Mabel gave her a confused look. "Adam and me," Kit clarified.

"You're wed to each other for life, so let's hope you do."

"He could still put me away – you said so yourself."

"Do you think he would?" Mabel gave her a slight smile. "The man is in love with you. He just needs to admit that to himself so that he can forgive you for lying to him."

"That was not my idea – you yourself made me swear not to tell." Kit chewed her cheek. "And once I…well, once I began to care for him…" She squirmed under Mabel's amused gaze. "I didn't know how to tell him the truth," she finished. "I feared he'd be angered."

"And he was," Mabel said. "Somewhat excessive, that anger."

Kit shrugged. "I don't think he trusts easily, so when he does and finds he's been lied to…" She exhaled, fingering the laces of her shift. "I want things to be like they were – before he found out about Katherine and me."

"Well then, you'd best do something about it." Mabel waggled her brows. "Now."

"Now?"

Their present surroundings were not conductive to tender moments, but Kit allowed Mabel to help her with her hair, shook out her rumpled kirtle and slipped it on, recalling that this was the gown she'd worn at her wedding.

"A morning ride, perhaps?" Mabel winked, propelling Kit towards the door.

"He's got company. Lionel and William are sharing his room." She looked about for her veil, but Mabel shook her head.

"He'll get rid of them – if you look enticing enough." Mabel tugged at Kit's neckline, making it a tad wider, low enough to show the world she was wearing a shift of the thinnest linen beneath. She handed Kit a cloak. "In case he misunderstands and takes you for a gallop on the moor instead."

"Or doesn't want to understand." Kit tried to readjust the neckline but had her hands slapped away by Mabel.

"Go on." Mabel pushed her over the threshold.

There was no one outside the door. A dark landing, the narrow and steep stairs to the left, and straight ahead the room Adam was sharing with William and Lionel. Something moved in the corner. A rat? No, a cat, a scruffy feline that darted by her legs and flowed down the stairs. Kit hesitated. What if he thought her too forward, or if he chose not to take her up on her offer, brushing her off in front of the others? From the other side of the door came laughter. Kit took a deep breath, gripped the handle and entered.

The tableau before her didn't quite make sense. William on a stool, Lionel sitting by the window with Adam's boots in his lap, and on the bed, side by side, Adam and Jeanine. He was only in his shirt, the linen riding up to display strong, lean thighs, covered by golden hair. On the floor were his braies and hose, thrown into an untidy heap as if he'd been in a hurry to get them off. Jeanine was as undressed as he was – well, almost – and had her hand on his leg. At Kit's entrance she smiled, that ugly duck's mouth of hers curling into a triumphant grin before she leaned forward to kiss Adam on the lips.

Kit barely registered how her husband jerked away from the whore's mouth. Her eyes were glued to his face, to the dark red flush that flew up his cheeks. All she wanted was to disappear, have the floor swallow her whole. Instead, she stood rooted to the spot.

"It's not what you think," Adam said, standing up.

"Oh, of course not," Jeanine purred, looking as if she intended to rub herself against Adam. Kit strode over, sank her hand into Jeanine's undone hair and pulled – hard. Jeanine screamed as Kit dragged her across the floor, cursing her loudly when Kit shoved her outside.

"Next time I break your nose," Kit snarled, banging the door in Jeanine's face.

Her husband was fastening his hose, looking discomfited.

"You said you didn't bed with whores," Kit said.

"I don't."

"And I'm blind, deaf and dumb, am I?"

"It's customary to knock," he said, "not barge in like you just did."

"And how was I to know you were making love to another woman?" Her voice was far too high, far too breathless, revealing just how hurt she was. Kit took a couple of deep breaths.

"He wasn't—" William interjected, but Kit waved him silent.

"Let's end this farce right now, my lord," she said to Adam. "You go your way and I go mine." She had no notion how she would survive on her own, but she was too hurt to think straight. A slut, a whore, and he'd been fondling her in his bed, when just across the landing was his wife!

"You're my wife," Adam said stonily. "We are bound together for life."

"And I can see just how happy that thought makes you." She fisted her hands.

"Not at present it doesn't," he snapped back, eyes like miniscule sheets of ice. "But the sacraments of marriage cannot be undone."

"Most unfortunate, is it not, my lord? So maybe it would be best if I find an adequate cliff to jump off, thereby relieving you of the burden of an unloved wife – a wife you've even suspected of being faithless." She kicked at him, angry with herself for crying, with him for making her feel so worthless. "But I never was. It wasn't me thrusting my tongue down someone else's throat."

"I did no such thing! You misconstrue!"

"And you lie! But go ahead, suckle Lady Duckmouth's lips dry. I don't care." She stalked towards him. "But as you make your bed, you must lie in it, my lord. You lie with whores and you will not come anywhere close to me. God alone knows what unsavoury diseases you might have picked up from her and others like her."

"I told you," he said, his voice ragged. "I have never bedded with any of them."

"Difficult to believe at present, my lord." He extended his hand towards her, but she backed away, shaking her head. "No. Besides, I have a cliff to find." With that she fled, banging the door in her wake.

"God spare me a scolding wife," Adam muttered, sinking down to sit on the bed.

"What was she to think?" William said, coming over to join him.

"She should know me better than that!" Anger flared through him, sputtered and died.

"And if it had been you, coming upon Lord Roger and Katherine in a similar situation?" William asked.

"I don't know." Adam dragged a hand over his face. He beckoned Lionel to come over with his boots, and stood to stamp his feet into them. On the floor lay a ribbon, one of the pair of green ribbons that had decorated her braids. He picked it up, running the silk through his fingers. She'd been quite a sight, his wife, that dark red hair gleaming in the morning sun, her kirtle hugging her supple figure. And her eyes...he winced as he recalled the look of astonished hurt in them, but couldn't suppress the jolt of pleasure at the jealousy he'd seen, bolts of blue ice directed at Jeanine.

"I'd best go and find her." He smiled slightly. "Before she finds that cliff."

"Yes, that would be most unfortunate," William replied.

The door crashed open, a breathless stable lad nearly falling into the room. "M' lord, m' lord," he gasped.

"Yes?"

"Your lady wife," the lad went on. "I tried to stop her, m' lord, but—"

"Stop her doing what?"

"Your horse." The lad threw Adam a despairing look, and a cold fist closed round an indefinite point in Adam's chest. "She took your horse, m' lord. Yon devil Goliath, she's astride him and long gone."

"What?" Adam ran – no, he flew out the door.

When Kit escaped Adam's room, she hurtled down the stairs, wanting to run as fast and as far away from all this as possible. She rushed through the hall, barged into Jeanine, who cursed her and shoved at her, yelling that Kit had torn her hair out, and finally she was outside, having to reduce her speed not to slip on the cobbles.

Damned man! She sobbed, sobbed again, but converted the sound to a cough, hiding her face from the curious men by the simple expedient of wrapping herself in the cloak and pulling the hood up.

On the other side of the yard, their horses stood saddled and waiting. As always in the absence of his master, Goliath was throwing a tantrum, tail swishing as he lunged at the unfortunate stable boy given the task of holding him. Today, however, her temper matched his, and Kit marched over and snatched the reins from the surprised boy.

"My lady," he protested, eyes going very round in his dirty face. "That's not your mount."

"Today he is." She didn't even lead him over to the mounting block, and was proud of herself when she swung herself up unaided to sit on his broad back. He was huge – and restive, his head ducking up and down repeatedly.

"My lady," the stable boy squeaked. "That's a dangerous horse, my lady!"

"And I'm a dangerous lady," she replied, showing him her teeth. "A very dangerous lady – at least today." She clapped her heels to the horse's side, feeling how every muscle beneath her bunched. "Oh, no you don't," she told him, collecting the reins in a firm hold. The horse snorted in reply, and at her command set off at a canter that quickly became a headless gallop, straight into the surrounding wilderness.

Chapter 12

"What is happening?" Mabel stumbled out of her room, colliding with Adam at the head of the stairs.

"Kit," he said, suppressing an urge to shove the old woman aside. "The daft woman has ridden off on Goliath."

"Sweetest Virgin!" Mabel gasped, leaping after him down the stairs, with surprising agility for one so old. "Oh, dear Lord! What if she falls off? What will it do to the babe?"

"The what?"

Mabel blanched and swallowed. "I…" She looked away. Adam gripped her by the shoulders and gave her a little shake.

"Are you telling me my foolish wife is risking not only her neck, but that of our unborn child as well?"

"It's not certain," Mabel mumbled, "but yes, I think she may be carrying."

Adam released her. "A horse!" He grabbed at the man closest to them. "Get me a horse, now!"

In the far distance, Goliath and Kit were still visible, her cloak whipping behind her like a tail. If the horse threw her… Goliath had a savage streak, and had scraped more than one rider off against an overhanging branch, or a suitably situated wall.

The stable boy came running with a horse, and Adam leapt astride.

"Ugly but fast," the boy said, standing aside when Adam dug his heels into the flanks of his mount. With a snort, the horse set off, a jarring trot switching to a fluid canter, and then a gallop.

Following Goliath's tracks was easy. The sodden ground showed clear marks of iron-shod hooves, a dotted pattern running like an incomplete cross-stitch over the fading autumn grass. Catching up with Goliath was another matter, no matter how much the gelding laboured. A stone wall, and the ground bore clear signs of where Goliath had taken off, a deep indent where he had landed. A tussle between horse and rider, he concluded, taking in an area of kicked-up turf, as if Kit had ridden Goliath in circles, bending him to her will. Off again, aiming for the nearby wooded hill. Adam pounded his heels into his mount, urging him on. Goliath and copses of trees did not go well together. Adam swallowed, recalling the Bible story of how Absalom's hair had got tangled in the overhead branches of an oak, leaving him hanging and helpless.

She had succeeded in turning the horse before they entered the woods. And not much longer after that, Goliath had managed to throw his unwelcome rider, at least to judge from the loud and angry invectives Adam heard as he approached. Katherine – Kit, he had to remember to call her that – was covered in mud, trying to regain her feet in the shallow, dirty pool of water. To one side, Goliath was grazing, ears twitching for an instant in the direction of Adam.

"I'm going to flay you, eat you and throw your hooves to the dogs," Kit told the horse once she'd reached firmer ground. "And what are you staring at?" she demanded, scowling at Adam.

"He threw you off, did he?" He couldn't help the little spurt of satisfaction at the fact that she hadn't managed his horse – not now, when he could see she was safe and sound, no matter how bedraggled she looked.

"No, I felt like wallowing in the mud." She gave him a cold look. "It's your fault." She took yet another step, slipped and overbalanced, landing on her knees. "Ow!"

"My fault?" Adam dismounted, sliding gingerly down the slope, and held out his hand to her. She ignored it, levering herself back to her feet on her own.

"If things had progressed as planned, you'd not have had Jeanine sitting on your lap – it would have been me." She threw him a blue look, quickly hidden by her long lashes, and Adam regretted not having been alone when she entered. Her on his lap, her arms round his neck, while he…He shook his head, dispelling these pleasant but distracting images, and concentrated his attention on his muddy wife, who averted her face.

"But I wasn't thinking properly, was I?" Kit continued. "Clearly you prefer her to me."

"What have I done to make you think that?" Jeanine was buxom and warm, had a laugh that gurgled from her, and breasts that begged to be fondled – but he wasn't interested, and ever since yesterday all he could see were the poor woman's lips, swollen into a permanent pout. Not, perhaps, a duck's bill, but enough to make him want to laugh when he saw her, a whispered 'Duckmouth' echoing through his brain.

Kit glared at him. "I don't know, what do you think? Maybe it was seeing you almost naked in bed, with her just as undressed? Or do you make a practice of talking to people in only your shirt?"

"I was asleep!"

"Yes, I saw that – asleep and sitting up straight, eyes stuck to precious, simpering Jeanine."

"Jesus and all his saints, give me patience," he muttered. "She brought me a mug of spiced wine. Aye, likely she was hoping for more, but I wasn't."

Blue eyes met his. "She had her hand in your lap."

"Aye." He twisted. Jeanine's hand had not been inactive, and his member had stirred – slightly.

"And you just let her?" Kit bent down, scooped up some mud and threw it at him. "You're a hypocrite, Adam de Guirande, pretending to be so full of righteous indignation, and yet you'll allow a woman like her to fondle you!"

"She was not! And had you not come in—"

"You'd have pulled the bed-hangings," she interrupted. Yet another dollop of mud landed on his tunic.

"I'd have thrown her out. And stop throwing mud at me."

"What else can you say?" This time the clod of wet earth struck him straight in the chest. "I hate you, you hear? For making me love you, and then treating me like soiled, discarded linen – or even worse, treating me as if I didn't even exist." She wiped her muddied hand down her skirts, and grimaced.

"And what about you?" Adam demanded, swallowing a smile. She loved him! "What did you do but the same?

Seducing me, making me care for you, and all the time you were living a lie."

"I would have told you. I wanted to tell you." She rubbed at her face, leaving garish streaks of mud behind.

He took a step towards her. "And when you tried to ride off in Oxford? You were going to steal away like a shadow in the night, and leave me behind. And even worse, you would have stolen my child with you."

"Your child?" Her hands dropped to her stomach. "She told you? That old crone drives me out of my wits."

"Why didn't you tell me?" he asked.

She gnawed at her lip, hands picking at her mud-encrusted girdle. "How could I?" she finally said. "It would have been the equivalent of taking your choice away from you. Knowing I was with child, you'd not have put me aside – you're too honourable to do so." She looked away. "And I wanted you to choose me, not the child."

Adam slipped an arm around her waist and drew her close enough to kiss her on her nose, the single un-muddied part of her face. "I don't want to put you aside. I've never wanted that. Even at my angriest, I never wanted that." He tightened his hold on her. "You're my choice, sweeting." He kissed her, ignoring the taste of mud on her lips. "And don't you dare close your eyes when I kiss you," he murmured.

She opened her mouth to his, eyes the colour of forget-me-nots locked into his. Her hips grinding against his, her arms tight round his neck, and that wonderful, welcoming mouth – it made his blood race. Had it not been for the fact that the ground was wet and cold, and that he could hear the sound of approaching horses, he would have taken her there and then. He pulled free, leaned his forehead against hers, and tried to calm his thumping pulse.

"Not here, not now," he said hoarsely. He nibbled at her neck. "They say it is a grievous sin to lie together for other purposes than that of procreation, but I will not be able to abstain."

"Nor me." She melted, shivering, into his arms. "Whatever penance I am given, I will do it gladly."

Adam chuckled. "I don't think that's how penance is supposed to work, Kit." It was the first time he'd called her that, and he saw a pleased smile flash across her face.

"And I don't think God would have given us such a wonderful gift if it is a sin." She moved sinuously against him and kissed him hungrily. Adam decided then and there that whatever penance he was given would be worth it.

Someone hailed them, and with a rueful smile, Adam broke away from her, retaining a hold on her hand. "Later," he promised. He tightened his grip on her hand. "Besides, there's the slight matter of chastisement as well, wife."

"Chastisement?"

Adam nodded in the direction of Goliath. "I told you, did I not? You ride my horse and I will have to punish you."

Kit's throat and face went a deep red. "Punish me?"

"Oh, yes. I'll not tolerate a disobedient wife — even less when she places my child at risk." He was hard put not to burst out laughing at the expression on her face. As if he would ever raise his hand against her again. Adam tweaked her cheek. "It was a foolhardy thing to do," he said softly. "What if you had fallen and lost the child? Or broken your neck?"

Kit hitched a shoulder. "I was too hurt to think that far." Her eyes flashed. "Besides, I am an excellent rider. He didn't throw me, I decided to slide off."

Adam threw his head back and roared with laughter.

They arrived at Adam's castle, situated outside of Cleobury Mortimer, just as the sun dipped out of sight behind the western horizon, this as a consequence of the morning's escapade. For most of the way, Kit had ridden beside Adam, while a sulking Jeanine had retired to ride further down the line. Why she insisted on accompanying them was something of a mystery at first, until Adam explained she was making for Lichfield, and was hoping to find another party with which to ride on the morrow.

"Well, she isn't staying with us if she doesn't," Kit said.

"Of course she is. The rules of common courtesy apply — especially for a woman travelling alone." His tone indicated this was not up for discussion. Kit made a face. Alone was an exaggeration. Jeanine had one maid, one groom and two burly men armed to their teeth – not exactly an unprotected waif.

"So where do we put her? In the solar?"

Adam raised his brows. "The hall will do. The castle is old, there is but one solar, and that is mine – ours."

Compared to Wigmore, Toot Castle was a sad little thing. A high curtain wall enclosed a small bailey, there was a range of low buildings hugging the wall to one side, a stone keep on the other. Steep wooden stairs led up to a large door, and on the inside was a dark and gloomy hall, inadequately lit with torches and a smouldering fire.

"It's not pretty," Adam said defensively. He beckoned to a boy and flung himself down in the large carved chair that presided over the central table.

"Not home either," Kit said, taking in the bare walls, the lack of anything resembling comforts.

"Home?" Adam downed the wine the boy had brought him. "I think not. I don't have a home, have never had a home. This…" he gestured at his surroundings, "…is not mine. I hold it for Mortimer – it defends the crossing over the River Rea."

"Ah. So where will we live?"

Adam shrugged. "As I hear it, Tresaints is a right pretty place."

"Tresaints?" Kit's throat clogged.

He gave her a quizzical look. "Does that not please you?"

Kit couldn't quite speak, but nodded repeatedly, blinking her eyes free of tears. "It's my home." The house her mother had adored, the only place she truly loved. She was suffused with longing for the small manor house, her chapel and her people. "When can we go there?"

Adam sighed. "Not for a long while yet. I must muster my men and return to my lord. I aim to leave you at Wigmore when we ride off – you'll be safer there." He looked glum, and Kit went over to touch him, placing a hand on his shoulder.

"And then what?"

"Then we ride to war," Adam said bitterly, "and this time Lord Roger stands mostly alone."

"Alone?" Kit tightened her hold on him. "What about that earl, the one up north?"

"Lancaster?" Adam spat to the side. "He refused his aid in the matter of Leeds Castle, saying he would not risk himself – not for Badlesmere. There's bad blood between the high and mighty Lancaster and the Lord Badlesmere. Besides, even Lancaster would baulk at riding against his royal cousin, and as I hear it, the king himself has taken the field."

"He has?"

"Yes." He turned to face her. "How am I to ride against the king? But how can I refuse to ride with my lord, the man who has made me what I am?" He inhaled, held his breath and expelled it slowly. "Ah well, there's still hope. Our lord will try and reach an accord with the king." For some time he was silent, fingers toying with his empty cup. He made a visible effort and cocked his head at her. "Shall we inspect the solar, my lady?"

"Is there much to see?" Kit teased, anxious to help him dispel the sombre mood.

"A bed, as I recall." Adam grinned. "What else should it have?" He swept her up and carried her up the stairs, ignoring her loud insistence that he set her down. As they reached the top, Kit caught sight of Jeanine, scowling at her from the other side of the hall. Kit smiled triumphantly, making Jeanine toss her head and stick her tongue out.

Adam banged the door closed with his foot and carefully laid her on the bed. Stormy eyes regarded her as he tore at his clothes, at hers. There was an urgency to him, a heat that seemed to sear him from within and spill over onto her, causing an agonising shortness of breath, an oppressive sense of limited time. His legs between hers, his breath on her cheek, a pounding force that joined him to her, had her clinging to him like a shipwrecked to a spar. A reconfirmation of life, of strength, an immersion in a present that held no threatening tomorrows, no muted sounds of impending war, but contained only them. Him. Her. Nothing else mattered.

Much later, and she was curled on her side, head resting on his shoulder. "It's a very male room," she said, now at leisure to study her surroundings. Bare walls, bare floor, a table in a corner with a stool beside it, an earthenware basin with a matching pitcher and nothing much else but the bed, hung with bed-hangings that looked as if they hadn't been shaken in years.

"Male? Bare, I think." Adam tugged at her hair. "I don't keep much here, and when I am here, I mostly bed down in the hall with my men."

Kit rose on her arms to look at him. "Haven't you had any women here before?"

Adam laughed. "Here? No, but I didn't come virgin to our marriage bed – what man does?"

A green-eyed snake stirred in the pit of her belly, wondering just who had taught him how to love a woman.

He tweaked her nose. "But I am very glad you did, my sweeting." He settled himself beside her. "I could get used to this," he yawned, draping an arm over her to hold her close. "Hours spent in bed, with you."

"I'm hungry," she protested.

"Later." His breath tickled her nape. "When I say so." She could hear the smile in his voice.

Chapter 13

She didn't say much as he led her up and down the castle next day. Now and then, she nodded at what he was saying, the people she met were greeted with a fleeting smile, but Kit kept her thoughts about his castle to herself, which made Adam all that more eager to point out the improvements he had made. She stood for some time under the portcullis, head craned back as she studied the raised gate, and he could see her gaze flitting from the gatehouse to the keep, as if measuring the distance, the number of leaps required to run from the walls to the protective stone of the looming building, should an enemy overrun the battlements.

"What do you do for food and water?" she asked, hiking up her skirts as they crossed the yard. "If there's a siege, I mean." She sounded casual, but Adam could see that his comment about war last night had her concerned.

"There's a well in the cellar of the keep." He set a hand to her waist and directed her towards the keep. "And a secret passageway," he added in an undertone. Not that he would ever use it – Adam shied away from the thought of braving that dark, enclosed passage.

"How convenient. You can sneak out and attack your besiegers from the back." She mimed a stabbing movement.

"Or escape to fight another day," he said drily, allowing her to precede him up the stairs to the hall.

It was time for mass, and as Toot Castle had no separate chapel, a small space abutting the hall did duty as chapel. Adam stood and knelt, gave all the expected responses and added his voice to the communal prayers, but his mind was elsewhere, making lists of provisions and weapons, what men he should leave behind as a garrison and which he should take with him. And then there was his wife, a gnawing concern – especially now that he knew she was with child. How would she fare, should he die on the battlefield?

"What's this war about?" she asked once mass was concluded, verifying his suspicions that she was thinking as much about the impending war as he was.

"Honour."

"Honour?" She sounded incredulous. "Surely it must be about more than that. Only in the romances would someone value honour over life."

"A knight lives for his honour."

"Dies for it, you mean," she said sharply. "Must you go?"

Adam inclined his head. He was bound by his oath, by his love for Lord Roger, but first and foremost by his honour. "I am nothing without my lord."

He led her over to the window bench and settled himself on the cold stone, staring out at the wooded hills that stretched, endlessly it seemed, towards the west. The trees were bare, he noted, branches swaying in the wind. Dark clouds speeded across the sky, and there was a smell of wet in the air. It would rain before vespers – rain all night. Adam smiled crookedly, tapping at the worn wood of the bench. Rain always reminded him of his father.

"My father was not a good man," he said.

"Your father? I thought we were talking about you and Mortimer." But she sat down beside him, as close as she could get. He draped his cloak round both of them, relishing sitting this close to her while the wind came in gusts through the window, causing the shutters to rattle.

"I must start at the beginning." Adam sighed. "Maybe he was once good, but by the time I was seven, he was an embittered man who drank too much and took his spite out on his wife – or on us. For years, I'd seen him beat my stepmother to a pulp, terrorise my brothers, but one night something snapped, and I stepped between them, telling him to stop." He shivered. "It was some weeks past Michaelmas, and the skies had poured rain on us for three days straight, three days in which he hadn't left the house, using every excuse he could find to abuse my lady stepmother, belt me and my brothers."

"Didn't she fight back?"

Adam looked away. "No." If his father had been a bully,

his stepmother had been a coward, not once standing up for herself – not even for her own son, precious Guy whom she brought with her to the marriage. Guy had been five the time when their father had thrown him against the wall, and as to William, Adam couldn't count the number of times he'd been slapped so hard his head snapped back. But it was Adam who was their father's preferred victim – after his stepmother.

"He nearly killed me," he said, recounting an hour of pain, of savage kicks and punches. In the background, Guy was wailing, William tried to intercede but was thrown away, and his stepmother just sat and watched, as incapable of defending him as she had been of defending herself. He had never forgiven her for that.

"And then…" Adam's hand drifted to the thin white scar that slashed down the side of his face. "He pulled his knife. I don't recall it hurting much at the time, but William shrieked, my stepmother gasped, and Father threw me out, telling me that if I ever came back he'd whip the last remaining life out of me." By then, the rain had become hail, a fierce wind whipping the air. Adam was in only his shirt, barefoot and barelegged. He was bleeding from his mouth and his slashed face, he could scarcely walk and there was a tuft of hair missing from his head. "Fortunately, our young baron was in residence that night."

"You were at Wigmore?"

Adam shook his head. "Ludlow. My father was captain of the guard – had been for some years, after he lost the last of his manors at dice."

"He gambled away his land?" Kit shook her head.

"He blamed everyone but himself for his reduced station in life, and as I hear it Lord Roger was already considering replacing him – my father was not much loved by his men."

"I imagine not. Did he beat them as well?"

"Grown men?" Adam sneered. "I think not."

He went on with his story: a hurt lad crawling through the mud, making for the refuge of the stables; a pair of boots appearing in his field of vision, hands that hoisted him to stand. An exclamation, a curse, and Adam was swept up and carried towards the keep.

"Lord Roger called for his wife, for his squire, and they laid me out on a table in front of the fire in the hearth. I have never been as ashamed in my life as I was then, appalled at having my dirty, bleeding body displayed before my lord and his lady, but he called for water and clean clothes, holding my hand while Lady Joan sewed up the gash." He smiled. "That hurt. Lady Joan said she had to do it carefully, every stitch put in ever so slowly. But at least I didn't cry – I think I was too tired and frightened to do so – and once Lady Joan was done, she had me sitting up before the fire, as naked as the day I was born, so that she could inspect the rest of me."

Kit had taken hold of his hand and was holding it to her heart.

"No one had ever touched me as gently as she did before." Adam recalled fingers sliding over his broken skin, a hand on his cheek, his hair. Once she was done, Lady Joan straightened up, placed a hand on her protruding belly, and told Lord Roger that the lad was staying with them.

"So I did. I became Lord Roger's page, and a sorry excuse for a page I was, at least at first." Adam grinned at her. "I had no notion about courtly manners, but I was right good at telling him what wine was which, and Lord Roger quickly discovered I was good at fighting. Very good, even. That was my father's single gift to me, that he had taught me how to use both sword and bow."

"So what happened to your father?" She ran a light finger over his scar, his mouth.

"Nothing. A father has the right to discipline his children, and he told Lord Roger I was in sore need of regular beatings to keep me meek and obedient." He trapped her digit with his lips, biting down gently before releasing it.

"And your brothers? Your mother?"

"William was put to help Father Denis, having some aptitude for his letters. Father couldn't protest, not when Lord Roger took me as his page, or gave William the opportunity to become a priest." Adam looked away. "But my stepmother and Guy remained in Father's tender care for three more years, until that fortuitous day when he fell off his horse and broke his neck."

"Ah. No wonder Guy doesn't always love you."

Adam gave her a surprised look. "He doesn't?"

Kit snorted and sat up. "At times, Guy looks at you as if you're a big fat fly and he's a frog, waiting for the opportunity to swallow you whole."

"He does?" Adam frowned, recalling a number of recent incidents when his youngest brother had gone out of his way to be malicious, first and foremost with all his comments about Kit and Lord Roger. "But what could I do to help him? I was but a lad myself."

"I don't think Guy sees it quite that way, do you?"

"Most certainly he doesn't," William said, startling them both. He approached and sat down on the facing bench. "It's too cold to keep the window open, brother."

"It's too dark when I close it." Adam didn't mind the chill, not when he was sharing a cloak with his wife. "So you think he dislikes me?"

"Guy?" William pursed his mouth. "He loves you and hates you – as you well know. Loves you for being the big brother who stood up for him, who has taken care of him from the moment you could, hates you for having been chosen by Lord Roger, and for being in a position to help him." William rolled his eyes. "A complicated being, our beloved stepbrother."

"All people are complicated," Kit put in.

"More or less – Guy is more." William turned to Adam. "A messenger just rode in. Lady Joan wishes you to make as much haste as you can. Our lord is riding north to meet with Lancaster, and the king has issued a writ forbidding Lord Roger to meet with the earl, on pain of being declared a rebel." He gave Adam a bleak look.

Beside him, Adam felt Kit stiffen. Under the cover of his cloak, he placed his hand on her thigh and gave it a reassuring squeeze. She covered his hand with hers and gripped it hard.

"It's not going to go well, is it?" Kit asked William once Adam disappeared down the stairs, yelling for Lionel to come with him.

"It's in God's hands." William settled himself in the spot

vacated by Adam. "But no, I do not believe things bode well." He glanced in the direction of where his brother had disappeared. "It gnaws at him – and at our lord – to be forced into taking up arms against the king. A violation of oaths is not an easy thing to do."

"So why do they?"

"Because the king has violated his oaths," William said. "A king who doesn't feel bound by his coronation oaths, who so disregards the laws and customs of his realm – well, it is not easy to trust such a man." He shook his head. "Not yet two years ago, Lord Roger returned home from Ireland triumphant. That Bruce pretender to the Irish throne was dead, the Irish were pacified and revenues were yet again beginning to stream back into the royal coffers. The king was mightily pleased with Lord Roger then, even sent him to negotiate with that stubborn fool, the Earl of Lancaster."

"And then what?" Kit asked.

"Then? Well, then Hugh Despenser happened, didn't he? Dripping poison into that comely royal ear, whispering that some barons needed to be kept on a tight leash, or else they might outshine the king."

"As I hear it, Despenser has been doing more than that." Kit lowered her voice. "Is it true that he and the king—"

"Shush!" William frowned, looked this way and that, as if suspecting an eavesdropper might be lurking within earshot. Not all that probable in a room as bare as an abandoned church. "The king has a great fondness for the Lord of Glamorgan," he said after a while. "And yes, he has been seen holding Despenser's hand, even kissing him, but from there to insinuate other things…No, I do not believe our monarch is so full of sin, so depraved."

"Oh." Kit huddled underneath her cloak. From the bailey came sounds of metal being hammered, and she caught a brief glimpse of Adam's fair head as he hurried off towards the stables.

"Speaking of sin," William went on, "I cannot recall hearing your confession lately."

"My confession?"

William raised his brows. "All of us commit daily sins. All of us must confess and ask for absolution."

"I'm not sure I want to confess to my husband's brother. Things may become too explicit."

If she had hoped to shock him, it didn't work. William eyed her calmly. "I dare say I have heard worse. Much worse." He sharpened his eyes. "You imperil your soul, Katherine."

"Kit," she corrected him. "I am Kit now – not that flighty Katherine." She gave him a smile. "I never liked her much, anyway." Which, after all, was the truth, albeit not in the way William might interpret it – and she had no intention of ever telling him the truth.

"Ah." He nodded and rose to his feet. "A new life requires a new name. Well, dear Kit, I expect you to see me before vespers." He grinned. "Be prepared to spend some hours on your knees praying. All that lustful fornication with your husband comes at a price."

Chapter 14

Kit had barely blinked sleep out of her eyes the day they set off and headed back to Wigmore. Adam rode beside her, William and Mabel were some horse-lengths further down, and behind them came the men-at-arms, twenty more than when they arrived at Toot Castle, and all of them adequately armed.

The last few days had been a flurry of activity, an exhausted Adam tumbling into bed close to midnight. Kit had spent most of the time going over Adam's clothes, repairing a tear in his thick cloak before turning her attention to the gambeson, the padded tunic that he'd wear under his chainmail, a garment that had seen very little care in recent times.

He was wearing his newly repaired cloak today, and had complimented her for her work, his mouth softening into a pleased smile when he discovered the discreetly embroidered horse she'd added to the right-hand shoulder of the garment. As he rode, his movements made the embroidery ripple, and Kit's thoughts drifted to her mother. Alaïs Coucy had been an expert embroiderer, a skill she had passed on to her daughter, together with her love for water. Kit smiled, recalling distant summers in her childhood when her mother would take her down to Lymington – long, tedious days in a litter – and teach her to swim in the icy waters of the Solent. Those long-lost days had been the only times Kit had seen her mother truly happy, her linen shift stiff with seawater and covered in sand. She smiled sadly; all of that had ended when her mother's uncle had died.

"What are you thinking of?" Adam's voice interrupted her thoughts.

"My mother." Kit sighed. "I don't think I understood just how stunted and isolated her life was – until now. Day after day in Tresaints with only me for company – except for those few weeks she spent with her uncle."

"Uncle?"

"He's dead," Kit said. "Last time I saw him was the summer of my thirteenth year. My mother had a share in his saltworks – from her father – and once a year we'd travel down to Lymington and collect her share of the earnings." She frowned. "And then one year, we arrived to find he'd died and his son had sold everything and left for Gascony."

"So your mother was from Lymington?"

"Yes. She always said she was destined to be the wife of a salter – she grew up on the saltworks that bordered the shore. That's where she learnt to swim, that's where she taught me to swim – just in case I somehow ended up in the water. It's shallow but treacherous, and where one day there is solid bottom, the next it has disappeared."

"But instead of a salter, she met Sir Thomas."

"He saw her on the sands, fell in love and courted her over one long summer." Kit frowned. "Well, that is what she told me, but then she also told me that they wed and he died, so who is to know what is true and what is a lie?"

"Does it matter?" Adam asked gently. "By all accounts she lived a sad and restricted life, so let us hope there was some truth in her tale."

"I do think Sir Thomas loved her," Kit said.

"So it seems. And maybe she'd be happy to see you living the life she was cheated out of." Adam smiled at her. "Maybe she wanted you to have a husband like me." She could hear in his voice that he was hoping for something.

"She'd have loved you, Adam de Guirande." Kit leaned towards him. "And so do I."

They rode in silence for some time, Kit listening with half an ear to Mabel, who was talking in an intense tone with William.

"…And as I hear it, Lady Cecily is thinking of departing for France," Mabel said.

"France? Why is she going to France?" Kit asked. Mabel fixed her with a warning look.

"You know that well enough, my lady. She aims to visit her grandmother, Lady Jeanne."

Kit's brows rose. Lady Cecily had a grandmother? The poor woman had to be as old as the rocks. "How old is she now?" she asked in a casual tone. "I always forget."

"Three score and twelve," Mabel sighed. "Not long for this world."

Adam laughed. "As I recall, people have been saying that about her for the last ten years or so. Sir Thomas is mightily irate with her for not being polite enough to die, thereby passing all her lands to his wife." He shook his head. "Sad, is it not? Lady Jeanne blessed with but the one child, a daughter, and that daughter dead since many years back."

Kit was not entirely certain this was a bad thing. If Lady Cecily's disposition came from her mother's side of the family, the fewer of them there were the better.

"Lady Eleanor died in childbirth," Mabel said. "Too narrow around the hips."

Kit could feel the old woman's gaze assessing her own hips. "Well, clearly my lady mother did not inherit that defect," she said out loud.

"Nay. Lady Cecily has proved most fertile." Mabel urged her mount into a trot, coming up alongside with Kit. "I am sure you will be too, my lady."

"Oh." Kit caught the pleased look on Adam's face and decided to change the subject.

The moment Wigmore Castle's massive walls became visible, the party grew silent. It was as if each plodding step was bringing them closer to a point of no return, to the inevitable confrontation with the fact that war was upon them, and in a matter of days Adam would be gone, riding off to join his lord. Kit couldn't help it – she just had to ride close enough to Adam to clasp his hand – hard. His fingers closed round hers, and they rode like that for some time, in silence and holding hands.

The guards at the gatehouse greeted Adam with curt nods, and the large bailey was strangely deserted, sunk into a restless silence, as if the castle itself was waiting for news as to the events occurring several days' ride from here. A couple of dogs, the ancient smith leading a horse, and only a dozen or so of men-at-arms were in the yard, even if Kit could see a number of men strung out along the walls.

"Where is everybody?" she whispered to Adam as he lifted her off her horse.

"Gone." He motioned for a boy to come and take Goliath. "What men Lady Joan could spare she's sent off to join Lord Roger." Adam frowned at his own men: six mounted men-at-arms, and two dozen on foot. Not, in Kit's opinion, the most impressive of fighters, but she supposed that sometimes one had to make do with what one had, and at least the men looked determined and healthy.

"Ah, Adam, at last!" Lady Joan's voice floated down from the hall's main door, and with the grace of a flighty girl she came running down the stairs.

"My lady." Adam bowed deeply. "I trust—"

"We've had word," Lady Joan interrupted. She twisted her hands together. "You'd best join me in the hall."

Kit wasn't sure if she was included in this sweeping invitation, but decided to follow her husband up the stairs. Lady Joan sat down in her husband's chair and motioned for Adam to take a seat beside her. Kit she ignored, thereby leaving her standing.

"Leeds Castle?" Adam asked.

Lady Joan nodded. "The king himself led the final charge. The garrison surrendered in exchange for their lives, but were hanged, every one of them. And as to Lady Badlesmere…" Lady Joan looked away. "He's thrown the poor woman in the Tower – with her young children."

Heavy silence greeted her words. Kit sidled closer to Adam.

"But you said—" Kit began.

"I was wrong!" Lady Joan turned to face them, eyes blazing. "I believed there was some honour in the man who sits on the throne, but I was wrong – so wrong. And if he does this to the wife, what will he do to the husband? What will he do to my husband, should he not prevail?"

"He will, my lady," Adam said, "of course he will. Is he not one of England's most capable and experienced generals?"

"He rides against the king." Lady Joan shrank before their eyes, looking tired.

"And we both know how inept a soldier King Edward is." Adam sounded calm. "Brave and strong, most certainly, but a warrior he is not."

Lady Joan gave him a grateful smile. "No, he isn't, is he?"

"And where is Lord Roger now?" Adam asked.

"He never entered Kent – Pembroke warned him not to. Instead, as you already know, he and Hereford are riding north, to meet with Lancaster." Lady Joan clapped her hands, telling the young page who appeared to bring wine and bread.

"I shall ride to join him tomorrow," Adam said, getting to his feet. His broad shoulders bowed for an instant, as if carrying an unbearable weight.

"No," Lady Joan said. "Not yet. I have sent my household knights off to muster more men, find more horses. My lord husband needs all the men he can get, and I mean to send you off with at least one hundred." She gave Adam a fleeting smile. "So for some days more you remain at Wigmore." Eyes as sharp as cut glass settled on Kit. "Best make the most of them."

Adam immersed himself in work. Horses to be shod, swords to be tempered, men to be fitted and trained – his tasks kept him busy from well before dawn to just before compline. As long as he kept busy, he could keep at bay the overpowering sensation of premonition that he felt every time he looked due east, in the general direction of London and the king. This would not go well for Lord Roger, not when the king was raising the royal arms and calling his nobles to help him punish his rebel barons, that ingrate Lord Roger Mortimer and that old warhorse Humphrey de Bohun, Earl of Hereford.

All previous supporters of Lord Roger had melted away, as ephemeral as a snowdrift in May. Lady Joan swore and raged at them, but mostly she raged at Thomas, Earl of Lancaster, who had refused his support in the matter of Leeds Castle, and who remained a passive presence in the north. Even more she raged when news came back of Lord Roger's fruitless meeting with Lancaster. Yes, Mortimer had his support, but for now Lancaster had no intention of bestirring himself sufficiently to join forces with him.

"Why is he staying away?" Kit asked Adam in an undertone, keeping a cautious eye on Lady Joan, who was wandering up and down the room with a silver goblet in her hand.

"Lancaster believes he is invincible," Adam said. "True king of the north, he styles himself, and so he believes his dear cousin will not move against him, unless provoked."

"And do you think he is right?"

Adam sighed. "The king does not forget a slight – ever. And his dear cousin, Thomas of Lancaster, has on more than one occasion twisted the royal nose out of joint. He may have convinced himself the king has forgotten, but if so the earl is a greater fool than most."

Over the coming days, Mortimer retainers came riding to Wigmore, the men to fight and the womenfolk and children to remain within the protective embrace of the fortress. Adam was kept busy from dawn to dusk, and only at night and at mealtimes did he have the luxury of spending time with his wife. After yet another exhausting day he was glad to find Kit waiting for him just outside the armoury, and they crossed the yard together, making for the privacy of their room. There was a nip to the air that brought out roses in Kit's cheeks and promised frost later on, and Adam was promising he'd kiss the cold from her fingers when they collided with someone in the doorway.

"Why, if it isn't my son-in-law," a grating voice said.

Beside him, Kit inhaled. Adam tightened his hold on her hand.

"Ah, my sweet Katherine! Step into the light, my child, that I may see you." Lady Cecily held out her hand to Kit, who shied away like a horse about to bolt. As she did so, lingering daylight struck Kit full in the face. "You!" Lady Cecily's eyes narrowed into slanted streaks of blue. "How can you—" She blanched, and with an audible snap she closed her mouth, eyes burning into Kit. "Where is—" She slid Adam a look.

"Your daughter?" Adam filled in, and Lady Cecily paled even more, leaning heavily against the nearest stone arch.

"You know?" she asked.

"I know everything, Lady Cecily." He eyed the woman with distaste. Lady Cecily's long, narrow face froze into a mask, her overlong nose casting a shadow over her compressed mouth. "Poisoned almond paste is a novel way to rid oneself of an unwanted child," he added. Her mouth fell open, causing her chin to all but disappear into her wimple.

"Rid?" she croaked. "How rid?"

"Your daughter is dead," Adam told her brutally.

"No! No, no, no. She's on her way to you. She's your true intended, not her!" She stabbed her finger at Kit. "She's an impostor! She drugged my poor child and—"

"Quiet!" Adam roared. "Your husband tells a different story, Lady Cecily – as does my wife." He placed heavy emphasis on the last word.

Lady Cecily's chest heaved – up and down it went, those thin, long-fingered hands of hers tightening into fists at her side. "Disobedient to the end," she said, closing her eyes. "Dear God, why couldn't she do as I asked?" She opened her eyes, turning the full force of her glare on Kit. "You should have been dead! You, not her."

"Me?" Kit sounded so surprised Adam realised she had never considered that Katherine might not have been the intended victim. In response, Lady Cecily spat in her face. With an expletive, Kit recoiled.

"I will kill you!" Lady Cecily screeched, making as if to launch herself at Kit. Adam stepped between them.

"You'd best beware, Lady Cecily," he said. "I'll have no compunction in exposing you as a murderess if I have to."

Without another word, Lady Cecily shoved by him and darted through the door.

Kit could not stop shaking. After escorting her to their room, Adam had disappeared in search of Lady Cecily, promising Kit the lady would leave – whether voluntarily or not – before mass the next day.

"How could she?" Kit asked Mabel, who trailed her up and down the room like a protective dog. "Poison?" She shook her head.

"Lady Cecily is formidably single-minded," Mabel said, making a grab for Kit. "Sit down, m' lady."

"But to kill your own child...how could she take the risk?" Kit slumped deeper into the window seat, trying to peer through the yellowish, near-transparent skin that filled the role of precious glass in the less luxurious rooms.

"She didn't mean to," Mabel reminded her. She sat down, leaning her elbows on her knees. "Lady Katherine must have found the casket, hidden away in one of the satchels. She'd have seen her brother's name on the letter, and known immediately this was yet another of her mother's gifts to her precious eldest son. I dare say Katherine only intended to take her share – Lady Cecily's almond sweetmeats are quite delicious."

"And lethal," Kit put in. "She wanted to kill me! Me! As if any of this...this...dung pile was of my making. "

"Oh, Lady Cecily has quite forgotten her participation in the events," Mabel said. "An admirably selective memory, she has." She patted Kit's hand. "You need not concern yourself, m' lady. From the look on your husband's face, Lady Cecily will be far gone by tomorrow."

"But she may return."

"She may." Mabel sighed. "A posset, m' lady? With all this upheaval you've missed supper."

Kit nodded. Something hot and nourishing would help soothe the agitation that had her belly tightening in knots.

Upon his return, Adam threw himself across the bed and groaned. "Like an adder," he said. "No, like an entire nest of adders. God must be punishing Sir Thomas for multiple sins by burdening him with that harpy." He raised his head and looked at Kit. "She'll be gone at dawn. I have men escorting her all the way to Bristol, and they have orders to set her aboard the first ship that sails for Bordeaux and remain until the ship leaves before returning here."

"Bordeaux?" Kit sat down on the bed.

"For her long overdue visit to Lady Jeanne. May the old lady have pity on us and die – slowly – ensuring Lady Cecily remains with her." He sat up. "I will also inform Sir Thomas. He must rein in his wife or I will accuse her of murder." His boots came off, he unbuckled his belt, drew the tunic over his head and fell back against the pillows, gathering her to him. "Thank the Lord you're not her daughter," he said fervently.

"Amen to that," she replied.

Chapter 15

Two weeks after returning to Wigmore, Adam stood halfway up the stairs to the keep and inspected the teeming bailey. Five score men, most of them on foot, but all of them hale and strong, although some not as young as he'd like them. He scanned the stacked panniers, the loaded carts and nodded to himself. It was time.

With a shout he brought them to order, waiting until they were silent before telling them they'd ride out just after daybreak on the morrow. There were some attempts at cheers, but they fell flat, his men just as aware as he was of how badly all of this could end. He urged them to spend these last hours wisely, grinning as he explained that this did not mean fornicating in the hay, but rather kneeling before the priest and asking for absolution. This brought a roar of laughter, the sound converting to loud applause when Lady Joan appeared, promising them all the wine they could drink.

Adam took his own advice and retreated to spend some time in the chapel. Old Father Denis was ailing, and the only other priest available at present was William, which made Adam decide to leave his confession until later – Lord Roger always had a high-ranking churchman or two among his companions. But when William invited him to pray with him, Adam complied, his gaze stuck on the dancing light beams that filtered through the small stained glass window.

"I must tell Kit," he said as he got off his knees.

William nodded and surprised him by enfolding him in a hug. "God be with you," he said, his voice cracking.

Adam attempted a laugh. "I'm not gone yet."

"I know." William grasped his hand. "I will be there for your wife."

"Are you insinuating I might not be?" It came out harsher than Adam intended.

"Well, not for the coming weeks, you won't," William replied, giving him a placating smile. Adam wasn't fooled; he could see his own fears mirrored in his brother's eyes.

"Pray for me," he said as he exited the chapel.

"Always," came the reply. "You are always in my prayers, my brother."

Adam entered their bedchamber and sank down on the bed, feeling too tired to take off his boots and tunic. It was happening. Dear God, they were riding out to war, and should they fail…

Kit set down her sewing and came over to sit beside him, taking his hand in hers. "What's the matter?"

"I leave on the morrow. Baron Mortimer has sent word that he and Hereford are riding towards the Marches – and the Severn. He needs me with him when he takes the field against his king. God help him. God help us all."

She leaned her head against his shoulder, slipping her arms round his waist. It made him relax to sit thus, his nose in her hair, her warmth soothing the chill in his gut. She smelled of rose petals and wool, of dried herbs and clean linen.

"I have to pack," he said after some minutes, reluctant to break their embrace. She tightened her hold, sighed deeply and released him. Adam stood and wandered over to his chest, staring at the contents without registering any of them.

"How long will you be gone?" Kit asked.

"I don't know." It might be weeks, months – or an eternity. Since he was old enough to wield a battle sword, he had followed his lord into battle. In Ireland, in the north, wherever Lord Roger was, there was Adam, at first as his squire, then as one of his personal knights, and now as one of his captains. Adam flexed his hand. What Lord Roger had told him to do, he had done, obeying his lord's command without hesitation. He had killed, he had maimed. He had chased after fleeing foot soldiers and ridden them down. He had dispensed martial justice, he had risked his life and his body in the service of Mortimer. Not once had he questioned the wisdom of Lord Roger's decisions – not even when he had them marching on

London last spring. But this time…Adam swallowed down on a heaving sense of unease, a premonition of bad things to come. A man who took up arms against his king was foresworn.

"Sweetest Virgin, help me in this, my moment of need," he whispered.

"What?" Kit gave him a concerned look.

"Nothing." He glanced down at his chest. "Lionel can do this. He knows best what I need."

"Oh." She sounded hurt. "I can do it."

"You've never sent me off to battle before. Lionel has." He raised his voice and called for his squire, who appeared instantly in the doorway. "We leave on the morrow."

"I know." Lionel grinned, cheeks flushed with excitement. "I have most of your belongings ready, my lord, but I can't find your gambeson, and as I recall it requires mending."

"Here." Kit went over to her chest, rummaged in it and produced Adam's quilted tunic, the linen layers stuffed with horsehair. "I found it and mended it." She held it out. "I added some decoration to it." She had embroidered an intertwined K and A on both the cuffs, and along the neckline ran an exquisite decoration consisting of miniature stars.

Adam touched the little K that she'd embroidered over his heart. "No one has ever embroidered anything for me before."

"Well, you haven't had a wife before, have you?"

"No." He smiled slightly, caressing the cuffs. "But now I do." He met her eyes, dark in the weakly lit chamber. "I've never had someone to come back to."

"That is good, isn't it?"

Adam nodded, although he wasn't entirely sure it was. This was the reason for the heavy dread that paralysed his limbs and congested his lungs. Never before had he had anything truly important to lose, but this time…

Kit moved closer and took his hand. "And it's not only one, it's two." She placed his hand on her belly. His son. Adam cleared his throat. A child. A wife. A future life. But first there was this matter of a war.

She was fast asleep when he finally made it to bed, lying on her side with her back towards him. He fitted himself around her, his naked body close to hers. Her skin was soft and warm, her hair tickled his face, and one part of him considered loving her, while the other just wanted to hold her, feel the steady beat of her heart under his hand. She turned towards him, no longer asleep but wide awake. No words, just hands and mouths, teasing, touching. He immersed himself in her, losing himself in her eyes and her body. He took – he could do no other. She gave – everything she had, she gave him. Afterwards, she fell asleep. He didn't, spending the night in lonely vigil, while on the little table the hour candle burnt lower and lower.

When she stirred, he drew her into his arms, nuzzling her neck. "And how is my wife today?" The room was still sunk in shadow, dawn no more than a faint promise.

She burrowed her face into his warm chest. "I don't want you to go."

"I know, neither do I." He rested his chin on her head, and they lay like that for some time, tightly entwined. His heartbeat thudded steadily below her ear.

"If I…" He cleared his throat. "Should I…"

"Shush." She put a finger to his lips. "Don't tempt fate."

"But we must speak of this," he said, raising himself on his elbow. "We can't ignore the darker sides of life." She made as to interrupt but he waved her quiet. "I may die, sweeting. Many men do, when armies crash together."

"Not you," she pleaded.

"We never know. It is in the hands of God, and you must pray, every day, for my safe deliverance."

"If anything happens to you, if you don't return to me, I'll come looking – just so you know."

"If I don't return, you must go to Tresaints, claim your dower rights and keep them safe. For the babe." He caressed her belly, as yet flat.

"My dower rights?" She stared at him. "How do you mean, my dower rights?"

"If we lose, we will all be attainted. Our land, our titles – all revert to the crown."

"You won't lose."

119

Adam ran his finger down her nose. "One never knows, sweet Kit. And if we do, it isn't only our lands. It is our lives as well that are forfeit." He looked tired – and frightened – and belatedly Kit realised he had probably lain sleepless most of the night. She opened her arms to him and held him close to her heart, whispering silly nothings into his hair. He drifted off to sleep, and Kit tightened her hold, wanting nothing more than to keep him here, with her – safe from battlefields and ambitious noblemen, from vindictive kings and certain death.

When he woke, he called for Lionel and had him send for the barber. He washed, had his face shaved and his hair shorn short, telling Kit with a wry smile that long hair was a nuisance under the helmet. She helped him dress, shooing Lionel out of the room to have these last precious minutes with him alone. She tightened the drawstring of his braies, fastened the points of his hose, and knelt to help him with his boots. He didn't speak, neither did she. But his eyes seemed to be eating her, and she just had to touch him everywhere, imprint his body on her skin, in her mind. His tunic and belt, the surcoat with the Mortimer arms, the heavy winter cloak that she had repaired so carefully, and she was done, taking a step back to look at him, drink him in.

He reached out and tugged at her hair. "A lock," he said, sounding very hoarse.

Kit nodded, incapable of speech. She found the shears and snipped off a curl, tying it together with one of the green ribbons he loved so much. When she handed it to him, he gripped her hand and pulled her close, almost crushing her to his chest. She was crying as he kissed her, crying as he told her that he loved her.

"As I love you," she managed to say, giving him a shaky smile.

Adam tugged a ring off his finger and gave it to her. "A keepsake," he said.

"I don't need a keepsake." She brushed at his hair, now far too short, making him look stern and cruel. "I carry you here." Kit placed a hand on her heart.

Adam made an inarticulate sound and left, and Kit sank down on the bed, covered her eyes with her hands and cried.

She stood on the battlements and watched them ride off, her man and the handful of knights in surcoats that displayed their coat of arms, the men-at arms in bright green tunics with a yellow sleeve. Banners snapped in the wind, the November sun glinted on polished harnesses and sword hilts, and from a distance it looked like a festive parade, this impression reinforced by the drums and the flutes, the tooting horns and the barking dogs.

In truth, Kit saw only one man: Adam. Riding at the head of the line, he sat astride Goliath, facing away from the castle, from her. Turn around, she thought, please turn around. Let me see your face one more time before you ride off, one last glimpse to conserve forever in my memory. Just as he crested the hillock, he did. As if drawn by lodestones, his eyes flew to hers. He raised his hand. She lifted her arm in reply, her veil held like a banner to stream behind her. One last look and he wheeled his horse around, spurring it away.

"Come back to me," she whispered, "please come back to me."

The men were long gone, but Kit still clung to the parapet, her gaze locked on the spot where she had last seen him. The wind had an icy edge to it, her fingers were blue with cold, and yet she remained where she was, futilely willing them back – him back.

"They'll not be back any time soon."

The voice startled her. Kit attempted a reverence – difficult to achieve while holding on to the wall.

"I know. Adam did not think they'd be back before Christmas."

"If then." Lady Joan sighed, lifting her second youngest to rest more comfortably against her shoulder. "She is devastated," she said with a little smile. "To Beatrice, the sun rises and sets with her father."

"Papa," the child said, hiding her face against Lady Joan's woollen gown.

"There, there." Lady Joan set her back on her feet, motioning for the nurse to collect her charge. "Papa will be back, my sweet. Now, go with Agnes here, and she will give you some honey wafers." Beatrice brightened, kissed her mother's proffered cheek and took hold of Agnes' hand. "And don't forget to share with little Blanche," Lady Joan admonished.

Kit smiled at the thought of Lord Roger's youngest child, a plump baby far too young to want anything as solid as a wafer. Beatrice bobbed her head a couple of times and was carried away, her high voice asking Agnes when Papa would come back.

Lady Joan sighed. "That has been her single litany these last few weeks: where is my papa? And then, with time, she will forget him." Her eyes acquired a distant look. "I hope to God he returns before that happens."

"So do I," Kit said.

"My husband?" Lady Joan's voice was very sharp.

"No, mine," Kit replied. "Yours too, of course, my lady, but—"

Lady Joan waved her silent. "My lord husband says that you care for him, this man you so loudly protested was too low-born, too poor, to make you an adequate husband."

Kit shrugged. She couldn't very well tell Lady Joan that it hadn't been her doing the protesting.

Lady Joan gave her a penetrating look. "You have changed, Katherine. The will-o'-the-wisp that entranced my husband seems a thing of the past, that flighty young woman converted into a devoted wife." She narrowed her eyes. "A true change of heart, or a convenient mask?"

"People change, my lady," Kit said. "Even irresponsible and inconsiderate girls reach a point in time when they must grow up and shoulder their responsibilities."

"And now you must shoulder the burden of seeing your newly-found husband ride off to war, maybe never to return."

"Don't say that, my lady!" Kit rounded on her. "Adam will come back – he must come back."

"Let us hope so. Let us hope our Lord sees fit to return both our men to us." Lady Joan exhaled. "But sometimes I'm not so sure…" She broke off and muttered something in Latin, which Kit recognised as a snippet from the Lord's Benediction.

"May He turn His countenance upon you and keep you

safe," Kit murmured to herself, her hands clasped together as if in prayer. "Adam said Lord Mortimer hopes to treat with the king."

"Since when do kings treat with their barons?" Lady Joan sounded bleak. "My husband humiliated his liege back in summer. Kings have long memories, and Roger may end up on the receiving end of the king's vengeance."

"But why did you let him do this then? Couldn't you have made him see reason?"

Lady Joan held up her hand. "My lord husband knows the risks. He is far too astute not to. He also knows the risks of not doing anything, thereby allowing that vile serpent, Hugh Despenser, back into the country. He had no choice, Katherine. Crushed between a rock and a hard place, what could Baron Mortimer do but ride out to defend what is his?"

"And if he loses?"

Lady Joan gave her a sad smile. "Then there will be nothing left to defend. There will only be fragments of life left to pick up and put together as well as we can." She shivered in a sudden gust of wind. "It is cold. Come inside with me before you catch your death out here."

Kit shook her head. "I'll stay up here a bit longer."

Lady Joan placed a light hand on Kit's shoulder. "As I said, they will not be back."

"Ever?" Kit choked on tears.

"That, my dear, is in the hands of God. You and I can but pray, hoping our men succeed in keeping themselves alive." Lady Joan gave herself a little hug. "Times of tribulation lie ahead. We must bear it as well as we can." With yet another little pat she was off, her veil lifting in the wind.

Kit's hand closed round Adam's ring, now hanging off a chain round her neck.

"Stay alive," she said. "Whatever happens, stay alive. And I will do whatever it takes to find you and bring you home." For some strange reason, it made her feel better to say that. She wasn't going to be a passive bystander while fate dealt her man God knew what blows. No, Kit de Guirande would do what it took to keep her husband safe – no matter the cost.

Chapter 16

Adam found Baron Mortimer encamped some miles west of Deddington and approached the camp just as day shifted into a dark December night. Adam greeted the sentries, dismounted and handed Goliath's reins to Lionel.

"Make sure he's fed and watered, and then get yourself some food too," he said to his squire, clapping the lad on his shoulder. Four days riding in a constant drizzle had dampened some of Lionel's exuberance, but even so, the lad turned a bright smile his way.

Adam made his way through the camp, now and then stopping to exchange a greeting. The tents drooped in the damp, as did the men and the horses, looking tired and wet after the recent enforced march from Pontefract. Small fires lit up the ground like miniature beacons, and everywhere men were working, some mending harnesses, other polishing armour and weapons. An air of quiet determination permeated the camp; soldiers spoke in low voices while sharing a jug or two of ale, here and there came the unmistakeable sounds of a man swiving a wench, or of a woman laughing.

The ground had been trampled into a muddy slurry, and by the time Adam reached Lord Roger's tent, the rain had become snow.

"It will be cold tonight," Adam commented to Richard de Monmouth as he entered.

Kit's brother gave him a grim smile. "Like all recent nights." He gestured in the direction of the small table. "He is waiting for you."

Not only Lord Roger, but also his uncle, Lord Chirk, and the Earl of Hereford were at the table.

"My lords." Adam bowed and remained standing.

"Ah, Adam, at last!" Lord Roger motioned for him to sit. "And have you brought us victuals as well as men?"

Adam grinned. "Lady Joan has piled the carts high, my lord. And there is wine as well." He dug into his tunic and produced a document, carefully sealed. "From your lady, my lord. As she commanded, I have kept it by my heart."

Lord Roger looked abashed. "She said that, my Joan?"

"Or she'd have my hamstrings for garters." Adam laughed.

Lord Roger tucked the document into his sleeve and invited Adam to help himself to wine and food.

"So, what news?" Adam asked, biting into the leg of a chicken.

"News? Well, none of it is good, lad," Lord Chirk rumbled.

"We heard about Lady Badlesmere," Adam said.

Lord Roger frowned and shook his head slightly, jerking it in the direction of the pallet bed. Someone groaned, and what Adam had assumed to be a pile of bedding stirred, revealing the Lord Badlesmere. The man glowered at Adam.

"Thrown into the Tower," he spat. "My wife, incarcerated by the king." He rose and came over, dragging the blankets with him. Adam bit back on an exclamation at the sight of him. Bloodshot eyes, hair a dirty, tangled mess, and his previously rotund exterior had melted away, leaving a sinewy man who looked years older than he was.

Lord Chirk handed Badlesmere a brimming goblet, patting him gently on the back. Hereford invited him to sit, but Badlesmere refused. He downed the wine, burped, and with a mumbled "Good night" left the tent, still trailing Lord Roger's blankets.

"The king has gained an enemy for life," Hereford commented.

"As has Badlesmere," Lord Roger sighed. "And at present, it seems the king has the upper hand." His face set. "How could things turn so quickly?" he muttered, addressing the billowing canvas wall of the tent rather than his companions.

"They may turn yet again, nephew." Lord Chirk clapped him on the shoulder.

"Or not," Hereford put in morosely. "The king is mustering at Cirencester, drawing men from all over his kingdom. Only the northern barons have as yet not heeded his call."

"They wouldn't," Lord Roger said sourly. "Not unless Lancaster tells them to – and he won't, so we can at least be grateful for that." He swallowed down his wine and poured himself some more. Adam studied him in the flickering light of the candles. His lord looked dishevelled, a shadow of a beard on his cheeks, dark hollows under his eyes. Tension rippled through him like a current through a churning stream – invisible to those that did not know him well, but Adam knew and loved his lord, and noted the twitching of his right eye, the constant finger-drumming.

"We all know the king can't command an army," Adam said, helping himself to a dried fig.

"No, but Pembroke can." Lord Chirk speared a slice of venison. "I wonder how he squares it with his prickly conscience, to go after us."

"His conscience?" Lord Roger laughed harshly. "Why, Pembroke is but doing his duty – to the king. Not necessarily to the realm, though, nor to the laws and customs that govern the kingdom." Once again, he refilled his goblet.

"And our Lord Lancaster?" Adam asked, hoping there would be some good news.

"Lancaster has declared his full support for us," Lord Roger said. "At least, that is what he said when we met in Pontefract."

"And yet Lancaster sits on his arse." Hereford hawked and spat. "What is he playing at? Doesn't he understand that united we stand, splintered we die?"

Adam swallowed at the earl's bald statement, but found a smile for the young lad that came over to serve Hereford some more wine. The bright red hair and the blue eyes marked the lad as a Monmouth, and Adam had to trawl through his brain to remember his name – ah yes, Thomas, named for his sire and, as Adam heard it, Lady Cecily's particular favourite. He wondered what his Kit would make of this brother, a child of downy cheeks and long, angular limbs. The lad was wearing a tabard embossed with the Hereford arms over his woollen tunic, and from the way his eyes darted from Lord Roger to Hereford, Adam surmised this was yet another eager fledging warrior, longing for the chance to prove himself in battle.

Little Thomas de Monmouth would last no longer than the time it took for a man to spit in the wind, should he be faced with a proven warrior.

Hereford muttered something and young Thomas nodded, darting off to do his bidding. By the entrance he collided with his big brother. Richard de Monmouth smiled down at his sibling, said something that made Thomas beam at him, and gave him a quick hug before sending him on his way. It made Adam somewhat jealous to watch this casual interplay between the brothers. He couldn't recall Guy ever fixing such adoring eyes on him.

"We must send to him," Lord Chirk said, forcing Adam's attention back to the conversation. "If Lancaster understands our plight, he will come to our aid."

Yes, Adam agreed with some relief, of course he would. The greatest magnate in the kingdom had little love for his fickle royal cousin – and even less for the Despensers, hating the elder Despenser almost as much as he detested the younger.

"Maybe." Lord Roger sounded unconvinced.

"We could still throw ourselves at the king's feet and beg for mercy," Lord Chirk said.

"We could. And would we get it, do you think?" Hereford asked.

"So far, we have committed no rebellious acts. Pembroke acted in good faith when he warned us not to enter Kent." Lord Roger sighed. "But this is not about Leeds Castle, is it? It is about the king wanting his favourite reinstated, and damn whoever stands in his way." He scrubbed at his face and gave his uncle a bleak look. "I have no choice. If Despenser returns to bask in the royal presence, he will destroy us."

"Or we beg for mercy," Lord Chirk repeated.

"And if he gave it to us, would you believe him? Would you trust the king to not renege on this promise as he has reneged on so many others?" Lord Roger shook his head. "I have tried to serve the king to the best of my abilities. We were even knighted together, all those years ago in Westminster." His mouth curled into a slight smile. "Well, the king, me and hundreds of others." He emptied his goblet and set it down with a bang, gesturing for Richard to fill it up. "But the prince of my youth has grown into a weak and incompetent king, a man for whom an oath is an inconvenience that can be broken at his whim, a man who throws gentle women in a cell. And therein lies the conundrum, my friends." Lord Roger took a sip or two of wine. "I don't trust him. God help me, but I have a king who kicks at his faithful servants and showers his favourites with gold, with lands and estates that by law belong to others. How can I submit myself to him? How can I place my life in the hands of a man who has no honour?" He frowned at nothing in particular. "Thank the Lord he has a goodly son. May God grant me the miracle of seeing Edward of Windsor crowned as king – soon."

"My lord!" Adam threw a furtive look over his shoulder. "To talk such is treason."

"I know." Lord Roger waved his hand at Hereford and Lord Chirk. "Go, seek your beds. I will sit here with my wine and think dark and maudlin thoughts for some time more. And you…" He sloshed some wine into Adam's cup. "You will keep me company."

Hereford exited the tent, looking relieved. Lord Chirk lingered some time longer, eyeing his nephew with concern. They were close, the two Mortimer men, with Roger having spent most of his childhood serving his uncle. Lord Roger raised his cup to his uncle and gave him a crooked smile. Lord Chirk gripped his shoulder and squeezed.

"The Lord provides," he said as he left.

"Not always," Lord Roger muttered to his back.

They sat together in silence. Adam had no need to say anything and reclined in his chair, eyes never leaving his lord and master. Never had he seen Lord Roger so afflicted by doubt, and this only served to settle an ice-cold weight in his innards. Lord Roger had the look of a man who no longer believed in victory, and in Adam's experience, the moment a captain began to doubt his capacity to win, he lost.

Lord Roger cleared his throat and asked Adam for news from home, listening avidly as Adam told him about Lady Joan and his children. He shook his head at the news that Father

128

Denis was ailing, but commented that Lady Joan had an able chaplain in Richard Judas, and as always they shared a chuckle at the poor priest's name.

"And your wife?" Lord Roger asked, giving Adam a cautious look. "How is little Kate, these days?"

"My wife does well," Adam replied dismissively.

"She loves you," Lord Roger pronounced, nodding his head slowly.

"My lord?" Adam was quite taken aback.

"You heard me." Lord Roger chuckled. "Your wife, she loves you. I didn't think sweet Kate was capable of such profound emotions." He downed his wine and called for more. "One of her more attractive qualities if you ask me, this penchant to live for today with no thoughts for tomorrow."

"You're talking about my wife, my lord," Adam said icily.

Lord Roger regarded him over the rim of his cup. "Not much happened, you know."

Nothing happened, Adam thought, grinning inside. At least not with his Kit. "My lord?" he said out loud, sounding disapproving.

Lord Roger shrugged. "Some pleasurable moments for me, a welcoming wife and a fat dowry for you. All in all, not bad for a landless knight."

Adam tightened his hands round his goblet, fighting the urge to throw his wine in Lord Roger's face. "I would prefer not to discuss this further, my lord."

Lord Roger sighed. "I am drunk, Adam. I am also remorseful." He laughed hollowly. "Most apt, don't you think? A man facing potential death should consider his sins." He straightened up from his slouch and beckoned for Richard to pour them some more wine before waving his squire out of earshot. Richard threw Adam a baleful look, clearly unhappy at not being included in the conversation.

"A good wife is an asset," Lord Roger continued. "A wife besotted with her husband is a precious gift. I'll tell you, I was sorely tempted to belt you some weeks back, when you went about glowering like an enraged bear while Kate wilted like a crushed violet." He sipped at his wine. "What did she do to so aggrieve you? Because I can assure you, it did not involve me."

"It is between my wife and me," Adam replied stiffly.

Lord Roger didn't seem to have heard – or care. "I am fortunate in my wife," Lord Roger mumbled. "So, so fortunate. A loyal companion, a fertile wife and good mother – what else can a man want?" He gulped his wine and slammed the goblet down on the table before getting to his feet. "May God keep her safe." He fixed bleary eyes on Adam. "And God help me that I don't cause her too much grief or sorrow."

"Amen to that," Adam said.

Next morning, Lord Roger was his normal, capable self. Freshly shaved and attired in clean clothes, he informed his captains that he had decided to ride for the Severn and retreat beyond it, using the river as a natural protection against their advancing enemies.

"We must make haste," he said. "Once the king sets his men moving, we will be trapped, far from our powerbase and lands."

Adam nodded in agreement. Cirencester was an excellent choice for mustering the royal army, allowing for quick forays due north and west. Lord Roger would have to lead his men in uncomfortable proximity to the royal forces.

Camp was struck in a matter of hours, the heavily loaded carts trundled off one by one, and the men marched after them, setting a steady pace due west. Adam was responsible for the rearguard, and kept a group of mounted sentries with him, men on fleet horses that were sent off due east to keep an eye out for any approaching enemy forces. Nothing, and as the day progressed, Adam relaxed. No one was giving chase, and at this pace they would be safe and sound beyond the Severn come next morning.

Despite the weather, Lord Roger refused to set up tents, saying no one had died of a night out in the drizzle, and damned if he intended to remain one hour more than necessary on the wrong side of the river. Adam spent an unhappy night huddled into his thick cloak – but so did all the others, and it was a tired and sullen army that rose on the morrow to continue marching. Bread to break their fast and then they were off, making for an ancient bridge just north of Gloucester, Lord Roger saying he would be a fool indeed to ride his men through the town itself.

Lord Roger had his mounted knights form a loose protective circle round his retreating men and the heavily loaded carts. Hereford was put in charge of the right, Lord Roger took the left, and just like the day before, Adam captained the small rearguard – fifty men, at most.

Most of the men had made it across when out of nowhere swooped a company of mounted knights, flying the Pembroke colours. Adam yelled out commands, forming his men into a loose arrow formation, and rode to meet the ambushers.

Goliath powered into a gallop, snorting and heaving below him. The visor of his helmet made it difficult to see much beyond the ground directly in front of him, and to his right came the sound of horses, many horses. He heard someone scream. A lance shattered against his shield, he rose in his stirrups and swung his sword, yelling himself hoarse as he called his men to him. He tore through the attackers like a sickle through hay, and with him rode the core of his men, yelling as loudly as he did.

They were through. Adam brought Goliath to a halt and turned him neatly. His men; dear God, what had happened to his men? Adam raised his visor. At most thirty men were still with him, most of them decorated with the same shallow gashes he himself sported. There were dead men everywhere, riderless horses galloping back and forth. In the distance he could see Lord Roger's banner, flying over a writhing mass of fighting men and horses.

Just before him, the Pembroke men he had just attacked had regrouped and were charging towards him, while another group of knights were riding hard towards Lord Roger's banner. So many men – to Adam it seemed their attackers had multiplied from a mere hundred to close to three hundred, even if well over two dozen lay dead at his feet.

The ground shook with the approaching horses.

"*A moi!*" Adam called, spurring Goliath into action. The

huge bay neighed and reared, and when Adam yelled in his ear, the stallion surged forward, carrying Adam straight towards the centre of their enemies. His sword cleaved through an unprotected shoulder, it hacked at an arm, a leg. To his left, Lionel was riding with his shield held high, his voice raised in a constant high-pitched bleating. Adam yelled orders, screamed encouragements to his men, abuse at his attackers. A surcoat drenched in blood rode by. He hacked at a leg, ducked at the last moment when a sword came his way, and unseated one opponent by swinging his shield in his face.

With no more knights barring his way, now there was only an open stretch of ground separating him from Lord Roger's banner, flying in the press of men. Adam drove Goliath in a circle, counted his men. Still approximately thirty, while their opponents were mostly dead or wounded.

"Go!" he commanded, using his sword to point in the direction of the banner. Yet again, Goliath thundered over the muddy ground. Adam slowed his pace, called his men to order so that they rode in a close formation, thirty men who struck the unsuspecting enemy in the back.

Half an hour later, it was over. Those of Pembroke's men who had survived had fled for their lives, while the field was decorated with the dead or dying. Lord Roger was covered in blood – not his, thanks be to the Virgin and all the saints – Adam felt as if he'd been pounded by multiple mallets, and Hereford was grinning from ear to ear, his sword bloodied to the hilt. No wonder de Bohun was reputed to be the fiercest warrior in England, Adam reflected as he took in the earl. To judge from the blood that decorated him, he must have killed several men singlehandedly.

"The river," Lord Roger said, cutting through the general cheering. "We must cross the river – now."

"But our men," Adam protested. "I have men out there, dead or wounded."

"Well then get them, now!" Lord Roger scowled at him. "I'll have the bridge burnt in an hour. Make sure you're across by then."

"An hour?" Adam looked at him.

"Leave the dead, man!" Lord Roger pointed to the east. "How long, do you think, before the rest of Pembroke's men get here? And what were you doing? Why didn't you see them?"

"They came from the right," Adam protested. "They were lying in wait, my lord."

"I don't care! How many men did this cost me?" He rode his roan right at Adam. "I can't afford to lose men, y' hear?" With a loud curse he was off, making for the river. Richard de Monmouth gave Adam a curt nod and rode after him, holding Mortimer's banner high.

Adam spent most of the afternoon fuming at Lord Roger's unjustified rebuke. Twelve men dead, eight wounded, two of whom badly, and Adam sent Lionel to fetch the surgeon and a priest before retiring to inspect his own wounds.

His right sleeve was stiff with blood – not his. He struggled with the ties of the coat of plate, sighing with relief when the cumbersome garment slid off his torso. The surcoat snagged as he pulled it over his head, tearing when he tugged it free.

"Help me," he said to Lionel. "I can't move my left arm."

Lionel was all eyes and trembling hands, still pinched around his mouth after his repeated bouts of vomiting. The lad had done well, Adam thought, eyeing his young squire. Scared almost senseless, Lionel had kept his wits about him and managed to survive unscathed due to diligent use of his shield.

"All of us have been afraid," he said as Lionel lifted the heavy hauberk off him. Here and there, there were dents in the chainmail, but nothing serious.

Lionel nodded but looked unconvinced. "I did not fight," he whispered. "I but cowered behind you and hid under my shield."

"And so you are alive when others are dead." Adam hissed when Lionel loosened the gambeson. His left shoulder hurt, as did his left arm. His linen shirt stuck to his skin, damp with sweat. No blood, though, and Adam relaxed.

Lionel relieved him of his shirt, leaving Adam in only braies and hose. "They died with their swords in their hands."

"I am sure we can arrange such an end for you as well,

should you want it," Adam said sarcastically. He regretted his comment immediately. "They were tried in battle. You were not. Next time you will be a little less fearful, the time after even less." He shivered, grateful when Lionel brought him his cloak.

"You showed no fear." With careful hands, Lionel explored the huge bruise that decorated Adam's left side. It made Adam wince.

"What one shows and what one feels are two different things, lad. Only a fool rides into battle without a twinge of fear. It is fear that will keep you alive, not excessive bravery."

"Well said, Adam," Lord Roger said as he ducked into the tent. "No serious damage?" He unbuckled his vambraces and threw them to clatter on the rickety table.

"No, my lord. And you?"

Lord Roger grinned. "Not a scratch on me." He gripped Adam's right hand. "I spoke out of turn before. It wasn't your fault."

"I know." Adam lowered his voice. "They knew we would ride for the river."

"Of course they did. A newborn babe could work that one out."

Adam shook his head. That wasn't what he meant. "We have to secure the other bridges, my lord. Before they come across." After months of autumn rains, the Severn was swollen with water, affording some protection against their enemies. But should they get across…

Lord Roger frowned. "Best make sure you are healed by tomorrow. We ride for Worcester."

"Yes, my lord." Adam moved his shoulder gingerly. A sore left arm was no major hindrance.

Once Lord Roger left, Adam asked Lionel to fetch him hot water and poultices. He lay face down on his narrow pallet bed as Lionel covered his shoulder and arm with hot, steaming cloths.

"How old are you, lad?" he asked.

"Sixteen." Lionel placed yet another hot rag on his skin, making Adam yelp in protest. Nine years younger than Adam, no more.

"I was eighteen when I first rode into battle," Adam said. "In Ireland, and a sad and dismal campaign it was." He laughed into the pillow. "As I recall, that first time I ducked and hugged my horse's neck, hoping the beast would have the sense to see us through what to me was an incomprehensible jumble of men and horses." He raised his head and looked at Lionel. "There is no hurry in learning to kill."

Lionel grunted something and went on with his work. Adam yawned and buried his face in his pillow, wishing it had been Kit's hands on his back, not Lionel's. With a little smile he groped for the leather thong round his neck and the small pouch that hung from it, containing Kit's lock of hair. He closed his hand round it and wondered if maybe she was thinking of him, as he was thinking of her.

Chapter 17

Ever since Adam rode away, Kit seemed to spend her days in endless vigil. Not so that she stood on the curtain wall all the time – Lady Joan would not have allowed it – but her mind was always with him, wondering if he was cold, if he was well and alive. Outwardly she maintained a rigid calm, submerging herself in her sewing to allow her thoughts to wander, unimpaired, to him.

It struck her sometime during the third week of his absence that with the exception of her mother, she had never felt this strongly about anyone before. Now it was Adam she thought of first thing in the morning, Adam she dreamed of last thing at night. Mostly she fell asleep with her hand on her belly, caressing the child that with every day grew more tangible. Would he know his father? It made her guts gripe to consider the possibility of her child being born fatherless. It made her heart stutter to contemplate a life without him.

Sometimes, she'd lie awake for hours in her bed, encased by bed-hangings, and she would slide her hands over her body, pretending they were his hands, not hers. It never worked, as her own hands never generated the sizzle that his touch did. She felt starved, somehow, like walking about with a clamouring hole inside of you that demanded to be fed. She yearned for the sound of his voice, for the scratchiness of his cheeks, for the curve of his mouth when he smiled at her. The memory of his hand on her back would have her preening like a lovesick cat, the faint recollection of his scent – leather and sweat, horses and steel – had her sighing with longing.

Mabel laughed at her. In a kindly way, but still, reminding Kit that not so long ago Kit had been appalled at the thought of being forced to wed a veritable stranger.

"It was awful," Kit protested.

"Not so awful now," Mabel teased.

"Very awful now," Kit corrected sharply, making Mabel apologise and explain she hadn't meant it like that, more that my lady did, in fact, love this most unwanted husband, did she not?

"Yes." Kit felt herself blushing. "Will he come back?" she asked – like she did a hundred times each day. Christmas had come and gone, with no Adam appearing in nothing but his skin to warm her bed. It made her smile – if only slightly – to imagine Adam thus.

"In God's hands," Mabel sighed. "Best you pray, my lady."

So Kit did, becoming a recurring visitor to the little chapel. The small space was whitewashed, with a well-scrubbed brick floor laid in a herringbone pattern. A beautiful statue of the Virgin with her infant resided in one niche, while in another was the same Virgin, now weeping over the broken body of her adult son. Time and time again, Kit's eyes would lock themselves on this morbid but evocative little sculpture, and she would intensify her prayers and redirect her gaze to the stained glass window that flooded the chapel with multihued light – when the sun shone.

"I did not expect such a devout sister-in-law," William said with a little smile, when yet again he came upon her on her knees before the altar.

"I did not expect to live through the fear of losing my man in warfare," she retorted.

"You didn't?" He sounded surprised. "Men of noble birth have always ridden to war with depressing regularity." He helped her to her feet and led her over to the bench that stood along the northern wall. "Our Adam knows how to take care of himself," he said, patting her hand.

Kit looked away. Every day or so, a messenger would ride in carrying news of the latest developments. Even she understood that matters were dire, with the Mortimer men forced into a constant defensive position. They had retreated beyond the Severn, and since then it seemed to Kit that they'd spent their time racing from bridge after bridge, attempting to ensure the royal forces couldn't cross.

Last they heard, Mortimer had managed to secure the bridge

at Worcester, but this victory had come at substantial losses, and to further plague Mortimer's men, the Welsh had taken the opportunity to do their own rebelling, sweeping down in quick raids on Mortimer's encamped men.

Now and then wounded men arrived at Wigmore, some of them laid flat in the carts, others on horseback. Most of them were sent off to the nearby abbey, where, according to Mabel, the monks were capable healers. Some remained at Wigmore, and Kit found some relief from her gnawing anxiety by helping Lady Joan tend to them. It also created a tenuous bond between Kit and Lady Joan, and after afternoons spent cleaning sword wounds, days holding a stranger's hand while Lady Joan set a long row of stitches, it happened quite often that Lady Joan would invite Kit to accompany her for a last walk along the battlements. Two women standing side by side like silent sentinels, winter winds causing their cloaks to billow behind them as they stared due north. They rarely spoke to each other, Kit lost in her thoughts, Lady Joan's face settling into a mask of concentration.

"I pray," she said when Kit asked her why she looked so determined. "I send my prayers off in his direction." She smiled faintly. "For all that my husband enjoys the company of learned church men, there are times when he is quite remiss in matters of faith. An extra prayer or two on his behalf won't come amiss, I think."

"Probably not," Kit said. "Do you think they will be home for Twelfth Night?"

Lady Joan lifted her shoulders in a helpless gesture. "How can they?"

Kit was steeping feverfew and willow bark into a tea when the dogs began to bark. Loud, joyous barks, and there was the high voice of Beatrice warbling a loud "Papa" over and over again. Kit ran out of the makeshift infirmary, skidding to a halt at the sight of the ten horsemen who had just ridden in.

He was here. She licked her lips and extended her hand in his direction, but made no further move to go to him, content for now to look at him, safe and sound astride Goliath. She did a quick inventory, taking in the sharper planes of his face, the bandage that peeped from under his right sleeve. There was an ugly bruise on the side of his face and he looked in serious need of a shave – and of sleep, his eyes smudged with purple shadows.

His gaze found her. She straightened up, hands dropping to her belly. He followed her movement with his eyes, raised them to meet hers and placed his right hand over his heart before bowing slightly in her direction. He could have thrown a fortune in jewels at her feet and it would not have made her happier. No sooner had his feet touched ground than she was in his arms, and his hands slid down her back to her waist, pressing her close.

"Is it over?" she asked, incapable of keeping the hope out of her voice.

Adam shook his head, something dark flitting through his eyes. "It has just begun."

"But you're here," she tried.

Adam released her, keeping hold of her hand. "A brief visit, sweeting. We return on the morrow."

What? She wanted to cry – or kick at something – but took a deep breath instead. One day and one night was better than nothing, and suddenly the hitherto so dreary winter months were brightened somewhat.

"Lord Roger wanted to surprise his lady wife," Adam continued. "And as we needed to replenish our stores, he thought we could ride escort to the carts."

Kit didn't really care. Out of the corner of her eye, she saw Lord Mortimer approach his wife, watching with some amazement when Lady Joan threw herself around his neck. The normally so contained Lady Joan was weeping, her face hidden against her husband's chest, and the discomfited baron was holding her close and hushing her, while their large household politely averted their eyes. After some minutes of this uncharacteristic behaviour, Lady Joan pulled herself together, smiled brightly at her husband and promised him there would be food and wine in half an hour – for everyone.

Kit groaned. "We can eat in our room," she suggested, not

wanting to share as much as a heartbeat of their allotted time with anyone else.

"There is time," Adam said, raising his free hand to her cheek. "After weeks of badly cooked meat and cold bread, I could do with a meal in the hall – and the company of all the people I love."

"Love?" Kit felt a flare of jealousy. "I thought you only loved me."

Adam laughed softly. "Carnally, yes." He squeezed her hand. "But I have other people in my life – as do you."

William appeared out of nowhere, embracing his brother with tears in his eyes. Kit reluctantly let go of Adam's hand.

"And Guy?" William asked. "Is he not with you?"

"Guy?" Adam pulled his brows together. "Isn't he here?"

William shook his head. "Why would he be? He rode off with you."

"Maybe he defected," Kit suggested. It seemed like something Guy would do if he considered life too uncomfortable.

"Or changed sides," Adam growled. "He left us three weeks ago, to ride back here with a group of wounded. Did they not arrive?"

"Who were the wounded?" William asked.

Adam rattled off some names and Kit shook her head. None of the recent arrivals had names that matched.

William paled. "What has he done? Dear Lord, has he left those unfortunate wretches on the road? Ridden off to join the king?"

"We don't know." Adam gripped William by the shoulders and gave him a small shake. "He may have been attacked himself, killed or captured while he defended the wounded."

William wrenched himself free. "Not our Guy," he said scornfully. "You know as well as I do that Guy de Guirande only risks his hide if it can benefit him."

"What is it?" Mortimer demanded, appearing by their side. "What?" he repeated, frowning at Adam. "Why are you looking as if someone has rammed a red-hot poker up your arse?"

"Because someone has," Adam replied grimly. Briefly, he explained their suspicions to Lord Mortimer, whose dark countenance grew even darker as he listened.

"Ingrate," he snarled, once Adam had finished. He drew in a couple of long breaths. "Not today," he said, throwing an arm round Adam's shoulders. "These few hours we make merry. Matters such as these we put aside until tomorrow."

Except that he didn't. No sooner had they sat down to eat than Lady Joan started questioning the men as to the progress in the war. With each question, Mortimer's mouth hardened imperceptibly, but his wife demanded answers, and Mortimer had no choice but to give them to her. The mood plunged from merry to lukewarm to concerned to fearful, and what had begun as a loud and happy meal ended in silence and grim faces.

Kit sat back, reeling inside. There was no hope. Everything Mortimer told them pointed to an inevitable defeat – unless Lancaster joined forces with them. With the Welsh at their backs and the king in front of them, Lord Mortimer and his men were effectively trapped, especially once the Severn reverted to more normal water levels.

"So where is Lancaster?" Kit asked, her voice loud in the quiet hall.

Mortimer scowled at her. "Where? Sitting on a fence is where he is." He slammed his hand down on the table. "Doesn't he understand that once the king has squashed me, he will go after him?"

"Apparently not," Kit muttered in an undertone.

Mortimer sighed heavily, sank his face into his hands and groaned. "I have sent Hereford to him, so let us hope he can sway that stubborn northerner to come to our aid. Soon." He straightened up and called for more wine. "No more. Now we talk of other things."

It took two men to lug the tub upstairs, and God knows how many men to fill it, but when Kit and Adam escaped to their room, the fragrant bath was waiting for them. Kit whispered a thank-you to Mabel, who beamed and shooed out maids and pages before taking Lionel by the arm and telling him he needed a purge against worms – anyone could see that.

Kit closed the door and bolted it. Alone at last. By the bed, Adam was standing in hose and tunic, having kicked off his boots. In a reversal of that morning when she had dressed him as he was leaving, now she undressed him, starting with his belt. The tunic came off with a loud rustle of damp and dirty wool, and she knelt down before him to help him undo the points of his hose. He smelled of sweat, of grime and smoke. His braies were thrown to the side, the shirt followed it, and Kit rocked back on her heels, studying him for any permanent damage. A fading discolouration on his shoulder, the bandage on his forearm and the ugly bruise on his face – a sword on his helmet, he told her – but all in all, he looked whole. She leaned forward and kissed him softly on his belly.

"Not now." He backed away. "I must reek."

"Which is why I have ordered you a bath." She smiled.

He almost fell asleep in the bath, head lolling back as she washed him.

"Couldn't we just ride off somewhere?" she asked, breaking the quiet.

"Hmm?" He opened an eye to look at her.

"We could go to France," she suggested.

"France?" Two grey eyes regarded her steadily. Kit ducked her head and pretended great concentration on his lower extremities.

"I can't bear it," she whispered. "To see you ride off tomorrow."

A hand cupped her chin, raised her face. "I must." He leaned forward, sloshing water over the edges. "But I will come back."

"Promise?"

He just smiled and placed his mouth over hers in the softest of kisses.

She dried him in front of the fire, rubbing each limb until he glowed ruddy in the light from the hearth. Her hands softened as she approached his groin, and there was a gratifying loud gasp when she took him in her mouth.

Moments later, she was on her feet, her back against the wall as he kissed her. Voraciously, like a starving beast he attacked her mouth with his lips and tongue. Her knees dipped, blood rushed from her head, and she had to grip his shoulders to remain upright. Such beautiful shoulders, strong and rounded.

"I want you naked," he said, and she fumbled with laces, with uncooperative garments that got stuck as she pulled them over her head. There, down to her chemise and hose, and he batted away her fingers, kneeling to undo the garters that held her hose in place. Once she was naked, he took hold of her hands and drew her to stand in the middle of the room. Kit shivered, not sure if with cold or expectation. His hands brushed her mound, rose to rest on her belly. "You've rounded," he said, and she almost laughed at how possessive he sounded.

"That's what happens when you are with child," she said, covering his big, warm hand with her own.

"It makes you beautiful." His hands slid up to her breasts, decidedly much rounder than the first time he caressed them. He smiled down at her. "Let me show you something." He walked over to the window and opened the shutters. Ice-cold wind whistled through the room. "Come." He held out his cloak, draping the heavy material over her before leading her to stand by the window. The yard below was bathed in the light of the moon. "Almost full," he said, hugging her from behind. Kit turned in his arms, enveloping them both in the heavy cloth. She nestled into him and tilted her head back to see his face. In the moonlight he looked as if he had been dipped in silver, aloof somehow – until he smiled.

"These last few nights I have watched the moon wax fuller, thinking of you." He kissed her nose. "It is too cold to love you by the light of the moon, at least tonight, but one day – night – I will love you in the moonlight, and the air will be balmy and fragrant with the scents of summer. That, my Kit, is a promise."

A promise he might not be able to deliver on, she thought with a shudder. But it was a beautiful promise, and she pressed her face against his hairy chest, placing the lightest of kisses over his heart. "I will hold you to it – over and over again."

Adam closed the shutters and led her towards the bed. Without the light of the moon, the room was a collection of shadows, the embers in the hearth spreading a weak glow, no more. Not that it mattered – he needed no light to find his way around her body. His hands on her limbs, his lips on her mouth, her breasts. The sensation of his stubble on her belly, her thighs. His tongue, strong hands holding her still as he loved her with his mouth, making her quiver and twist, fists clenched in his hair. Skin on skin, his body atop hers, a heavy, welcome weight that she wrapped her arms and legs around, wanting to fetter him to her, keep him with her, never let him go. His thigh between hers, that almost unbearable moment when his cock nudged at her, and then he was in her, groaning her name in time with the flexing movement of his hips.

It was well on its way to dawn when Kit at last drifted off to sleep, cradled in his arms. "I love you," she mumbled through a yawn.

He gently bit her ear. "As you should, good wife that you are."

When Kit woke, he was gone, the shallow imprint of his body on the mattress the only indication that he had been there at all – that, and the scent of him, covering every inch of her body. Kit rolled over on her side and decided not to wash – at least not today.

Chapter 18

Lancaster wasn't coming. Adam had no need to hear Lord Roger say it – he could see it in his lord's face. With a curse, Adam threw himself down in a chair. They were doomed, and unless there was some sort of miracle…Adam swallowed, his hand straying to his neck. He didn't want to die – especially not a traitor's death, because how could any man die with dignity while submitted to such iniquities? He closed his eyes. Only once had he witnessed the execution of a man condemned to be hanged, drawn and quartered, and all he could properly recall was the rancid stench of fear, and the screams.

"So now what?" he asked.

Lord Roger rubbed at a new permanent crease on his brow. "We parley."

Too late for that, Adam thought. Had they done so in December, the king could perhaps have been persuaded to show some leniency, but now, well into January, King Edward knew beyond a doubt that he was winning, despite considerable losses at the recent confrontation in Bridgnorth. Adam massaged his hand. It had been a brief moment of triumph, Lord Roger and his uncle riding side by side as they charged the bridge and wrested it out of royal control. But it had all been in vain, and now, when he had at last found someone he loved and cared for, he was to die.

A hard clap to his head had him sitting up straight. "You must have some faith in me," Lord Roger said. "I will do my utmost to minimise the consequences – for my men. For me, I fear there is little hope."

Lord Chirk snorted. "Don't be a fool, Roger. We will parley until that craven sodomite of a king grants us our lives. His nobles will baulk at putting us to death if we submit."

Adam was not as sure, but felt a spark of hope surge through him at the old man's tone. Lord Chirk sounded anything but defeated.

145

Lord Roger gave his uncle a fond smile. "What would I do without you?"

"Despair, apparently," Lord Chirk replied, punching his nephew lightly on the shoulder. "It might be time to send a message to the qu—"

"Shush!" Lord Roger scowled. He lowered his voice. "You will never – and I mean never – mention her again. A missive in the wrong hands could put her in the gravest of dangers."

"*We* are in the gravest of dangers," Lord Chirk said. "So grave, in fact, that we might need her help to make it out alive." He sat down beside Lord Roger. "It is said she has some influence with her husband."

"Not recently. She tried to plead with him when Lady Badlesmere was put in the Tower, to no avail – he wouldn't even allow her to help the hapless children."

"So you have been in correspondence with her." Lord Chirk grinned.

"A couple of times." Lord Roger fingered one of his rings. "She fears the return of the Despensers as much as I do."

"She hates Hugh the younger," Lord Chirk said. "Is there truth, do you think, to the rumours that he's—"

"No." Lord Roger gave his uncle a cool look. "Queen Isabella would rather impale herself on a sword than submit to being raped. Besides, bedding the queen is high treason, and not even Edward could save his favourite should such charges be made."

"Hmm." Lord Chirk looked pensive. "Best to keep that in mind."

"Keep what in mind?" Lord Roger sounded irritated.

"That bedding the queen is treason."

"I have never…" Lord Roger broke off.

"That's not what I hear. Not that it matters much now." Lord Chirk rose to his feet. "Let us hope your relationship with Her Grace will save us instead."

"Have you?" Adam asked once they were alone.

"What does it matter?" Lord Roger snapped.

Adam shrugged. "She is a formidable woman."

Lord Roger's mouth quirked. "Ah yes, most formidable."

He eyed Adam. "I have never bedded her – I have but enjoyed her company, hours spent in discussions rather than in bed-sport, no matter how enticing our fair queen is. I have been tempted, and so, I dare say, has she. But it would be a foolish and dishonourable thing to do. Besides, I love my wife."

"Of course. What is there not to love about Lady Joan?" Adam couldn't help the slight tone of reproof. It was one thing to take the odd wench or two to bed while spending months away from his wife, but it was another matter entirely for Lord Roger to develop feelings for another high-born lady – and Adam could hear from the timbre of Lord Roger's voice that he was attracted to the queen. Adam regarded his lord, thinking that ambition could be a most potent and dangerous drug.

"Once you've been married twenty years, you will understand," Lord Roger said.

Adam suppressed a mirthless chuckle. Twenty years? He'd be fortunate if he lived to celebrate one year. He got to his feet, thinking that never before had he felt so drained, so utterly exhausted.

"Still making for Shrewsbury, my lord?" he asked.

"Yes. If we hold that bridge, we can hold off a further few weeks." He gave Adam a twisted smile. "We need all the bargaining power we can get."

It wasn't only the king's forces that hounded them.

"A plague on the accursed Welsh!" Adam scowled, inspecting the damage from last night's raid. The Welsh came not so much to fight as to steal, and this time they'd made off with five horses and as much weaponry as the beasts could carry – which was a lot. The unfortunate sentries had been found hogtied and badly knocked about, but alive.

"At least they didn't steal Goliath," Lionel said.

"Only a fool would try to steal that horse." Richard de Monmouth laughed.

Adam grinned. "Goliath is particular when it comes to his riders." His horse was a mean-spirited bastard, but Adam loved him, and now and then he thought Goliath might love him back – or at least like him. He offered the horse a wrinkled winter apple, patted him on his neck and went to find Lord Roger.

Adam came to a halt just before Lord Roger's tent. Outside, a group of four mounted knights were eyeing the surrounding men nervously. They were all in full armour, their surcoats proclaiming them to be Pembroke's men, and with a sinking feeling in his guts, Adam strode inside.

The Earl of Pembroke had come himself. Aymer de Valence was standing in front of Lord Roger, hands clasped behind his back, his head nodding at whatever Lord Roger was saying. The earl looked as tired as Adam felt, his back bowed, his face furrowed.

"There is no other way," Pembroke said, frowning down at his muddied boots.

"That is no way!" Lord Roger yelled. "I am no traitor, and you know that, Aymer. I have ever worked diligently on behalf of the crown, and it is only those Despensers – and our royal liege's inclination to give them whatever they might desire, no matter to whom it may belong – that has brought us to this. You know that."

"I do." Pembroke uttered a sound like a disgruntled horse. "But His Grace has another opinion, and it is not I, nor you, but Edward II who rules this land."

"Take it to Parliament," Lord Chirk said. "Convene all our peers and let us have it out there."

Pembroke raised his bushy brows. "The king will not agree to that. He has no need to." He lowered his head and stared Lord Roger straight in the eye. "We both know how this will end, Roger: in ignominious defeat, or with submission. The Mortimers are true Marcher lords, born with their swords in their hands and with the courage of a mountain lion, but this time it will not help."

Adam sneered at Pembroke's sop; did he truly think Lord Roger could be swayed by flattery?

"No," Lord Roger said. "I will not submit – not without a promise of a royal pardon."

"A promise? Don't be a fool!"

"Do you truly expect me to throw myself on the king's

mercy?" Lord Roger laughed. "Despenser would beg him to give him leave to use my guts for sausages – and the king would gladly give them to him."

Pembroke looked away. "What do you want?"

"Our lives," Lord Roger said. "And I want you to guarantee them."

"Me?" Pembroke blustered. "How can I—"

Lord Chirk emitted a bark of laughter. "If you won't pledge your honour, we will not submit." He strode over and gave Pembroke a hearty embrace. "You, de Valence, you're a man of honour. The king is not – as we all know."

"We all live to serve the king," Pembroke said coldly, disengaging himself from Lord Chirk's arms.

"I have done so all my life," Lord Chirk replied. "But it was easier to serve the royal pleasure when Edward Longshanks, may he rest in peace, wore the crown."

Aymer de Valence sighed deeply. "Yes, that it most certainly was." He shook his head at the goblet Lord Roger offered him. "I must return to the king. I will give him your conditions."

"My conditions?" Lord Roger shook his head. "I am not in a position to impose conditions, Lord Pembroke. If I were, they would be very brief: that the king honour the promises he made last September, no more, no less." He sipped at his wine, dark eyes never leaving Pembroke. "As it is, I will settle for my life and a promise that my hereditary lands will pass to my sons."

"That will not happen. You submit and you may save your lives – and that of your sons. But your lands…" Pembroke waved his hand in the air, "…they are lost. Fortunately, your wife is an heiress in her own right."

"Fortunately," Lord Chirk echoed. "Except that these days the king has his lords make war on women as well."

Pembroke's face was flooded by a wave of red. "She refused entry to the queen."

"The garrison submitted – and were hanged. And you wonder we want promises?" Lord Roger bowed in dismissal, remaining in an inclined position until Pembroke had exited the tent.

"Did that go well?" Lord Chirk extended his cup for a refill.

"I'm not sure." Lord Roger's brows pulled together in a concerned frown. "What do you think, Adam?"

"I think submitting for your life is a foolish thing to do, my lord. In fact, I fear submitting for any reason to our king is to play with fire – or an enraged lion, if you will."

"And what choice do I have?" Lord Roger gave him a tired look. "Our men are deserting – as would I, were I them. The royal army swells daily, with those spineless lords and barons who so loudly voiced their support of our cause not yet a year ago, but who now cower before the king and whisper that they were all misled – by me. So what should I do, Adam?"

"Ride for Ireland, my lord. Or France, biding your time. One day, the Despensers will overreach, and then…"

"Flee?" Lord Roger scowled. "And what of my wife, my children? What of your wife? Should we leave them in the tender care of Edward of Caernarvon, our just and glorious liege?"

Adam dropped his eyes to the trodden grass beneath his feet. Kit. His breath hitched. If something happened to him…She's strong, he reassured himself. She will find her way on her own. Kit, he moaned inside – would she find someone else to love when his own head decorated a spike? He rubbed at his neck – he did that frequently lately, plagued by gruelling images of just what he'd have to suffer before that final blow released him from pain and life.

"I think your lady wife would prefer you alive than dead," he said quietly. "I know mine would, even if it were to cost her imprisonment."

"Oh, I aim to come out of this alive," Lord Roger said.

"Then do not place trust in the worthless word of the king!" Anger flared red-hot through Adam. "That man lies as easily as he draws breath, and his honour is as battered as his arse."

"Adam!" Lord Roger's jaw dropped. And then he began to laugh, as did his uncle.

"This is no jesting matter, my lord." Adam frowned.

"No, of course not." Lord Roger gave him a long look, eyes

the colour of slate. "Which is why I will not take the king's word alone. Unless Pembroke pledges his honour, I will not submit." He chuckled and placed his arm round Adam's neck, bringing their heads together. "Battered arse, hey? Best not repeat that outside of this tent, lad."

Adam felt himself flush, not sure if he was irritated at being called a lad, or pleased that Lord Roger should show him such overt affection.

That night, the Welsh changed tactics, slipping into the camp before attacking the sleeping men. Adam stumbled to his feet, grabbed his sword and rushed outside, calling for Lionel to bring his shield. Two tents were on fire, as Adam watched yet another flaming arrow landed in a third, and men ran like witless hens from one tent to the other trying to stamp the fire out before it spread.

The horses. There was a burst of angry neighing, and Adam leapt towards the picket lines, calling for men to follow him, but not stopping to ensure if they did. He could make out the shadowy shapes of the thieves and roared in anger, threatening these half-heathen Welsh savages with one death more painful than the other should he get his hands on them. Something whirred through the air, slammed into his flank. Adam sank to his knees, halfway through yet another curse.

A horse reared and screamed. Goliath. Adam staggered to his feet, trying to run despite the arrow shaft that protruded from his side. He looked about for his men, but found none – except Lionel. There was a loud thump, a muted cry. Several horses streamed past, ridden by men who crouched low over their necks. Goliath. Adam's vision was clouding and he fell to his knees. There was something familiar about the man astride his horse, and when the rider was illuminated by a burst of light, Adam realised this was no Welsh attack, staring slack-mouthed from the burning nearby tent to his traitorous stepbrother.

"My horse," he croaked, trying to rise to his feet. God's blood, but his side hurt when he tried to straighten up! Lionel rushed to his side, propping him up.

"Mine now." Guy leaned forward over Goliath's neck. He gestured at the arrow. "You're a dead man anyway, brother. You'll never need a horse like him again."

"This won't kill me," Adam vowed in a cracking voice, "and then, little brother, I'll come looking."

"You do that." Guy yanked at Goliath's reins, and the horse snorted and tried to unseat him. "But if that broadhead doesn't kill you, the king will."

"Damn you!" With a hoarse shout, Lionel charged Guy. Without his support, Adam collapsed to the ground and could only watch as Guy raised his sword.

"Lionel!" Adam yelled – no, screeched. The sword came down, but at the last moment Guy twisted his hand, bringing down the flat of the blade rather than the honed edge. The effect was all the same horrifying: Lionel crumpled to the ground, making a series of whimpering sounds while he cradled his right arm.

"A lad!" Adam roared, spitting in the direction of his brother. "May you burn in hell, Guy de Guirande."

Guy sneered. "You'll be in hell much sooner than me, brother." He forced Goliath's head around and plunged off.

Adam wasn't quite sure who supported whom, but somehow Lionel and he made it back to the tents. Lionel's forearm seemed to be broken, while Adam's flank was one throbbing, bruising pain.

"Adam?" Lord Roger came towards him. "What—"

"The horses," Adam said. "They took the horses." My horse, he meant, not caring a whit about the other mounts they may have taken.

"Damned Welsh scoundrels!" Lord Chirk scowled. "Once we have this matter sorted, I will have them pay, every single one of them. Where is their loyalty to their lords and masters?"

Adam was tempted to laugh. The few Welshmen he knew expressed little but resignation when talking about their English lords. And mostly they would speak in Welsh, now and then forgetting that most Marcher lords were as fluent in this language as they were, having been raised by Welsh nurses. But laughing hurt – badly – and Adam wheezed instead, clapping a hand to his side to contain the pain. He had attempted to break off the shaft, but nearly fainted when the broadhead sank deeper into his flesh. Now he could feel blood seeping through his spread fingers, fearing that maybe Guy was right, maybe a rogue arrow would be the death of him.

Someone took hold of his arm, holding him steady. Sir Thomas. Adam blinked at the man. Another pair of hands. Richard de Monmouth. It almost made Adam laugh; his married kin were hurrying to his aid. Kit was remarkably like her brother, Adam reflected, squinting slightly to blur Richard's features into Kit's face. Kit. He wanted her here, her hair tickling his face.

Lord Roger was talking to him, in the same reassuring voice he had used all those years ago, when Adam was a bleeding, weeping lad with nothing but a torn shirt to his name. Adam slumped in his arms, safe in his lord's embrace. Loud voices, the flickering light of torches, and Adam was being carried towards the closest tent. Someone ripped his tunic, and Adam wanted to protest – he only had two – but closed his eyes instead, trying to visualise the arrowhead. A shallow wound, the point lodged in muscles rather than organs, and Adam drew in a relieved breath – until the surgeon took hold of the shaft and tugged.

"That won't work, man," Lord Chirk said, shoving the surgeon aside. He gripped the shaft, muttered an apology to Adam and broke it off. "Now you cut out the head."

Adam breathed in short, shallow gasps, eyes locked on the long shadows that danced across the canvas ceiling above him.

"If you kill him, I'll tear out your heart," Lord Roger told the surgeon, who stuttered and said he would do his best – he always did his best.

"Lionel," Adam said.

"Here, my lord." His squire leaned over him, eyes wet. He was still cradling his arm, but otherwise looked composed. Behind him hovered Sir Thomas, smiling encouragingly.

"Your arm." Adam gestured vaguely in Lionel's direction.

"It will be seen to." Lord Roger nodded at Lionel. "Go on, have Richard help you. Young de Monmouth knows a thing or two about broken bone."

That made Adam laugh, despite the pain it caused. Richard had seen more than his fair share of breaks, having been uncommonly clumsy as a young adolescent.

What seemed an eternity later, and Adam's jaws ached from his efforts not to cry out. The broadhead was lying in a bowl, covered with fragments of Adam's flesh. By his side, the surgeon was murmuring and shaking his head, studying the welling blood.

"God's truth! Don't you know anything?" Lord Chirk shoved him aside. "Such wounds need to be cauterised."

"No, uncle." Lord Roger shook his head. "It's too deep, too wide. Leave the surgeon to do his work – he does not question your ability with the sword, you should not question his skills with a needle." He held a goblet of sweetened wine to Adam's mouth and helped him drink. And just like he had done when Lady Joan sewed together Adam's cheek, he held Adam's hand while the surgeon did his stitching.

Once the surgeon pronounced himself finished, Lord Roger called for burnt wine and vinegar, upending first one, then the other over Adam's flank. It burnt like the fires of everlasting hell, but then it was over and Adam was bandaged, dressed in a clean shirt and transferred to his pallet bed.

"Sleep," Lord Roger suggested. Adam closed his eyes and did as he was told.

Chapter 19

For some strange reason, having had Adam visit and then leave made her feel his absence even more. Kit moped for some days until Lady Joan reprimanded her in a sharp tone, wondering if Kit thought she had more to lose than any of the other ladies present.

"No, of course not," she muttered, while screaming inside that of course she did.

Mabel tried to distract her by teaching her Welsh – a rather laborious process involving multiple unfamiliar sound combinations and words that in no way resembled words in either English or French. But as the days passed, Kit found herself understanding more and more, even if she generally restricted herself to using a few standard phrases.

When William discovered she could read and write, he was at first very impressed, pressing her for details as to who had taught her until Mabel bit him off by telling him Lady Cecily was a great believer in educating her girls.

"She is?" Kit murmured once William was out of earshot.

"No, not as such. Our Katherine could at most read her name." Mabel eyed Kit. "Was it your mother who taught you to read?"

"My mother did not know how. I was an only – and lonely – child," Kit replied with a shrug. "Father Luke took it upon himself to fill my days with something." And now he was as dead as her mother, both of them dying within days of each other.

Once over his initial surprise, William set Kit to work, having her help him in sorting and cataloguing Baron Mortimer's correspondence.

"And Lady Joan? Doesn't she write?" Kit asked, carefully blowing dust from an old deed.

"She does. But John and Walter have no need of our services," William said, referring to Lady Joan's clerks.

"And Mortimer? Doesn't he have clerks?"

"They're not here, are they?" William shrugged, but Kit suspected all this archiving was mainly motivated by his desire to keep her occupied rather than by any real need.

Most of the deeds and documents were in Latin, and the more complex of these she piled to the side for William to deal with. What she was left with were copies of letters Lord Mortimer had written, letters he had received, the odd set of accounts, receipts for cattle, for horses, for houses – this man owned more houses than she owned garters.

"A chessboard painted with gold?" Kit waved the receipt at William. "What capital sin does that fall under?" This was a new game of theirs, classifying various items under any of the seven capital sins. So far, pride and greed were winning, although William kept insisting that fur-lined garments, exotic gaming tables and expensive wines were necessities where nobility was concerned, as were Arabian steeds, Saracen weaponry inlaid with gold, and embroidered tapestries. "So where are Adam's rings? His tunics in fur-lined velvet?"

William laughed. "Adam has no such belongings – how could he? What gold he has earned he has invested in arms and that devil of a horse he's so proud of. Now, of course, things are different. With your dowry and Lord Roger's generous gift, he may be able to stretch himself to a glass goblet or two." His mouth pulled down. "Assuming things go our way, of course."

Which, in Kit's opinion, would be the equivalent of a miracle. William sighed but agreed; the first few weeks of January had not been good, and as he heard it Mortimer was considering pleading for mercy.

"He is?" Kit's heart raced with hope. Peace; Adam back home, with her.

William gave her a wary look. "Pleading and getting are different things. Our king is not inclined to be magnanimous."

Kit rose from her stool, scattering documents around her, and left the room at a run.

He came to find her on the wall, standing as she was wont to do with her eyes lost in the peaceful landscape to the north-east. A scattering of sheep dotted the faded green of the surrounding moors, and clouds so dark they shifted into purple were blowing in from the distant sea, tingeing the air with the scent of approaching rain.

"You must prepare yourself for the worst," William said without preamble, coming to stand beside her.

"Or I make plans to stop the worst from happening." What plans, a little voice in her head jeered. How are you, Kit de Guirande, to stop the king from executing your husband for treason? "They could run away to France," she said out loud.

William raised his brows. "They could. But you forget Despenser controls the seas, pirate that he is."

Kit hugged herself. "It isn't fair. I've only known him since September, and now I may lose him forever? And what about him?" She caressed her belly. "Is he to grow up without a father?"

"Life is not fair. If it was, none would be born as barons or villeins, we would all be born equal. And yet, God has ordained that some are masters, some are servants, some live long lives while some die young."

"Not my Adam," she said, making him smile.

"Your Adam?" He touched her face lightly. "He would be pleased to hear you speak of him thus."

She shrugged away his hand. "He won't die. I won't let him die."

"It is out of your hands," William sighed. "It is out of all our hands but those of the king."

"You've given up on hope," she said harshly, backing away. "Aren't you supposed to give people hope, not smash it to pieces? What kind of a priest are you, croaking prophesies of doom? Why don't you speak of miracles, of divine intervention? Why do you want me to imagine him dead, gone, instead of alive, with me? Why? Why, God damn you?"

"Child," he said, extending his hands towards her.

"I'm not your child! I am Kit de Guirande, and I will not become a widow. Not yet. And you…" She pointed at William. "You're supposed to help me."

"I will," he soothed, "of course I will." But she could hear it in his voice that he was only humouring her.

Two days later, Lionel rode in on a sad excuse of a horse, his arm bandaged to well above his elbow. The boy who had ridden out seven weeks ago, exuberant at following his lord into the field, returned a quiet young man, his face set in an expression of sad determination.

"What news?" Kit asked, rushing towards him.

"Let him get off his horse first," Mabel chided, making Lionel throw her a grateful smile.

"My lady." Lionel slid to the ground. He bowed and raised a pale face in her direction, every single one of his freckles visible. "The king has granted them a safe-conduct. They ride to Betton Strange to negotiate with the king."

"A safe-conduct? Can he be trusted to allow them to leave?" The voice came from behind them, Lady Joan nodding her head in the briefest of greetings before fixing Lionel with a hard stare. "Answer, lad!"

"Six earls have signed their name to it," Lionel said. "Lord Mortimer thought that good enough."

"And Adam? Does he ride with him?" Kit asked.

"No, my lady." Lionel stared intently at the ground, and Kit had the distinct impression he was attempting not to cry. Oh God; he's dead. The ground swayed below her feet.

"So where is he?" She forced the words over her lips, not sure she wanted to hear his reply.

"In Shrewsbury."

Thank God. He wasn't dead.

"He took an arrow to the side," Lionel continued in a low voice, "and despite the surgeon doing his very best, he became fevered and delirious, so Lord Mortimer sent him off to the monks at St Peter and Paul."

"And is he any better?"

"I don't know. My lord baron sent me back here, to deliver this to his lady." Lionel extended a sealed roll to Lady Joan, who took it, broke the seal and retreated some paces to read it in private. Lionel sighed, a sound of utter desolation, and scraped at the ground.

"What is it, lad?" William said, placing a hand on his shoulder.

158

"It was Guy," Lionel whispered. "It was Guy who captained the Welsh scoundrels who shot Sir Adam, it was him who stole Goliath and who broke my arm." He gave William an anguished look. "How could he do that?" He clutched at William's sleeve with his good hand. "Why would a man want his brother dead?"

Kit's legs gave way. Mabel crouched down beside her and gave her a hug.

"Will he die?" Kit asked her, but Mabel only shook her head, telling her it was in God's hands. "Will he die?" she repeated, directing herself to Lionel.

"I don't know," the boy said, giving her a helpless look.

"The abbey has a reputation for good healers," Lady Joan cut in. Her eyes were red and wet, the parchment she had received clutched to her chest. "But we should pray, I think. For Adam, for my lord husband and all the men that ride with them." She swept away, her brown everyday kirtle swishing as she moved with speed, making for the chapel. They all followed. In silence they trudged after her, as sombre as if they were attending a wake.

Praying didn't help. If anything, standing squashed together in the small chapel intensified the suffocating fear. It drove Kit witless, to stand and mutter Latin sentences when she should be on a horse, galloping for Shrewsbury. No sooner was the impromptu service over than Kit was out of the door, making for her chamber.

"Kit!" Lady Joan's voice brought her up short. "No," Lady Joan continued, "you will not set out for Shrewsbury. I cannot provide you with an adequate escort, not now, and besides, we do not know what you may find."

"You cannot stop me," Kit said.

"Oh yes I can." Lady Joan locked eyes with Kit. "We send Lionel. Give him some days to recuperate, and he can set off with one of my knights."

"I ride with them," Kit tried.

"No you do not. You are with child and should not be on a horse for several days straight – and particularly not now, when Welsh rogues and bandits plague the roads."

"But—"

"I said no. In the absence of your husband, you owe your obedience to me, and I am quite sure Sir Adam would not want you gallivanting about the countryside in your condition."

Kit scowled at her.

"I will lock you up if I have to," Lady Joan continued, unfazed by Kit's glare. She stared at Kit, light blue eyes boring into her. "Well?" she finally asked. "Do I have your promise, or must I put you under lock and key?"

Kit scowled some more, but knew herself beaten. Lady Joan had but to snap her fingers and every man, woman and child at Wigmore would come rushing to do her bidding – including hindering Kit from leaving.

"I promise." She twisted her hands into her skirts to stop them from trembling. "But what if he dies, and I'm not there to hold him?"

Lady Joan looked away. "Don't you think we all carry the same fear?" She frowned down at the scrap of parchment that contained her husband's message to her. "We must trust in God," she said quietly. "Our cause is just, and God will lead us through it." Lady Joan sighed and lifted her face to the grey sky. A kite soared in splendid isolation, a harbinger of sorts. Lady Joan crossed herself, and Kit followed suit. "I do not think I will see my husband for a long, long time." She turned a brilliant smile on Kit, her eyes glittering with tears. "But I will see him again. Someday."

Chapter 20

They came to fetch Adam early on a dim January day.

"My lords?" Adam sat up carefully, dizzy with fever.

"Are you feeling any better?" Lord Roger stood looking down at him, with Richard hovering in the doorway.

Adam shrugged. He no longer felt at death's door, and while he was not fit for much more than sitting or lying in bed, daily he felt stronger. But the wound in his side flared and itched, and at times he felt as if there was a thorn gnawing its way deeper and deeper into his body. Brother Francis told him it was his imagination. They had cut him open, tsked at the surgeon's clumsy handiwork, and then they'd cleaned the open wound with water that smelled of mint and chamomile, before sewing it together and applying poultices of crushed yarrow and comfrey.

By now, there was no red, irritated skin, and yesterday Brother Francis had pronounced that Adam was healing remarkably well for a man so infected, even if he had best remain in bed another few days for the fever to properly abate.

"What is the occasion?" Adam asked, indicating his lord's clothes. Roger Mortimer was in scarlet and green, silk for his tabard, velvet for the tunic he wore below. The cloak was lined with fur, what was visible of the chainmail was polished to shine, and as far as Adam could see, Lord Roger was wearing every single ring he owned.

"We present ourselves to the king," Lord Roger said lightly, but Adam knew him too well, could hear the tightly controlled tension in his voice.

"What? No, my lord, please do not do this! He will—"

Lord Roger held up his hand. "Lord Pembroke has pledged his honour – we will not be harmed." He gave Adam a crooked smile. "Well, beyond a humiliating submission, no doubt forced to grovel at the king's feet."

161

"And you believe him?"

"The king?" Lord Roger shook his head slowly. "Lord Pembroke?" He nodded, twice.

"My lord, I don't…" Adam clasped Lord Roger's hand and knelt clumsily before him, ignoring just how much that made his side hurt. He could feel one of Brother Francis' stitches tear, but at present he couldn't care less. "Please, my lord. Ride the other way, ride for Ireland, ride to freedom."

"It is too late, and I must do this for my family." Lord Roger snapped his fingers, and Richard ducked into the cell, giving Adam a nod. "You need to get dressed," Lord Roger said. "Your presence is also required."

Adam's innards quivered. Why would the king insist a wounded minor lord attend the meeting?

Lord Roger gave him yet another crooked smile. "I dare say our liege wants you all to witness my abject submission. An apt lesson in humility for a man as proud as I am." His eyes slid to the side, but not before Adam saw a glimmer of fear in them. Christ and all his saints! Adam licked his lips.

"Please," he repeated hoarsely. "Do not place your life in the fickle hands of the king. What if he changes his mind? What if you…" Die, he intended to say, but chose not to.

Lord Roger sighed. "It is in the hands of God." He bent low enough to whisper in Adam's ear. "And the queen's." For an instant, his dark eyes sparkled with amusement.

"Is she here?" Adam managed to stand, lifting his arms over his head as Richard pulled on a clean shirt over his bandaged torso.

"Queen Isabella?" Lord Roger shook his head. "But her son is." His eyes crinkled at the corners. "Now that is a lad born to be king."

"Not king yet," Adam warned.

"No, and as yet a child. But one day…"

Adam made one more attempt. "So why not flee into exile until that day, my lord?"

Lord Roger gave him an uncompromising look. "My honour would be in shreds. Besides, didn't I just tell you Aymer de Valence has promised us it will be no more than a slap – a

162

most painful slap, for sure." He fiddled with his gloves and stood back to regard Adam, now fully dressed. "You'll do." He reached forward to tousle his hair, and Adam was overwhelmed by a wave of affection for this man who had been more than a father to him, despite only being ten years his senior.

"My lord," he mumbled, not knowing how to phrase this urgent need to tell his lord just how much he cared for him.

"I know," Lord Roger said with a little smile. "Now, can you walk on your own, or do we carry you?"

Adam stood up straight. "I walk, my lord."

"Thank the Lord for that," Richard muttered from behind him. "Carrying a man as big as you would have me split a gut or two." It was a weak jest, but Lord Roger and Adam laughed all the same.

They rode into Shrewsbury Castle and were met by silence – and an impressive display of royal might, men-at-arms wearing the royal arms standing in silent lines along the walls. All of them armed, Adam noted, hastily brushing his hand over his upper lip to rid it of the sheen of sweat he could feel on it. The day was cold, but he was hot – and near-incapable of remaining on his feet when he slid off his horse.

Stable boys appeared out of nowhere to claim their mounts and lead them away. Lord Roger set out for the hall, crossing the bailey with his men at his back, and all the time this silence, oppressive as a mountain of rocks. Adam shivered. He had once seen a man executed by weights, one rock at the time placed on the wide plank that covered his chest, and as he walked slowly, step by step, up the stairs that led to the hall, he felt as if his own lungs were being pressed together, every gust of precious air being driven from his body.

The hall, at last. Once again, silent men-at-arms lining their way, standing along the walls, around the dais. The large room was filled with gaudily dressed lords and nobles, but they were just as silent as the soldiers, keeping their eyes fixed on the dais and the imposing figure that stood waiting for them, hands resting on an unsheathed sword. King Edward, second of that name, regarded them with ice-cold eyes, his face implacable. In burgundy velvet, with ermine trimming his cloak and sleeves, Edward looked every inch the king he wasn't, that fair and brave exterior hiding a weak and pliable man. Adam felt an urge to spit at his sovereign's feet. This was his fault. A good king, ruled by his own counsel and that of the peers of his realm, would never have allowed things to escalate to this point.

Adam scanned the faces closest to the king. Prince Edward was standing with the Earls of Richmond and Arundel, Surrey and Norfolk, all of them as silent as their royal master, while on the other side of the king, quite alone, was the Earl of Pembroke. Something wasn't right. Aymer de Valence had the look of a whipped cur, and to his left, Adam heard Lord Roger's hissed intake of breath. Too late, too late! They should not have come! He staggered, crashing into Thomas de Monmouth who steadied him, giving him a supporting pat to the back as he released him to walk those last few yards on his own two feet.

They were going to die. He could see it in the eyes of the assembled nobles, in the stern visages of the earls, but most of all in Pembroke's crumpled face. Adam's legs dipped, his head was fit to burst, and he was sweating all over, having difficulty drawing breath. His flank was on fire, every step driving shards of pain through his lacerated muscles. What did it matter, he thought sarcastically? By tomorrow he would be dead anyway.

"My liege." Lord Roger knelt, his eyes never leaving the king. In his feverish state, Adam was tempted to laugh out loud. This was not a grovelling submission, this was a man bowing to a greater power with his dignity intact.

"My lord king," Lord Chirk said, kneeling down beside his nephew. Yet again that refusal to bend his neck, the old man almost contemptuous in the way he regarded his liege. King Edward's mouth twitched, his long fingers clenching round the hilt of the sword.

One by one, Lord Roger's men knelt behind him, until it was only Adam left standing. He tried to lower himself to the ground, but his head was spinning, the room was tilting from side to side. With a grunt he collapsed, set his hands on the floor and retched.

"The man is ailing!" Lord Pembroke's voice came from somewhere above Adam's head. Adam cackled quietly. Ailing? He was doomed to die, and all because of Pembroke's worthless promises.

"My liege," Adam said through cracked lips, and managed to get to his knees. Not for him a defiant staring contest with his monarch. Adam concentrated on the floor in front of him, trying to stop himself from fainting.

"I submit myself to your mercy," Lord Roger said quietly. "I would remind you, my liege, that ever have I served you faithfully, that—"

"Faithfully?" King Edward's voice was sharp with anger. "Does a faithful subject take up arms against his king? Does he impose his will on his king, forcing us to be parted from our most beloved subjects?"

"Parliament ruled that—"

"And you set them up to it!" Not much of a king now, with spittle flying and those eyes burning with hate.

"You were in breach of your coronation oaths," Lord Chirk said.

The king just looked at him. "Take them away. Strike our lords Mortimer in chains and transport them to London, where they are to languish in the Tower until their execution."

A collective gasp ran through the room, making the king throw his assembled nobles a furious look. Men approached Lord Roger and his uncle, hoisted them to their feet and began dragging them from the room. Neither Lord Roger nor Lord Chirk said a word. They just kept their eyes fixed on Pembroke, who was sweating like a whore in a bathhouse. With them went Richard de Monmouth, manhandled roughly towards the door.

"My dearest lord," Adam groaned, extending his hand in the direction of Lord Roger. "May the Lord keep you," he whispered, "and may He give you the strength to live through this, your final ordeal."

"You promised!" Thomas de Monmouth was on his feet, pointing at Pembroke. "You, my lord, you swore on your honour that we would keep our lives."

"Silence!" thundered the king, striding across the dais to

strike Thomas over the face. "Lord Pembroke exceeded his authority. It is I, not he, who decides who lives and dies."

"Begging your pardon, sire," Sir Thomas said, "it is the court, not the king who decides such. Or is this yet another English law you no longer intend to honour?"

Adam closed his eyes. From the look the king gave Sir Thomas, his death was imminent – and would be most unpleasant.

"Take him away," the king barked. "Take them all away." His men leapt to it with alacrity.

Adam didn't fight, but he was no longer capable of getting to his feet, his vision blurring into a collection of bright colours. A hand, a concerned face. Pembroke. With the last of his energy, Adam spat in the earl's face.

"Perjured," he hissed, and had the satisfaction of seeing Aymer de Valence go the colour of day-old porridge. That was the last he registered, apart from the agonising pain as his wounded side was scraped along the floor.

"Are you awake, then?" a voice slurred beside him. Adam opened an eye, then closed it just as quickly to contain his shock. He peeked. Sir Thomas looked as if he'd been kicked in the face by a horse, repeatedly.

"Where are we?" Adam asked, sitting up carefully.

"We are still in the castle," Sir Thomas told him. "Our liege has accorded us food and accommodation." He grimaced, gesturing at their squalid surroundings. A dungeon, dark and damp, with straw on the floor as their bedding and a bucket in the corner for their bodily needs.

"Lord Roger?"

Sir Thomas shook his head. "They had us watch as they struck him in chains, and then they set him and his uncle astride a horse and set off for London."

"And Richard?"

"With them. Also manacled, as are we all – except for you, but that will change once they realise you've regained consciousness." Sir Thomas fretted at his chains. "I didn't think it would end like this."

"I did. I never trusted Pembroke."

"Pembroke committed the mistake of trusting the king," Sir Thomas corrected.

"Then more fool him." Adam swallowed, feeling just how dry his mouth was. Sir Thomas handed him a ladle with water, and helped him sit up sufficiently to drink it.

"What will happen to us?" Adam asked.

"Happen? The guards tell me they've been busy at the gallows. Any day now and we will dangle by our necks." Sir Thomas gave a shaky laugh. "At least we are spared being hung, drawn and quartered."

"Somehow I do not find that much of a comfort." Adam groped for his leather thong, but found it gone. Kit. He would never see her again, never tell her that he loved her.

"I do," Sir Thomas said. "The king wanted me to die a traitor's death, but his earls prevailed upon him."

"Oh." Adam felt himself slipping away again, fever burning through his veins.

"Adam?" he heard faintly, but he couldn't summon the energy required to reply. Instead he fell, into that deep, dark hole within himself where fire raged and from which there was no escape. None at all.

When next he woke, it was to a booted foot in his side, making him gasp. He tried to drag himself out of reach and was kicked again. He curled together, protecting himself with his arms, but his tormentors took hold of his hands and pulled him to stand. Adam wheezed.

"No need to waste chains on him," one of the guards said.

"The constable said everyone," a small man said, frowning up at Adam. "Look at the size of him – he claps me one and I'm dead."

"Well, we can't have that, Harry, can we?" the third guard chuckled. "Bring him along, the smith is waiting."

"Sir Thomas?" Adam asked through a woollen mouth.

"Dead," the small guard said. He eyed Adam with some sympathy. "What is ailing you?"

"Arrow," Adam mumbled.

He didn't protest as they fitted him in irons – there was no point – and afterwards he was given a bowl of watery porridge and a jug of ale. The porridge was hot, and Adam ate slowly, not wanting this source of delicious warmth to end too soon. His new cell was smaller than the previous one, and furnished with a light-gap. It was set too high in the wall for him to reach it, but at least there were streaks of pale light on the grimy stone floor, allowing him to keep track of the days. Not that he knew what for, but his guards explained that Pembroke refused to hang him without a trial – all the others had been accorded a trial – and until he was somewhat healed, Pembroke also refused to have him brought to trial.

"Taken a liking to you, he has," one of the guards said. "Doesn't please our constable much, but the king left Pembroke in charge while he set off north, and so…" He lifted a shoulder, indicating just how incomprehensible the ways of the rich and powerful were.

A monk was brought to see Adam, and once again the wound to his side was opened and cleansed, and yet again the scents of yarrow and mint tickled his nose.

"It is healing as it should," the monk said, some days later, holding yet another cup of willow-bark tea to Adam's mouth.

"I am so glad," Adam said sarcastically, even if he had to admit the monk had done a good job, the fevers occurring but rarely. He settled down to live through days of utter boredom, trying to push away all thoughts of death. With each day that he woke alive, the hope inside him grew, further nourished by the casual kindness with which the guards treated him. And then came the day when Despenser arrived.

Adam didn't know, of course. Not until afterwards. Apparently, Despenser had been livid at hearing one of the accursed rebels still lingered, alive, and had commanded Pembroke to hang him immediately. Upon which Pembroke had yelled at Despenser that some things one did not do, however depraved one was, and that was to hang a man so sick he was incapable of standing on his own two feet before his judges.

So instead, Despenser came to visit. Adam expected kicks and punches, but Despenser smirked and shook his head, saying that as Pembroke insisted on keeping Adam from the hangman's noose by referring to his wound, then Despenser intended to inspect it – with a knife. Sweet Jesus, but it hurt! Adam couldn't breathe, nor scream, when Despenser dug the tip of his knife into the unhealed scar. But he did scream when the damned Hugh Despenser set his knife to his skin and cut him, decorating his flank with a series of shallow cuts that were never allowed to heal.

"You do understand that I am only doing to you what I am not allowed to do to Roger Mortimer, don't you?" Despenser wiped his bloody knife on Adam's tunic and sat back on his heels, dark eyes studying him intently. "But alas, my most hated personal enemy is not available, and so you, Adam de Guirande, traitor to *my* king, trusted captain to *my* enemy, will have to do instead."

Even worse was when Despenser touched him, shushing him as he gently washed the gashes he himself had made, but now and then applying so much pressure that Adam couldn't contain a sob. At times, Despenser's caresses became much too intimate, and there was nothing Adam could do in his weakened state to avoid that intrusive hand, those glittering eyes and that wet, soft mouth.

"Tell Pembroke," he pleaded with the guards, but his previously friendly captors were gone, replaced by men with eyes as cold as Despenser's.

In between these cutting sessions with Despenser, Adam lay slumped in his cell, hanging somewhere between wakefulness and sleep. He could feel his body weakening, day by day, the life force leaked away from him, and instead he fled into dreams of other places, of a smiling wife and a gurgling babe.

"Kit," he would murmur as an unusually bright beam of sunlight came dancing through his cell. "My Kit."

Sometime in the last half of February, Despenser brought company. Adam recognised Guy's voice, laughing at something Despenser said, and for a couple of moments he was suffused with hope, until he recalled that Guy had betrayed them, jumping ship like a mangy rat.

The door swung open, and it wasn't only Despenser and Guy – there were other men as well, and the fear Adam always felt upon seeing Despenser was compounded by the look in his brother's eyes. Stepbrother, he reminded himself; he didn't share a drop of blood with this sorry creature, and strangely enough it gave him some comfort.

Guy had the grace to pale at the sight of him, his mouth falling open before he collected himself. "And now what?" Guy asked Despenser.

"Oh, I amuse myself with your brother," Despenser said, coming over to stroke Adam's hair out of his face. Adam's muscles bunched in protest at this invasive touch, so much worse than the fleeting pain of the cutting knife.

"Stepbrother," Guy replied immediately, making Adam think of St Peter and his repudiation of Christ.

"Brother, stepbrother, it doesn't really matter, does it?" Despenser said, eyeing Guy avidly. He chuckled. "It is time for you to prove once and for all that you have cut all ties with your rebellious kin, and will hold yourself only to me."

"I will, my lord, of course I will," Guy said, dipping his head up and down like a thrush looking for a worm.

"So prove it." Despenser beckoned for the men behind them to enter.

A stool was set down and Adam was hoisted to sit, his back to the wall. A brazier was set on the floor, and Adam stared at it. Now what? Hot coals on his body? His skin shrank at the thought.

"Seeing as that old fool Pembroke repeatedly stops us from hanging him, we have to make sure he is permanently incapacitated. Just in case." Despenser smiled at Adam, brushing his knuckles down his face, down the side of his neck. Adam tried to shift away. Despenser took hold of his chains and yanked, bringing Adam's head in uncomfortable proximity to Despenser's groin.

"Just in case of what?" Guy said.

"Someone might try to free him." Despenser gave Guy a guileless look. "You, for example."

"Me? I would never—"

"Yes, yes," Despenser waved him quiet. "It is a risk I am not prepared to take." He cradled Adam's head. "We can't have that, can we?" he crooned, his fingers massaging Adam's scalp. "Well, get on with it," Despenser barked.

"What do you want me to do?" Guy asked, sounding defeated.

"A hand or a foot," Despenser said.

Adam jerked back, but those fingers sank into his head, holding him immobile. "Not my hand," he mumbled into Despenser's tunic. "Please, not my hand."

"Ah," Despenser said, releasing his hold sufficiently to gaze into Adam's eyes. "The prisoner has made his choice. The foot it will be."

"The foot?" Guy looked at Adam, at Despenser, and licked his lips.

"Are you some sort of fool?" Despenser jerked his head in the direction of the brazier. "A red hot stake through his foot, that's all you have to do." He laughed. "It will ensure he never walks again – at least not without a limp."

"No!" Adam pushed and shoved, kicking wildly as the other men approached him. "Guy, don't do this, for the love of God, don't! Please, Guy!"

"If you don't do it, I will do it – to him and to you," Despenser said.

"I have to," Guy said. "Forgive me, Adam, but—"

"Forgive you?" Adam landed a kick on Guy's leg. "What should I forgive? That you betrayed us? That you attacked us?" He sank his teeth into Despenser's hand and had the distinct pleasure of hearing his tormentor shriek. "I will never forgive you, you hear? And if you do this—"

Despenser grabbed him by the hair and knocked his head against the wall. "Silence! And you, do it now!"

"No!" Adam bucked and heaved. Despenser's hand in his hair immobilised him, holding him still as the royal favourite rubbed his lower regions against Adam's face. Oh God; Adam gagged, kicked out yet again, and felt a weight settle on his leg. His hose was torn off, and here came Guy, mallet in one hand and pliers round a red-hot stake in the other.

"Please!" Adam screamed. Despenser laughed, twisting Adam's face round towards his swollen groin. Adam squeezed his eyes shut, clamped his mouth closed and prayed. For death, for release from the pain, but most of all for an opportunity to one day avenge himself on Hugh Despenser, the man who caressed his head as his brother repeatedly slammed down the mallet on the red-hot stake he held to Adam's right foot.

They were gone. Adam couldn't move, didn't dare to look at his staked foot, at present feeling as if he'd caught it in a wolf-trap. One of the guards came in.

"What did they…" His voice tailed off. "Mother of God," he groaned, before stumbling over to the bucket and retching. Had it not been for the situation, Adam would have laughed: his guard vomiting his innards to pieces while it was his, Adam's, foot that stank of scorched meat.

"I hope they hurry up and hang me," he muttered to the guard. "I much prefer dying in the sunlight than down here, killed ever so slowly by your dear lord and master, that bastard Despenser."

The guard met his eyes. "I will speak to Pembroke."

"You do that." But Adam didn't believe him. He resigned himself to death, and over the coming days, he slid into a deep and restless slumber, waking only when one of the guards shook him awake to offer him food – or when Despenser entered the room, knife in hand.

Chapter 21

Lionel rode off with a squat Welshman named Owain, and Kit stood looking after him until he was no more than a speck to the north.

"Find him," she'd said to Lionel as they bid their farewells. "Tell him I love him, and will come to him soon."

"But my lady…" Lionel threw a wary glance in the direction of Lady Joan.

"I will," Kit told him. Somehow she had to set off and find her husband, because her every nerve was telling her he needed her. Ridiculous, she told herself as she clutched at the parapet. *You're being foolish. People cannot feel what other people are experiencing over miles and miles of distance.* But she could, God help her, and it made her stomach churn, because none of the images were of a well-cared-for patient – they were all of a tormented man.

Her reverie was interrupted by Mabel. "Lady Joan has need of you."

"Again?" Kit sighed. These days she lived at Lady Joan's beck and call, the lady setting her one task after the other in an effort to distract her.

"We're leaving," Mabel said.

"Leaving?" Kit wasn't going anywhere until she knew how her husband fared.

"Not far, just to the abbey." Mabel gestured to the north. "Our lady desires a few days of peace and contemplation."

A few days of peace and contemplation? Several hours later, Kit studied the bailey, filled with packhorses, with carts and people.

"Does she have to take everything with her for this little retreat?" she murmured to William.

"Retreat?" He frowned at her. "This is no retreat."

But, it suddenly struck Kit, it was. Not a retreat in the

spiritual sense, but this was Lady Joan trying to salvage what she could from the impending disaster.

"If the king wins—" she began.

"When," William interrupted sharply. "You heard the messenger. Lord Roger and his men ride as we speak to submit themselves to the king's mercy."

Sometimes, Kit didn't like her brother-in-law, but the way his eyes regarded her made her realise just how concerned he was. For Mortimer, for their men, but most of all for Adam.

"The king's men will be here any day," William tried to explain. "But when they do, Lady Joan wants them to find a castle empty of treasure."

"But they'll just go to the abbey." Everyone knew the Mortimer family considered Wigmore Abbey but an extension of their favourite castle.

"Yes, of course they will." Lady Joan appeared beside them, and Kit and William made their courtesies, him much lower than her. "And there they will find me surrounded by all my treasure and be mightily pleased to have discovered my ruse." Her face set. "Except, of course, that they will not find it all." Lady Joan pointed at three small chests, each of them the size of an infant's coffin. "They will not be there."

"They won't?" Kit eyed the locked chests.

"No, they will be with you." Lady Joan placed a hand on Kit's sleeve. "I commend them into your safekeeping. Take them with you to Tresaints, hide them there, and with that final service I release you to ride to Shrewsbury to look for your man." She looked about the bustling yard. "All our lives, reduced to this: some carts and horses and a collection of frightened people. Even I am frightened, and my lord husband would be the first to tell you I don't frighten easily."

"Frightened of what?" Kit asked.

"The king's revenge," Lady Joan replied. She looked to the north. "By tomorrow, my lord husband will be stripped of all his possessions. I hope to God he will keep his life."

Kit's throat closed. "But you said..." She whirled to face William. "Pembroke promised them mercy. You said so."

"Pembroke may promise, but the king must deliver." Lady Joan sounded bleak, her hands adjusting her wimple.

And so it was that just after noon on a January day that was bright and sunny after weeks of sullen rain, Kit rode off towards Tresaints, accompanied by William and Mabel, two packhorses and four men-at-arms, one of whom was Mabel's cousin and went by the name of Egard.

Kit wiped her eyes. It had been difficult to bid Lady Joan farewell, to smile at the silent Mortimer offspring and wish them a safe journey. Even Blanche had been silent, the normally happy baby hiding her face against her mother's kirtle. Lady Joan had no illusions as to the fate of herself and her children. They would be incarcerated at the king's pleasure, and her hands had fluttered over the heads of her daughters as she had muttered that she hoped at least to be allowed to keep them close, her girls. The boys she had no hopes for. Her eldest was a man grown, commanded by his father to stay away from the events in Shrewsbury, and as to her younger sons, they were old enough to be ripped away from her.

"Only Geoffrey is safe," Lady Joan had said, giving Kit a lopsided smile. Geoffrey was in France, out of the king's reach. "And Maud and Margaret, God bless them both," she'd added as an afterthought. "The king will not deprive their husbands of their wives."

"And you?" Kit had clasped Lady Joan's hand.

"Me?" Lady Joan straightened up. "I am Joan de Geneville. Let the king try his worst."

"We're going the wrong way," Kit grumbled once they were safely on their way. Tresaints was close to Worcester, and so they were riding away from Shrewsbury, not towards it. But even as she said it, Kit felt a little thrill at the thought of seeing her home again, no matter that at present she had a constant mauling ache in her belly whenever she thought of Adam. If the king chose to be lenient, he would be destitute, and if the king chose to be merciless, he would be dead.

"He'll be all right, won't he?" she asked William, begging him for a smile and an affirming nod.

Her priest brother-in-law looked away. "I don't know. Whatever the case, he will be imprisoned – at least for a while. The king has need to set some examples, and Adam is one of Lord Roger's closest men."

"Set some examples?" Kit's heart cramped.

"Rebels require punishment," William said bleakly.

Kit drew her horse to a halt. "We must go the other way! Now, before it's too—"

"…Late?" William shook his head. "It already is, Kit." He took hold of Kit's reins and clucked her horse into a walk. "We must discharge Lady Joan's wish, and then we will ride north to find my brother." He smiled at her. "We will find him." But whether dead or alive, he had no idea, his tone told her, and Kit seethed with frustration that there was nothing she could do. The men had their instructions from Lady Joan, and William would no more consider disobeying Lady Joan's command than he would set fire to the Bible.

Two days later, they arrived at Tresaints. As the landscape became more familiar, Kit's mood picked up, and by the time the dirt road did its last turn up the hill, Kit was jumping up and down in the saddle, so eager to set eyes on her home. Tresaints had always been a haven, a place of peace and quiet – according to her mother, because of its name and origins. The small chapel had been built well over a hundred years ago, honouring three saints, one Welsh, one English and one French.

"St Winefride the chaste," Alaïs would murmur, running her fingers over an effigy worn featureless. "St Wulfstan, defender of the poor…" Alaïs would stoop to place a kiss on a lump of stone she insisted was the saint's foot, "and St Odo." She never did more than nod at St Odo's statue, confiding to Kit that in her book Odo was more interested in earthly power than was appropriate for a true saint.

Just thinking of her mother had Kit's hands tightening on her reins. She would never see her again, and thereby her entire family was gone. Or not, she reminded herself with a little cough, because she had new people in her life, first and foremost her Adam – assuming he was still alive, of course. It gnawed at her like a rabid rat, this constant uncertainty, and not even the beauty of the surrounding landscape, a collection of undulating hills as far as she could see, could soothe the constant cramp in her chest.

There was the lane with its hornbeam hedge, there were the meadows and pastures, and there was her home, a sturdy stone house with a rough slate roof, surrounded by wooden buildings of various shapes and forms. Home. Kit rose in her stirrups and inhaled. Yes, this was home, and for the first time in weeks the constant sensation of dread that inhabited her heart abated. A bit.

"It is good to be home, is it not?" Mabel asked.

"Oh, yes." Kit had by now found the chapel, a staid building in grey stone that stood apart from the rest of the manor. She looked at the chests on the packhorses, at the chapel, and knew exactly where she would hide the entrusted treasure.

As they rode into the front yard, Kit's exuberance at being home faltered. What before her abduction had seemed a grand place, now looked paltry and unkempt compared to the grandeur of Wigmore. She eyed the ramshackle fence with a frown, thinking that in times of unrest something more robust was required to keep the wolf from the door. She sighed, her gaze sweeping the stables to her right, the byre and the pigsty. From the squat building that housed the kitchen old Mall came running, arms opened wide, and Kit slipped off the horse and fell into her welcoming embrace.

The people of the household swarmed around her, and it was only after several greetings that Kit was capable of disentangling herself sufficiently to greet John. He'd been standing to the side, watching with a smile, but when she approached the wizened man bowed and gave her a gap-toothed smile.

"You're back, my lady," he said. "Finally!" He turned to beam at Mabel, who beamed back, using her sleeve to wipe at her eyes.

"Brother!" Mabel bussed John on both cheeks before standing back to eye him critically. "You're not wearing your years as well as I am."

John laughed. "And you're still like a rose in the first flush of summer, are you?"

Mabel huffed. "No need to be impertinent."

What had once appeared the finest of halls now looked exactly what it was: a sad little place in need of repair, the single gigantic fireplace doing little to dispel the damp. Kit made notes to have John look into the cracks in the wall, and ascended the stairs to the solar. The door protested at being thrown open, the floors were in grave need of a good scrub, but Kit didn't care, already at the window to open the shutters. The view was unchanged, a combination of dips and folds in the encircling hills, and in the nearby orchard the trees stood silent and denuded under the winter skies, but John and the lads had already been at them, pruning and sawing.

"It hasn't changed much." Mabel was already busy unpacking.

"It hasn't?" Kit ran her hand down the decorated bedposts, frowning at the dusty state of the bed-hangings. It looked as if no one had entered the room since the day she'd been abducted. She shivered in a sudden gust of wind, but was reluctant to close the shutters and shut out the light.

"It's nice and big," Mabel continued. "That's good as you'll be spending a lot of time here during your confinement."

"My confinement?" Kit laughed. "I am no high-born lady, Mabel. I will not go into confinement."

"Of course you will. Expecting mothers must retire to a life of quiet and comfort to soothe the child's passage into the world."

Kit snorted. "I am needed in the daily running of things. I don't have time for a confinement."

Mabel set her jaw. "It is unseemly—"

"I don't care."

"Your husband—"

"He's not here, is he? Chances are he'll never come here."

Kit turned away and placed her hands on her belly. "My baby should have a father."

"Oh, child." Mabel bustled over to her and gave her a clumsy hug. "We will do right by the babe – and by its father."

"Truly?" Kit gave her a teary smile.

"Well, God save us all if you don't find him alive. I dare say you'll set out to impale the king in revenge."

"Something like that." Kit laughed, and for the first time in days she felt a glimmer of hope.

She waited until well after dark before stating that she intended to visit the chapel. Mabel and William went with her, all three of them loaded with linen bags of treasure that they carried under their cloaks.

"Why the subterfuge?" William asked, puffing as he hastened after Kit across the yard. The poor man was straining under his load – as were they all, Kit's arms feeling about to drop off.

"The fewer who know, the better. You never know when a secret hiding place can come in handy, do you?"

"A hiding place?"

"What did you think? That I aimed to pile these bags in front of the altar and pray to God to make them invisible?"

William huffed, looking displeased.

Ever since childhood, Kit could remember waking in the night and going to find her mother, knowing she would find Alaïs not in her bed but here, praying.

"Keeping vigil for my people," Alaïs would say sadly, lighting yet another candle. Now Kit understood: candles for Sir Thomas, for the man Alaïs loved enough to allow herself to be immured in solitude with only her daughter for company.

The tiled floor smelled of beeswax, the altar was as plain as always, decorated only by a set of candlesticks and a small silver chalice. But behind the altar was a triptych, three panels of wood that depicted the passion of the Christ, his burial and resurrection. The colours vibrated in the otherwise plain space, a glory of reds and blues, of gold leaf and muted greens. Brought home by an ancestor from the Crusades, Kit's mother would say in hushed tones, tracing a gentle finger over the exquisite frame, an elegant pattern of ivory and ebony squares, each one marked with a miniature cross.

William sank to his knees, Mabel did the same and Kit followed suit, finding comfort in William's voice, a low and rumbling baritone that prayed for God to help them, to carry them through their hour of need. In Kit's experience, God rarely did, but sometimes ritual offered solace, and she intensified her prayers, begging God to keep her Adam safe.

She was almost asleep on her knees, lulled by William's droning voice and the flickering lights of the candles, when William decided he was done and helped her to her feet.

"So where is this little nook of yours?" he asked.

"Behind the altar." Kit led the way and sank down in a crouch, running her fingers into a narrow gap at the base of the altar. The lever was where she'd expected it to be, and when she pressed on it, the floor section behind her swung downwards, revealing a hole. Quite the large hole, adequately ventilated and lit by a number of miniature slits, invisible from above as they formed part of the decorated tile floor.

William was most impressed, as was Mabel, expressing over and over again that never had she heard of such a hiding place.

"It's a secret," Kit said with a smile. "Secrets are meant to be kept secret."

"An excellent secret." William smiled broadly. "And somehow I think it will come in very useful." He set down the last of the linen bags and brushed the dust off his dark gown.

"So do I," Kit replied, activating the mechanism that lifted the floor back into place.

Chapter 22

Kit had every intention of setting out for Shrewsbury on the morrow after her arrival at Tresaints. Unfortunately, the powers that be conspired against her, and she woke to a howling blizzard that made any attempt at travelling futile. For four days the storm raged, and when it was over, Kit was sick, chilled to the bone after days in her frigid hall.

"It's just a cold," she protested when Mabel insisted she had to stay in bed.

"It is more than that." Mabel knocked her on her chest, making Kit cough. "Hear that? That's a bad cough, m' lady, and we will not go anywhere until you are recuperated from it."

"But Adam—"

"If he's dead he's beyond our help anyway, and if he's alive I dare say he'll remain alive a couple of weeks more. Whatever the case, it won't help if you sicken and die, will it?" Mabel pushed Kit down into the bed. "Sleep. I will bring you possets."

Elderberry cordial laced with linseed oil was just the thing, Kit reflected a fortnight or so later, sitting up in bed as she drank yet another of Mabel's concoctions. Her chest was free of congestion, and for the first time in days she could inhale through her nose.

"Any news?" she asked William when he entered the room. He gave her a heavy look and came over to sit on the stool beside the bed.

"In chains," he said. "Egard heard it from someone down in the village, how the king had Lord Roger and his uncle fitted with chains before all the assembled nobles, and then they were sent off to the Tower."

"The Tower?" Kit whispered, a sinking feeling in her stomach. "And Adam?"

"The rest of Lord Roger's men have been incarcerated in Shrewsbury, there to lose their lives as rebels."

"No!" Kit struggled up to sit. "No. We have to—"

"Lie down," William said, pushing her back down among the quilts. "There is no word as to these executions, so maybe they've been stayed. Besides, king or not, the men deserve a trial, and the king knows better by now than to attempt to circumvent the course of justice."

"I have to—"

"I know. So do I." Her priest friend took her hand. "We leave tomorrow, and until we find him, I will pray constantly for Adam." He bent down and kissed her forehead. "I would suggest you do the same."

"This is foolhardy," Mabel said next morning, using substantial force as she braided Kit's hair before covering it with a coif and heavy veil. "You're not fit to set off on a week-long ride, and as to the baby…" She shook her head.

"I am an experienced rider, so my baby travels safely with me." Kit replied. "I am not yet five months gone, and women much further along than me have ridden great distances." Like the sainted Virgin, she thought to herself, but wisely chose not to voice it.

Mabel gave her a disapproving look. "I don't like it."

"You know as well as I do that I have to do this. I have to find Adam." Kit patted her belly. "He lies safe in here, but Adam, well…" She choked.

"He?" Mabel said with a little smile.

"Definitely a he. Only a boy would give his mother heartburn before he is born."

Once they made it out into the bailey, Kit complained that she'd been swaddled, with Mabel insisting on one garment after the other to ensure she was safe from anything the weather might throw their way.

Egard boosted her up onto the horse, large hands holding her steady as she settled herself in the saddle. She felt faint, tremors rippling up her legs and back after the short walk from the hall to the horse. Mabel fixed eagle eyes on her, so Kit gave her a little smile and tried to look unaffected.

It was the third week of February, and no matter how Kit

counted, that gave the king ample time to try, condemn and hang all the men who had been arrested with Mortimer.

"He isn't there," William said when she shared this with him. "The king rides north to deal with the Earl of Lancaster."

"Justly deserved," Kit muttered. If haughty Lancaster had ridden down to join the Mortimers, none of this mess would have happened.

"It will keep the king occupied for some time," William said. "The earls of Lancaster and Hereford are experienced battle commanders."

"And the king isn't." Kit nodded, even if by now she wasn't quite sure she agreed with this general statement. After all, King Edward had rather ably turned the tables on his victorious barons, which indicated some capacity for leadership.

William must have seen what she was thinking, because he smiled wryly. "A fast learner, " he said, before reverting to the original subject by telling her it was Pembroke who had been left in charge of administering the royal justice. "No doubt to teach him not to make promises on behalf of his liege," William finished.

"Very subtle," Kit murmured. God forgive her, but she hated Pembroke! Most of all she hated the king and the Despensers, a consequence of her recent exposure to the Mortimers. Now and then, it struck her that the Mortimer version of events might not necessarily be the truth. After all, she'd never met Sir Hugh Despenser, and for all she knew, he might be a kind and upright man, defending his family and lands as tenaciously as Mortimer was defending his.

"It may be to your advantage that the earl twists in shame." William chewed his lip. "You need to have him confirm your ownership of your dower lands."

"And how do I do that?" At William's urging, Kit was carrying the deeds to her four dower manors with her, plus a copy of the wedding contract that clearly stated these manors were to be her jointure should anything happen to Adam.

"He has to validate the wedding contract – and preferably the deeds to the manors as well." William mimed a seal coming down.

Kit nodded, at present not all that concerned about her manors, but when she said that out loud, William glared at her.

"And how aim you to live, without your land?" He reached across and placed a hand on her belly, making Kit shrink away. "How will you support this one, with nothing to your name?"

They said nothing more for the next few hours, both of them lost in their own thoughts.

The first night they spent in Thornbury, then pushed on to Ludlow the day after, riding in silence along the Treme as they approached the former Mortimer stronghold. Ludlow was now under royal control, the English lions flying from the castle that until recently had displayed the azure and or arms of the Mortimers. It made Kit sick to the stomach to see the Mortimer banner torn down and trampled in the mud, a most evocative testimonial to how low Lord Roger Mortimer had fallen.

At William's urging, they spoke little to anyone, keeping very much to themselves in the little inn in which they were to stay the night. Still, Kit was more than aware of the glances the men in the room threw her way, interested glances that sharpened as they took in her clothes, her hands and face. Fortunately, Egard hovered like a protective shadow at her back, but she was discomfited, as was William.

"They eye you like starving wolves would eye a wounded ewe," William muttered.

"Don't be silly! Who looks at a woman with child?" Kit attempted to laugh his comment away.

"Men," he replied drily.

Kit laughed and caressed her slight bulge. "I will dress like a frumpy old wife."

"Frumpy?" William's teeth flashed in a smile. "You could not be frumpy even if you tried." His eyes moistened. "My brother is fortunate in his wife – in every way that matters."

"Hold on to that," Kit said.

"Eh?"

"You said *is* fortunate, not *was* fortunate." Kit smiled at him. "And now let's get some sleep. We have several long days before us."

They had decided to ride up via Church Stratton, wanting to avoid as many curious eyes as possible. This meant long stretches of riding through empty, uninhabited moor, which suited Kit, because with every step their horses took towards Shrewsbury, the more agitated she got. She tried to hide her anxiety from her companions – with little success, as evidenced by William's solicitous presence and Mabel's attempts to cheer her up by talking about the markets and all the other sights that would be waiting for them in Shrewsbury.

"As long as they don't include gallows." Kit bit her off, immediately sorry for the sharpness of her tone.

"All towns have gallows," William pointed out.

"Yes, but most towns don't have my husband lined up to be hanged from one," Kit flashed back, setting her heels to her horse for a quick gallop on her own.

Under any other circumstances, Kit would have enjoyed the ride through the dramatic landscapes that surrounded her. Endless moors shifted into gorges and sheer cliff faces, and some days of warmer sun had left the shrubs with a promise of green, with here and there an early anemone presenting a white head to the world. A stiff wind made her eyes water, the horse between her legs was surefooted enough to take her careening across the uneven landscape, and yet no matter how she tried, these occasional bursts of speed on horseback did nothing to alleviate the growing dread that inhabited every wrinkled corner of her brain.

Five days after setting out, they saw Shrewsbury on the horizon, a collection of buildings clambering up a series of hills outlined against the light blue of the February sky. They'd passed Bridgnorth the day before, and Kit had insisted they stop and silently honour Lord Mortimer and his companions, here where they had won their last victory against the king.

"Where do you think Lady Joan is?" Kit asked William, holding in her horse to wait for Mabel, who seemed increasingly reluctant to enter Shrewsbury the closer they got. By now, Kit could make out the walls and the imposing gatehouse on the bridge, guarding the entry to the city.

"I don't know. Last I heard, she was escorted to Hampshire."

"And the children? Did they go with her?" There was a large church and accompanying buildings this side of the Severn which Kit supposed to be the abbey. Would Adam be there?

William shook his head. "They've been sent hither and dither. Edmund and Roger are in Windsor, and all the lasses have been incarcerated – except Maud."

Kit turned from her inspection of her surroundings. "All of them? Even baby Blanche?"

"She, I believe, remains with her mother." He looked away and mouthed a prayer, ending it by crossing himself. "They are all in God's hands, and there they lie safe."

"Let us hope so," Kit said, beckoning for Mabel to catch up.

At the last bend of the road, Mabel yet again held in her horse, eyes darting in the direction of William.

"What?" Kit asked, wrinkling her nose at the sickly sweet scent of rot that came in wafts from somewhere to her right.

"The gibbets." William took hold of Kit's arm. "Not a sight for a woman with child."

Kit sniffed. "Being with child doesn't leave you witless and useless."

"No, but maybe more sensitive," William said.

Had she had any notion of what she would see, Kit would have followed William's suggestion and kept her eyes closed all the way to the city walls. But she had never seen a gibbet before, and had but the vaguest comprehension what it might entail. Until she saw the first ones.

"Oh my God, oh my God, oh my God." Kit had to slide off her horse, retching until her insides felt about to tear themselves apart. Mabel and William joined her, leaving Egard in charge of the horses. Slowly, Kit straightened up, only to clap her hands over her eyes in a futile effort to avoid seeing the macabre spectacle that adorned the last stretch of the road to Shrewsbury.

Everywhere, swinging corpses, in various states of decomposition, all of them crammed into metal cages. Invariably, the eyes were gone, as were most of their faces, but here and there a nose held on, an ear or even part of a mouth. Most of the men had been hanged, some were no more than boys, and nowhere – thank the Lord, nowhere – did she see a body of Adam's proportions. But there were others she recognised, and when they reached the bridge, Kit mewled, pointing upwards to the head of Sir Thomas de Monmouth, displayed from a spike on the gatehouse.

"My fath—" she croaked, her gaze stuck on a tuft of distinctive curly hair.

"Shush!" Mabel hissed. "It does you no good to claim kinship with an executed traitor."

"And Adam?" She couldn't move, tremors rushing through her limbs. "My Adam?" she whispered, giving William a pleading look.

"I don't know," he replied, his voice close to breaking.

"Well, we haven't seen him, have we?" Mabel pointed out, settling a strong hand round Kit's wrist. "Now, lass, first we find an inn, and then we set about finding this husband of yours."

Chapter 23

They found an inn just off St Chad's, a church so ancient it looked as if it had risen from the hill it stood on. It was a clean enough place, even if the three of them had to bed down in one room, with William fortunate enough to get the smaller of the pallet beds while Kit and Mabel squashed down on the other, lying almost on top of each other.

"We have to find Lionel," Kit said the next morning.

"You have to find the Earl of Pembroke," William said. "Mabel and I will keep an eye out for young Lionel."

Kit nodded. "But first we go to the abbey."

A man in dark robes and with a hesitant smile came to greet her once she had stated her business. "I am Brother Francis."

"My husband," Kit asked bluntly. "Is he here?"

"Your husband?"

"Adam de Guirande."

"Ah." The monk tapped his mouth with an ink-stained digit. "He was here. But he's not here any longer."

"So where is he?"

The monk sighed. "I do not rightly know, Lady de Guirande. The man should not have left his bed, but was commanded to attend on the king with the Mortimers." He wrinkled his brows. "In late January, I believe. And since then, I am sad to say, we haven't seen him."

"But where can he be?"

The monk gave her a pitying look. "Dead?"

Kit staggered back, clutching at her skirts.

The monk hastened towards her, helping her to sit. "I am sorry, my lady, but that is one possibility."

"But…" Kit wet her lips. "We didn't see him," she said hoarsely. "Not among the gibbets."

"My lady," the monk took her hands, "your husband was

ailing. The wound to his side was healing, but he was nowhere close to full recovery. And if he has received no care, well then…"

Kit shook her head. "No." She fixed the monk with a stubborn look. "You don't die of an arrow to the side."

"Men die of lesser cuts every day." The monk sighed.

"Not my Adam." She stood, ignoring William's outstretched hand. She had to be strong and resourceful, hold on to hope when everyone around her seemed to have given up. "So if he isn't dead, where would he be?"

"I do not know," the monk replied, "but I'd hazard the castle – in the dungeons."

Once outside, Kit threw William a wild look. "The castle?"

"On the other side of the river, to your right."

Kit set off at half-run. "Come on," she threw over her shoulder.

"Kit!" William took hold of her arm. "Walk, woman. And take a deep breath or two." He placed her hand in the crook of his arm. "No need to draw undue attention to ourselves, is there?"

He was right. Kit slowed her pace, while attempting to stop her heart from racing. Not much success there, and even less when, upon turning the corner, they bumped into Guy de Guirande.

He looked as if he'd seen a ghost. Guy's face blanched and he retreated, arms flung out to steady himself. His dark hair had been newly cut, the hooded velvet tabard in deep red was lined with fur, and his long legs were encased in black hose and brand new boots. He was unarmed – except for the dagger slightly to the back of his left hip – and a leather pouch jangled at his abrupt movement.

"It pays, does it?" William asked with a sneer. Kit took a firm hold of his arm, surprised to feel just how much muscle bunched along his forearm.

"What pays?"

"Being a traitorous whelp," William snarled, shaking Kit off. His resemblance to Adam grew more marked with every step he took towards Guy, who retreated before his enraged stepbrother.

"A traitor?" Guy straightened up. "I was but doing my duty to my liege."

"Only because you suspected he would win," Kit said. "You're not exactly motivated by convictions, are you?"

William snickered, while Guy puffed up like an angry cockerel.

"I'll not have you talk to me like that!"

"No?" Kit slapped him full in the face. "Prefer me to do that instead? Or maybe I should kick you in the balls, craven whoreson that you are!" She swung for him again, but this time Guy managed to get hold of her wrist, squeezing down so hard Kit emitted a whimper.

"I'll not have the wife of my traitor brother hit me," he said, lowering his face to her. "Because, dear Kit, that is how it is: Adam is the traitor here, not me."

"Let her go!" William shoved at Guy, sending him flying backwards. "In my book, a man who shoots his own brother is a faithless, spineless worm. Our Adam followed his lord, while you followed your purse."

"I followed my king!" Guy scrambled to his feet, dagger in hand. "And as to Adam, I didn't shoot him. It isn't my fault that Welsh archer chose to use him for target practice, is it?"

"You stole his horse," Kit said.

"His horse? Damned animal!" Guy sneered. "He doesn't need him anymore, does he? Your precious Adam will be dead before the week is out."

"What?" Kit hated it that her voice broke. "When?"

"On Friday," Guy mumbled, ducking his face. "And even if you don't believe me, I am sorry that he is to die."

"They're going to…" Kit couldn't complete the sentence, her head filling with gruesome images of extended executions involving nooses and knives and skilled executioners.

"By mercy of the king, he is to hang – assuming he is still alive by then."

"Mercy of the king? And what do you mean, assuming he is still alive?"

Guy shuffled on his feet.

"Answer me!" Kit gripped him by his shoulders and shook him. "What ails him?"

"Everything," Guy said, disengaging himself from her hands. "He rots, I fear."

"We have to help him." Kit looked Guy up and down. "You have to help him, you seem to have the means to do so."

Guy backed away, hands raised in a placatory gesture. "I will do everything I can," he said, before darting off.

"Oh God." Kit's legs seemed incapable of supporting her weight. She turned anguished eyes on William. "What do I do now?"

"Well, whatever you do, don't count on Guy," William said bitterly. He led her out of the busy, cobbled street, ducked into a nearby church and helped her sit. The dim interior smelled of incense and damp wool, weakly lit by a distant candle. "Are you all right?"

Kit shook her head, incapable of speech.

"He isn't dead," William tried. Kit was overcome with a wave of exhaustion and bent forward, supporting her head in her hands.

"Friday," she said, glancing at William through her splayed fingers. Four days from now, and no matter how she racked her brain she couldn't think if one single thing that might save him. And he was ill, so ill Guy thought he might die before…and…Kit inhaled, held her breath, did it again, all the while blinking madly in an attempt to stop herself from crying. One tear plopped down onto the dusty floorboards below her feet, another followed suit, and Kit held herself tightly and wept, while William sat silent beside her, his hand making slow rubbing motions over her back.

"I have to see him," she said, sitting up. Kit wiped at her face with her sleeve. "And then I'm going to see Pembroke."

An hour later, and Kit was desperate. The guards had refused her entry to the castle, telling her curtly that the traitor Adam de Guirande wasn't allowed any visitors.

"But he is to hang on Friday," she said. "Please let me see him, please! Just an hour, but at least let me tell him farewell."

"You can do that at the gallows," the guard said. "I have my orders from the constable." He jerked his head in the direction of a rotund man, who was rushing across the bailey. "You'll have to ask him, not me, for permission."

The constable looked harried. He frowned at Kit, inspected his feet and then told her she would not be allowed to see her husband. "Probably for the better, if you ask me," he added with a sly grin that made Kit want to kick him.

"But why?" she asked.

"My Lord Despenser prefers it that way," the constable said. Once again that sly smile, transforming into a genuine expression of pleasure when the constable's eyes alighted on a small boy who came running towards him.

"Your son?" Kit asked, smiling at the redheaded child.

"My very own little prince," the constable replied, lifting the boy high.

"And isn't he a fortunate boy?" Kit said bitterly. "He gets to know his father."

"Not my fault," the constable told her, setting his son down.

"And it isn't mine either – or his." Kit caressed her belly.

"Your man took up arms against the king."

"My man held to his pledged loyalty and followed his lord." She swept him a reverence and left, her mind a hive of activity as she tried to find some way out of all this.

William listened, he listened again, and when Kit began on her third repetition of how unfair all this was, and what were they to do, because there had to be *something* they could do, he interrupted her and told her they had to eat.

"Eat?" She gave him an angered look. "Eat while Adam dies?"

"You are not doing yourself any good." He propelled her to a nearby market stand and bought them a pasty each, so hot they burnt her fingers. When she opened her mouth to say something he held up a hand. "First we eat, then we talk."

As a consequence of their discussions, Kit returned to the castle just before noon, demanding to see the Earl of Pembroke.

"Not here," the guard told her, directing her down a nearby street towards an imposing residence, the upper floors protruding over the street. Kit made her way carefully; a brief shower had left the gutters overflowing and the cobbles covered in mud. Children and hens, pigs and dogs, here and there a woman with a basket on her arm, a man laughing, another talking to a friend – all in all a normal life, a life of small pleasures and daily problems, none of them anywhere close to being as grave as the conundrum Kit was facing. She gnawed her lip and rehearsed her little speech, while things the size of hairy caterpillars crawled up and down her gullet, causing her now and then to have to stop and take a couple of breaths or two.

There was a banner hanging limply by the gate, white and blue stripes decorated by a number of bright red birds that looked like overweight swallows – martlets, she corrected herself. A couple of guards eyed her as she approached, standing aside to let her enter with a nod. The inner yard was full of people, and at the top of the stairs that led to the entrance stood the man Kit assumed to be the earl, at least to judge from his clothes. Full-length robes in the same blue that decorated his banner, a richly wrought belt, a hooded silk tunic in madder rose, and visible below the hem of his robes, soft, ankle-high shoes.

"My lord," Kit said, waving her deeds to catch his attention. The earl looked at her, heavy brows pulled together in an inquisitive frown. "I am Kit de Guirande," she continued, and the earl backed away, eyes flitting in all directions but hers. "I have matters I need your help with."

"You may deal with my clerk," the earl said, retreating from her in haste. He clapped a young man on the shoulder. "Peter here will help you with everything. Everything, you hear, Peter?"

And just like that he was gone.

Peter the clerk never bothered introducing himself. He listened in stony silence to Kit's requests for the earl to help her husband, before saying such matters were no longer in the earl's hands – she would do better trying the constable.

"I already have," she said.

"Try again," the clerk said, lifting narrow shoulders in a shrug. He made as if to move away.

"Wait!" Kit grabbed at him. "I have these as well." She handed him the deeds and saw a look of relief flit over the young man's face as he scanned the documents, before he told her that here the earl could most definitely help. Moments later, her documents contained several lines of minute handwriting in Latin conferring permanent ownership of the manors to Katherine de Monmouth.

"It will not be much to live on," the clerk said as he affixed the earl's seal to the documents. "Four manors will not keep you in furs and silks."

"At least there will be mutton and wool," she replied, making the clerk smile.

"Why won't he listen?" she asked Peter as he escorted her out of the house.

"If he were to speak to all the widows coming to claim on him he wouldn't do much else," Peter replied, his protruding Adam's apple bobbing up and down. "Any matters pertaining to the traitors are no longer his responsibility – the king fears my Lord Pembroke's conscience will get the better of him."

"It should," Kit said. "After all, it's because of his lies that Shrewsbury is decorated with rotting men."

"The king's will," Peter sighed, before giving her a courteous farewell.

Yet again, Kit trudged up to the castle, this time demanding to speak to the constable. The guard at the gate sighed. "He'll not see you, my lady."

"But he must! I insist that he see me."

"Insist all you like," the guard said, not unkindly. "Our constable prefers to avoid strife."

"Strife? I just want to see my husband." To her shame, she began to cry.

"I'm sorry, my lady. It isn't me who makes up the rules." The guard gently pushed her away.

She found William at St Mary's, and from the look on his face he had had no success in gaining access to Adam, despite his priestly garb. Kit looked him over; at present, William didn't look all that much like a priest, his tonsure resembling a normal bald spot rather than the severe hairless circle that had adorned his scalp when first she met him. His cheeks bristled, there was something very sticky on his right sleeve, and since he'd insisted on carrying a dagger while they travelled, he looked more like a potential rogue in disguise than a devout churchman.

"What do we do?" she asked, turning to look back towards the castle.

"I don't know." He craned his head to look at a nearby spire. "We need a miracle, I think."

"We need an invitation to the castle," Kit replied, watching a small redheaded boy come skipping down the street with a slight woman at his side. The constable's son – and his lady wife, given that the boy addressed the woman as Mama. With a wrinkle between her brows, Kit watched them until they were out of sight.

Mabel greeted them at the inn with a wide smile, tugging Kit in the direction of a very dishevelled but entirely healed Lionel, at present sitting with Egard at one of the trestles and slurping soup as if he hadn't seen food in days. He rose at the sight of Kit.

"My lady," he said through his full mouth. She waved him to sit and sank down on the bench opposite, cradling her head in her arms. William and Mabel filled Lionel in, bits and pieces of their recent adventures, and when they'd finished Lionel began to talk, a longwinded description of his unsuccessful quest.

"Do you know the constable's wife?" Kit interrupted, without lifting her head from her arms.

"Lady Maude?" Lionel wiped his mouth on his sleeve. "Everyone knows Lady Maude. Twice a day she drags her little son down to the abbey, there to pray at her recently departed father's grave."

"Her father was a monk?" Kit asked, surprised. William frowned at her.

"Not when she was born, but it is said old man Gilbert saw the light some years ago – coincidentally when Lady Maude married the constable – and signed over all his lands to her before retiring to the abbey." Lionel scraped his spoon over the bottom of his bowl, chasing the last remnants of his food. "I dare say she suffers remorse – one of the monks told me how Gilbert was most unhappy, complaining loudly that his only daughter had cheated him of everything."

"She did?"

Lionel sucked his spoon, eyeing the innkeeper's wife hopefully. "No sooner had he made his sign on the deeds than she threw him out, so what could he do but turn to the monks?"

"Quite the dutiful daughter." Kit sat up; there were fragments of a potential plan in her head, but it required some reconnoitring. "Come with me," she said, leading the way outside and down Wyle Cop to the bridge.

It was an impressive bridge, straddling the Severn with several arches. The water was scummy and smelled of rancid fats, which William explained was due to all the tanneries located upriver.

"Mmm." Kit nodded distractedly. "Is it deep?"

"What are you planning?" William asked.

"A rescue operation," Kit replied, going on to outline her plan.

"You can't do something like that!" William said once she had finished.

"I just told you, there's no risk." That was a lie; to judge from the frothy waters below, there was definitely a risk, but Kit could see no other way out of her dilemma. None. A desperate and foolish plan to be sure, but it was the only plan she had.

"No risk? Of course there's a risk! Look at it, it's in full spate, and the current will—"

"Shhh!" Kit scowled at him. "No need to shout, you fool." She pursed her mouth. "I see no alternative. I have to get into the castle, put myself in front of the constable's eyes in such a way that he can't refuse me."

"But not like that," William moaned. "Not by risking—"

"I'm not risking anything! I know how to swim. And so, Adam tells me, do you."

William gave her a look of pure dislike. "And if things go wrong?"

Kit stamped her foot. "They won't. But if they do, and I end up dead, well then…"

William scowled. "I wasn't thinking of you, I was thinking of the innocent—"

"Why thank you. And let me remind you that the only reason I'm considering this is because my husband, your brother, is rotting away in a dungeon. For some strange reason, I care more about him than I do about—"

"I can do it," Egard interrupted. He peered down at the water.

Kit shook her head. The man was the size of an ox, and had a face it was difficult to forget, what with his huge, twisted nose. "You're too distinctive. They'll find you in less than an hour and then—"

"Quiet!" Mabel hissed. They stood silent until the little group of men-at-arms had passed them, making for the gatehouse. "I think it will work," she went on once they were alone again. "Lionel and Egard can hide well down the river to help William, and I'll be just below the castle walls." She grinned at Kit. "And I do know how to swim, should you need help."

Kit smiled back, hoping she would never have to place her life in the hands of a woman more than twice her age and half her size.

Early next morning, Kit had her team of five in position. William had protested well into the night, but faced with one rational argument after the other, he had finally succumbed, and was now standing just where Wyle Cop joined with the bridge, dressed in dirty sacking, a piped hood in bright green and multicoloured hose.

Lionel and Egard had ridden off well before dawn, and Mabel had set off shortly after, ambling along the river in the general direction of the castle. Kit was sitting on the bridge parapet, pretending great concentration on the faraway horizon while silently praying to the Virgin for protection. Her belly was doing somersaults, and she was no longer all that sure this would work. She eyed the water with some trepidation. It looked cold and dark, with several unidentified objects bobbing along in it. Her nerve was failing her, and Kit was just considering whether to call all of this off, when from the direction of the castle came the constable's wife, yet again with the son at her side.

"Don't take your eyes off him," she whispered to herself. "Whatever you do, don't take your eyes off him."

The little boy laughed and talked – he danced along the streets, and his mother laughed with him, now and then shaking her head in amused exasperation. They were almost at the bridge. Time for William to do his part, but he hung back, slouching against a wall.

"Come on, come on," Kit muttered, wiping damp hands against her skirts.

A yell, a shriek, and William stepped howling into the street, arms raised towards the skies. "The end of the world," he screamed, "the end of the world is upon us!" People came to a halt, and doors and shutters in the adjoining houses popped open. "I tell you," William yelled, swivelling on his toes with his arms extended, "I tell you we must die. Die and burn!" Someone laughed. William turned, face so scrunched up he resembled a gargoyle. "Laugh," he hissed, dropping his voice. "Laugh now and sizzle in eternity."

The people began to mutter, some edging away, some looking amused. William clasped his hands together and prayed out loud: "*Pater noster qui es in caelis…*" All around people fell in, which was when William howled again and pointed up the street, towards St Mary's. "Fire! The fire of heaven is upon us! Run or be burnt, run or die!" And just like that he leapt forward, grabbed hold of the little redheaded boy, and jumped off the bridge into the waters below.

"My son!" screamed the constable's wife.

Kit rose to her feet. "I'll save him," she said, and jumped. She landed just in front of one of the arches, and was swept under the bridge. With one arm William was hanging on for dear life to the net Egard had affixed earlier, the other holding the boy. Kit grabbed hold of the child, William let go and was carried downstream, howling and kicking.

"Roderick!" someone screamed, and out of the corner of her eye Kit saw the constable's wife running along the riverbank. There was a terrifying moment when Kit's feet tangled in the net, but then she was free, dragged along by the current. The child in her arms screamed, they were pulled under, came up coughing and went down again. A small foot kicked Kit in the hip.

"Agh!" Her mouth flooded with water, she tried to kick for the shore, but the current drove her out towards the middle, and it was far too cold. Her skirts weighed like lead, and the boy in her arms clung to her neck like a limpet, making it impossible to breathe. Down. Water closed over her head, over the boy's head, and for a moment her grip on the little body slipped. She clutched at the wool of his tunic, kicked and surfaced, spitting like a drowning cat. The boy coughed and sobbed, tightening his hold on her neck.

Something struck her foot, her skirts snagged and they were sinking again, imprisoned by whatever it was that had got caught in her kirtle. Bubbles. Everywhere bubbles. Red hair floated before her eyes. Kit tightened her hold on the boy with one arm and used the other to grip at her skirts and pull. She kicked and thrashed, and seconds later they broke the surface, bobbing along in the current. Dearest Virgin; she was going to die, the poor boy was going to die, and…Once again they were tugged under. No. She couldn't die. Adam. The babe. Swim, God help me, swim! So she did, water streaming from her nose and mouth when she succeeded in thrashing her way up into the wonderful, wonderful air.

Before her loomed the walls of the castle. The river did a slow turn to the right, the current weakened and Kit struck out for the shore, to where she could see a whole crowd of people, one of them Mabel, who was being held back by an elderly man.

Her foot hit the bottom. Two men waded towards her.

"Here," she said, arms trembling as she handed them the boy. Step by step she dragged herself towards the bank.

"You saved him!" Lady Maude gave her a teary smile, arms round her drenched son. "How can I ever repay you?"

Kit coughed and shivered. "A cloak," Lady Maude commanded. "Give her a cloak, and then take her up to the castle."

"M' lady?" Mabel popped up beside them. "What were you playing at? You nearly got yourself killed is what you did," she scolded.

"I had to," Kit croaked. "The boy would have drowned."

"And your babe?" Mabel's voice grew shrill. "What if you have saved one child to lose the other?"

"Hush," Kit said.

Lady Maude took hold of Kit. "Well, we can't let that happen. Come with me, my lady, you need dry clothes and something warm to drink." She smiled again at Kit and drew back her hood, revealing a pockmarked face that must once have been very beautiful. "My husband will want to thank you in person," she continued. "Our Roderick is precious to us both."

Chapter 24

For the coming hour, Kit was the centre of attention. Mabel was sent off to the inn for dry clothes, and Kit was served one warm posset after the other, while Lady Maude just wouldn't stop thanking her. Kit smiled weakly and was very relieved when Mabel returned, rushing in behind the constable, who had the panicked look of a parent expecting dire news about his child.

Lady Maude hastened to her husband and drew him forward, insisting he had to thank the woman who had saved their son. The constable's eyes widened in recognition, and then he was bowing and thanking her, promising he would do whatever was in his power to repay her. Kit bit back a little smile, thinking things were working out according to plan, when there was a commotion by the door. The constable threw a look over his shoulder, stiffened and straightened up from his obsequious stance, hurrying to greet the man who now strode into the room, accompanied by a gaudily dressed company.

"Who's that?" Kit whispered to Mabel. She studied the man, who was taking his time walking through the large room, now and then stopping to converse with a bowing man or simpering woman.

"That's Despenser," Mabel hissed. She spat discreetly in the rushes. "May you die soon, Hugh Despenser, and may it be painful."

Kit felt a tremor rushing through her, but wasn't sure whether to attribute it to fear or to her damp clothes. The man approaching them looked quite ordinary, of an age with Lord Mortimer but with receding dark hair and pasty skin. In contrast to Baron Mortimer and her own Adam, Hugh Despenser looked soft – a misleading impression, she suspected, at least to judge from the hushed silence in the room.

The man oozed wealth. Silk hose, newfangled shoes, sweeping robes and an impressive cloak, slashed through to reveal a lining that was also silk, a deep red that contrasted with the black and gold of the rest of his clothes. Every finger held a ring – one had two – gold adorned his chest, his shoes, and even the buckle of his belt seemed to consist of some precious metal, decorated with a glittering jewel. One step behind him came the Earl of Pembroke, head bent towards the constable who was talking rapidly, pointing at Kit.

"And what have we here?" Despenser came to a stop, regarding Kit. His gaze revealed nothing but a mild interest, but she could see him registering everything about her, his brows rising infinitesimally as he took in her belly. He had a beautiful voice, low and musical, it slithered through your brain. Kit inclined her upper body in a bow, and Mabel nearly dropped to the floor.

The Earl of Pembroke whispered something to Despenser, who nodded.

"Ah, yes. Mistress de Guirande, the brave saviour of hapless children." He smiled as he said it, but there was little warmth in Despenser's voice.

Kit straightened up, which left her at eye level with Despenser. He didn't seem bothered by her height, studying her with the keen interest of a hawk regarding a fat and juicy coney. Dark eyes regarded her from under equally dark brows, his teeth worrying at his plump lower lip. Kit met his gaze calmly, aiming to appear unperturbed. Despenser circled her. Kit was sorely tempted to turn her head when he was behind her, but fixed her eyes on the Earl of Pembroke and smiled instead, receiving a weak twitch of his lips in return.

Even the earl looked frightened. Aymer de Valence was the colour of soiled linen, his brow glistening with sweat. Kit scrutinised Despenser, trying to understand what it was about him that had the entire room quaking. No massive chest, no bulging arms, Hugh Despenser looked puny compared to de Valence, and as to Roger Mortimer, he could have fought this man with one hand tied behind his back and still come out on top. Except, of course, that Hugh Despenser would never do anything so foolish as to place himself within reach of Roger Mortimer. No, this man worked through the king, behind the king, and therein lay his strength; what he wanted done, the royal chamberlain whispered in the royal ear, and Hugh Despenser's wish became royal command.

Kit supposed it was but a matter of weeks before Roger Mortimer was dragged out from his cell in the Tower and executed, thereby leaving the stage entirely to the man before her. It saddened her, but her present concern was Adam, not Mortimer. She swallowed. Adam's execution was set for Friday, and besides, he was apparently seriously ill, so even if she succeeded in getting him a reprieve, who was to know if he'd survive?

"Is it a habit of yours?" Despenser asked, having apparently completed his thorough inspection of her.

"What, my lord?" Kit tried to stop herself from shivering, not wanting him to think she was frightened when she was wet. And frightened.

"Saving unknown children from a certain death. Most commendable, I'm sure, but why would you risk your life?"

"I didn't stop to think. Besides, he could have drowned."

"So could you."

"I swim like a fish," she replied with a smile.

"Really?" Despenser drawled. "How intriguing. And where has Katherine de Monmouth learnt to do that?"

"In water," she said, making him break out in laughter – for an instant. He glared at her.

"Your brother lies awaiting his death in the Tower, your father adorns a spike on this city's walls, and your husband faces a traitor's death. How propitious that you should save the constable's son in these circumstances, don't you think?"

"For the boy, at least," she replied. "He'd have died if I hadn't leapt in."

"And what do you expect in return?" Despenser demanded. "Your husband's life? His freedom?"

Kit licked her lips. "How can I demand his freedom? He rode with his lord against the king, obliged by his oath to do something he knew was wrong." She twisted her hands together and knelt before him. "But his life, yes, for that I beg you. Please don't kill him, my lord."

"And would you have saved the boy had your husband not been rotting in a dungeon in this castle?" Despenser smirked. "As I hear it, he is in a bad way, Lady de Guirande. That wound of his is most infected, it hurts him just to move, and should one set a finger to it, he screams in pain."

"How do you know, my lord?"

"I know everything. It helps, if one wants to stay alive."

"I meant about the finger. How would you know it makes him scream?"

Despenser's eyes glittered. "Guess." He smiled widely, showing small, neat teeth. "I visit him every day, my dear." Beside him, the Earl of Pembroke muttered in protest, but a sidelong look from Despenser shut him up.

Kit felt sick. "They say that ultimately you pay: every wrong you do down here, you pay for up there, my lord." She pointed upwards. "Or down there." She pointed downwards.

Despenser roared with laughter. "Ah yes, the devil incarnate, that's me – at least according to Mortimer and his cohorts." He sobered up, facing Pembroke. "And you, my lord? What do you think? Am I the devil come to earth?"

De Valence gave him a tired look. "You serve the king's pleasure – as do we all." He rubbed at his face. "And a great king combines harsh justice with mercy."

"Not this king," Despenser said. "But then, my liege does not aspire to greatness. He aspires to peace and happiness – for him, at least."

"An unburdened conscience would help." Pembroke glanced at Kit. "This woman's husband is no longer a danger to the realm. The man may die anyway, and should he recover, he will never ride to war again – you've made sure of that."

Kit's heart plummeted. "How ill is he?" What had they done to him, to be so certain he would never be able to fight again?

Pembroke raised his bushy brows. "Have you not seen him?"

"No! I have been forbidden to see him!" She rose, and turned all her fury and despair on the earl. "You lied to them! You pledged your honour that they would be severely punished, but given their lives in return for submitting to the king. And they did – all of them – and now Lord Mortimer awaits imminent execution, my father and so many more are already dead, and my husband...All at your word, your worthless word!" She spat at de Valence's feet. "You owe me, my lord. Just as you owe every widow, every orphan."

The earl backed away from her, and to her right she heard Despenser explode in laughter. Kit turned his way, wanting nothing much as to punch the royal favourite's face. Instead, she sucked in her breath, counting to ten before releasing it.

"I want to see my husband."

Despenser wiped his eyes, still grinning. "Of course. And just for the sheer pleasure of watching dear Aymer cringe, I give you his life."

"Thank you, thank you..." Tears welled in her eyes.

"Not his freedom. He stays behind walls." With a little nod Despenser moved off, calling for a clerk.

"My walls – not these," the earl said. He approached Kit and gave her a little bow. "Despenser is a fickle man, and what he gives today, he may take back tomorrow. Your husband is safer with me. Once, very many years ago, my honour was besmirched when a man under my care was taken from me and killed – I'll not allow that to happen again."

"It won't? It already has, my lord – and with far more deaths this time," Kit said, glad to see the earl flinch. "But you refer to Piers Gaveston, don't you? His predecessor." She jerked her head at Despenser. "If we're fortunate, he'll end up the same way."

"My lady!" Mabel gasped, knotting her hands in her skirts.

"Shush!" Aymer de Valence took a firm grip of her arm, propelling her towards the door. "These days, such statements are tantamount to treason." He released her. "I will have your husband transferred to one of my castles. It is a small compensation for all that you've lost, but it's all I can do." He sagged, looking quite ancient. "And I didn't lie. I truly believed the king would be magnanimous in victory."

"Kings rarely are – and kings that continuously break their

oaths, even less." She felt a twinge of compassion for this man, not yet old but with the carriage of man disillusioned with life. "And thank you, my lord, for promising to take care of my husband."

"Take care?" Despenser appeared like an inquisitive bird. "Here." He handed Kit a document. "A reprieve – and permission to visit him tomorrow. And if he lives – which I think unlikely – Pembroke here can carry him off to whatever castle he wants to hold him at. As a prisoner, not a guest." He made a dismissive gesture with his hand, placed an arm round Pembroke's shoulders and led him away. "And you, dear Aymer, must make haste. Our liege demands that you join him up north. It seems he has Lancaster at bay – at last." Despenser made a gleeful sound.

"Will you not ride with me?" the earl asked.

"Me?" Despenser laughed. "I'm not even in the country yet – at least not officially." He tapped his nose. "Best keep out of sight for now."

Kit hastened through the castle, wondering just where in this large building her husband might be. So close, so damned close, and still not allowed to see him – not until tomorrow.

"We have to get you back to our room," Mabel said. "Get you out of those damp clothes."

"I don't care about my clothes." Kit tightened the cloak around her shoulders. The February day was uncomfortably cold, with a biting edge to the wind. "Any news of William?"

"Safe and sound, back at the inn. Now properly tonsured and garbed." Mabel grinned. "And still most upset with you for forcing him to risk a child's life."

"It wasn't a risk!"

"No?" Mabel sniffed. "We both know you almost drowned, I saw you swept away like flotsam." She gripped Kit's hand. "I'm so glad you didn't."

"Me too," Kit said, shuddering at the recollection of just how helpless she had been in the swollen waters.

"Lady de Guirande?" The speaker sounded breathless.

"Yes?" Kit came to a halt. A woman in a dark cloak stepped

out from under the protective shadow of the gatehouse.

"I just wanted to thank you again." Lady Maude gave Kit a tentative smile. "For saving my boy."

"Ah." Kit made a depreciating gesture. "It was nothing. I am sure you would have done the same."

"Me? I can't swim." The constable's wife handed Kit a pouch. "My son's life cannot be valued in gold, but maybe this can be of help to you – and to your husband."

"I…" Kit didn't know what to say.

"Thank you m' lady," Mabel said, giving her a series of small bows, "that was most kind of you. And although my mistress will not admit to it, it will ease her burdens."

"Mabel!" Kit hissed.

"Poor as paupers," Mabel sighed, "what with the husband being attainted and all that." She set a hand on Kit's back and more or less pushed her through the gate, while repeating over and over just how grateful they were. "You're daft," she said to Kit once they were out of earshot. "You need every piece of silver you can get your hands on. Unless he has ready money, that husband of yours faces a dire existence, no matter who holds him captive." She rolled her eyes. "He wants to send a letter – a piece of silver. He needs a clean shirt – a piece of silver. He wants to eat other than gruel and mouldy bread – a piece of silver. It all adds up, m' lady."

Chapter 25

"I have permission to visit him." Kit waved the document in the face of the guard. "From Lord Despenser himself." The guard didn't even glance at the deed – he just stood to the side and waved her and Mabel through. William, however, he stopped, saying that as far as he knew the prisoner was in no need of a priest, at least not quite yet.

Adam was alone, lying on a pile of straw in a dark room the size of monk's cell. This far down in the castle, the walls were damp and covered with fuzzy green growth, and what little light there was filtered in from a narrow slit just below the ceiling. The first thing that struck her was the stench. In a corner stood a covered bucket containing his waste, but it was the smell emanating from his body that made Kit gag.

"Adam?"

He mumbled incoherently, thrashing on his bedding. His hands were in manacles, deep sores cutting into his wrists.

"My love?" She knelt beside him, gesturing for Mabel to set down her burdens. The straw rustled as Adam turned towards her voice. Kit bit back on a gasp. The man she had last seen back in early January was reduced to a wreck, eyes sunk into a face hollowed out by illness and hunger. "They've been starving him!" she exclaimed, her hands running over wasted limbs, over a ribcage where every rib was a tangible ridge.

"Or he has been too ill to feed himself." Mabel wrinkled her nose. "He has soiled himself."

Kit unslung the water skin from her shoulder and gestured for Mabel to pass her the clay pot with glowing coals which Mabel had carried with her, wrapped in damp leather. Moments later, Kit had a smaller clay pot balanced atop the coals, filled with water. She tore his shirt open, baring a dirty bandage and grimy skin.

"Eh?" Adam's eyes fluttered open for an instant, enough for her to see the fear in them.

"What have they done to you?" she said as she cut away the bandage, revealing a badly stitched wound, the length of her dagger. The area around it was shiny and red, streaks of vivid yellow visible through the taut skin. It was apparent at first sight that the wound had been slashed open – repeatedly, several unhealed gashes criss-crossing the original wound.

"They've cut him quite a few times," Mabel said. "Bastards."

Kit nodded, using gentle hands to inspect the damage. No gangrene, not yet, but things weren't healing as they should. Some more probing, and Adam shrieked like a flayed cat, sitting up straight for some seconds before slumping back into semi-consciousness.

"Scalded Saracens!" Kit sat back on her heels and pressed her trembling hands together. "I assume that's where Despenser poked him."

Mabel grunted and produced vinegar, a small, sharp knife and various packets of herbs. Kit gripped Adam by the shoulders and shook him, hard. "Adam?"

A grunt.

"Adam, it's me, Kit."

"..it" he slurred.

"I have to cut you, and it's going to hurt."

"…it." He smiled faintly.

"Adam!" She slapped him, and he opened his eyes to blink at her. "Listen to me!"

"Kit?" He tried to sit up, giving her a bleary look. She just smiled and nodded.

"I have to cut you," she repeated.

Adam looked at her and licked his lips. "There's been plenty of that. Despenser enjoys wielding a knife." His voice was not much more than a whisper, but at least he seemed fully awake.

"I can see that. But I have to clean it properly." She held the knife in the fire.

Adam slumped down. "What for? They'll hang me on Friday."

"They won't." She handed him a small leather flask and urged him to drink. "Wine."

"No milk of poppy?" He tried to wipe his mouth, rubbed a hand through his bristling beard.

"Not now. I need you awake." She helped him to lie down.

"I won't hang?" He gripped her hand, his dirty fingers almost crushing hers.

"I have it in writing," she said, extricating her hand from his hold.

His breath whistled in and out of his mouth, his teeth gritted, as she sank the knife into his side. Pus spurted, it welled from one abscess after the other, and while Kit cut, all Adam did was breathe and breathe, his gaze stuck on the ceiling. At last she was done. Adam slumped and closed his eyes, his tongue darting out to wet his chapped lips.

"All done?" Mabel asked. Kit nodded, inspecting the wound for any more abscesses before upending the vinegar over it all. Adam inhaled and squeezed his eyes shut.

"I'm sorry," she said, "but—"

"Am I free?" he interrupted.

"Not as such. But you're to be transferred into Pembroke's care."

"De Valence!" Adam's eyes snapped open. "He lied to us!"

"Not knowingly." Kit crumbled meadowsweet into the boiling water. A scent of crushed almonds permeated the room, making Kit think of Alaïs, who swore by meadowsweet as the single most important herb one could find in the wild. She washed Adam's flank repeatedly with the infusion, and as a final precaution she poured what was left in the pot over the open wounds.

"Right, and now for the embroidery," she said, producing a length of catgut and a bent needle. She cupped Adam's cheek. "I have to do this first. Then we'll clean you up."

Adam didn't reply, but a weak smile flitted over his mouth. He didn't as much as twitch when she stitched him together, but once she was done he slumped, a harsh exhalation escaping his compressed lips. More water, more clean rags, and Kit turned to the task of washing him.

His braies were stuck to his skin. Kit held her breath as she relieved him of them, trying not to cry as she washed his groin and buttocks clean. Days of lying in his own waste had effectively corroded his skin into non-existence, leaving behind bright red patches of oozing flesh. She wept and he flinched, his hand stroking her head. But he didn't utter a sound – not when she cleaned him, not when she applied the ointment that she knew had to sting.

It was only when Kit began cutting off his hose that she discovered his other injury. When she lifted his right leg, he exclaimed, motioning towards his foot.

"It looks swollen," Mabel muttered.

"It is," Adam gasped, "and it hurts like the devil."

Kit pulled off his hose, clapping a hand to her mouth to stop herself from exclaiming out loud. Someone had driven something straight through his foot, leaving an ugly gaping hole surrounded by a bruised mess.

"What..." She cleared her throat. "Who?"

"Guy," Adam whispered. "Despenser made him do it, to prove his loyalty."

"Do what, exactly?"

"He drove a stake through it," Adam said, turning away from the look in her eyes. "It will stop me from ever taking the field again. In fact, it will stop me from doing anything that requires two whole feet, such as walking, or running, or—"

"How could he?" Kit ran her fingers over his foot, feeling several splintered bones. Impossible to set – besides, it was too late, the body was already attempting to heal the injury by knitting together what bones it could find. Her husband was doomed to walk with a severe limp.

"He said he had no choice." Adam's voice was harsh.

"Of course he did. You always have a choice." At least there was no infection – the hole left by the stake was surprisingly neat, and very dark around the edges.

"Iron," Mabel muttered. "An iron stake, and red-hot, I'd warrant."

Kit felt sick. "To his own brother!" she hissed, not wanting Adam to hear. "First he has him shot, then he tortures him."

"No love lost there," Mabel said.

"I swear, somehow he'll pay," Kit vowed. Just as she'd done with his flank wound, she covered the ghastly hole with honey before bandaging the foot with trembling hands.

To undress a man in chains was easy; you just slashed his clothes off him. To get a clean shirt on him was impossible, and it was only after half an hour of tearful wheedling and begging that the guards agreed to strike off the chains so as to allow her to dress him in clean clothes.

An eternal hour later, and Adam was sitting up against the wall, a blanket round his shoulders. He was in a clean shirt, with clean braies and clean hose. The soiled straw and clothes had been exchanged for a new pile of bedding brought in by the guard after Mabel threatened him with one ailment after the other unless he made sure the soiled rags and straw were burnt. Kit had done what she could for Adam's hair and beard, using her knife to bring some semblance of order to his facial growth. But despite these obvious improvements, he was but a shadow of his former self, his gaze returning over and over again to his bandaged foot. It wasn't the foot that could potentially kill him – the wound to his side was far more serious – but Kit could see in his face just how stricken he was by the insight that he would never be whole again.

"There are horses, you know," she said, moving closer to him. Mabel had left them alone, telling them she would ensure the guards were kept well and truly busy so that they could, well…Not that there was much possibility of anything beyond the odd caress, what with her man being as weak as a mewling kitten, and in chains to boot. Adam took hold of her hand, holding it to his chest.

"I thought I'd never see you again," he said.

"Our Lord had other plans." She snuggled closer, careful not to rest too much of her weight on him. "So here I am."

"Aye, that you are." She heard the smile in his voice. He rested his free hand on her belly. "I dreamt of you. When reality became too unbearable, I could escape into my dreams, and you were always there."

"Right now, I'm here in the flesh. This isn't a dream, Adam."

"No." He shifted his bandaged foot. "But you'll be gone shortly." He craned his head back, looking at the little light-shaft. "You'll go outside, see the sun, and I will remain trapped in the dark."

"Not for much longer. In two weeks, you'll be out of here."

Adam laughed bitterly. "I'll be exchanging one dungeon for another, Kit. Pembroke may promise to ensure I am not badly treated – as far as prisoners go – but don't expect him to lodge me in comfort, allow me the run of his castle. Even should he want to, he'd not be allowed to." He extended his hand upwards, as if attempting to capture the light. "You have won me a reprieve, wife. But you have not won me my freedom. I fear it will be many years before I go anywhere without these." He jangled his chains, refastened the moment Kit had finished dressing him and bandaging his wrists.

"I'll get you out." She knelt beside him. "Somehow, I'll set you free."

"How? There is nothing you can do, nothing anyone can do, not now that my lord—" He choked. "Is his head adorning London Bridge yet?"

"No, so far it remains atop his neck. He's in the Tower, and the king is busy to the north, quelling the rebellious earls of Lancaster and Hereford."

"I pity de Bohun, but all of this is Lancaster's fault. He should have made common cause with us. Instead, his petty grievance against Lord Badlesmere made him hold back, and now that the king has Lord Roger in the Tower, Lancaster will bear the full force of the royal rage."

"Serve him right," Kit said.

"Aye. But it doesn't much help, does it?"

There was a banging on the door. "Time!" yelled a guard, and Kit reluctantly got to her feet.

"I have to go."

Adam nodded, looking down at his fettered hands.

"Remember, you have to keep the wound clean. Not water, wine is better."

He nodded again, fiddling with the pouch of silver pennies she'd given him.

"I'll try to see you again, before they take you somewhere else."

Yet another nod.

"Adam, please," she whispered. "This is hard for me too. It's not only you that despairs."

He raised his face at that, eyes wild with anger and fear. Kit recoiled, finding no comfort in his contorted face. He took a couple of deep breaths, and closed his eyes for some seconds before opening them again. He extended his hand.

"Come here."

She placed her hand in his, his calloused fingers caressing her wrist, her downy forearm.

"I'll stay alive," he promised, his lips curving into a slight smile.

"And so will I." She kissed him softly on the mouth. Adam moaned, gripped her face and kissed her back, a forceful kiss that left her with a pounding heart and a throbbing need.

"There will be other tomorrows," he said. "There will be a night when the moon shines bright and the air is soft and balmy, and we will lie together, you and I, and it will be like it should be. Hold on to that, my sweetest Kit."

"To a future night of moonshine," she said, smiling through her tears.

"Many moonlit nights," he whispered back.

Kit stood for some moments outside his cell, regaining her composure. Three deep breaths and she smoothed the heavy cloth of her kirtle to lie as it should before stalking over to the guard.

"If you let anyone as much as tweak a hair on him, I will have your guts," she hissed. "My lord husband has been treated like an animal, left to lie in his own filth, and I tell you…I tell you…" She fisted her hand and shook it in his face. "I will come after you, your wife, your children, your goddamned dogs and even your chickens, you hear? So for your own sake, keep my man safe."

The guard's eyes had widened during her little speech, the large lout shuffling backwards until he was stopped by the wall.

"I didn't—" he whined.

"You did! You let them in, and it wasn't only Lord Despenser was it? No, it was his snake of a brother as well, coming to gloat and have his little sport with a wounded man."

"I—"

"Silence!" She leaned towards him, glad of her height. "It happens again and…" She drew her finger over her throat.

The guard blanched.

Chapter 26

"One visit," the guard repeated, giving her a mulish look. He had clearly not forgiven her for her threat yesterday.

"But he needs me!" Kit tried. The guard shook his head. "Fine. On your head be it if he dies," she said, scowling at him.

"He won't," the guard replied. He fiddled with his sword. "I can't stop Lord Despenser from entering, but I promise to look out for him, do what I can to keep him hale."

"You will?" Kit gripped his gloved hand.

"I'm not partial to torturing dying men," the guard muttered, throwing her a glance from under stubby, fair lashes.

"Which is to your credit," she said, giving the entrance to the dungeons a longing look. "Just some moments?"

He straightened up. "I have my orders, my lady. To break them would be to risk Lord Despenser's displeasure." He shivered as he said it.

"That man…" Kit broke off.

The guard just nodded and held out his hand for her basket. "I'll make sure he gets this."

Kit took her time making her way back to the inn. Shrewsbury was a busy little town, clearly divided into the pleasant part and the malodorous part, the Mardol running like a cobbled boundary between the tanneries to the south and the more affluent merchant quarters to the north. She was loitering by the stalls that lined the square, when someone took hold of her arm. Kit turned.

"Take your hand off me," she spat, jerking her sleeve from Guy's hold. "Lay as much as a finger on me, and I will tear off your hand and leave you as maimed as you've left your brother."

Guy paled. "How do you—"

"Know? You thought I wouldn't find out that you drove

a stake through your brother's foot?" She was being too loud, too shrill, attracting the attention of the passers-by. "How could you?" she continued, now in a much lower voice. "How many silver pieces did they pay you to do that? Thirty?"

Guy flushed. "The lands were attainted anyway. This way they stay in the family." He tried to touch her. "I'll see you and the child safe."

"We don't need your help. I have my dower lands – and the charters have been confirmed by the Earl of Pembroke himself."

"Your dower lands?" He frowned. "But Tresaints—"

"Is mine. Just as the three adjoining manors are mine." It pleased her to see his features tighten into a displeased scowl. Brother Guy was not only surprised, but disappointed by this turn of events.

"A widow still needs some protection," he said.

"A widow? Well, you'd best go and find someone else then. Haven't you heard? Adam has been reprieved, thank the Lord!"

Guy's mouth fell open. "How?"

"Divine intervention?" Kit leaned towards him. "Someday, you will sorely regret what you did to your brother. And I won't raise a finger to save you."

"He's not my brother."

"Something I thank the Lord daily for. I would be most concerned had my future child been in any way related to you." That dart struck home, she thought, watching Guy hurry off.

Their days had settled into a predictable routine: every morning Kit would walk up to the castle and attempt to wheedle the guards into letting her through. Every morning they would shake their heads and say they weren't allowed to give her entry. She would sigh, she would huff, and would end up handing over her basket, exchanged for the empty one from the day before, and slowly walk away, ensuring she looked just as dejected as she felt.

After this mandatory visit to the castle, Kit and Mabel

would invest efforts in keeping their few pieces of clothing looking presentable, through hours spent with a fuller's brush and sand on their woollen garments. William insisted they attended church at least twice a day – and pestered Kit about that confession she was always putting off. Finally, she went to St Alkmund's and spoke to one of the priests, returning with a severe penance involving several hours on her knees for having risked an innocent child's life.

Lionel was fed back into shape, and submitted with much grumbling to being thoroughly deloused, the process involving hours with a comb and large quantities of a reeking potion Mabel made with vinegar and mustard. Egard struck up a friendship with the castle guards and returned with endless amounts of gossip about the Lord Despenser, most of it vile and, Kit hoped, exaggerated.

Halfway through March, Kit woke to a terrible noise. Every single church bell in Shrewsbury seemed to be clanging, and from every door people poured out into the narrow streets, some fearing fire, others taking the sound for good news. William and Lionel disappeared outside, Mabel and Kit following as fast as they could, having to push their way through to the street. Kit hung back from the crowds, intimidated by the loud men, that sheer mass of humanity.

"It's the king." William popped up beside her and gripped her by her elbow to lead her aside. "Lancaster and Hereford have been defeated, all is lost. Now the king can execute our Lord Roger at his leisure and then…" He made a slashing gesture over his throat, looking as morose as he sounded.

There was no unanimous revelling on the streets. Young men cheered and slapped each other on the shoulders, older men sighed and shook their heads, saying this only meant one thing: Hugh Despenser, Lord of Glamorgan, was back in his own, and God help the kingdom. Kit tugged at the coarse material of her veil and followed William through the press of people, relieved when they reached the slow curve of the Severn. They walked along the water for some time, William looking grim.

"There is no hope for Adam now," he said. "They'll never set him free."

Kit was sorely tempted to slap him. "Don't say that!" She eyed the water, far more placid today than during her recent life-saving effort. All she'd done, it couldn't be for nothing – she wouldn't let it be for nothing, although to be quite honest she had no notion as to how to achieve her husband's freedom. She placed a hand on her belly. The child deserved to know its father – its father deserved to know his child.

"Things change," she said. "The wheel of fate is a fickle thing, and who is to know when next it turns?" She gave William a stubborn look. She would not give up hope. Ever.

Next afternoon there was a terse message from the constable that the traitor Adam de Guirande was now sufficiently healed to be transported to Goodrich Castle, there to be held under the strictest of conditions by the Earl of Pembroke.

"What does that mean?" Kit asked William.

"The constable is merely making the point that Adam remains a prisoner." William peered down at the document. "They leave tomorrow."

"Tomorrow?" Kit rose. "But I haven't been allowed to see him, and—"

"You'll see him as he sets out," Mabel said. "We'll be up at the castle before dawn, just in case."

Not quite the farewell Kit envisioned, but she realised she was being foolish. She would not be allowed to do anything more than wave and smile at her man as he rode by. She hoped that would be enough to survive on – for him and for her.

That evening, Lionel stumbled into the inn, righted himself and rushed over to Kit. "He'll kill him!"

"Who? When?" Kit looked about for the potential murderer.

"Guy." Lionel sank to his knees. "It is Guy who is to captain the troop that transports Adam to Goodrich Castle, and I heard Despenser tell him to make sure Adam dies along the way." He hiccupped. "And you, once a widow, will be forced to marry Guy."

"I'm not a widow yet," Kit told him. "Damn them, damn them all to hell!" She rose to her feet. "When do they set off?"

"At first light." Lionel eyed her from under his unkempt thatch of hair. "What will you do?"

"I don't know!" She paced back and forth to the door a couple of times. If only Pembroke had been here. Kit wrung her hands, eyes darting from Lionel, to the door, to the table and the remnants of their meal. Being Lent, it had been yet another fish dish, somewhat improved by the spicy mustard sauce. Mustard…

"Is Guy still riding Goliath?

Lionel dragged his arm under his snotty nose and nodded at the same time.

"And I presume he will ride him tomorrow," Kit mused out loud.

"To rub things in," Mabel agreed, before reverting to sucking her fingers clean of fish and sauce.

"Right." Kit turned to Lionel. "Find me some mustard seeds. A handful or so."

"Mustard?" Mabel looked at her, a slow grin spreading over her face. "Yes, that could work."

Early next morning, Kit stood in the bailey of the castle, having insisted on being allowed to bid her husband farewell. The guards had been reluctant at first, but when the constable's wife appeared, demanding to know what all the commotion was about, they'd done as she bid them and let Kit, Lionel and Mabel through the gate.

Men were milling round the six assembled horses. Guy was already astride, his eyes clouding when they alighted on Kit. "What are you doing here?" he barked.

"I have come to wish my husband Godspeed. And you, why are you here?"

Guy grinned. "Me? Oh, I'm in charge of the prisoner's safety."

"His safety?" Kit spun to face Despenser, who was lounging against a doorway, an amused look on his face. "He wants to make me a widow," she said harshly. "And it was him that maimed my husband."

"I know," Despenser said. "I made him do it, remember?" He yawned and pretended interest in his nails.

"I will not have my husband's wellbeing entrusted to one of your lackeys, my lord," Kit said.

"Lackeys?" Guy's voice rose. "I'm Sir Guy to you!"

"Don't make me laugh! To me you're nothing but a flea-bitten cur, so busy licking the balls of whatever mongrel that sits atop you your own balls have shrivelled into non-existence."

Guy cursed, set spurs to Goliath and made as if to charge her. Kit stood her ground, fists clenched round her precious ground mustard seeds.

Despenser laughed. "She has you there, Sir Guy. What aim you to do, ride a defenceless woman down before witnesses?"

Guy drove Goliath in a circle around her. "I'll make you pay," he swore. "One day you'll pay for every insult."

"Oh, I think not." Kit raised her hands as if to pat Goliath. The horse shied away, but when she crooned his name, he dipped his head, ears pricked forward in recognition. There was blood seeping from the corners of the stallion's mouth, and from what little Kit could see of the mouthpiece, it had been sharpened into a wicked wedge.

"Whoreson," she muttered under her breath. She took a big breath, apologised to the poor stallion, and under the guise of caressing him hastily spread a liberal amount of crushed mustard into his mouth and nose. She stepped back as the horse snorted and shook his head.

Another snort, accompanied by wild head-ducking. Guy yanked at the reins, and Goliath exploded across the bailey, bucking, jumping and rearing. The horse made for the quintain pole, with Guy hanging on for dear life. One massive jump and Goliath scraped Guy off against the pole, going on to do a series of stiff-legged jumps before coming to a halt, head bowed and sides heaving.

Kit hastened across the cobbled yard to where Guy was lying sprawled on his front. It would have been nice had he been permanently incapacitated, but from the way he was groaning and moving his legs, she concluded he was at most bruised, even if he did seem to have hurt his shoulder. Guy set his hand on the ground to heave himself upright. Kit brought down her heel, grinding it into his hand. Guy howled.

"What? What?" Kit yelled. "Are you hurt?" She pretended to bend down to help him, and brought her foot down again, for once finding the pattens Mabel insisted she wear in a city as dirty and muddy as Shrewsbury useful. There was a distinct crunching sound. Unfortunately, it was his left hand.

She straightened up, chin raised defiantly as Despenser came striding towards her. Over his shoulder, she could see Adam, his arms held by two guards. He met her eyes and grinned, a wide, genuine grin.

"Get up," Despenser snapped, regarding Guy as if he were a slimy worm.

"She did it on purpose," Guy said, getting to his feet. His shoulder hung awry, and his hand was a trampled, bloodied mess.

"Me? I was only trying to help." Yet again, her gaze darted over to her husband, shoulders relaxing when she took in his general appearance. Still thin, still very pale, but all in all a definite improvement from when she'd seen him last.

"My hand!" Guy yelled, holding up his damaged extremity. "Look what you did to it."

Kit shrugged. "I'm clumsy at times."

"Or too shrewd for your own good," Despenser said. "What did you do to the horse?" He loomed over her, eyes flat and cold like a lizard's.

"Nothing! I suppose it's a matter of poor horsemanship. Goliath requires a steady hand." She smirked at Guy, who looked as if he'd gladly strangle her.

"I can ride any horse," Guy said.

"Yes, we just saw that, didn't we?" Despenser made an amused sound. "Most entertaining, however unfortunate the outcome." He swivelled to face Kit. "Are you a good rider, Lady Katherine?"

"Very." Where was he going with this? Kit threw Goliath a glance. Lionel was standing close to him, talking softly as he stroked away any remaining evidence of Kit's little ploy.

"Get on the horse then." Despenser gestured at Goliath.

"Why should I?" She placed a hand on her belly.

"I think you doctored the horse," Despenser said, eyeing her as a fox might study a trapped hen, considering just what part to rip off first.

"Really, my lord! Why would I do that?"

"To stop him from accompanying your husband." Despenser jerked his head at Guy. Kit took a step away from him, curling her mouth in an expression of distaste.

"I did no such thing."

Despenser followed her. "Either you get on the horse, or I'll have your husband hanged – here, now."

"You pardoned him his life!" This was not developing as she had hoped.

"And so I can unpardon him." Despenser crossed his arms. "What is it to be, Lady Katherine?"

Guy snickered. Kit turned her head to find Adam, standing on the other side of the bailey.

"You are a cruel man," she said to Despenser, "and in case you haven't noticed, my lord, I am with child."

"And do you think I care? If the horse throws you and you miscarry, that is none of my concern."

Kit sucked in her cheeks. No choice, not really. "I have one condition."

"A condition? And what makes you think you're in a position to demand one? And before you ask, I will not free Adam de Guirande."

She gave an irritated shake of her head. Why ask for the moon? Nobody ever gave it to you. "I get to keep the horse."

"That's my horse," Guy protested.

"That's Adam's horse." Kit looked him up and down. "Too big for you to handle, I reckon. Just as his boots are too big to fill. How does it feel, to live your life in hand-me-downs?"

Despenser snorted with laughter, while Guy glared at her. "Quiet, woman!"

"Why should I? How does it feel to be nothing but a warped and soiled copy?"

"I said be quiet!" Guy made as if to hit her, but Despenser grabbed his arm.

"Now, now – a lady is always a lady…at least in front of witnesses." He inclined his head to Kit. "If you ride him twice round the bailey, he's yours."

"He's mine!" Guy screeched, and Despenser gave him an annoyed look.

"I'll get you another one – a rouncey, perhaps?" Despenser waved his hand in Guy's direction, multiple rings winking in the sunlight.

"I want my stallion," Guy said through his teeth.

"As the lady has already said, he is too much for you to handle," Despenser replied. "To each his own, Sir Guy." He clapped Guy on the back, so hard he stumbled, clutching his damaged shoulder. "Get yourself to the infirmary. And, now, Lady Katherine, we are all waiting." Despenser bowed courteously, arm extended in the direction of Goliath.

"Kit!" Adam's voice cut through the air. "You will not mount that horse. I will not have you risk our unborn child."

Despenser turned to face him, shielding his eyes with his hand. "You best hope she does, Adam dearest. If not…" He mimed strangulation and laughed at Adam's shocked exclamation.

Adam had been woken just before dawn by one of his guards and been told to get ready – he was to be transported to Goodrich Castle. Adam sighed, moving gingerly around his cell as he attempted to bring himself into some sort of order. He was still weak, shuffling to keep as much weight as possible off his right foot, but these last three weeks had seen him regaining some of his strength, and no matter that he was but exchanging one prison for the other, he was looking forward to seeing the outside world again.

While Kit had not been allowed in to see him, the guards had diligently passed on her foodstuffs, making Adam wonder just what his wife had threatened them with to make them so cooperative. Or maybe she was bribing them, a silver penny here, another there.

Only once during these last weeks had Despenser come, and when Adam had steeled himself for yet another session with the knife, Despenser had surprised him by saying he had tired of that particular game. Instead, Despenser had amused himself by describing to Adam just how attractive he found Kit, stopping now and then to study Adam's face intently. Adam had managed to keep his face blank, even when Despenser whispered that while Adam lingered in his cell, there was no one to protect his comely wife, was there? Despenser was partial to redheads, he confided to Adam, and especially fiery women such as Lady de Guirande – it was so much fun to tame them. Adam stared straight ahead. Finally, Despenser had given up.

"I have given you your worthless life," he said coldly. "You, a traitor to *my* king, a despoiler of *my* lands, a vassal to *my* enemy. And one day, I intend to exact my revenge on you – or your wife." He leaned over Adam, dark eyes far too close. "I reprieved you your life – for now. Go with the fear of God, Adam de Guirande, for you will never know when I come for you – until it is too late." With that he had kicked Adam in the foot and left.

A bowl of cabbage soup to break his fast, and then Adam was helped up the stairs, having to lean heavily on the guards to make it to the open doorway and the bright spring dawn beyond. The first thing he saw when he exited into the bailey was Guy, astride Goliath. The second thing he saw was his wife, crossing the bailey at a half-run with a determined look on her face. From a distance he had followed the altercation, not hearing more than the odd word, but when Guy spurred Goliath towards Kit, he had tensed, leaning towards his wife as much as his guards would let him.

And now, after seeing Guy hit the ground, after watching Lionel rush over to calm Goliath, after hearing Despenser's threat, Adam could do nothing but pray as his wife approached his stallion. She was wearing green today – he liked her in green, and he wondered if it was for his sake she wore the kirtle he recognised from their wedding – her dark red hair neatly braided into one thick plait that was visible under her thin veil. His fingers itched with the desire to undo her hair, sink his fingers into it and pull it free to lie like a fiery mane across his pillow. Not today, but someday, he promised himself – assuming the foolish woman didn't break her neck in the very near future.

Out of the corner of his eye, Adam caught Despenser watching him with ill-hidden glee, no doubt hoping to witness Kit take a spill from Goliath and lie writhing on the ground. He squinted, trying to see what his wife was up to. She was fiddling with the bridle, calling for one of the men to come and help her. Despenser came over, saying something in a low voice. Kit shook her head, pointing at the bridle. Despenser pointed at the saddle, scowled and threw his hands up in the air.

A groom hurried across the yard, bridle in hand, and minutes later Kit was leading Goliath to the mounting block, all the while talking to the stallion. Whatever Guy had done to Goliath over the last months, it seemed to have robbed the horse of a sizeable part of his temper, and his normally so proud neck was held low. Like me, Adam reflected, a wild thing permanently tamed. Except that as far as he could see, no one had driven a stake through any of Goliath's hooves.

Kit sat up. Pride rushed through him at the sight of her, regal almost, on his horse. Her veil lifted in the wind, the deep green of her gown moulded itself to round breasts and a much rounder belly, and Adam promised himself that once more, at least, he would hold her in his arms. Kit tightened her hold on the reins, bent forward to whisper something to the horse. And that was when Adam whistled.

The neck shot up, small ears pricked forward. Here came his horse, carrying his wife towards him, and the men in the bailey cheered and called her Lady Godiva. Kit laughed, leaned forward and rose ever so slightly in the stirrups, urging Goliath into a canter. The horse snorted. Massive hindquarters bunched, the hooves skittered over the cobbles, and for an instant Adam feared the horse would throw her as spectacularly as he had unhorsed Guy. But then he was off, a controlled canter once, twice, thrice round the yard.

He had never loved her as much as when she finally brought the horse to a halt just in front of him. She slid off the broad back, met his eyes and swept him the deepest of reverences, head bowed as she greeted her lord. To the side, Despenser glowered, arms crossed over his velvet tunic, for the day in a bright blue shade that exactly matched the sky.

Kit rose unaided and made her way up the few steps that separated them. "My lord," she said, mouth soft with need.

"My lady." Adam bowed, raising his manacled hands to his heart. "My love," he added in a tone meant for her ears only. He heard her intake of breath and smiled, thinking it took very little to make her happy – at least for this fleeting instant.

"Are you feeling better?" She approached him, placed a hand on his arm.

"No touching the prisoner!" Despenser roared. Kit lifted her hand so that it hovered over his sleeve no more.

"Goes for him as well," Kit muttered under her breath. "Has he…?"

Adam shook his head. "No, not since you visited." He held her eyes with his. "He is a dangerous man to rile," he said softly.

"I know." She clasped her hands over her belly.

"If…" Adam wet his lips. "Promise me that no matter how bad, you will always tell me the truth. I could not bear to have you lie to me, even if it is to protect me."

She gave him a wary look. "The truth about what?"

"Should Despenser—" He broke off, nearly gagging on the rage that surged through him at the thought. "If he harms you, touches you in any untoward way, I want to know."

"Why?"

"So that I can make him pay." Adam banged his fisted hand against his thigh. "I keep score, and I will make him pay, for every cut and every kick. And should he harm as much as a hair on your head…" He looked down at his manacled hands. "Will you promise?"

"To always tell you the truth?" She smiled. "Yes, I promise. And will you promise to do the same?" She had him there, blue eyes burning into his. After what seemed an eternity he nodded, once.

"I will. But please be careful with the questions you ask."

"Oh, Adam…"

He heard the tears in her voice and gave her a little smile. "It is of no matter now. I live – and will continue to live. I've promised you that, haven't I?"

Moments later, Adam was gone, escorted by six grim guards. But one of them had turned to smile at Kit just before they rode out of sight. Kit smiled back, very pleased with herself for having added this little failsafe to her plan. Egard would keep Adam safe, no matter how many of Despenser's men were riding in the little troop.

Chapter 27

Halfway through April, Kit sat on a bench in her herbal garden. After days of hard work, things were back in order, the mints brought harshly back to heel so as to stop them from suffocating the rosemary, the sage and even the vigorous lemon balm. The lovage was already well over a foot high, the chervil seemed to be thriving, and she'd just cut back the lavender. She eyed the yarrow, standing side by side with comfrey and pennyroyal, and wondered where the borage had got to – she couldn't quite remember where it was supposed to sprout. Right at the back was her mother's precious rose, clambering over a large wooden trellis. In a month or so, the bush would be covered in tight, dark pink buds that would open into scented white blooms, decorating the borders below with scattered petals.

Since they'd returned from Shrewsbury, Kit had concentrated her efforts on her home, trying to drown out the constant concern for Adam that hummed through her brain from the moment she woke to the instant she fell asleep – followed by nights dominated by dreams of her husband, mostly as he'd been before that day in December when he'd ridden off to join Mortimer, now and then as he'd looked when she'd found him in the dungeons of Shrewsbury Castle.

By now, every floor in the manor had been scrubbed, John had been set to making the necessary repairs to stop the wind whistling straight through the cracks in the walls, and Lionel had been placed in charge of the stables, complaining loudly that he was a squire, not a farmhand. But he did it well enough – especially when Kit sweetened the bid by allowing him to ride Goliath, now that she was forbidden by both Mabel and William to as much as set her foot in a stirrup.

Twice since they'd come back home, Kit had sent William to Goodrich Castle, a mere two-day ride away. Twice he had returned with news of Adam, his eyes alight with relief when he told her he was mending. Her letters had been delivered, but Adam was not allowed to correspond in return – at least not openly, and so it wasn't until William's second trip that he'd returned with a scrap of parchment on which Adam had written a brief message, telling her to heed his brother and take care of herself and the child, and that the child, should he be born a boy, was to be named Thomas. There was a scrawled heart at the bottom, accompanied by what she assumed to be a picture of a crescent moon. That had made her cry, wondering if there would ever be future nights in moonlight, with him.

She rose at the sound of the dogs and made her way slowly to the neat, well-ordered bailey. These last few days, there'd been a constant sound of hammering as William led the work on reinforcing the wooden fence, raising it to be at least man-high and stout enough to offer some protection.

A cart was trundling down the lane, accompanied by two men on horseback. There was an elongated object on the cart, and for a terrifying instant Kit thought it might be Adam's body, until she took in just how small the bundle was. Lady Joan? But why would anyone send her the body of Roger Mortimer's wife?

"Lady Katherine?" one of the knights asked.

"Yes." Kit's eyes hung off the surcoats the men wore, both of them displaying the royal arms.

"I am charged with returning you your brother," the knight continued, pointing at the narrow bundle.

"My brother?" But Richard was taller than she was, while this object wasn't.

"He died after Boroughbridge," the knight explained. "Hanged with most of the noble prisoners."

"Hanged?" Kit asked, gesturing at the frail little shape. "A boy?"

The knight's face reddened. "A traitor, my lady – as is most of your family. But my lady queen insisted he should be buried by his family, not placed in a gibbet."

"The queen?" Why would the queen show an interest in a dead lad?

"He was so young," the knight said, as if that clarified everything.

"Thirteen," Mabel put in, her voice thick with tears. "Lads that young should not take part in battle. What was Earl Humphrey thinking of, allowing Thomas to accompany him up north?"

"Rebellion?" the knight suggested acidly. He motioned for the drover to unload the wrapped bundle, gave Kit the briefest of bows and ordered his companions to follow him back up the long lane.

Mabel insisted her Thomas had to be adequately prepared for his grave, and Kit reluctantly offered to help, unwinding the long lengths of linen, drenched in aromatic oil, that were wrapped around the body. A boy, all knobby limbs and pale, freckled skin, hair the same shade as hers, eyes now permanently closed. Kit was overwhelmed by just how fragile life was, and even if she'd never known Thomas de Monmouth when he was alive, she wept at the waste of it all.

"Lady Cecily must be informed," she said. Despite everything, she felt a twinge of pity for the lady: first her husband, now her son. Kit sighed and undid the last bands from Thomas' narrow chest and a folded square of precious parchment fell out. It was sealed and addressed to Adam.

"Open it," William said.

"I can't open Adam's letter!"

"And I cannot hand it to him next I visit. Look at the seal, Kit, that's Queen Isabella's private seal."

"It is?" So it was true then; the queen was no more enamoured of her husband the king and his royal favourite than were the rebel barons.

The message was brief. Lord Mortimer remained alive, and the queen intended to keep it that way, even if the king was presently venting his spleen by executing every rebel baron he could get his hands on. Next in line, the queen wrote, was Badlesmere, who was to be hanged, drawn and quartered in Canterbury, and everywhere the king went, he was leaving a bloody wake behind, imprisoning widows and orphans under the direst of circumstances.

"And how is she planning on keeping Lord Mortimer alive?" Kit asked.

"The queen has her ways," William said, smiling happily.

The best part of the letter came right at the end, where the queen advised Adam she was working on a pardon for him, and hoped to get one, on the basis that the king had not approved the mutilation of a belted knight.

"So the king will gladly hang and disembowel his nobles, but pardon Adam because of his foot?" Kit shook her head in incomprehension. "And why does she want him pardoned?"

"The queen foresees a time when Lord Roger will have need of him," William said with a shrug.

That did not go down well with Kit. "I will not have him risking his life again."

"That is not for you to decide," William told her sharply. "Adam will do as his duty bids him."

Kit looked away; he was right, of course. Maybe it was better for them all if Adam remained locked up at Goodrich. But she didn't say that out loud – nor did she believe it, as she suspected her husband pined for his freedom, every day locked away behind those thick walls adding to his despair.

They buried Thomas on a quiet April morning when the dew glittered on the grass and the nearby fields smelled of earth and growing things. The little graveyard was quiet, with only the odd chirping of a bird disturbing its fragrant peace. Kit sat on a bench and prayed for the soul of a boy she had never known, thinking that it was a fearful world indeed when a mere child could be hanged as a convicted traitor.

Some weeks later, William rode off for yet another visit to Adam, this time to share with him the news from the queen. He returned to tell her Adam was getting his fair share of sun and air, as at present Earl Aymer was rebuilding his castle, and as a consequence anyone able-bodied enough to help among the handful of prisoners were allowed outdoors, albeit under strict guard. He went on to tell her he looked well, and Kit felt a sting of jealousy that William should see her husband, while she was stuck here, more or less imprisoned in the house now that her time drew near.

Kit refused to be locked in her solar for her confinement. Mabel scowled and yelled, but retaliated by forbidding Kit to venture any further than the herbal garden.

"I can go wherever I want," Kit countered, but more out of obligation than anything else, as the child lay heavy inside of her, a heaving, kicking presence that had her complaining loudly while grinning as she stroked her stomach.

Three days into July, Kit woke to drenched sheets and a mauling pain in her back.

"I think…" she said, but couldn't quite finish, doubling over as an excruciating pain tightened round her belly. "Sweetest Virgin!" she gasped when the pain receded.

"That?" Mabel snorted. "That was nothing, m' lady. Just you wait."

Hours later, Kit was prone to agree. The contractions were relentless, one following upon the other with ever-increasing intensity. Her linen shift was by now as drenched as the bed had been, and she no longer prayed to the Virgin for an easy delivery – she was willing to settle for a delivery, soon.

"Women's lot in life," Mabel said when Kit groaned that she couldn't take anymore. "We open our legs to our men, and this is the price we must pay."

"Never again," Kit said hoarsely.

Mabel laughed, wiping at Kit's face. "All women say that in the birthing chamber. Rarely do they mean it."

Just before sunset, Kit was delivered of a son – a big, lusty boy who bawled in protest at having been expelled from his mother's womb. Kit fell back against the pillows, so tired she couldn't quite make the effort to lift her hand to wipe away the hair that stuck to her brow.

"Meet young Master Thomas," she told William when he came to inspect the child some hours later. He smiled and lifted the baby from her arms.

"A handsome lad," he said, inspecting the little face. "I will baptise him tomorrow morning."

"As soon as possible," Kit agreed. "We must safeguard his soul." She held out her hands for her boy. At present, she couldn't get enough of him, enthralled by the rosy perfection of his toes, the soft roundness of his head. Her son. Adam's son, what little hair he had as fair as that of his sire.

Mabel was scandalised when six days later Kit informed her she was riding down to Goodrich Castle. "It's too soon," Mabel said.

"Too soon? I haven't seen him in over three months."

"But the babe…"

"Tom?" Kit moved over to the cradle and smiled down at her son. "Why, he will come with his mama."

"A puling babe to ride across the moor?" Mabel fixed Kit with a flinty stare. "I think not."

"I think yes," Kit retorted, lifting the baby to her chest.

It was not an easy life, being imprisoned at Goodrich. Earl Aymer had left strict instructions for the care of his prisoner, and these instructions left little room for air or exercise, at least initially. Adam spent days, nights, weeks in his little cell, viewing the world through the arrow-slit that was his only source of light.

The boredom of his days was only broken by William's infrequent visits, and in between he spent his time daydreaming, imagining different outcomes to the recent war, all of them ending with Lord Roger in charge and Despenser dead. Unfortunately, at times those daydreams became nightmares, sweaty sessions when he recalled in far too much detail what Despenser had done to him, and what he had threatened to do to Kit.

In May, Adam's life changed for the better. The castle became home to a company of builders, led by a loud, bluff man who went by the nickname of Boulder, this on account of his bald and polished head. Boulder was a master mason, responsible for the large additions Pembroke planned to make to Goodrich, first and foremost of which was a new barbican. To speed things up, Boulder had been authorised to use every pair of hands available, including those of the prisoners.

Adam was good with his hands, and was also unbothered by heights. Where some of the guards went green when clambering up the rickety scaffold, Adam had no problem at all, his damaged foot causing him little discomfort when climbing upwards. It was another matter entirely when he attempted to walk, or to stand for any length of time. The badly-knit bones in his foot would start by sending prickles of pain up his calf. Moments later, those prickles became knives, and it was either sit down or stand still with his damaged foot in the air until it passed, shouting to the world that Adam de Guirande was a cripple. Much better, therefore, to clamber up using the strength in his arms.

"So why are you here?" Boulder asked him one day, offering Adam a piece of fried rabbit.

Adam eyed the big man cautiously, but Boulder sounded genuinely curious. "I am Lord Mortimer's man," he said simply.

"Ah." Boulder tipped his head back and drained the last of his wineskin, burped and turned to smile at Adam. "So why are you still alive?"

"Alive?" Adam shivered at his tone.

Boulder nodded. "Badlesmere is dead, Lancaster is dead, Clifford and Mowbray are dead, Montford and Willington too. And that's just the peers and barons – if we start counting all the knights that have followed them to death, we are talking many, many more."

Adam hugged himself. "I was fortunate." And gifted with a wife who had somehow managed to gain him a reprieve. He frowned, gnawing at his lip. He had never thought to ask William just how Kit had saved his life.

"Well, enjoy it for as long as it lasts," Boulder said, getting to his feet. "The land rests uneasy, and the king is not done yet." He helped Adam to stand. "And beware of Despenser's man," he added in an undertone, nodding discreetly in the direction of Egard.

"Him?" Adam shook his head. "You must be wrong."

"He has an unforgettable face." Boulder shrugged. "And last I was in Gloucester he was there as well, drinking with Despenser and a young knight."

Some things were best handled by confronting them directly. No sooner had Adam finished for the day than he went to find Egard, ensuring he was standing out of reach.

"So you serve Despenser now," he said.

"My lord?" Egard turned confused eyes in his direction. "Who told you that?"

"Never you mind. Do you?"

Egard scowled. "Of course not!" He lowered his voice. "You forget, my lord, just what the Despensers have done to me and mine."

"But I've heard—"

"Heard? From who, from Boulder?" Egard spat to the side. "Now there you have Despenser's man, my lord. And if I were you, I'd avoid standing too close to him while on the scaffold."

Adam's guts coiled into knots. "I go up with him every day."

Egard regarded him in silence. "I know. And the moment he gets an opportunity, he'll push you off, claiming you lost your balance, what with your foot." He spat again. "I will never serve Despenser," he vowed. "The man who murdered my uncle and stole the land from my people – do you truly think I can forget?"

Adam relaxed. He'd forgotten that Egard was close kin to Llywelyn Bren, the Welshman Despenser had executed on a whim.

Egard beckoned Adam to come closer. "No need to tell Boulder you've asked me."

Adam gave him a long look. "I'm not a fool, Egard."

"Fool enough to give credence to his lies," Egard snapped.

"Or frightened enough," Adam replied in a low voice.

Egard gave him a grudging nod. "Watch your step," was all he said as he flitted off, remarkably silent for a man the size of a carthorse.

Over the coming days, Adam studied Boulder surreptitiously, while maintaining a careful distance to Egard. The builder was a cheerful man, much given to slapping his men on the back – a powerful slap, causing most of his workers to stumble forward. He also had the disconcerting tendency to approach noiselessly, popping up just behind you when you least expected it. It made Adam's skin crawl, and even more once he noticed just how often Boulder happened to appear beside him.

"I think you may be right," Adam told Boulder one afternoon, handing the mason his chisel.

"Hmm?" Boulder frowned down at the block of stone, tapping his chisel carefully across the surface.

"About Egard," Adam said, studying Boulder's face. The mouth twitched, twice, as if a smile wanting to burst forth was held back. "It breaks my heart," Adam continued, "but the way Egard watches me chills my blood."

Boulder glanced at Egard, standing some distance away. "I told you, didn't I? These days all you need is a heavy purse to buy somebody's loyalty." Or a murder, Adam thought.

Adam never went up the scaffolding again – not unless Boulder was somewhere else entirely. But he could feel the bald man's eyes following him, just as Egard's did, and some days he had no idea which one of them to trust.

When William rode by a day or so later, bringing with him word from the queen, Adam shared his concerns with him, but made his brother swear he wouldn't burden Kit with them.

"Egard is our man," William told him as he was leaving. "Him you can trust with your life."

Adam just looked at him. "The only people I trust with my life are my wife, my brother and my lord."

Living constantly on your guard was exhausting. Adam retreated into silence and isolation, ensuring always to keep some space between himself and the other men. The best way to achieve this was by working on the wall, and so it was that Adam was balancing on a ledge, twenty feet up in the air, when he saw the horses approaching. He recognised William immediately, and the hooded woman riding beside him could only be his wife, confirmed by the sudden appearance of a dark red lock, escaped from her braid to dance in the wind.

She was riding very carefully, at a plodding pace unlike any he had seen her acquiesce to before, and as she got closer, he saw that her horse was on a leading rein, while she was cradling a bundle to her chest.

A sensation of utter joy rushed through him. His wife, with his child at her breast. Had someone asked him back in Lent whether he would ever live to see the sight, he would not have thought it probable. And here he was, four months on, watching the woman he loved come riding towards him. Adam couldn't tear his gaze away from her, following the shape of her body, the way her arms were holding his child, so close to her heart.

They came to a halt before the gate. William talked to the sentry and was waved through. Adam wiped his hands against the cloth of his tunic. For the first time in four months he was to see Kit, and he would have preferred it to happen in privacy – plenty of privacy, involving a bed and her body in his arms – not in full view of guards and builders.

There was a soft crunch as someone trod on the crumbling mortar that lined the ledge. Adam wheeled, nearly overbalancing as he put his weight on his right foot. Boulder was coming towards him, graceful like a mountain goat. Adam cursed; a couple of moments off guard, and the mason had made it all the way to the top, without Adam noticing him.

"Your wife?" Boulder asked, pointing at Kit, now visible in the bailey. She had drawn back her hood and was looking about, her uncovered hair gleaming in the sun.

"Yes." Adam eyed the trowel Boulder was holding and tightened his grip on the chisel.

"Pretty." Boulder grinned. "No wonder my Lord Despenser has his eyes set on her."

"Well, he won't get her – ever." Adam shifted on the ledge, putting his weight on his good foot.

"And who is to stop him? You?" Boulder laughed and swung at him with the trowel. Adam fell back. The ledge was not quite a foot across, too narrow for him to attempt an attack, not with only one good foot, but if he could make it to the new part of the wall, he could leap across to the scaffolding.

"So you're Despenser's man," Adam said.

"One of them," Boulder replied. "Hugh Despenser has deep pouches, and most men will do anything for gold."

"And Egard?"

"What do you care? You'll be dead shortly." Boulder lunged again, Adam ducked, keeping his weight on his left foot. His left hand gripped at the top of the wall, fingers clawing for purchase. He shuffled backwards. Boulder swung again and again, the trowel slicing through the air. Too close. The man was getting too close. Adam didn't stop to think, he merely prayed and kicked, using his right leg. His foot made contact with Boulder's thigh, and excruciating pain rushed up Adam's calf. Boulder staggered, looking surprised. Adam yelled, he yelled again, and the sounds of raised voices floated up from below, principal among them that of his wife, calling his name. Boulder threw their spectators a look and Adam launched himself at him, chisel raised.

Boulder screamed when Adam sank the chisel into his exposed throat. Still screaming, Boulder toppled off the ledge, somersaulting through the air before he landed with a thud in the deep ditch below. By then he was silent. Adam clung to the wall, his eyes closed as he tried to calm his breathing.

Kit couldn't take her eyes off her husband, who was carefully making his way down the wall.

"Why?" she said in an undertone to William. "Who wants Adam dead?" Out of the corner of her eye, she studied the dead man, lying in a broken heap among the stones below. Several guards were converging round the body, fingers were pointed at Adam, at the wall.

"You know that as well as I do – Despenser," William replied with a grimace.

"But why?" She hefted Tom close, inhaling the clean scent of her son to block out the pungent smell of ordure that emanated from the nearby garderobe tower. "He reprieved him."

William puffed out his cheeks. "And regretted it immediately. Some cats don't like it when someone steals away their mouse."

"Mouse?" She kept her gaze on Adam, now safely on firm ground.

"As I hear it, Despenser enjoyed toying with Adam – his revenge on one of Mortimer's most trusted men for every single perceived wrong done our Hugh by Lord Roger. He had probably hoped to toy him to death."

Kit's stomach roiled. "He's a man beset by the devil."

"He's a powerful man." William studied her with a concerned frown. "And he doesn't like to lose."

"Best he get used to it," Kit said with a confidence she didn't quite feel.

Adam came limping towards her. His hair stood like an unruly haystack of spun gold around his head, and his eyes were alight with life, with hope. He was stopped by a guard, said something in a low voice, spitting in the direction of the dead man. The guard nodded, patted him on the back, and moments later Adam stood in front of her, more or less whole, all of him alive. She grazed his hand, his fingers closed around hers, calloused finger-pads rubbing softly over hers.

"My lord," she whispered. This close, she could see he was dirty, that the tunic he wore was the same one she'd dressed him in back in February. He was still far too thin, his legs were bare, his feet encased in simple shoes made of worn leather and tied together with twine, and instead of a belt he wore a length of rope. And still, when he smiled, he took her breath away, and she forgot about the men, about the corpse in the ditch, and rose on her toes to kiss him.

Time stopped. His lips, his tongue, his warm, warm mouth, his free hand cupping her face, holding her still as he deepened the kiss. She closed her eyes, he drew back, shaking his head with the slightest of smiles hovering over his mouth.

"Don't close them. My wife kisses me with open eyes."

She half-sobbed, half-laughed, rubbing her wet cheek against his shoulder. He nudged her face up and kissed her again, and this time she kept her eyes open, drowning in his pools of silver. There was a whistle, some catcalls and a burst of cheering. Adam grinned against her mouth and released her.

"Is this…" He placed a finger on the cloak that hid his child.

"It is. Here, hold him." She handed over the baby, helping Adam adjust his hold until the head rested safely in the crook of his arm. She retreated a pace or two, not wanting to intrude when Adam made his first acquaintance with his son, but she ate them with her eyes, her husband and her son. At first, Adam just looked, rocking his child gently in his arms. His mouth quivered, fair lashes swooping down to hide his eyes from her view. And then he smiled, lifted little Tom closer and kissed his forehead.

"My son," he said.

"My nephew," William put in, hugging brother and baby both.

Adam raised his face to look at Kit. "Thank you."

"My pleasure," she said, wondering how long it would be before she would lie in his arms again, hold him as he came inside of her.

Chapter 28

To be without him, when he was so close, was driving Kit to the borders of despair and beyond. July shifted into August, Tom grew and thrived, and Kit fell into a deep dejection, spending most of her time staring off towards the south, where Adam was.

Mabel tried to cheer her up, William told her to stop moping and make herself useful – harvest was in full swing, and even the lady of the manor should contribute, as well as she could. Lionel would sigh and nod his agreement, stroking Goliath's nose as he expressed the hope that Adam would be home soon.

"Where is that pardon?" Kit complained, settling herself side by side with William. She lifted up her skirts and dipped her feet in the little stream, wondering, as she always did, what Adam might be doing now. At least Boulder was dead, even if both William and Egard were of the opinion that it was an easy matter for Despenser to place a man or two within Goodrich, journeymen came and went throughout the summer, and who was to know which one of the masons, of the carpenters, was in fact a Despenser spy?

The incident with Boulder did bring some benefits, such as the entire garrison keeping a protective eye on Adam. The general instability of the times, however, caused Pembroke to tighten the security, and where before visits had been allowed, these days they required prearranged permission, so far difficult to get.

"The pardon may take some time to arrange," William said, reclining against his arms. He paddled his feet. "The queen must somehow sweet-talk the king, and do so without antagonising Despenser."

"Near on impossible. Anything not thought up or approved by Despenser antagonises him." Kit kicked at the water, smiling at the resulting spray. "Do you really think he feels cheated of killing Adam? He was the one who pardoned him."

"When he thought he would die anyway. And then you foiled his little plan with Guy, further vexing him. I fear Despenser has developed a fixation on Adam."

That did not sound good – in fact, it sounded very bad. Kit sighed and leaned against William. He no longer stiffened when she showed him physical affection, but the priest was constantly present in her brother-in-law, causing a reticence in him whenever she got too close. But today he remained where he was, not shifting away from her.

"It is in the hands of God," he said after a while. He moved his shoulder until she sat up. "So far, it seems our Lord has other plans for our Adam than to let him die in captivity."

"Let us pray it stays that way," Kit said.

She wasn't all that sure God was anywhere close when their visitors arrived the next day. Lionel came running down the lane as if he had the hounds of hell behind him, gasping that it was him, it was Despenser, and with him came Guy.

"Well, they'll just have to turn right around and ride off," Kit said.

"You can't deny Despenser," William told her. "He holds the overlordship, and as such you owe him hospitality."

"And Guy?"

"Guy is another matter." William's jaw clenched, eyes hardening into shards of light-blue ice.

"It does not do to rile him," Mabel said with a frown. "They cannot intend to stay but a night, not here."

"So where do you think he's headed?" Kit asked, a leaden weight in her belly. "Goodrich Castle?"

Mabel snorted. "He'd be a fool to do so. According to Egard, the Earl of Pembroke and his lady are in residence. Not much love lost between the earl and the royal chamberlain."

"Not much love lost between Despenser and anyone – except for the king," Kit muttered, her eyes on the approaching cavalcade. Twenty men and counting – it would leave her food stores sadly depleted, and even worse, she'd be feeding the enemy. She scratched distractedly at her arm, wishing she could lace the food with monkshood or hemlock. Painful deaths, the both of them, and Kit entertained herself by visualising a writhing Despenser, hands extended in imploration.

Despenser held in his horse and took his time inspecting the house, the stables and the chapel. Dark eyes roved over the yard, the well and the hencoop, mouth curling into an amused smile.

"Is this truly what you aspire to?" he asked Guy. "A life in the country, scratching at the earth like a hen?"

"It's good land," Guy replied evasively.

"My land," Kit reminded them both, dipping her head in a minimal bow in the direction of Despenser. "My lord."

"For now." Despenser leaned forward over his horse. "But once you've wed Guy, then the land will pass to him."

"I'd not marry Guy if he was the last man on earth," Kit retorted. "I have better taste than that." She regarded Guy with distaste, noting with considerable satisfaction that his left hand looked awry, fingers in a permanent half-curl.

Despenser laughed and leapt off his horse, throwing the reins at Lionel. "You are most refreshing at times, Lady Katherine – or may I call you Kate?"

"You can try. I don't respond to that name."

"Ah, so little Kate died with Morimer, did she?"

"Is he dead?" Kit managed to keep her voice under control.

Despenser glowered at her. "Sadly, no. The king has chosen to give him his life." He clasped his hands behind his back. "Aren't you going to invite us inside?"

"Do I have a choice, my lord?" Kit said.

"Not really. Not unless you want to witness my men slaying your household."

Kit knotted her hands, hating him for being so casually intimidating. "May I offer you something to eat, my lord?" she said, succeeding in sounding cool rather than frightened.

Despenser gave her an amused look and swept inside, followed by his men.

Kit sat hemmed in by the two men she hated the most. To her right, Despenser settled himself in the best chair of the house, while to her left, Guy was sitting far too close, his arm constantly brushing against hers.

"Not bad," Despenser said, studying the hall. The walls had been recently whitewashed, and the old tapestries Kit had found in a chest had been carefully repaired and cleaned before being hung to decorate the walls. "It will make you a nice home, Guy."

"It will not." Kit shoved at the meat on her trencher. "This is my home, not his, and I have no intention of inviting him to stay."

Despenser raised his cup and sniffed at the wine. "Once you're wed—"

"First of all, I will never marry a man with the integrity of a toad, and secondly, I am married. Or are you proposing to make bigamy legal, my lord?"

Despenser snorted, spraying wine all over the tablecloth. "Bigamy?" he croaked in between bouts of coughs and laughter. "Now that does raise some interesting possibilities, doesn't it?"

"It does? To me it sounds immoral. But then, I don't think morality is your strongest side, my lord."

"Do not dare to presume to judge me." Fingers closed on her wrist, closed and squeezed until she feared she might hear the bone snapping. Kit gritted her teeth and stared straight ahead. After interminable seconds, his hold released.

"Once we have sorted the matter of your married status, Guy will take you as his wife. I've promised him these manors, and sadly they come with you."

"You can't sort my married status," she protested. "And even if you could, you can't force me to marry him."

"You think not?" Despenser snickered. "Tell her, Guy."

"It wouldn't be too hard," Guy said, leaning towards her so that she was squashed between them. "I'd just lock you into the solar, have my way with you until you ended up carrying my child." His eyes drifted over to Mabel, who was sitting with Tom in her lap. "The brat would have to go, of course. If you're good and compliant, to a nice home. If you're not..." He shrugged.

"No matter how much with child, I still wouldn't marry you!" she hissed, squirming wildly in an attempt to avoid his deformed hand on her breast. He pinched, hard.

"A month or so in my tender care would change your mind," Guy said coldly. "There is only so much pain a woman can take – and then there is the babe. Vulnerable creatures, babies."

"You wouldn't!" But she could see it in his eyes that he would. She threw a desperate look at Mabel. Get my boy out of here, she tried to signal.

"Not unless you force me to." He grinned at her. "You'll not see him much anyway, but you'll soon forget him." His hand was shoving at her skirts. Kit slapped at it, which resulted in him sinking his fingers into her thigh, hard enough to make her gasp.

"He's my son – Adam's son. He stays with me."

"Once you're a widow, the boy is nothing but a nuisance," Despenser said into her ear. "Guy will want his sons to inherit, not his brother's whelp." He ran his finger along her neckline.

"I am not a widow!" She pushed at him.

"For now, but that is so very easy to rectify." Despenser gave her a wolfish grin. "In fact, as we speak it may already have happened."

"No!" She dug her elbow into Guy, tried to free herself from the arms that fettered her to her chair. "Get away from me, don't touch me!"

"I think not," Despenser chuckled, sticking his tongue in her ear.

"Please, my lord," she said, "do not humiliate me before my household." Out of the corner of her eye, she could see William, arms held tight by the two Despenser men who were marching him out of the room.

"I do as I wish," Despenser said. "What was it you said? That morality is not my strong side?" He laughed softly. "You were entirely correct."

Kit's hand closed on the handle of her eating knife. "Let me go!" she yelled, sinking the knife into Despenser's arm. Lord Despenser fell back with a curse, clutching his bleeding arm. He raised his arm and hit her, once, twice across the face. She tried to protect herself, but Guy's hands had closed on her upper arms, holding her still.

Despenser leaned over her. "I'll not have the wife of a traitor cut me!"

"I'll not be fondled by a depraved bastard, lord or no lord!" she yelled back, her head ringing with the force of his slaps.

"Fondled? You'll be more than fondled." Despenser jerked his head. "Take her to the solar."

"Don't you dare!" Kit heaved, she stomped and kicked, as Guy dragged her from her chair.

"If you don't behave, I'll cut your son's throat," Despenser told her. Kit froze, having no doubt whatsoever that he'd do it. Despenser snickered. "Get the brat," he told Guy.

Guy looked about the hall. "He isn't here."

Kit closed her eyes in relief. Mabel had understood. A moment of relief, no more, because now Despenser and Guy were manhandling her across the floor, and no matter how much she yelled and fought, she was dragged, inch by inch, towards the solar and the waiting bed.

"Help me!" She got hold of the surcoat of one of Despenser's men. "For the love of God, help me." The man averted his face, but not before Kit saw a look of utter shame on it. She clung to him until the garment ripped. Up the stairs. Kit tore at Despenser's hands, she raked her nails over Guy's face, hearing him grunt. The door. She clung to the doorpost, she screamed and kicked, until Despenser got hold of her hair and yanked, sending her tumbling inside.

"Alone at last," he sneered, banging the door closed. He was breathing heavily, his clothes dishevelled and torn by the recent tussle. Guy was bleeding from his cheek, from his neck, looking at her as if he wanted to throttle her. Kit backed away, looking for something – anything – with which to defend herself.

"No way out of this one," Despenser told her, eyes shiny with lust. He came towards her, and she retreated, thinking that if she could only get hold of her shears, then…She sidled towards the basket where she kept her sewing.

"Is that what you're planning to do?" she asked Guy. "Share your women with him?" She jerked her head in Despenser's direction. "So it won't be your son either, will it? It will be Despenser's bastards that you will have to raise as your own."

"Hold your tongue." Despenser made a grab for her; she ducked and darted away.

"And when you ride away from here, what do you think I will do? Forget it ever happened? Oh, no, I'll ride straight for Pembroke and shout to him that I've been raped. He may not be able to do something about Lord Despenser here, but you he will squash – and I will cheer him on."

"Pembroke can't touch us," Despenser sneered.

"Not you. But Guy...Besides, if Pembroke doesn't, William will. How does that feel, Guy? Years and years looking over your shoulder, wondering when your enraged priest brother will show up, to avenge his brother and me." She backed into the corner. Only a couple of yards or so to go – she could see the shears.

"We'll kill the priest." Despenser sounded unconcerned, but Guy was beginning to look uncomfortable.

"Yes, one more murder won't make that much of a difference to your immortal soul," Kit said.

"Careful," Despenser warned, moving towards her.

"But you, Guy, how many men have you murdered?" Almost there.

"No one!" Guy replied, glaring at her.

"And how many women have you raped, how often have you held down your brother's wife and taken her against her will?"

"Never." Guy lifted his hand to his bleeding cheek.

"But now you plan on doing both these heinous deeds." She spat at him. "You will go to hell, Guy. But maybe you won't mind spending eternity side by side with Lord Despenser."

"Silence, woman!" Despenser lunged, and Kit fell backwards, fingers scrabbling for the shears. "Oh, no you don't!" Despenser kicked the basket out of reach, took hold of her and flung her on the bed. She was pinioned to the mattress by his weight, his breath on her face. "I enjoyed myself with your husband," he said, wet lips far too close. "Let's see if I'll enjoy myself as much with you." She heaved, trying to dislodge him. In response, he gripped her gown and ripped the fabric apart.

"Let me go!" She pushed at him, was slapped, slapped again, leaving her head ringing. She fell back, arms passive.

"That's better," Despenser grunted, his invasive hands on her breasts. "See?" he threw over his shoulder. "All they need is to be treated firmly." Kit could hear Guy approach the bed, his footsteps loud on the wooden boards. Despenser's wet mouth again, now on her neck. It made Kit gag. She whimpered, which only made him laugh and rub himself against her while he pawed at her bared skin. Kit closed her eyes, lying like a broken doll beneath him. All she needed was an opportunity – please God, give her an opportunity. Yet again that mouth, those hands, travelling all over her breasts. It hurt when he twisted her nipple, and she couldn't bite back a gasp, making him laugh.

"Just you wait, Lady de Guirande, this is but the beginning," Despenser said. He rose on his knees to fiddle with his clothes. Kit slammed her hands into his groin, twisted until he screamed, pitched him to the side, and leapt out of bed.

Despenser drew a series of loud breaths, clutching at his privates, and then he came towards her, his eyes narrowed into slits. Kit took hold of the chamber pot and lifted it high. It was full, making Kit frown until she realised that might not be a bad thing – at least not at present.

With all her might she swung at him with the chamber pot. It broke, the earthenware shattering when it connected with Despenser's head. There was blood running in rivulets down Despenser's face from a jagged tear just below his hairline, the room filled with the stench of urine, and Despenser reeled, collapsing to his knees with a grunt.

"What have you done?" Guy rushed over to help his lord, but hovered, nose wrinkling at the stench that emanated from Despenser's clothes. Kit shoved past him and ran for door. A hand on her braid, another on her shoulder, and Kit was sent stumbling across the room, her face crashing into the wall.

Fuzzily, she watched Guy stalk towards her, dagger in hand. Kit didn't stop to think. With what little strength was left to her, she staggered to the window, wrenched the shutters open and jumped.

Chapter 29

They wouldn't let her get up. Kit had no time to lie in bed: she had to warn Adam, Pembroke, someone, before Despenser had her Adam assassinated – if he hadn't already achieved his goal. But no matter how she begged, Mabel just shook her head, saying head injuries were not to be taken lightly. Besides, William had sent Lionel off to warn Adam immediately upon seeing Despenser. That didn't help. Kit needed to see Adam with her own eyes, but from the mulish set to Mabel's mouth, that wasn't about to happen.

"It's just a concussion," Kit said, touching the huge discolouration that covered the right-hand side of her face. Not quite true. She'd torn her skin against something sharp, so there was a jagged tear down her face that she hadn't quite dared to look at, beyond the odd peek. The jump as such had left her with a bruised leg and a twisted ankle.

"You could have died!" Mabel replied, looking as if she was about to begin crying – again. "To leap out of a window like that!"

"But I didn't." Kit shivered. She took a big breath. "They were going to—"

"Rape you," Mabel finished for her, placing yet another poultice on her face. She smoothed at her hair, slow, long strokes that made Kit relax against the pillows. "But they didn't. I believe they think they killed you. We all thought that when we found you crumpled on the ground below your window." Mabel made a disgusted sound. "Besides, what fun is there in ravishing an unconscious woman? Despenser is the type of man who enjoys the chase more than the kill. He wants to see the light go out in his victim's eyes."

Kit turned her face to the wall. Had Despenser seen the light go out of Adam's eyes?

"M' lady?" Mabel said.

"And they just left?" Kit still found this incomprehensible.

"They did. Like greased rats, which was why we feared they'd killed you." An aggravated squeal from the cradle made Mabel grin. "Ah, Master Tom awakes." She beckoned for the wet nurse, who hurried over to her new charge. Kit frowned, still not entirely happy with these new arrangements for her son – arrangements made by Mabel just after Despenser's visit. When Kit had protested, Mabel had brusquely cut her off, reminding her that high-born ladies did not nurse their babies much beyond the first month, and as far as Mabel knew, she had far more experience when it came to the welfare of babies than Kit did.

"All he does is eat and eat," Kit said with a little smile, having watched her son attack first one, then the other, of the offered teats. Gingerly, she eased herself up to sit, arms held out to receive her son. Her breasts ached and throbbed under the swaddling bands, causing her substantial discomfort, even if Mabel assured her it was worst the first week or so.

"And a thriving lad he is, aren't you Master Tom?" Mabel cooed. Kit stroked her baby's head, covered by wisps of fair hair, and lifted him close enough to inhale his scent. She gave Mabel a considering look.

"If Lionel doesn't come back tomorrow, I'm riding to Goodrich." The only reason she could think of for Despenser and Guy to leave so abruptly, was to ensure Adam was killed – after which they could return to torture her at leisure. Her throat closed up.

"We'll see," Mabel said, her jaw jutting.

"No we won't." Kit sighed. "He should have been back by now."

"He'll be fine," Mabel assured her. "Big strong lad like that, who's to harm him? Besides, you can't leave your babe."

"Yes I can. After all, Tom has Amy now." She grinned at the sour expression on Mabel's face.

William was no more enthusiastic than Mabel, but had to agree that it was strange that Lionel had not returned. At first, he tried to convince Kit to stay at home, but she wasn't having any of it, telling him over and over again that she just had to reassure herself that Adam – and Lionel – were all right. With a loud, theatrical sigh William gave up.

They set off at dawn. It was cold, it was wet, and the moment Kit swung herself astride the horse she knew she should have stayed abed. Her cheek flamed, her head thudded angrily, and a cold sweat broke out along her back and arms. But she didn't say anything, ignoring Mabel's concerned look. Instead, she nodded to John to set them moving, her hands gripping the saddle to hold herself upright.

It was John who found him. By then, Kit was feeling somewhat recovered, capable even of conversing William. John was riding some distance ahead of William and Kit, bow in hand, when Kit saw him pull his horse to an abrupt halt. Despite looking as if he was about to keel over and die any moment, John was a nimble man, and he was off his horse in a matter of seconds, leaping through the deep heather towards something that lay immobile some distance from the track. At his approach, there was a flurry of wings, several carrion-eaters taking flight.

Lionel was lying on his front, three arrows sticking out of his back.

"They must have left in haste," William said. "They didn't retrieve their arrows."

Kit couldn't reply, staring down at the immobile shape of her husband's squire. "Why shoot a boy?"

"Why do you think?" William sounded grim. "They didn't want him to reach Goodrich Castle."

Kit clutched at the mane of her horse and filled her lungs with air, expelling it slowly as she counted to fifty. He'd be all right, she tried to tell herself, of course he'd be all right.

"We can't leave him lying here," she said. William nodded and gestured for one of the accompanying men to help him load Lionel onto a horse.

Adam was lying on his pallet when a loud grating noise made him start. It had to be well after midnight, and visitors this late could only mean one thing: bad news. He groped for the sharpened chisel he had pilfered from the builders and clenched his hand round the handle. As quietly as possible he rose from the rustling straw and hobbled over to stand on the other side of the cell, flattening himself against the wall as the door opened and swung towards him.

A man entered, carrying a lantern, and Adam's shoulders slumped when he recognised Egard.

"My lord?" Egard whispered.

"What?" Adam kept his voice low.

"We must get you out of here." Egard motioned towards the darkened passage.

"You first." Ever since the incident with Boulder, Adam kept his back free – all the time.

They made their way over the uneven stone floor, Adam setting his damaged foot down carefully. Even through the thickness of the stone walls, Adam could hear the sound of men and horses, and from the way Egard was rushing him along, Adam supposed they were here for him.

"Here." Egard pulled back a heavy grate and gestured at the space below it. Adam's hair stood upright. He had no love of cramped, pitch-black spaces. His breathing quickened, becoming loud in the silence of the passage. "My lord!" Egard hissed. "There's no time."

"I don't like the dark," Adam muttered. "I…" He wet his lips. "And it's very small." He'd have to sit crouched to fit. Egard regarded him steadily.

"There's no choice, my lord." He grinned, a brief flash of teeth visible in the light of the lantern. "You shouldn't share your fears with your enemies."

"Enemy?" Adam tightened his hold on the chisel.

Egard shook his head. "Not me, my lord, never me." There were shouts from somewhere just above them. "Please, my lord, get in, now."

Adam did as he was told, lowering himself into the hole. Egard pushed the grate back into place, grunting with the effort.

"And what if you die, or if you're wounded or taken prisoner?" Adam placed his hands against the grate and tried to heave, but it barely budged.

"I'll be back as soon as it's safe," Egard whispered, moving off.

"Egard!" Adam hissed. "Please don't leave me to die, not like this!"

There was no reply but the fading sound of Egard's footsteps.

Adam shrank together in his cramped space, his hand clenched round his chisel. The stone at his back was cold, damp seeping in through his tunic. He tried to sit, but he was stuck in a crouch, his right foot already beginning to throb. He closed his eyes, counting his breaths. His windpipe shrivelled, sweat formed like dewdrops on his chilled skin. Adam stuffed his sleeve into his mouth and moaned, overcome with far too many graphic memories of the old well-shaft in Ludlow, hours spent in utter darkness as he begged his father to please pull him out. His foot. Pain rushed through his toes, up his calf. Pain was good. Pain was better than the memories of Father, of his own snivelling and the sound his fingers made when Father forced him to release his grip on the sill.

A noise from above recalled him to the present. Light flared against the stone walls, voices rang out and feet rushed by. Steel clanged, doors were wrenched open, and then there was a loud commotion, steel grating against stone, a solitary voice raised in anger. The feet returned.

"Where is he?" a voice demanded. Guy. Adam pressed his head back against the wall behind him, tried to see through the grate, but could only catch a glimpse of booted feet.

"Who?" Egard sounded confused, as if he'd just been woken from heavy sleep.

"The prisoner!" Guy snarled. "Adam de Guirande – we are here to fetch him."

"Fetch him?"

Adam muffled a guffaw. Egard sounded as dim-witted as a cow.

"What is it you don't understand, fool?" Guy's voice again, his foot on the grate. "Where is the prisoner?"

"There is no prisoner here," Egard replied. "Not that I can see."

Guy cursed. "You're a lying cur, man! Tell me where he is, or I'll—"

"Look wherever you want," Egard said. "I swear, my lord, you'll find no prisoner here."

Guy stomped off and Egard shuffled forward, planting his considerable bulk over the grate. He kept up a low, monotonous humming as Guy's men yet again searched the lower level of the castle, but from the sound of things they found nothing but the odd heap of straw, an empty pallet bed and a chipped earthenware mug.

"You!" Guy's voice echoed down the passage.

"My lord?" Egard said.

"Come with us. We go to search the rest of this infernal pile of stone. And I'll not want to be in your shoes if you don't produce the prisoner. Lord Despenser has ridden far for him."

"My lord?" Egard repeated.

"Are you dense?" Guy asked.

Adam could almost see Egard's little smile as he assured Guy that he didn't think he was.

Off they went, taking the flickering torches with them, and Adam was submerged in darkness. His foot no longer hurt; now it was numb. His knees scraped against the stones and he tried yet again to lower himself to sit, but his big frame was stuck. Adam sucked in air, did so again. His bowels cramped, and in his head his pulse thudded far too loud and far too fast. Think of something else, he urged himself, and he forced himself to bring forth an image of Kit, but no matter how he tried, he couldn't quite visualise her beyond her hair and eyes, seeing instead the looming shape of his father, the man who knew just how afraid Adam was of the dark.

He couldn't have been more than six, he reckoned, the first time his father threw him in the well. His mother was recently dead, the baby sister dead as well, and Father had been deranged by grief, drinking himself into a stupor every night, every day. William had been no more than three, a dirty thing in smocks and bare feet, while Adam was old enough to wear a tunic and braies – but not quite old enough to cope with hose and points.

During the day, Adam ensured he and his brother kept well away from his father, mostly by hiding in the kitchen where Adam would help with what he could, whether it was fetching wood or turning the spits. Come the evening, there was no choice but to return to the rooms allotted to their father. It was the wine, people said. Wine and grief drove Walter de Guirande over an edge, and the previously conscientious father became a monster, demanding that Adam do this, or that, and if Adam wasn't quick enough, that resulting slap would have the lad reeling.

It irked Walter that Adam never cried. He'd yell that there was something wrong with his son, and slap him again. And again. But Adam wouldn't give Father the satisfaction of seeing him weep – until the first time in the well. And once Walter had realised just how frightened his son was of the dark and narrow old well-shaft, by now mostly filled in with rubble, he took the greatest pleasure in manhandling his son to spend hours in the dark, telling Adam that men weren't afraid of the dark.

Adam laughed hollowly in his cramped space. Some men were most definitely scared of the dark, especially when stuck in a rounded space that reminded him far too much of his childhood prison. He pillowed his head as well as he could against his arms and tried to escape into sleep. Impossible. He would die here, stuffed into a hole. He filled his lungs with air, trying to combat the constricting sensation around his chest. No air. He sucked and sucked, hearing his inhalations wheeze their way down his windpipe. He was cold. He was sweating. So cold, so damned cold, and his right foot was no longer numb – it felt as if there were rats gnawing at it. Were there rats? Adam shuffled his feet and rapped at the enclosing walls with his chisel, but nothing furry and warm squeezed by him. He groaned and rested his head against the wall. He hated the dark.

A loud clanging had him jerking awake. He must have dozed off. The chisel. He had dropped his chisel. Some groping, and his fingers closed round the reassuring softness of its worn handle. In the distance, he heard a horn. A lot of noise, from somewhere above his head.

Someone was coming down the stairs. Adam blinked at the sudden burst of light, like bright sunlight after hours trapped in the dark. Heavy footsteps coming his way, and then the grate was pushed aside and Egard's hands took hold of his arms and heaved. Adam couldn't stand. His damaged foot was aflame and he was incapable of straightening out of his crouch. He bit back on a yell when Egard forcibly pulled him up.

"Our lord is back and demands your presence," Egard said.

"Our lord?" Adam tried to pull himself free from Egard's hold. "My lord languishes in the Tower, so who is this lord of yours?"

"You'll see soon enough." Egard more or less carried Adam along, through the passage, up the stairs, up yet another set of stairs, and then Adam was shoved into the great hall of Goodrich Castle, nearly landing on his nose by the feet of the Earl of Pembroke.

Aymer de Valence was in a foul mood, bushy brows pulled so low his eyes were reduced to dashes of blue. The cause of all this anger was slouching against the wall, looking entirely unconcerned as the earl yelled at him, voice cracking when he told Hugh Despenser that he wouldn't have it, and Despenser had best have a very good excuse for attempting to steal away his prisoner while Aymer himself was elsewhere.

"Not your, prisoner, dear Aymer," Despenser said, "the king's."

"Entrusted to me!" Pembroke spluttered.

"By me, you buffoon!" Despenser yelled back.

"You had no right," de Valence continued. "How dare you ride into my castle and demand that he be turned over to you? With what authority, eh?"

"Royal authority," Despenser said coldly.

"Really? And where is your writ?" Pembroke advanced upon Despenser, who scowled at him before admitting he didn't have one.

By now, Adam had managed to get to his feet. Despenser gave a bark of laughter. "Ah, there you are! Now where might you have been hiding all night and all morning? My men and I have looked everywhere for you."

"With little success," Adam replied, glancing at Guy, who was standing several yards behind Despenser.

"There will be other opportunities to play this little game," Despenser said, "and next time you will not be quite as lucky."

"Fortune is a fickle thing, my lord." Adam locked eyes with Guy. "Next time, it may be me searching for you, brother dearest."

Guy paled.

"You'll be dead first," Despenser said.

"I will not have you threatening my prisoner," Pembroke broke in. "While he is here, he remains under my protection."

"So you say, Aymer my dear, so you say. And yet look at what happened to Piers Gaveston. One moment safe in your protection, the other…" Despenser mimed a chop to his head. "Besides, you can't remain here to keep Adam protected – you are expected at court next month, and once you're gone, who is to know what misfortune may befall our Adam?" He chuckled and moved towards Adam. "We could take off where we left off, you and I. You know – you in chains, at my mercy." He gestured at Adam's left foot. "I could have your brother stake your other foot this time – I do so aspire for symmetry in life."

"You are a vile, heartless bastard," Adam said, trying to sound unconcerned. But he wasn't, his hands clenching as he recalled the hours of pain Despenser had submitted him to.

"I am, aren't I?" Despenser replied with a little shrug. He smiled, bowed to Pembroke and apologised for having to cut his stay short, but he had pressing matters to attend in Bristol – the king's matters – and so, alas, he had no choice but to set pleasure aside and hasten off. With one last lingering look at Adam, he left, with Guy hurrying after him.

Chapter 30

Aymer de Valence accorded Adam the privilege of a bath, calling for his squire to find Adam some clean clothes. It was the first time in months that Adam submerged his body in hot water, and he watched with some disgust as the water turned scummy with grime, here and there dotted with a drowned louse or flea.

An hour or so later, he rejoined his host, freshly shaved and dressed in a clean brown tunic with matching hose. His scalp tingled from its recent close encounter with vinegar and the bather's hard brush, and he had to suppress the desire to scratch at it.

Pembroke was standing in his hall, accompanied by his countess, the Lady Marie. She gave Adam a polite but cool smile, regarding him in much the same way as he had regarded the dead lice in the bath water.

"Better?" de Valence asked, offering Adam a goblet of wine.

"Yes, my lord." Adam sipped at the wine, taking in the splendid tapestries that adorned the walls closest to the main entrance.

"You were fortunate." Pembroke slammed down his cup on the table. "Had they found you, they would have hanged you – or worse." He sat down on the long stone bench that ran below the three large western windows, and regarded Adam from under his heavy brows.

"Probably worse," Adam replied lightly. He was giddy-headed with hunger and lack of sleep, and the wine was going to his head, so he set the goblet down and, at the earl's invitation, joined him on the bench. Soft fleeces padded the bench, a white alaunt slept in front of the hearth, and from the beams hung de Valence's colours, four large banners that moved slightly back and forth. Adam threw his surroundings an admiring look, all the way from the carved pillars to the whitewashed walls, decorated with red martlets and a border of blue squares. Goodrich was a modern castle – nothing like the old heap Lord Roger called home – built by de Valence's Lusignan father on the site of an ancient fortification of which only the old keep remained, its greyish stone contrasting with the deep red sandstone of the rest of the buildings.

From where he was sitting, Adam had a glimpse of the sunlit courtyard and the chapel beyond, situated on the opposite side of the drawbridge from the barbican. A strange place for a chapel, Adam had expressed to Egard some time ago, only to be informed that this was yet another fortifying feature, ensuring God stood safely with the defenders in case of an attack.

Not that any such attack was imminent. Only a fool would attempt to breach Goodrich's impressive defences, with a deep ditch protecting the castle to the south and the east, while the river Wye and a series of sheer cliffs held the castle's back.

"I'm not sure what to do." De Valence sucked in his lip. "Do I take you with me to London, or do I leave you here?"

"In his present mood, I prefer to stay well away from the king." Adam threw the earl a look. "And Mortimer? Any news of my lord?"

Pembroke's face acquired a ruddy hue. "I didn't set out to trick him, I—"

"I know," Adam interrupted. "Is he still alive?"

"Yes, hale enough, as I hear it, though careworn after all these months in captivity. The king is not exactly feeding him on capons and dates, it is more bread and gruel."

"Ah." Adam looked away. "Why?"

"Why what?"

"Why hasn't the king executed him?"

"Even a king must listen to his people at times. Too much killing, too much mutilation…" The earl looked away. "It suited the king to show Mortimer and Chirk leniency – for now."

"For now," Adam repeated bitterly.

Pembroke turned to face him. "Of course for now.

Despenser and the king mean to rid this world of Mortimer – someday soon he'll be murdered in his cell."

"And me? Will I also be murdered?"

"Not if I can stop it," Pembroke said.

"You can't stop it." Adam eyed his host levelly. "The only way to do so is to let me go."

Over the following days, Pembroke elected to treat Adam as a guest rather than as a prisoner, ignoring his wife's displeased expression. From sleeping on straw, Adam was suddenly back to mattresses and linen sheets, the little chamber he'd been given abutting the hall itself.

They were at dinner some days later when a servant hurried in and whispered something to the earl, who nodded. Moments later, the door opened and Kit came in, followed by William. She came to an abrupt halt at the sight of Adam, eyes flying up and down his body. Her lower lip wobbled for an instant before she caught it with her teeth, and when she turned to greet the countess, Adam gasped.

He crossed the room in a couple of strides. "Who did this?" he asked, setting a gentle finger to the angry scar that marred her face. His hand lingered, cupping her cheek. Such smooth skin, such pretty ears, and eyes as blue as cornflowers gazing up at him. She swayed towards him, her breasts brushing his chest.

"Despenser – and Guy," she replied in a voice meant for his ears only. His grip tightened, she inhaled.

"Sorry." He released the pressure, but couldn't take his hand from her face, needing to touch her, verify that she was real. She leaned into his touch, her breath tickling his palm.

"Did I hear you say Despenser?" Pembroke joined them. Reluctantly, Adam dropped his hand. Her fingers found his, hooking them together. He placed his thumb on her wrist, where he could feel the steady beat of her pulse.

"He visited us a week or so ago," Kit said. "I dare say he did not find his welcome as warm as he wanted it."

Adam tightened his hold on her hand. "What did they do to you?"

"Not now," she murmured, before turning to frown at

Pembroke. "He is a murderer, Earl Aymer. We found the body of my husband's squire a day's ride north of here – on your land."

"Lionel?" Adam looked at her, at William. "He's dead?"

"Shot." William looked tired, fair stubble decorating his cheeks. "But we don't know if it was Despenser – the lad was lying quite alone in the heather."

Kit's face went a deep pink. "Of course it was him! He wanted to stop Lionel from warning you that—"

"Warning who of what?" Pembroke interrupted.

"Despenser aims to make me a widow," Kit said, and once again her lip wobbled. "And once I'm widowed, he intends to force me to wed Adam's despicable stepbrother."

No. Adam ignored their audience and pulled her close enough to kiss her brow. "It will not happen." She hid her face against his shoulder and made a strangled sound. "It won't, my sweeting."

She drew herself up straight. "You think not?" Kit turned to the earl. "That's twice that Despenser almost kills my man while he is in your care."

Adam winced at her tone, and the countess stiffened, eyeing Kit with dislike. The earl, however, sagged.

"I do as well as I can," he said

"Not good enough, my lord." Kit folded her arms over her chest.

"I shall double the guard," Pembroke told her.

"And that won't help, will it? Every man you bring inside is potentially an assassin hired by Despenser," Kit said.

"Kit." Adam frowned at her. "Earl Aymer is on our side."

"Your side?" The countess snorted. "My lord husband is the king's man, has always been the king's man. You, on the other hand, you're a traitor, as is Roger Mortimer, for now rotting in the Tower."

"Where he wouldn't be if it hadn't been for the false promises your honourable husband gave him." Kit advanced on the countess. "Despenser is a tyrant, supported by this besotted king of ours. How many widows has he robbed of their land? How many orphans has he cheated of their inheritance?

Do you think you'll fare any better at his hands should your husband die?"

The countess retreated, hands trembling.

"Kit!" Adam took hold of her arm and pulled her to stand by his side. "My apologies, Countess Marie. My wife is distraught, and—"

"Distraught? Of course I'm distraught! They almost killed you – again." Kit's eyes filled with tears that she angrily wiped away.

"But they failed." He cupped her face and met her eyes. "Again. And they will keep on failing."

"Not if you remain here," Kit said.

"So what do you propose?" Earl Pembroke asked. "That I just let my prisoner go?" He raised his brows, giving Kit a haughty look.

"Yes."

The countess laughed. "Don't be ridiculous! To do so could put my lord husband in the gravest danger."

"To not do so is to gamble with my husband's life." Kit glared at her, before focusing her attention on the earl. "Or will you swear on your immortal soul that he will come to no harm?"

Earl Aymer met her eyes, opened his mouth to say something, but desisted. Finally he shook his head. "I cannot."

"Exactly." Kit sighed, shoulders rounding.

"I can't just let him go," Pembroke said. "The moment he rides out of that gate, Despenser will hear of it."

"There is a solution, my lord." William stepped forward. "We do an exchange."

"An exchange?" Adam frowned at his brother. "I'll not have you stuck in a dungeon, pretending to be me." But he was tempted – sorely tempted, even – noting just how similar William was to him.

William grinned. "Not me. Lionel."

"But Lionel is dead," Kit protested.

The earl gave a short bark of laughter. "Even better, one could say." He eyed William thoughtfully. "It might work. You ride off with a corpse, I give out that my prisoner has died and bury him hastily, and Despenser is none the wiser."

"There is but one hitch," Kit said. "I am suddenly a widow, and Guy…" She clasped her hands together. Adam covered them with his own.

"One day at the time, Kit," William said. "If Guy comes looking, you will tell him that you refuse to believe that Adam is dead unless he can prove it to you." He laughed. "We can have Adam write to you, telling you he's safe in France or something."

"And when Despenser finds out about this ruse, what then?" the countess demanded. "I will not have it, Aymer, that you risk your wellbeing – mine as well – on behalf of a traitor."

Lord Pembroke gave his wife a fond look. "It gladdens my heart to hear just how much you care for me, dearest wife." He glanced at Kit. "Almost as much as Lady de Guirande cares for her husband. But as to your concern, that is easily handled. We leave for London today, and any events that take place here are done without my knowledge." The earl pursed his lips. "You'd do best to escape the country, Adam. Because once Despenser finds out, he'll come hunting."

"But what about the pardon?" Kit asked.

"Ah." Earl Aymer nodded a couple of times. "The pardon. Well," he said, directing himself to his wife, "it seems we must make haste to London, my lady. We have a queen to visit."

Two hours later, they were on their way. The shrouded corpse lay balanced across William's horse, and they departed in silence, Kit riding first. She caught Egard's eyes when she rode by him and received an infinitesimal nod in reply. He would do his part, ensuring Lionel was buried on the morrow – as Adam de Guirande. It sat uneasily on Kit to steal poor Lionel's name away from him, but Egard had promised he would pray for him under his true names and ensure the ivory crucifix Lionel always wore would accompany him to the grave.

John murmured something to Egard as he rode by, and Kit heard Egard chuckle, telling the old man he'd be home soon enough. Kit would welcome him with open arms, because if there was something Tresaints lacked, it was capable defenders. Well, beyond John. The man was as old as the hills and then some, but give him a crossbow and a quiver of quarrels and he'd drop any man you pointed at.

As if he could sense her eyes on him, John turned and grinned. "I'll keep you and yours safe, my lady – just as I've done all of your life."

Kit shared a smile with him, recalling a number of incidents in which he'd rushed to her aid, most of them involving horses. "Thank you." She gave him a wide smile. "Will that include my husband? Or do we have to smuggle him into Tresaints?" She leaned over to pat Adam on the rump. He was playing dead, as William had insisted it would be wiser to do so until they were safely away from Goodrich.

"They'll not tell, m' lady. If they do, I'll have their guts for garters."

"Oh. Well, that sorts things, doesn't it?" Kit replied. John cocked his head to the side and gave her a frank look.

"They'll do it for you, m' lady – and your grandmother. Your lady grandmother was much loved by the people of Tresaints, and you, m' lady, you look just like Lady Marjory."

"I do?" Kit shifted in her saddle. "How do you know—"

John broke out in laughter. "That you're Sir Thomas' daughter?" He crossed himself, commending the poor man's soul to the keeping of the saints. "We knew the moment we saw you, all that dark red hair peeping out from under your little coif. Besides, why else would he have installed your lady mother in his childhood home? And now you're the living image of his sainted mother – but in temperament you take after *her* mother, Lady Alicia."

"Lady Alicia?" Kit was intrigued, never having heard anything about her paternal family before. She supposed it was her mother who had forbidden the people of Tresaints to talk to her about her father and his family, depriving her of any roots but the ones Alaïs herself could offer. Was it perhaps Alaïs' subtle way of avenging herself on Sir Thomas for abandoning her? Kit would never know.

"Has not Mabel told you of the time Lady Alicia, a chit of a lass at the time, rode all the way to London to demand that Prince Edward – old Longshanks as was – free her man?"

Kit shook her head.

"The prince had judged Lord Gerald a traitor, accusing him of serving under Simon de Montfort," John continued.

"But he hadn't?"

"He had. But just like your own lord, it was a matter of pledged fealty, of honour. A man has no choice but to follow his chosen lord whence he leads."

Kit nodded gravely. That was how things were ordained in the world: that some men led and others followed. She gestured for John to go on.

"We don't know what she said to the prince, but some months later she came back to Tresaints, with her lord husband. The poor man was in a bad way, having suffered harsh imprisonment for months."

"Oh dear – some sort of family tradition," Kit muttered, making William grin.

"You come from a line of strong women, m' lady," John said. "According to Mabel, too strong. I dare say your grandmother's husband wouldn't agree, and nor would your own."

"Hmm." Kit eyed the bundle that contained Adam. "I think there are days when he would prefer me meeker."

"Always," came the muffled reply. "But I'm not about to complain. Not now."

Chapter 31

They arrived at Tresaints late in the evening of the second day. After one whole day disguised as a corpse, Adam had refused to spend yet another day rolled into the heavy cloaks, and instead had mounted Kit's horse, settling her in front of him. All day, they'd ridden like that, his thighs rubbing against hers, his arm around her waist. A good way of getting accustomed to each other, Kit reflected as she toyed with his fingers, smiling when he pressed her that much closer, close enough that he could kiss her head.

Mabel led the welcoming party, her wrinkled face wreathed in a wide smile as she bowed to Adam, hugged Kit, punched John on his arm and went back to smiling at Adam, commenting that he didn't look as if he'd been fed all that well lately, what with how his clothes hung off his frame.

"Well enough," he protested, but allowed her to drag him off in the direction of the hall, where she and Mall the cook served him chicken cooked in wine and spices, tender greens and roasted lamb, freshly baked bread and cheese, rounding it off with fresh berries. Adam ate. He drank, he ate, he inspected his sleeping son, presented to him by Mabel, he ate some more, and all the time Kit sat glued to his side, her leg pressed to his, her hand on his thigh.

And then, at last, the meal was over. Adam complained of being tired and held out his hand to Kit, leading the way up the stairs to the solar. She was shy. It was close to eight months since he'd last seen her naked – or she him – and her fingers were clumsy on the laces of her clothes. Her mouth was dry, her skin prickled when his fingers brushed her neck, and she had no idea what to do with her eyes when he slowly undressed, revealing a body that was a collection of muscle and sinews, the scar to his flank a dark, bubbly decoration on his pale skin.

"You may look," he said with a tinge of bitterness. "I return to you a lesser man."

Kit shook her head, incapable of speech. Her hands rose of their own accord to smooth their way over his shoulders, down his arms. He was standing with most of his weight on his left leg, still in his braies, and when Kit undid the drawstring his breath hitched. She kept her eyes on his as she knelt before him, tugging the linen garment with her until he was entirely naked. The hair in his groin was a darker shade of fair than that on his head, substantially darker than the fuzz on his chest, on his legs. She ran her hands down his legs, all the way to his feet, and he stiffened. Kit touched first his whole foot, then the damaged one, fingers probing gently as she inspected the discoloured skin, the lumpy bones beneath.

"Don't," he said softly. "Not tonight."

"Not tonight," she agreed, bending low to place a kiss on his foot before allowing her hands and her mouth to travel upwards.

In the bed, and she was now as naked as he was, aware of his eyes on her belly, her breasts. He brushed a finger over her nipple and it hardened, making him smile.

"I wish I had seen you when you were big with child," he said, hands on her belly. "I would have wanted to see my wife, distended with my seed."

"God willing, Tom won't be our only child, will he?" She wanted to give him many sons, many daughters.

"No." He kissed her belly, her mound. He rubbed his face against her, and she relished the sensation of his unshaven cheeks against her skin, his hands on her hips, his mouth on her privates. So many months without him, so many nights wondering if she'd ever have him this close again, feel his weight, the warmth of him.

He loved her slowly, long, steady movements that had her throwing her head back, hands gripping the closest bedpost.

"Look at me," he commanded, so she did, eyes locked on his as he picked up pace, rocking the bed with his thrusts. Suddenly, he pulled out.

"What…"

"Shhh," he said, kissing his way down her body. Sweet Mary and the angels! His fingers, his tongue, and she fragmented, like shards of dazzling coloured glass. He touched her again, and her body nearly rose off the bed.

"Let me," she said, wanting to give him as much as he'd given her. He lay back on the bed, a hand on her head as she touched him and kissed him, tasting herself on his member. He quivered, his buttocks tensed, and wordlessly he urged her on top, holding her steady as she sank down on him. His eyes never left hers, not even when he finally climaxed, mouth open in a silent shout.

"That was…intense." Kit had yet to normalise her breathing, lying side by side with him and holding hands.

"Intense, indeed," he laughed, pulling her closer.

Hours later, and Kit stirred from sleep, a wave of fear rushing through her at finding Adam's half of the bed empty. Had she but dreamt it? But no, he was there, in the room, standing by the un-shuttered windows. Soft, silvery light spilled into the room, causing his shadow to lie like a block of darkness along the floor. In the hearth, the embers of the fire glowed a dull red, but it was the moon that lit up the room, casting everything in pale whites and greys, devoid of any colours.

"It's a full moon," he said when she padded over to join him, shivering slightly in the breeze.

Yes it was, a heavy moon hanging like a giant silver orb over the hills.

"It's beautiful," she said, remembering his promise back at Wigmore.

"As are you, my lady." His mouth came down on hers, his tongue driving into her with force. She clung to him and kissed him back, was lifted onto the top of the window seat, her back pressed against the chilly stone behind her, her feet on the cushion she'd normally sit on. He spread her legs and took her, hard. She gasped when he slammed into her, grinding his pubic bone against hers. Again. Yet again, and Kit held on to his shoulders, his hot breath in her ear, his hair tickling her face. He pounded into her, pinioning her against the wall, until at last he shuddered and groaned into her neck, repeating her name over and over again. Kit smoothed his hair and caressed his naked back, assuring him that she was here, very much here. She squirmed against him. That made him laugh, and he raised his face to look at her.

"I didn't do right by you," he said. No, he most certainly hadn't, leaving her wanting for more. But she didn't care, not really, flattered at being loved so forcefully.

"I once promised you I'd love you in the moonlight," he said, nipping his way down her throat. They were still joined together, her legs round his hips.

"You also said it would be nice and warm," she laughed into his shoulder, "not quite as chilly as this. Look, I have goosebumps." And she did, but she wasn't entirely sure if it was the night air or the things his mouth was doing to her breast that elicited that reaction.

She yelped with surprise when he disentangled himself from her, swooped down and lifted her into his arms, limping towards the bed. Moments later, she was encased in quilts and man, her recent chill totally forgotten as he loved her until all she could do was call out his name, incapable of any other thoughts but those of him.

They lay close together afterwards, him holding her in his arms. His fingers teased at her hair, her face.

"What did they do to you?"

"Not now," Kit said, not wanting to tarnish this night of moonlight with her dark recollections.

"Now." He rose on his elbow. "I have to know."

Kit looked away.

"Kit," he warned, touching the raw scar on her face. With a sigh she turned to face him, haltingly describing that awful meal, the humiliation of being dragged up the stairs towards her bed, knowing full well they intended to violate her.

"But they didn't, and Lord knows that they tried."

"What did you do?" Adam's hand was stroking her back, up and down, as if he were soothing a restless horse.

"I hit Despenser with the chamber pot." Kit snuggled up to him. "It was full." She felt rather than heard his laughter.

"That did not please his lordship much, did it?"

"Being drenched in piss douses your ardour, doesn't it?" she said lightly. But not his spite, she thought, recalling blazing eyes, a mouth twisted into a snarl while he lifted his hand to his bleeding scalp.

Adam shifted, lying on his side so that he could see her eyes. "What did he do?"

"Guy threw me against the wall. That's when I got this." She touched her scar. "And then I jumped out of the window. I don't remember anything after that, but Mabel says they rode off as if the hounds of hell were at their heels, probably convinced they'd killed me." She pressed her good cheek against his chest, searching for the reassuring sound of his heartbeat. "They said they'd make me a widow and then force me to marry Guy."

Adam hissed.

"I would never have married him," Kit continued.

"Of course you would." Adam sounded bleak. "Eventually you would have done as they wanted."

Kit shook her head. "Never." But deep inside, she knew that he was right. They'd have used Tom to force her into submission.

Adam didn't reply, he just drew her closer and kissed the top of her head. "I am so sorry," he said in a tight voice.

"Not your fault," she murmured, loving being able to lie this close to him, even if his chest hairs were tickling her nose.

The moon dipped, casting the room in darkness. Kit was incapable of sleep, so she rose and lit one of her precious candles, setting it on the little table beside the bed. Beside her, Adam was awake but silent, his hands repeatedly touching her, stroking her, as if he needed to reassure himself that she was truly here, not a figment of his imagination.

"Your turn," she said, taking hold of his roving hand and placing it between her breasts.

"My turn what?"

"To tell me." She kissed the tip of his nose in encouragement, eliciting a crooked smile.

"I don't want to."

"I need to know – just like you needed to know."

Adam sighed and rolled onto his back. With his eyes on the roof beams he told her everything, from the humiliating submission before the king, to Despenser's endless visits with his knife. Kit didn't interrupt, she didn't exclaim, she just wept inside at this detailed description of what Despenser had subjected him to. He fell silent after having described how Guy staked his foot.

"Did he ever...you know?" This was the question she should never have asked, but she needed to know just how deep the damage went.

"Did he ever what?" Adam's eyes met hers, daring her to be more specific.

"He said...I know he lies, but all the same, he said that... err...he had had his way with you."

Her husband's frame tensed, every muscle standing like corded rope against his skin. "He did not." His voice was so low she almost couldn't hear him. "But the day Guy drove the mallet through my foot, my Lord Despenser pleasured himself by rubbing his groin against my face. And one day he will pay for that."

"He will pay for much more than that," Kit said, pressing herself to him.

"He will," Adam whispered, "and may the dear Lord grant me the pleasure of being the last face he sees in his sorry life."

Morning came with sun and Mabel, entering unannounced with a wide-awake Tom in her arms. Kit was embarrassed at being found stark naked with her husband, but Mabel seemed not to care, telling them they'd best hurry or they'd be late for mass.

"Give him to me," Adam said, holding out his arms.

Mabel beamed at him. "A big and healthy son, m' lord, and as covered in golden hair as his sire is."

"You make him sound like a bear cub," Kit protested, leaning over Adam's shoulder to smile at her son. "He isn't all that hairy, in fact, he's almost bald."

"Huh." Mabel scooped up used linens, the empty pitcher and left the room, telling them yet again to make haste.

"Am I that hairy?" Adam asked with a little laugh.

"No, you just have all of this lovely, light fuzz, covering your arms, your legs, your chest." She dropped a kiss on one of his shoulders. "Sometimes, it makes you look as if someone dipped you in golden dust."

"That's about the only golden thing about me," he said, his face clouding. "Poor as a pauper, that's me."

"Not all that important at present," Kit said. "And besides, we have my manors, and there's Goliath—"

"Goliath?" His eyes lit up.

"Most certainly Goliath, by now so recovered as to have reverted to his old happy, evil self." Kit rolled her eyes. "The other day he bit Lionel in the…" She broke off. Lionel was gone, dead before the age of seventeen. Kit cleared her throat.

"Yet another thing to add to my ever-growing list of grievances," Adam said darkly. He sighed, settling Tom against his shoulder before reclining against the headboard. Kit just nodded.

"What do you want to do today?" she asked, determined to change the subject. He regarded her in silence, lips brushing back and forth over Tom's head. All the while, his eyes burnt into her, his brows rising. Kit's face heated. "We can't spend all day in bed."

"No?"

"No. Mabel will scold me to death if we do." She rose, found her shift on the floor and slipped it over her head, tugging it into place. "Besides, we have mass to go to, and William will be most upset if we're not there." Her kirtle, her girdle, the veil and the braided circlet she'd made some weeks ago, and she was ready to go, holding out her arms for her son.

Adam pulled on braies and hose, found a clean shirt and looked about for his tunic.

"There." She pointed at the chest. "Your dark blue one is in there somewhere."

The lid squeaked when Adam opened it, and he stood for some moments looking down at the contents. Every single garment she had folded and refolded, smoothing at the fabric while pretending she was touching him. And right at the top was the new tunic she'd made him, in a soft grey fustian with contrasting embroidery decorating the sleeves, the hem and neckline. Miniature love-knots, intertwined As and Ks, and recurring throughout a crescent moon, flanked by two hearts.

"It must have taken you a long time." Adam rubbed his thumb over the embroidered collar.

"Hours spent thinking of you – my happiest hours these last few months." She brushed at his chest, smoothing the heavy cloth into place.

"You never gave up, did you?" he said, studying a sequence of hearts and moons.

"Of course not. You promised me, remember?" She handed him his belt. "We have to run. William has been practising his *Te Deum* for days."

"He has?"

"What? You haven't noticed? He was driving me out of my wits with all his humming on the ride back home."

"As I recall, I spent a large part of the first day rolled in a cloak," Adam said drily. "It muted all sounds."

"How fortunate for you." Kit led the way through the door. "That man couldn't hold a tune if his life depended on it."

"Neither can I." Adam grinned.

"No?" she replied with a wink. "I've never noticed."

Chapter 32

"It doesn't take much, does it?" William commented, coming to sit beside Kit. Some distance away, Adam was going through his daily sword routine, the heavy blade slicing rapidly through the air.

"No – some weeks of sun and fresh air, of good food and exercise, and just like that you have a healthy husband." Not quite as easy, because these days there was a darkness in Adam that had not been there before, and even worse, he preferred not to talk about it, retreating to sit in the chapel or on a nearby hillside with his eyes lost in the distance.

"It's Lord Roger," William said when she shared this with him.

"It's always Lord Roger," Kit retorted. "Now that he feels moderately safe himself, all he seems to think about is his lord – or Lady Joan."

"And you find that strange?"

Kit sighed – loudly. "Of course not." But sometimes she felt jealous, wanting him to focus all his attention on her and their son. "But he isn't safe," she added, throwing an anxious look up the lane. "And I fear what will happen when Guy comes storming down towards the house, intent on claiming me as his wife."

"We've gone through all that." William had taken to the role as captain of the guard with aplomb, running the household through multiple drills so that everyone knew just what to do should they have unwelcome visitors.

The hiding place behind the altar was always kept prepared, and Adam had been shown just how to open it and close it, even if he seemed disturbed by the notion of hiding below ground. When Kit had asked him, he'd waved it away, saying that after close to nine months in the dark he preferred to remain in the light, but she hadn't quite believed him and had gone to William instead, listening in horror when he told her of Adam's childhood experiences in an old well-shaft.

After insistent wheedling, Adam had allowed Kit to perform a thorough inspection of his foot, and as a consequence she had confiscated his shoes and boots, telling him to walk barefoot instead. She could see that it hurt him to do so, but after three days of grim silence he had gruffly admitted to believing she might be right, because no matter that it hurt like hell, he seemed to be regaining some flexibility. Every night, she'd lift his foot up into her lap and knead it, a long session that would start with grunts and muttered protests and generally end with her extending the kneading well beyond his foot – as a reward of sorts.

They slept with open shutters, and as August shifted into September there were nights that became uncomfortably cold, but Adam insisted he wanted to be able to see the sky. Kit didn't protest overmuch. She had Mabel produce pelts and extra quilts, and spent her nights within the safety of her husband's arms.

It was just after Michaelmas when Guy made an appearance. The lad sitting lookout came sprinting down the lane, bare legs blurring, and within seconds the household was rushing to do their respective tasks. One of the maids bounded up into the solar to clear away all signs of a male presence. John hid away Adam's weapons, Mabel and the wet nurse, together with Tom, were boosted onto a horse, disappearing out of sight just as the first unwelcome visitors became visible at the top of the lane. The storage sheds were emptied, foods and wines hidden elsewhere, and in all this commotion Kit hurried after her husband as he made for the chapel, eyes darting all over the place to ensure no one saw just where they went.

"I'll keep the altar candles lit," she whispered once he was hidden below the floor. She heard his muffled "Thank you" and busied herself with lighting the candles from the hour candle William kept burning just inside the door.

Kit knelt on the floor and pretended to pray, while her ears were strained outwards, trying to understand what was happening. Moments later, the door crashed open, and Guy entered, spurs jangling as he strode towards her. She ignored him, her gaze on the wooden crucifix that stood atop the altar. Guy came to stand beside her. She refused to acknowledge him.

"Praying for your departed husband?" he asked, breaking the silence. She glanced up at him, meeting dark eyes that studied her intently.

"My what? I am praying for Adam's continued health." She rose, maintaining her distance from him.

"Haven't you heard?" Guy laughed. "He is dead."

"Dead?" She took a step towards him and slapped him. "How dare you show up here with such vile lies?"

"Lies?" Guy gripped her hand. "I think not, and now, my widowed sister-in-law, you had best resign yourself to becoming my wife."

"I will never be your wife!" She jerked free of his hold. "No one has told me that Adam is dead, so why should I believe you?"

"They said—"

"Said? You expect me to take someone's word for his death?" She placed a hand over her chest. "My heart tells me he is alive, and I believe my heart much more than I believe anything you say." Further helped along by the fact that she knew her husband was lying only yards away, very much alive and breathing.

"Enough of this," Guy growled, making a grab for her. "It is time we finished what I came for last."

"You try, and I will gut you." Kit pulled her dagger, an elegant, slightly curved, Saracen blade. Over the past few weeks, Adam had taught her to wield it, and she held it now as he had taught her. Guy gave her an appraising look and backed away.

"Who taught you to use a dagger?"

"My father," Kit said. "And since last we met, I never go anywhere without one."

"Ah." His eyes flew to her face, lingering on the scar that marred her cheek. "Things got out of hand," he muttered. "I—"

"Silence!" She waved the dagger at him. "As I recall, you were just as hideous as he was – even more, as you're supposed to be some sort of family."

"What is this?" William's voice came from somewhere behind Guy. "Why is there a naked blade in my church?"

"Ask your brother," Kit replied.

"My brother?" William looked at Guy. "I see no brother here."

Guy flushed. "I am come to inform you that Adam is dead."

"And we are of course expected to take your word for it, given that we know you as such an upright, honest man," William replied scathingly. He approached, placing himself between Guy and Kit. "What proof do you have?"

"Proof? I have heard it from the guards at Goodrich."

"And that is nothing but hearsay." William shoved Guy, propelling him towards the exit. "Had he been dead, do you not think we would have heard?"

Guy growled. "Shove me again and I'll—"

"What? Hit me?" William chuckled. "You've never bested me in a fight before, Guy."

"There's always a first, dear brother." Guy set his hands to William's chest and pushed, sending him to the floor in a welter of long garments, bare limbs and sandals. He pointed at Kit. "I'll find you the proof you so desire, and then, dear Katherine, you will become my wife."

"Never!" she spat, shaking her dagger at him. Guy laughed, swept her a bow and was gone.

"Just as we planned it," William said, slowly getting to his feet.

"We're playing with fire," Kit muttered, darting over to door. Guy and his men were already horsed, cloaks fluttering behind them as they set their horses to a canter up the lane.

"Exactly – which is why Guy will now ride to Goodrich, demand that his brother be disinterred, after which he will tell everyone there that this is not his brother." William clucked. "Fool. It would serve him better to fabricate evidence proving Adam is dead, thereby making you a widow, but he is too impetuous to think that far, and so instead he will descend on us again, this time demanding that the traitor be turned over to him, an officer of the king."

There was a grating sound as the floor behind the altar moved, and moments later Adam stood beside them, brushing repeatedly at his sleeves.

"I detest being buried alive," he muttered when he intercepted Kit's look.

"Not buried. Hidden," William said. "Did you hear it all?"

"Everything." Adam stretched out his arm and pulled Kit close. "How long, do you think, before he is back?"

"A week?" William shrugged. "We must ensure your hiding place is adequately stocked, because next time round, Guy will not be quite as easily brushed off. You must prepare yourself, brother – next time, you may need to stay down there for days."

Kit felt the tremor that rushed through Adam, his arm tightening uncomfortably round her waist.

"It's not that small," she said.

Adam released her and moved over towards the door. "Small enough – and dark."

Four days later, Egard came galloping through the gate, on a horse so winded Adam scowled at him before yelling for one of the stable boys to come and see to the poor beast.

"They're coming," Egard said as he slid off the horse. "He is in a mighty rage, yon Guy."

"How many men?" Adam asked.

"Twelve – armed to the teeth."

"Ah."

"We're not about to fight them, are we?" Kit said.

"Not unless we have to." Adam scanned the horizon, but as yet there were no signs of any approaching men. He would have preferred to fight them than to crawl away and hide in a space the size of a large coffin, but the people of Tresaints could put up no resistance against trained men-at-arms.

Already Mabel was rushing the wet nurse towards the saddled rouncey, keeping up a constant chatter that grated on

Adam's ears. He limped over and lifted his son out of Mabel's arms. Tom stared up at him, one small hand waving aimlessly. Adam hugged the child close.

"It'll be all right." Kit joined him, placing a hand on Tom's head. "We just follow the plan."

The plan? Adam lifted Tom higher and blew him gently in the face, laughing when his son gurgled in response.

"Guy might not play the game as we've foreseen," he said, reluctantly handing Tom back to Mabel, now seated behind the wet nurse.

"What can he do?" Kit asked. "He can't very well force me to marry him now that he knows you're alive, and you he will never find." She gave Mabel a little wave, standing back to allow the horse to pass.

"And what if he decides to vent his anger on you – on them?" Adam gestured at the people in the yard. He watched his son retreating out of sight, relieved that he at least was safe.

"He won't," she said, but he could hear the tremor in her voice.

"I can't lie hidden, incapable of helping you should you need it," he hissed as they walked towards the chapel. As always, she stopped just inside the door, greeting the three small stone effigies with a reverence.

"You have to hide," she replied. "It's you he wants to kill, while me he—"

"…Wants to force into his bed," he finished for her, regretting his harsh tone when she blanched, one hand flying up to clutch the cloak tighter round her throat.

"He won't succeed," she told him, wetting her lips. "I'll cut him if he tries."

Adam shook his head. "Guy is a trained knight. That dagger of yours is not much of a protection against a man like that – not now that he knows you carry it."

"Why are you doing this?" She glared at him. "Why do you want to frighten me?"

"You have to be frightened. To underestimate the enemy is to lose." He touched her hair, her cheek, and his fingers lingered over her mouth. "I could hide elsewhere, jump on him as he passes by." Should Guy as much as lay a finger on his wife, Adam would tear him to pieces, limb by limb, no matter what it might ultimately cost him.

"Twelve men, Adam." She gestured towards the altar. "Either you hide there, or you take to the moors. Those are the only options." Raised voices from the bailey made her start, turning to him with huge eyes. "They're here!" She tugged at him. "For God's sake, Adam, hide!"

She was trembling all over when she knelt behind the altar, hand all but disappearing into the crack that hid the lever. The floor moved.

"Go on!" She was breathless, pushing at him. From outside came the sound of booted feet, and with a last, brief kiss, Adam slid into the hole, shivering inside when the floor closed above him. He heard her footsteps tip-tapping over the floor, there was a creak as she opened the door followed by a soft thud as it closed, and then he was alone.

Enough light filtered through the narrow cracks to allow him to make out his surroundings, find the foodstuffs and the water skins. But the space was cramped, the ceiling too low to allow him to stand, and already after a couple of moments he was aware of his breathing, his pulse, unbearably loud in the silence of this tomblike space. He retreated to lie on the pallet and concentrated on flexing his damaged foot up and down, the resulting discomfort distracting him for a while.

The door opened again, followed by the footsteps of a man. Adam strained his ears for other sounds that might reveal who was moving about overhead. There was a swish of heavy fabric, a grunt, and suddenly the light was gone.

"He is enraged," William murmured. Adam held his tongue, mindful of the instruction that he should never respond, in case it was a trap. His brother had to be kneeling just above him, the dark cloth of his habit effectively blocking out the light. "She, however, is playing the overjoyed wife with aplomb." William chuckled. "She even thanked him for bringing him such good tidings. Guy looked about to disintegrate."

Adam cursed silently. His Kit could at times be too

provocative, and she would be better served by not riling Guy unnecessarily.

"I'll see her safe," William promised as he got to his feet. How? Adam wanted to yell. "I do know how to wield a sword," William said, as if in reply to Adam's silent question. Adam almost laughed. His brother was a man who abhorred violence, but he knew for a fact that William could swing a sword, should he have to.

Hours of silence, and then the door was yet again pulled open, this time followed by the sound of many booted feet.

"Look everywhere," Guy commanded.

"Everywhere?" Kit sounded scornful. "That won't take you long."

There were a series of loud sounds as chests were opened, benches were moved. Adam heard his brother curse. "Where is he?"

"I have no idea, but I aim to ride myself to Pembroke and demand that he explain himself," Kit said.

"Pembroke! It is him who's spirited him away," Guy snarled.

"Then why are you looking here?" Kit asked. Adam heard the rustle of her heavy skirts as she approached the altar.

"Because I think he did it with your collusion," Guy said. "Quite the coincidence, is it not, that you come riding to Goodrich, and as I hear it, Adam dies the day after? Even more of a coincidence, I ride to Goodrich and demand to see the corpse and what do I find but this?" A small object skittered across the floor. "That's not Adam's, that's Lionel's crucifix! And from what I could see it was Lionel, not Adam, in that hastily dug grave."

"Lionel?" Kit produced a gasp. "Is Lionel dead?"

"Don't give me that! You know he is, which brings me back to my original supposition. You sneaked Adam out of Goodrich, and therefore he is hidden here, somewhere." There was a flurry of skirts, a scuffle and a suppressed whimper. "On your feet, woman. We go to search the rest of these sorry buildings, and we will keep on searching until we find him."

"Let go of me!"

"Not likely." Yet again the sound of footsteps, of someone being dragged along. The door banged. Adam stuck his hands into his armpits, struggling with the overwhelming urge to push the lever just above his head and leap out of his hiding place, sword in his hand as he rushed to protect his wife.

"Twelve," he muttered to himself. "You can't take on twelve men on your own." With a moan, he covered his face with his hands. Never had he felt so utterly useless.

Two days later, and Kit was exhausted. Guy prowled like an enraged wolf, forcing her to accompany him on every single futile search. Her home was a mess, every chest, every barrel emptied in Guy's determined search for Adam. The only upside was that at present Guy was too focused on finding his brother to do more than talk about what he would do to her – once Adam had been adequately dispatched. Kit pressed her hands to her side in an effort to stop them from trembling as Guy approached her, eyes raking her up and down.

"If we stay here long enough, he will starve in whatever hiding place you've got for him," he said with a smirk.

Kit rolled her eyes. "How many times must I tell you? He isn't here!"

"And how many times must I reply that I do not believe you?" He grinned, took hold of her arm and lifted her to her feet. "And I also have a good idea of where this hiding place is."

He frogmarched her across the yard, opened the door to the chapel and flung her inside. October sun filtered in through the glassed window, patterning the floor with greenish light, and on the altar two candles were burning, as they'd been burning constantly since Guy and his men arrived.

"Somewhere here," Guy said, breaking the peaceful silence.

"Here?" Kit snorted.

"You spend an inordinate amount at prayers," Guy commented, pacing up and down the little space.

"I pray for my husband – and my son."

He frowned at her. He had not been happy to find Tom gone, and had spent several hours last night detailing just what future he had planned for her son – once Kit was married to him. She swallowed. Poor Tom was destined for a monastery, Guy had told her, and it would be his sons, not Adam's, who inherited her lands.

"He's here, somewhere." Guy stamped at the floor. "I wonder if he can get out on his own?" he mused, strolling round the bare walls. "And if he can, what do I need to do to make him do so?" He gave her an amused look. "Will he lie still, do you think, while I ravish you?"

"This is a church!" she said, retreating from him.

"This is where you've hidden him!" he snapped, and just like that he was on her, dragging her to the floor.

She fought him in silence, groping for her dagger.

"You'll not pull a blade on me again." His hand closed over her wrist, banged it down hard against the floor. Kit gasped and the dagger clattered against the floor, out of reach. She heaved, she bit, she hit at his face, at his arms, but he had her pinned to the floor, her skirts shoved up to lie around her waist. Guy laughed when she tried to kick him, and there he was, his swollen groin pressing against hers. He undid his braies, tugged and grunted, holding her immobile by the simple expedient of twisting his hand in her hair and pulling it tight. She couldn't breathe, and now she could feel him, his engorged member prodding at her. Oh God; this was happening for real, and soon...She bit his ear, he howled and slapped her, twice, so hard that her head bounced against the floor.

He was gone. Kit blinked, tried to sit up. Guy was some feet away, struggling to his feet, while Adam was looming above him, bare hands clenched.

"Adam..." She tried to call his name, wanting to warn him that Guy was armed, but her voice didn't carry.

Guy pulled his dagger and grinned. "And so we meet again." He swiped at Adam, who backed away, clumsy in his movements. Two days below the floor must have left him stiff, and when Guy rushed him, Adam stumbled, put too much weight on his right foot, and went down.

"Here!" Kit sent her dagger sliding over the floor towards him. Guy's boot stomped down on it before it reached its target, and suddenly he had two daggers, one in each hand, albeit that his left hand couldn't quite close round the hilt. Adam rose, ducked Guy's daggers and punched him, causing Guy to stagger. A blade glinted in the sunlight, it swooped down and Adam cursed, clutching at his bleeding arm.

"I will kill you," Adam said in a low voice, circling Guy. "If I have to rip your heart out with my bare hands, I will kill you."

"You can try," Guy retorted. He lunged, Adam feinted to the right and brought up his left leg, slamming his knee into Guy, who staggered back. Adam came after, limping badly, and from Guy came a series of whistling sounds as he attempted to draw air into his lungs. Adam kicked at Guy's left arm, and one of the daggers clattered to the floor.

Blood stained Adam's tunic, it coloured his hand. When he bent to retrieve the knife, Guy howled and threw himself at him. Adam went down, with Guy on top. Kit kicked Guy hard, took hold of his leg and tugged – enough that Guy was distracted, and with a grunt Adam rolled them over. His fists flew, thudding into Guy's face. Guy snarled and gave as good as he got, squirming like a giant eel in an effort to dislodge Adam.

Up they came, both of them breathing heavily. Guy was till gripping his dagger, and Adam lowered his head like a bull about to charge. Guy sneered, using his free hand to beckon Adam on. Kit threw Adam a concerned look. Her man had all his concentration focused on Guy, every muscle in his body quivering. Guy laughed, but it came out high and breathless. He waved his dagger at Adam.

"Come then, big brother," he jeered. "Let us finish this, once and for all." But Adam did not budge, his piercing gaze never leaving his brother. "What? Afraid of me?" Guy said, his voice loud in the stillness of the chapel. Adam just shook his head, and for an instant his eyes darted over to the candlesticks on the altar. Kit tried to sidle closer, but a small shake of his head had her staying put. And then, at last, Adam struck. In a series of swift movements he grabbed the closest candlestick, leapt straight up in the air and brought the candlestick down on Guy's head. A crunch. Another crunch; the sickening sound of something hard splintering. Adam was standing over Guy, and on the floor Guy was crawling weakly, the back of his head reduced to a bloody pulp. There was a gurgling sound and Guy stilled.

The door slammed open, and Adam whirled, the bloodied candlestick held aloft.

"Dearest Lord!" William's face was ashen. "What have you done?" he said, sinking to his knees beside Guy. "Did you have to kill him? Here, in God's presence?" He lifted Guy into his arms, cradling him to his chest.

"I had no choice," Adam said in a low voice. William did not seem to hear, his voice rising in a wail.

"Shh!" Kit frowned at him. There was blood everywhere. On the floor, on the altar cloth, on Adam's boots. "We have to hide him, clean this up. If his men find him, we're all dead." She knelt beside William, tried to unlock his hold on Guy. "Help me, William. Any moment they'll come looking." He gave her a vacant look, then raised his eyes to Adam, who was standing awkwardly, one sleeve drenched in blood.

"Are you all right?" William asked, sounding like his normal self.

"Well enough." Adam gestured at the hole in the floor. "We will have to put him there, with me." He grimaced, bent over and took hold of Guy's legs, dragging him backwards. William got to his feet, slowly, and went over to help him, face averted from the body. Someone called for Guy in the yard, called again. Kit dropped to her knees and used her cloak to scrub at the thick smear of blood Guy's massacred head left behind, while whispering to Adam and William that they had to hurry.

There – Guy landed in the hole, and Adam lowered himself inside after him. Kit just had to touch him, extending her hand until their fingers grazed. The floor slid into place. Yet another voice, calling for Guy. Men outside the chapel's door, the unmistakeable sound of the door being pulled open. Kit bundled the bloodied altar cloth together and hid it under her skirts, sinking down on her knees before the altar with William by her side.

Chapter 33

Guy's men went into a frenzy at his disappearance. They tore Tresaints apart in their determined search for their master, but after four days they gave up. By then, Kit was a wreck and the chapel reeked of all the incense they kept burning to mask the rather more offensive stench of a corpse. Most of all, Kit feared for Adam, stuck below ground with dwindling food reserves and his dead brother for company.

"He's here somewhere," Guy's sergeant said on the day of their departure.

"So you say." Kit shrugged disinterestedly. "Personally, I think he's not. Last I saw, he was riding off in that direction." She waved vaguely to the south, congratulating herself yet again on having had the foresight of having William spirit Guy's horse away while she kept Guy's men busy searching the house.

"But why would he just leave?"

"I have no idea."

The man looked unconvinced. "He would have told me."

"He should have told you," Kit agreed. "But Guy is an unpredictable man."

By the time William judged it safe to allow Adam out of the hole, he was a pale copy of himself, telling them in no uncertain terms that he would never hide there again. Never. Without a further word, he'd held out his hand to Kit and led her to the solar, where he had submitted her to a very thorough inspection, relaxing only once he had verified that she was, in fact, unharmed by Guy's attack – well, beyond the nasty bump to her head.

For the days that followed, Adam kept a constant guard on the lane, and only once the weather turned truly bad, with day after day of ice-cold winds and rain, did he relax. At night, he slept with his unsheathed sword by the bed, loving Kit to sleep with a fierce passion that left her disjointed and spent, her sweaty body pressed close to his. One early morning he told her of his father, a slow and halting description of those childhood terrors that still haunted the adult man – her man. Spending several days underground in close proximity to a corpse had not helped, at least to judge from the expression on his face.

Guy's body was smuggled out of the chapel by William, who took it upon himself to ensure Guy was properly buried. He was gone for three days, returning drenched to the skin and silent. The day after, he took hold of Adam and led him over to the chapel, insisting that this time Adam would have to make his confession to him, right now.

Adam looked pale and tense afterwards. William had given him a heavy penance, saying that Adam's immortal soul had been severely soiled by the recent events.

"How can you say that?" Kit demanded. "Guy was the one at fault in all this, not Adam."

"He murdered his brother," William retorted. "No matter how provoked, that is a grievous sin."

"And if he hadn't killed him, Guy would have killed him!"

"Which would have been as grievous a sin." William sighed. "I know why Adam did as he did, but it doesn't take away the fact that he took a life."

"I think he is wrong," Kit told Adam, sinking down to lie beside him. No more nights of lying looking at the moon – by now it was far too cold for such romantic gestures.

"He is the priest, sweeting." Adam peeled off her shift and pulled her close, murmuring as he always did that he wanted to feel her skin against his.

"I don't want you to feel guilt – not over Guy." She snuggled up as close as she could, one leg draped over his.

"I don't. So maybe William is right, I must pray for forgiveness." He tugged at her braid. "No more talk about this."

William took to walking about with a severe expression on his face, insisting both Adam and Kit join him as he prayed for

Guy's soul, hours upon hours spent kneeling on the hard floor of the chapel. Adam humoured him – to a point, which led to heated discussions which always ended with William flouncing out to spend yet another night in vigil.

It was therefore something of a relief when two men rode in some days later, dressed in the black robes of friars. William rushed to meet them, and very soon Adam was included in the group as well, his fair head nodding in agreement with what the older of the friars was saying.

"Who is that?" Kit asked Mabel. The old woman was watching their visitors intently.

"That," she said, gesturing at the older of the friars, "is Richard Judas."

"Judas?" Kit suppressed the urge to cross herself.

"A most unfortunate name for a chaplain," Mabel said.

"A most unfortunate name no matter your profession." Now that Kit looked closer, she recognised the man from Wigmore. Lady Joan had always held him in the highest of regards, and Kit had supposed he'd stayed with his mistress to the end.

"He's a priest," Mabel reminded her when Kit expressed her surprise at seeing Richard Judas here when he should have behind lock and key. "The far more interesting question is why he is riding about disguised as a friar." She squinted at the other man. "And that, if I'm not mistaken, is one of Bishop Orleton's men."

William came bouncing towards them, as eager as a greyhound before the chase. "I'm leaving," he said.

"Now?" Kit shivered in a gust of cold autumn air.

"Now." He beamed at her. "Lady Joan has suggested that I may be of help to Lord Roger."

"Really? How?" She studied the supposed friars. It was a good disguise, allowing them to travel unquestioned throughout the realm.

"I shall be a friar too." William grinned. "A friar that keeps his eyes and ears open at all times."

"Oh." She touched his hand, ever so gently. "And what about us?"

"You will be all right. Adam is fully recovered, and Mabel—"

"Not them! What about me?" She gave him a little smile. "You're my friend, William. How am I to cope without you?"

William ducked his head, fiddling with the frayed end of the rope he used as a belt. "I am sure you will manage." He raised his face. "I am called to help our baron and his lady. I must go – I want to go." Yet again, she caught that look of eager anticipation in his eyes. "For once, the lad Mortimer so generously helped become a priest may be of use."

Kit could but smile at his enthusiasm. "Go with God, William. But please be careful – we need you too."

Tresaints was strangely empty without its resident priest. Not until William had left did Kit realise just how important a presence he'd become in her life, a constant companion during all those months when Adam was gone to fight or otherwise inaccessible to her.

"I miss him," she said with a shrug when Mabel came to find her in the chapel, where she was yet again praying for William's safety.

"So do we all." Mabel handed her Tom, all wet hands and a slobbering mouth. "He's teething."

"I can see that." Kit offered her finger to her son, who clamped down on it. "Will he be all right?"

"Hmm? Oh, William." Mabel produced a wooden rattle and handed it to Tom, who gripped it and banged it enthusiastically on Kit's head. "Of course he will. And he's not defenceless in himself, for all that he is a priest. " She lit a candle and muttered a hasty prayer. "As I hear it, they are making for London."

"Yes."

"For the best, I think. Guy's death drove a wedge between William and Sir Adam. Time apart may heal the rift."

"I hope so." Kit reclaimed her finger. "I'm glad he's dead," she added in a lower voice. "I'd have hated it, knowing he was out there." She wiped her free hand down her skirts. "He almost—"

"But he didn't," Mabel said, patting her on her arm. She cocked her head to the side and frowned. "Horses – many horses."

Kit almost ran outside.

The Earl of Pembroke was wet and covered in mud. He dismounted with a loud grunt, handed the reins to Egard and walked stiffly towards Kit.

"My lord." She bowed, son in arms.

"My lady." He looked happy somehow, and even more so when he snapped his fingers at his clerk, Peter, who winked at Kit before handing Earl Aymer a large roll from which dangled several seals. "Is your husband not here?"

"My husband?" Kit gave him a hesitant look. "He is in your custody, my lord."

"Not anymore." Pembroke grinned. "This is a pardon for Adam de Guirande, granting him his life and freedom. A small redress for the treatment he was subjected to while a royal prisoner." He looked surprised when Kit clasped his hand and sank to her knees, kissing his hand repeatedly between a series of loud thank-yous.

"And my lands?" Adam's voice was frosty, his eyes decidedly chilly when they settled on Kit. She released the earl's hand and went over to her husband.

"You've got straw in your hair," she whispered, but he just shrugged.

"Your lands remain with the crown – for now," Pembroke said, handing Adam the deed.

"So it is only half a pardon," Adam said.

"Adam!" Kit pinched his thigh, hard. He didn't even twitch, but the look he gave her from under his lashes promised retribution – later.

"It is better than nothing," Pembroke said with a frown. "Queen Isabella and I had to work hard to get this much."

"My apologies, my lord." Adam bowed low. "I am most grateful for your efforts."

"Hmph!" Pembroke seemed less than mollified.

"Truly," Adam said, bowing yet again. "Is the queen doing well?" he asked as he straightened up.

Pembroke pursed his mouth. "Not an entirely happy queen at present, despite having twisted Despenser's nose sorely out of joint with that pardon."

"And my lord? Have you any news of my lord?"

Pembroke's frown deepened. "Be careful, man. That pardon you hold requires you to forsake all previous loyalties and hold only to the queen."

"Not to the king?" Adam scanned the roll.

"No. It wasn't him who wrote it," Pembroke said, grinning. "He just signed and sealed it, after a rather sweet little scene with a weeping and distraught queen. She even played her trump card."

Adam nodded. "Scotland."

"Oh yes, Scotland. Queen Isabella will never let her liege live down the danger he put her in."

As Kit recalled it, the queen had accompanied her husband on his recent campaign against the Scots, and had somehow become separated from the main force, which had then retreated, leaving the queen and her retinue stranded just south of the Scottish border. She'd had to flee for her life, and two of her women had died in the fracas.

"And Lord Roger?" Adam asked, making Kit roll her eyes discreetly. Baron Mortimer cast a gigantic shadow over her husband, and now that Adam was well on the way to recuperation he had begun to speak much more frequently about his beloved lord and what he could do to help him.

"As well as can be expected – alive, at least." Pembroke rubbed his hands together. "It is mightily cold outside, don't you think?"

Adam flushed. "My apologies, Lord Aymer. May I be honoured with your presence in my hall?"

"About time," Peter muttered as he passed Kit. But he said it with a smile, so she smiled back.

Having an earl visit was hard work. First, Pembroke demanded mulled wine and ale for his men, then he handed over his soiled garments for immediate cleaning. He inspected the hall with a pursed mouth and told Adam that it would do – for one night – so he wouldn't claim the solar for his own.

"Our solar?" Kit whispered to Adam. "Why would he take our bed?"

"He's an earl, I am but a lowly knight," Adam replied in an undertone.

"But when Despenser was here—" Kit broke off. Despenser had never demanded the solar.

"He was expecting to spend his night there anyway – with you," Adam said harshly. She stepped away from him, overwhelmed by memories she worked so hard to keep at bay. Despenser leering, Guy blocking her escape, Despenser's face above hers as he pinned her to the bed, Guy shoving her legs apart, Guy dead on the floor…

Kit took a deep breath; she took two. Adam raised a hand to her face.

"It didn't happen, sweeting."

"No, but it was very close."

He just shrugged and ran a light finger over her scar, his eyes dark and soft.

Earl Aymer interrupted all this by calling for more wine and victuals. Kit ran like a harried mother hen from her hall to the kitchen, to her cellar, back to the kitchen and then one last dash through the rain back to the hall.

The men had seated themselves at the high table, but upon her appearance Adam beckoned for her to join them, so she slid in beside the earl, who gave her a brief smile, before continuing with his conversation.

"Old Lord Chirk is doing poorly," he said in passing, and Kit felt Adam stiffen beside her.

"Why?" Adam asked, using his knife to spear a dried fig. "Is he being mistreated?"

"He is old." Pembroke sighed. "Old, and ill-treated, and that leg wound he got back at Bridgnorth has never healed. He'll never see the outside world again, poor man – he'll die inside those walls."

Adam crossed himself and muttered a hasty prayer.

"If Despenser has his wish, so will Mortimer," Pembroke said. "But his gallant squire, Richard de Monmouth, is ever at his side. I hear it they take turns sleeping."

Kit shivered. "Why?"

"Why?" Pembroke gave her a patronising smile. "Because the smiler with the knife prefers to come and go unseen."

Next morning, Kit's daily communion with absent William was interrupted by the soft treads of someone trying to approach unnoticed. Kit retreated to stand just behind the chapel door, but was relieved when the person who entered was Peter, the earl's clerk.

"Can I help you?" she asked, thinking that was a foolish question to ask a man educated by the church in a chapel.

"Maybe." He dug into his sleeve and produced a folded document, wrapped in twine and sealed. "For your husband. But best not give it to him until Lord Aymer leaves." Light eyes regarded her steadily. "My lord is oversensitive when it comes to his duties to the king – as my lady queen well knows." He flitted away as silently as he had entered.

Kit was in two minds. Should she hand the letter to her husband or should she throw it away? She retreated to the privy and turned it over and over, trying to guess at its contents. Somehow, she suspected it would place her husband in danger, and as his wife she had an obligation to keep him safe. She held the missive over the privy pit and tried to convince herself it would be the right thing to let it drop into the stinking slurry below, but with a deep sigh she ordered her clothes and went to find him, knowing he would never forgive her if she kept the letter from him.

Adam read the letter, read it again and threw it on the table.

"What?" she asked. In response, he gestured at the letter, inviting her to read it. The queen kept things brief: Mortimer was alive and would so remain if she had anything to do with it. Queen Isabella seemed more concerned about his mental health than his physical state, but concluded that Mortimer had the fortitude required to bear his present reduced state.

"Close to a year," Adam said, interrupting Kit halfway through her reading. "A man like that, locked away from the sun and the wind – it's cruel, it's like caging an eagle." He took the letter from her and threw it into the fire, watching it burn with a concerned frown.

"But at least he's alive," Kit tried.

"For now." He poured himself some wine. "I…" With a frustrated sound he broke off.

"Yes?"

He scrubbed at his hair. "There's nothing I can do! The man who took me in when I was close to death, who gave me a home and a place at his side, and now he is laid low and I can do nothing – nothing! – to help him." The earthenware mug was sent flying, shattering when it hit the wall. "I would not have been here without him – I'd not have you as my wife, this as my home, if it weren't for him." With a groan he collapsed into a nearby chair, beckoning her towards him.

"Hmm," Kit said, thinking that Lord Mortimer had been acting out of self-interest when he proposed Adam de Guirande as a suitable husband for Katherine de Monmouth. Adam threw her a look.

"I know," he muttered, pulling her into his lap. "I am more fortunate in you than he intended, but all the same—"

"You love him," Kit finished for him.

"Yes." He tightened his hold on her. Kit brushed at his hair, sweeping it off his face.

"He'll be fine," she said, kissing his brow.

"Fine? How can he be fine, when at any moment the king could have him killed?"

"But he can't. He's pardoned him his life."

Adam gave her a sharp look. "You're such an innocent at times. Did you not hear Lord Aymer yesterday? Lord Roger and Richard take turns sleeping – they have to!"

"But would the king—"

"Of course he would! Or rather, Despenser is not a fool – on matters such as these, he ensures he has his royal master's approval before he proceeds."

"He's not much of a king, is he?" Kit said with a sigh, leaning into him.

"No. But he is the king, and as he has so clearly shown us all these last few months, a vengeful king is a dangerous king."

"So what does the queen want you to do?" Kit asked.

"Nothing."

Kit slumped, breath escaping her in a loud exhalation.

"For now," he added. "I shall be ready when she calls for me."

Kit made a face. It seemed Roger Mortimer and this unknown queen were going to have a major influence on their future lives.

Chapter 34

There was something very sensual about sharing a bath – especially when it was done before a roaring fire, with wine goblets at hand and handfuls of dried rose petals and lavender sprigs in the water. Kit slid deeper into the water and studied her husband, who seemed half-asleep, arms slung over the rim of the tub, head pillowed against the edge. For the first time in days she felt warm, weeks of rain having transformed into sleet and snow, the freezing temperatures chilling the house to the point where Kit felt compelled to wear a cloak while indoors.

These last few nights she'd kept the heavy bed-hangings tightly drawn, trying to extend her time in the warmth of her bed well beyond the limits of propriety – at least according to Mabel.

A foot sneaked up her legs, big toes caressing her inner thigh. Kit smiled. Winter and cold did have some very tangible advantages, one of them being the undivided attention of her husband for long periods of time.

"Come here." Strong hands closed on her wrists and tugged her through the water, until she was settled between his legs, reclining against his chest.

"You have such beautiful skin," he murmured, stroking her nape, her shoulder, with a finger. "As soft as fine vellum."

"I hope you're not thinking of flaying me and writing a book on it," she replied, almost purring when he massaged her shoulders.

"No. I prefer it like this, pink with life and heat." He nibbled at her ear, making her squeal. Arms like iron bands held her still as he kissed his way down her neck. She relaxed against him and closed her eyes, luxuriating in his proximity.

"Do you think we should call for more hot water?" she asked, wanting to extend their bath for as long as possible.

"No. The tub is too full as it is. Why? Are you cold?" A light finger traced patterns on her back, down her arm.

"Not yet." She wriggled until she was face to face with him instead, sitting astride his lap. "You taste good," she informed him, releasing his mouth.

"Do I now?" His hands rose to her head, cupping it gently as he did his own tasting. "So do you," he said, allowing her a second or two to breathe before he kissed her again, hands sliding down to her bottom to lift her that much closer.

"M' lord?" Mabel almost fell in through the door. "Riders – and they ride under Despenser's colours."

"What?" Adam rose so abruptly Kit fell backwards into the tub, water cascading onto the floor. Mabel glanced at his member, went the colour of a scalded ham, and threw him a linen towel.

"That will have to wait," she told them and retreated outside. 'That' had already wilted, Adam cursing as he limped about the room, picking up his clothes.

"What does he want?" Kit tugged on her chemise, pulled hose up her damp legs, and struggled with her garters, her fingers all of a sudden clumsy and uncooperative.

"I don't think he's here to celebrate Candlemas," Adam told her, pulling her skirts down. "Your hair," he added, looking about for his new boots.

At the door to the solar she came to a halt. "I…" She threw an anguished look at Adam. "I'm not sure I can do this. To see him here, where he…" She choked. Adam took her hand.

"I'm here this time, sweeting." He brushed at her scar. "I'll kill him if he hurts you again." This was not much of a comfort, filling Kit's head with images of an enraged, bloodied Adam, being dragged away in chains. He kissed her brow. "It will be fine, Kit. Had he intended to apprehend me, his men-at-arms would already be in here."

She gripped his tunic and rested her forehead against his chest, taking deep gulps of air.

"It will be fine," she repeated. She straightened up. "Fine." She even managed a wobbly smile.

By the time they entered the hall, Despenser was already there, seated in the large armchair usually reserved for Adam. With relief, Adam noted Despenser had not come alone. Standing some feet away, Pembroke was warming his hands by the fire, while his clerk, devious Peter, was lounging against a wall. Peter looked up, caught Adam's eyes and nodded once.

"My lord." Adam made a point of greeting Earl Aymer first, a low reverence in his direction. Kit swept the earl a deep reverence before turning to incline her head in greeting to Despenser. In her dark kirtle and her linen veil, she looked most respectable, not as much as a strand of hair visible. It was difficult to believe that not yet half an hour ago she'd been naked and wet, all warm pink skin and damp hair.

"And what brings you here, my lords?" Adam asked, once his guests had been served mulled wine.

"Oh, I was but passing by," Despenser said, "so I decided to drop in on Aymer here."

"Passing by, my lord?" Kit raised her brows. "Bristol is not precisely down the road, is it?"

Despenser frowned. "And how does Lady de Guirande know I was in Bristol?"

"Why shouldn't I know? Is it a secret?" Kit sipped at her wine. Adam gave her a warning look. No need to let Despenser know there was an entire flock of little spies who kept track of his movements.

"But why are you here, Lord Despenser?" Adam asked. "Goodrich Castle is a good two days' ride from here."

"Ah, yes." Despenser held out his goblet for a refill. "There is the matter of Guy de Guirande's murder."

"His murder?" Adam felt a wave of ice-cold fear wash through him. Had they found Guy's body?

"What other reason can there be for his absence? He's been gone for nigh on four months!" Despenser broke off a piece of cheese and studied it closely before grimacing and throwing it to the floor. A pity, as Kit had once told Adam certain types of cheese mould could be lethal to ingest.

"So you don't know if he's dead," Kit put in, politely serving Despenser some bread.

"I don't have a body, but that doesn't mean I don't know he is dead."

"Really, my lord?" Kit brushed some crumbs from her sleeve. "Have you been communing with his restless ghost?"

Adam suppressed a grin, torn between irritation and admiration for his wife, who seemed not to understand just how dangerous it was to goad this man.

"What sacrilegious nonsense is this?" Pembroke said, giving Kit a displeased look. "Ghosts, Lady Katherine?"

"But how else would Lord Despenser know?" Kit asked, face arranged into a mask of innocence.

"I know it because the man disappeared. Here one day, gone the next – or so his closest man tells me."

"I know," Kit sighed. "A true mystery."

"Even more of a mystery when one considers the fact that Guy's disappearance coincides with your husband's return from the dead."

"I'm not sure I understand." Kit pulled her brows together.

"Someone gave out that Adam de Guirande was dead!" Despenser hissed.

"That would be me," Lord Pembroke said, popping an almond fritter into his mouth. "I was tired of the repeated attempts on my prisoner's life, and so..." He gave Despenser a sly smile. "It worked, did it not? And now here he is, our Adam, and with a royal pardon at that."

Despenser looked as if he'd been force-fed cow dung. "Royal pardon? Edward is far too lenient, and if it hadn't been for that conniving wife of his—"

"The queen," Peter said loudly, glaring at Despenser. "Our liege's wife is our most beloved queen, is that not so, Lord Despenser?"

"A foreigner," Despenser spat.

"The mother of our future king," Pembroke said sternly. "Best you keep that in mind, Hugh. Edward of Windsor is most fond of his mother."

For once, Despenser seemed at a loss for words. Dark eyes studied them all in turn, lingering a bit too long on Kit before locking down on Adam. "So where is he?"

"Guy?" Adam shrugged. "I have no idea, my lord. But I hope for his sake that he stays well away from me. I have matters to settle with him."

Despenser chuckled. "Does it still hurt?" He gestured at Adam's foot.

"No," Adam lied. "But the memory of seeing my brother slam the stake through it does."

"You didn't see it. You fainted – well, not immediately, for which I am most grateful, as it would have interrupted such an enjoyable moment for me." Despenser winked and Adam fought down the urge to throttle him there and then. Despenser leaned forward and lowered his voice. "Best you keep well away from your beloved baron, dear Adam. Otherwise who knows? You may yet again find yourself the recipient of my tender affections." He placed a hand on Adam's sleeve, fingers moving insinuatingly. Adam willed himself not to move, not to flinch. "Now we both know I would enjoy it – but I am not so sure you would."

"More wine, my lord?" Kit sloshed wine into Despenser's cup, interposing herself between them.

Despenser laughed. "Such a protective wife you have, Adam dearest." He took hold of Kit's kirtle and pulled her close. "And she smells like a summer garden, doesn't she?"

Kit yanked her skirts free. "You most certainly don't, my lord."

"A bath," Despenser said with a little sigh. "That's what I need. And you, Lady Katherine, will be my bather."

"Your what?" Kit retreated so abruptly she overbalanced and sat down heavily in Adam's lap.

He folded his arms round her waist and held her still. "My wife will not perform such services for you, my lord," he said calmly. "I'll not have her anywhere close to her would-be rapist."

Lord Aymer's bushy brows came down in a dark frown. "Is this true, Lady Katherine?"

Kit just nodded, clutching at Adam's arm.

"Her word against mine," Despenser snorted. "What is to say she didn't offer herself to me?"

"Your reputation?" Pembroke suggested acerbically. "Is that how you got that scar?" he asked Kit, who once again just nodded. Pembroke spat in the rushes. "Best enjoy yourself while you can, Hugh, because one day all your sins will come back to haunt you."

"Really?" Despenser drawled, but he looked discomfited, his plump mouth wet and twitching. "I have an excellent confessor, dear Aymer. He ensures I am kept constantly shriven, my soul as white as driven snow."

"And who said I was talking about the afterlife?" Pembroke asked.

Despenser rose, dark eyes narrowed in anger. "Beware, Lord Aymer. You are speaking to the royal chamberlain, your king's most trusted advisor."

Kit cleared her throat. "Kings die, my lord. Best keep that in mind."

"And that, Lady Katherine, is borderline treasonous," Despenser snarled.

"It is? I was but pointing out a fact. All men die – eventually."

"Which brings us back to the matter of dear, dead Guy, does it not?" Despenser said, and Adam had to admire him for this drastic change of subject.

"Not dear Guy, not in this house. Nor is he dead Guy – unless you've found his body." Adam steadied Kit to her feet and rose, standing to look down at Despenser. "I would prefer it if you leave, my lord. Your presence here unsettles my lady wife – understandably, don't you think?"

Despenser rose, but no matter that he pulled himself up straight he was a good half-head shorter than Adam. "It isn't wise to antagonise me," Despenser said.

"It isn't wise to threaten me or mine," Adam retorted.

Despenser brought his boot down – hard – on Adam's damaged foot. For some seconds, all Adam felt was pain, his leg nearly folding under him. He could hear his own breath, whistling in and out of his nose, tears stung at his eyes, and his foot howled in agony.

"Hugh!" Pembroke roared, shoving Despenser backwards.

"Adam!" Kit's voice was low, her arms tight around him.

Despenser straightened up and brushed his disarrayed clothes into place. "Always a pleasure, dear Adam," he snickered, before bowing to Kit. With a curt command to his men he left, the heavy door to the hall banging closed in their wake.

Pembroke sat down with a grunt. Adam limped over to a nearby chair and collapsed, scowling a no at Kit when it seemed she intended to pull off his boot and inspect the damage. He flexed his toes and bit back on a gasp.

"He'll pay," Pembroke said. "The good Lord will hold that serpent of a man accountable."

"Let's hope it happens sooner rather than later." Kit sat down as close as she could to Adam and slipped her hand into his, hiding their clasped hands under her skirts.

"At present, Despenser rules this land." Pembroke gestured for Peter to serve him some more wine. "No one dare oppose him, for fear of losing their lives."

"Except for the queen," Adam said softly.

"Ah yes, except for the queen." Pembroke's mouth settled into a grim line. "She best beware. Despenser drips poison into the royal ear, and the king regards his wife with much less favour now than he did a year ago."

"She's his wife, a woman," Adam protested.

"Haven't you noticed?" Pembroke shook his head. "In this conflict, no one is spared. Lady Badlesmere was held for over a year at the Tower, and as to Lady Joan and her children…"

"What of the Lady Joan?" Kit asked.

Pembroke scrubbed at his face and gave her a tired look. "She and her youngest children are kept in harsh captivity. The Sheriff of Hampshire seems to delight in plaguing his prisoner, keeping her under very restricted circumstances. They feed her on a pittance, and as I hear it Despenser ensures word of how his wife and family are being treated regularly reaches Mortimer. Poor man."

"Poor man?" Kit's voice rose. "It is his fault! Didn't he stop to think? Did he not once consider just what he might be unleashing on them?"

"He thought the king to have some honour," Adam said,

rushing to the defence of Lord Roger. "To make war on women and children—"

"The king? What does he have to do with anything?" Kit's eyes narrowed. "This land is ruled by that serpent, Despenser, and surely Mortimer knew that vile man to be capable of anything."

"Shush," Pembroke warned, scanning the hall as if fearful that a contingent of Despenser men might suddenly appear.

"He didn't think he would lose," Adam said quietly. "At least not at first. He believed his fellow barons would support him – as they should have done." He threw Pembroke a heated look. Aymer de Valence was one of those barons. He had his heart with the Marcher lords, but had chosen to support the king.

"My oath to the king is sacred," Lord Aymer muttered, squirming in his seat.

"And look how well that has served the kingdom." Kit tugged at Adam's hand. "I have to see to your foot. Now."

He heard in her tone of voice that there was no point in protesting, and besides, his foot was throbbing. He rose, set his damaged foot down gingerly, and took one step. Sweetest Virgin! He staggered and was steadied by Kit, who had her arm round his waist.

"No," he muttered. "I must walk on my own. I will not be judged a cripple by the earl."

She released him, he stiffened his spine and made for the solar, one excruciating step at the time.

Next morning, Pembroke departed just before noon, his face set in a concerned expression. He had refused to divulge the content of the message the exhausted horseman who rode in just after dawn had delivered to him, but from Adam's private conversation with Peter, he had gathered it had to do with the king demanding Pembroke's presence in an upcoming interrogation with one of his rebellious barons. Not Lord Mortimer, Peter had hastened to add, before lowering his voice to inform Adam that the queen had contrived a meeting with Mortimer, and would do so soon again.

According to Peter, time was running out for Mortimer. Despenser was pressuring the king to have him killed, and sooner or later the king would cave in – which was why the queen was planning a rescue.

"Be ready," was Peter's parting remark, before he hurried over to mount his little jennet.

Be ready? A man who could scarcely walk up and down the stairs to his solar – what use could he possibly be in an attempt to rescue Lord Roger? But Adam nodded all the same, watching in silence as Pembroke and his men departed.

"It is no great matter," he snapped some hours later, irritated by Kit's concern and by how much his foot hurt.

"No great matter? It's one huge bruise, and I think he managed to break some of the fused bones." Kit knelt at his feet, her hands warm and gentle on his skin. He didn't need her to tell him Despenser had cracked the bones – he could feel it in every step he took, but he'd be damned if he intended to let his foot keep him from helping his lord.

Over the coming days, he concentrated on his training, spending hours under the denuded trees of the apple orchard as he worked with his sword and his dagger. His foot protested loudly when he put too much weight on it and at times he stumbled and fell to his knees, but he refused to succumb to the pain. If anything, every faltering step caused him to increase his efforts, push himself all that much harder.

"You have to rest," Kit scolded when he came limping towards her. Despite the chill of the February day, he was covered in sweat, every single muscle protesting after his recent tussle with his homemade quintain.

"I have to be ready," he retorted.

"Ready for what?" She pointed him in the direction of the hall.

"For when the queen sends for me." He hadn't told her about his conversation with Peter.

"To do what?" She sounded irate, pushing him down to sit while she called for a basin of hot water.

Adam lowered his voice. "Help free our lord, of course."

"That makes sense. A one-man army to free Mortimer from

the most secure prison in England." She snorted, undoing the linen bandages round his foot far less gently than she would normally do. He studied her head, her bare nape, so white in contrast to her dark red hair. In the privacy of their home, she preferred to go about unveiled, and as long as her hair was collected in braids or buns, he did not object – rather the reverse, as his wife had beautiful hair.

"Do you think me incapable?" he asked, inhaling when she set his foot to soak in water that was uncomfortably warm.

"It has nothing to do with you. But I won't let you set off on a mission that is bound to fail."

Adam frowned. "That is not your decision, wife." He saw her flinch, her shoulders tensing. "And when the queen calls, I will go."

"Oh." She got to her feet and wiped her hands on her skirts. "None of my concern, is it? Well then why don't you ask your precious queen to take care of your foot?" She kicked the basin and strode off.

He found her in the solar, sitting on the window bench with the shutters wide. The room was cold, but she was wrapped in quilts and cloaks, her face turned up to the weak winter sun.

"Go away," she said, without turning around. Adam limped over to join her.

"I must," he said.

"You must? And what about me?" She kept her gaze on the landscape outside. "Look at what you've already lost due to Mortimer," she continued. "Your lands, your income…"

"…my foot," he filled in. "But I can't do differently," he tried to explain. "I owe him everything. If I can help get him out of that accursed prison before they kill him, I will do so gladly."

Kit exhaled. "All this talk about obligations," she muttered, throwing him a look. "You have obligations here as well, my lord." In private, she only called him that when she was annoyed with him, and Adam knew better than to attempt to cuddle her out of her present mood.

"Of course I do," he said instead. "But first and foremost I must serve my lord."

"Go away," she repeated. "Leave me alone. Why not do some more of that precious training of yours instead?" With that she turned her back on him, staring intently at something he couldn't see. After some moments of sitting beside her, he gave up.

She remained in the solar for the rest of the day, and when the short day shifted to night he came to find her, hoping she'd had the sense to close the shutters before the room lost all its warmth.

Kit was sitting by the fire, her hair undone as Mabel brushed it. Tom was in her lap, chortling when his mother blew into his ear, those fat baby limbs of his waving wildly. Adam remained by the door, drinking in the sight of his wife and his son. Mabel noticed him first, halting her brushing mid-stroke. He jerked his head, and Mabel reclaimed Tom from his mother and made for the door, giving Adam a reverence as she squeezed past him.

"Will you walk outside with me?" he asked.

"Now?" She looked at him. "It is mightily cold, is it not? And dark."

"Not so dark," he said with a little smile. "There is a moon." He settled her cloak round her shoulders and took her hand, leading them down the narrow stairs, through the hall where the trestles were being set up for supper, and out into the dark.

Just as she'd said, the February night was cold, sheer veils of cloud covering the gibbous moon. A weak, soft light filtered down from the heavens, here and there glittering in a puddle. In the distance, a dog barked, but otherwise the night was quiet. Adam steered them towards the small copse just below the solar, drawing them both to a halt as a white shape rose before them, silently speeding away into the night.

"Owl," he said.

"I know." She opened her fingers to braid them with his. "I love you," she said. "That's why I am so upset by all this talk about riding off to save Mortimer. It makes me so angry – or fearful, rather." She turned to face him, eyes dark and unreadable. "Part of me would die if something should happen to you."

He kissed her forehead. "It won't."

"You don't know that."

No, he sighed, he didn't. "I'll keep myself safe. I have to – for you and for our son."

She tightened his hold on his fingers, but said nothing more. He pulled her close, tipped her chin up and kissed her softly on the mouth. Her arms slid round his neck, and he deepened the kiss until she broke away to draw in air in huge gulps.

"Bed?" he suggested, tightening his hold on her. In reply, she took hold of him and kissed him, as voraciously as he had just kissed her.

Chapter 35

With March came milder temperatures, cowslips and anemones – and lambs. Kit was in her element, and despite Adam's protests that the lady of the manor should not be quite so active a participant, Kit spent most of the first weeks of March – both day and night, it seemed – helping with the lambing. For the most part, the ewes handled things themselves, but now and then there was need of human assistance, and Kit's hands were smaller than the men's.

So she came home smelling of blood and other fluids, and Adam wrinkled his nose, saying he didn't quite like it when his wife smelled so ripe. But when she was called out one very late night, he insisted on coming with her, telling her that although he had little experience of sheep, he'd seen his fair share of foals being brought into the world.

"It's stuck," John said when Kit knelt beside him. The ewe was panting, eyes dilated with pain. It always impressed Kit how stoically the sheep – any animal – handled pain. No shrieking, just an increased pace in their breathing, a restless shuffling of limbs. Not that this ewe was doing much shuffling. Her belly was distended every which way, and Kit's quick examination made her conclude there were three lambs inside.

"We'll never get them out," she said after a careful examination. "I can't separate one lamb from the other." She wiped her slimy hand on her apron and sat back on her heels. "Poor thing."

"Aye." John stroked the ewe over her head.

Kit took a deep breath. "Nothing for it, right?" She gripped her knife, gestured for John to hold the ewe still and swiftly slit her throat. Blood gushed, the ewe kicked spasmodically and went still. "Roll her over," Kit said to Adam, who was looking stunned. He did as she asked, and Kit slit the ewe wide open, spilling organs and intestines all around in her haste to get to the womb. More blood, and three small lambs were lying on the grass, all of them wet and lifeless. "Here." Kit handed one of them to Adam. "Clean its nostrils and mouth, and rub it warm."

"They'll not live without their mammy," John commented, gently working one of the lambs into life.

"We can drip-feed them," Kit replied, smiling when the black woolly creature in her arms began to struggle. "We must try, at least."

"A lot of work," Adam warned.

"A lot of meat," Kit replied with a shrug. She bundled the lamb into her apron and handed it to one of John's grandsons before getting to her feet to stretch. To the east, the sky was shifting into grey, while overhead stars still twinkled brightly. It was cold, the night wind causing her to shiver, and automatically Adam rose to his feet, unclasped his cloak and draped it round her.

"Now you'll be cold," she protested.

"No matter." He looked down at her, his face a collection of shadows, no more. "I did not think you could be so ruthless."

"Ruthless?" Kit looked at her bloodied hand. "She was as good as dead. This way, it was quick."

"But still." He took her hand, touched each of her fingers. "Women are givers of life, not death."

"Sometimes, to give life there must be death." Kit gestured at the lambs. "They'd have died too." She set off towards the distant manor, longing for hot water and her bed.

"You didn't hesitate. You just slashed her throat open," he persisted. Kit came to a halt.

"You're shocked," she said. "Here you are, a belted knight who has done more than your share of killing and maiming on various battlefields, and you don't quite know how to handle the fact that I just killed a sheep." She took hold of his arm and gave it a little shake. "I was raised here. You don't grow up with sheep and chickens and rabbits without learning how to kill them. Besides, the ewe was in agony."

"If it were a woman, not a ewe, would you…" His voice drifted off.

"A woman?" Kit just looked at him. "Of course not! That would have been murder."

"But if she were carrying three babes in her womb..."

"She'd have had to birth them – or die." Kit crossed herself. "Probably die," she muttered.

"Aye." He was silent. "And if that had been Despenser?" he asked after a while. "Could you have severed his throat?"

Kit shivered, despite the heavy folds of his cloak. "I cannot say." She clenched and unclenched her hand a couple of times. "If he was threatening one of mine, then yes, I think I could."

He draped an arm round her shoulders and hugged her close. "You won't have to. I'll kill him first."

By now, night was morphing into day, a bleak March dawn transforming previously amorphous shapes into houses and sheds, fences and walls. Someone had already lit the fires in the kitchens, acrid smoke billowing from the chimney, and Kit was considering whether to detour for an early morning meal when Adam drew her to a stop.

"What?" she said.

"Listen!"

So she did, and at first she heard nothing, but then she made out the sound of hooves, coming at a pace down their lane. "Visitors?" One of the dogs growled. Another followed suit, trotting over to the gate.

"Now?" Adam shook his head. "Not likely." He was already moving at a limping run over the bailey, and by now all the dogs were barking. John materialised out of nowhere, crossbow in hand. Egard stumbled out from the hall, in only his shirt but with his sword at hand.

"Who goes there?" John demanded.

"Peter," a faint voice replied. "I am Peter de Amiens, Pembroke's clerk."

"What does he want?" Adam muttered.

"To break his fast?" Kit suggested.

Peter dropped off his jennet with the grace of a haystack. He looked tired and grimy, but at Adam's concerned questions he made a dismissive gesture, saying that as far as he knew he was not under attack – it was more a matter of slipping his leash.

"Your leash?" Kit eyed the scrawny clerk.

Peter tapped his nose. "Spies, my lady. Everywhere those accursed Despenser spies."

"And you led them here?" Adam frowned.

"I did not." Peter yawned. "I led them to Worcester, and once they thought me safely abed, I rode off."

"And how do you know they didn't come after?" Kit asked.

"I paid for their wine," Peter grinned. "Plenty of wine. Without them knowing, of course."

"Ah." Adam's lips twitched into a smile. "So why are you here?"

Peter sighed deeply, his features sombre. "I've just been to see Lady Joan."

"Lady Joan? How is she?" Adam sounded ridiculously eager, and Kit took a step or two away from him.

"Later." Peter yawned again. "First I need to sleep." He peered at Kit, eyes widening at her bloodied hands and skirts. "And you, my lady, need to wash. Been killing someone recently?"

Some hours later, and Peter was up and about, commenting that it was relief to find Kit nice and clean. She sniffed, had the maids serve them frumenty and bread, and sat down to listen.

It was a sad story he had to tell. Kit alternated between cursing the king to hell – loudly – and cursing Lord Mortimer – silently – for putting his wife in such a precarious position. Lady Joan was presently under house arrest, forbidden to have any communication with any others but her gaolers and the few members of her household who still remained with her. From what Peter told them, it was a harsh existence, with food being scarce and Lady Joan reduced to wearing the clothes she'd arrived in, despite these garments gaping wide over her reduced body.

"I was there on behalf of the queen," Peter explained. "Well, Lord Mortimer, indirectly." He smiled slightly and leaned towards Adam, murmuring that the queen had on two occasions seen Mortimer, and for all that he was careworn, the man was very much himself.

Adam shone like a beacon. Kit fiddled with her bread, keeping her face under control.

"Does the earl know where you've been?" Kit asked.

"No." Peter threw her a cautious look. "He thinks I'm in Wales – I felt it best not to tell him I've been smuggling coins to Lady Joan." He went back to his story, describing how he'd had to present a royal writ to be allowed in to see the traitor's wife. "She was…frail." Peter gnawed his lip. "Frail but adamant that her lord would come out alive of this as well."

"So the king gave you a writ?" Kit was somewhat confused.

Peter squirmed before admitting it had been a forgery – an excellent forgery, if he were to say so himself.

"Ah. And the queen asked you to do this?" Kit asked.

Peter nodded, eyes acquiring an adoring sheen.

"But you're Pembroke's man," Kit said.

"At times. But my true loyalty lies with the queen – and my Lord Aymer knows that, even if he pretends not to."

"Of course," Kit murmured. "So now what? I suppose the king will find out about your little errand to Lady Joan – if nothing else those Despenser spies you talked about will tell him."

Peter blew out his cheeks and nodded. "Our liege will not be happy should he hear his queen has taken it upon herself to succour those he would prefer to lock away forever."

"No, I imagine not – close to treasonous," Kit said, and both men glared at her. "Well, from the king's perspective it is," she added defensively.

"Aye. But the king is not much of a king, is he?" Adam sloshed some more ale into his mug.

"Rather our queen than our king," Peter agreed. "She's playing with fire, Queen Isabella. Despenser is driving quite the wedge between the queen and the king, and now that his wife has been placed in the queen's household, everything she does is reported back to the king."

"And still she takes risks like this?" Kit felt a twinge of admiration for this unknown woman.

Peter gave her a sly smile. "Lady Despenser is not the most effective of jailers. Too many children, too tired." He stretched for the cheese, and nodded his thanks when Kit offered him some more bread. "For now our queen still has her freedom. She has her dower lands, her household. But as I hear it, Despenser is urging the king to take it away from her, thereby reducing her to yet another royal dependent."

"She wouldn't like that, I imagine," Kit said.

"No." It came out clipped. "Let us hope it never happens." Peter belched, dug into his pouch and produced a tightly rolled piece of parchment. "For you." He handed it to Adam. "Lady Joan asked me to make sure it got to you personally."

Adam did not open the little missive at the table. Instead, he weighed it as if was made of gold before slipping it into his pouch. "I'll read it later," he said.

"You do that." Peter slapped himself on his thighs and rose. "I must be on my way."

Adam offered to see him to his horse, and the two men disappeared outside, still deep in conversation. Kit went to find the cook.

She was still in the kitchens when Adam came to find her, considering whether to have trout or salted herring for dinner. It would have to be salted herring, she decided, all the while aware that Adam was leaning against the doorpost, arms crossed over his chest. It made the cook go white and red in blotches, to have the master standing like that in her domain, so Kit took pity on poor Mall and left, squeezing by Adam and making for the stables.

"So what did she write?" she asked, as casually as she could.

"It's not a love letter," he replied, the shadow of a smile playing over his mouth.

"But precious all the same."

He frowned. "Of course it is, I was glad to have word from her. Lady Joan is a woman I admire greatly." He gave her a challenging look.

"Don't we all?" Kit muttered, feeling childish and petty. The poor woman was locked up somewhere, with her children locked up elsewhere and her husband facing imminent death.

And here she was, feeling jealous because Adam's features softened when he held her letter.

To his credit, Adam said nothing more. He just took her hand. "She fears for her husband," he said after some minutes. "She asked me to do what I can to help him, and she wondered if the treasures she entrusted to you remain safe."

"Of course they are. I have not stolen her gold!"

"She didn't mean it like that," he admonished. "But that gold will come in handy when planning Lord Roger's escape." He gave her hand a little shake. "Why didn't you tell me you had such riches in your care?"

Kit lifted her shoulders. "I forgot. This last year or so, I've had other things on my mind." Principally you and your welfare, she wanted to say, but she didn't need to, because his eyes lit up and he tightened his hold on her hand.

"Me."

"Yes, you." She leaned against him for an instant. "Anyway, all that gold lies very safe where it is."

He thought about that for a moment. "In the chapel?" he whispered. "In those linen sacks stacked to the back of the hiding place?"

"Where else?"

Chapter 36

Halfway through April, a party of eight men showed up at Tresaints, informing Adam that they had instructions from Lord Despenser to search the entire manor – and the neighbouring three – for the remains of Sir Guy.

"A wild goose chase," Adam scoffed.

"Not according to our master," the sergeant said. "And it is mightily strange, that a man so high in our lord's favour should choose to disappear."

"Maybe he was overcome by his conscience," Kit offered. "Maybe he's right now making a pilgrimage to expiate his sins."

The sergeant looked at her. "You don't know Sir Guy very well, do you?" he said in a dry tone. "The day he goes on a pilgrimage is the day I become a monk." He wiped at his hand with his mouth. "No, mark my words, he's dead – or held captive somewhere."

"Without someone having heard from him?" Adam said.

"Dead people don't talk much," the sergeant replied. "And as to captives, well it depends, doesn't it? On who is holding him."

"Not us," Kit told him.

"No." The sergeant did a little turn, taking in the manor. "That does seem unlikely – which is why Lord Despenser believes Sir Guy is dead." He cocked his head at Kit. "As I hear it, Sir Guy pressed his suit where he wasn't welcome."

"He did," Kit said coldly. "And he seemed to forget I was already married."

"Widows are easy to make." The sergeant smiled, showing a set of rather decaying teeth.

Three days later, William came walking down the lane. It took some time for Kit to recognise him, unused to seeing him in anything but clerical garb. The man making his way slowly down the slope was in tunic and hose, a hood covering his hair and features. Beside her, Kit heard Adam draw in breath in a surprised hiss, and then he was off, hastening to meet the stranger with open arms.

"You have done what?" Kit wiped at her eyes. William was back, looking thinner and older, with his tonsure entirely overgrown and a month's worth of beard covering his cheeks.

"You heard me." William beamed. "I am the queen's man now."

"You are?" Kit studied his scruffy appearance. "But isn't that dangerous? What if Despenser recognises you?"

"Lord Despenser has only seen me as a priest, never like this." William swept his hands down his tunic.

He had a point, but should Despenser look for too long or too hard at William, it would be difficult to miss his resemblance to Adam, and if there was one man Despenser would recognise in the densest of throngs, that was Adam. She regarded her husband in silence, wondering what it was about him that had attracted Despenser's interest. She supposed it was the combination of his obvious physical strength and his loyalty to Mortimer that had made it such sport for Despenser to humiliate him, leave him permanently marked. Or maybe Despenser had a preference for certain types of men – as she heard it, King Edward was also tall and fair.

William gave her arm a little shake, recalling her to the present. "We don't meet, Lord Despenser and me – I stay well away from the court."

William launched himself into a description of his new life in the queen's employ – albeit that officially he was working for a rich mercer in London. An exciting life, Kit gathered, unable to contain a smile at the way the words bubbled out of William. But her pleasure at seeing her brother-in-law vanished when she understood he was here to discuss certain aspects of Lord Mortimer's planned escape with Adam. Sitting side by side, the brothers looked remarkably alike, especially when they both had that eager look in their eyes.

Out of the corner of her eye, she saw the sergeant loitering by the fence, keen eyes studying William with avid interest.

318

"Shush," she warned, interrupting William's description of the Tower's kitchens.

"Hmm?" William glanced at her, at the sergeant, and turned to look at Adam. "What are Despenser's men doing here?"

"They're looking for Guy," Adam said.

"Is there any chance they'll find his remains?" Kit asked, gesturing at the soldiers.

"No." William's face closed up. "I pray for him," he added, looking at Adam.

"So do I," Adam replied.

"I don't." Kit stood up. "I hope he burns in hell forever." She stalked off, making for the chapel, with Adam at her heels.

"Kit." His hand closed on her arm.

"How can you say you pray for him?" She wrenched free of his hold. "He tried to rape me, twice!"

"He was not always like that," Adam said, holding the door to the chapel open for her. As always, stepping inside the little space was the equivalent of being wrapped in a soft blanket – apart from that awful day back in October when Guy had dragged her in here, so convinced this was where she was hiding Adam. She greeted the three saints, waited while Adam did the same, and led the way towards the altar.

"At some point one must forgive," Adam said in a low voice. "It drags at you, to hate."

"So you don't hate him for that?" She gestured at his foot.

"I do." Adam sighed. "But I try, Kit – not for his sake, but for mine." He gave her a lopsided smile.

"I can't." She choked. "Look at what he did to you – what he was planning to do to you, that night at Goodrich Castle. And me he was going to force into marriage, and Tom…" She couldn't go on.

"None of it happened," he said gently. "And Guy was ever a misguided soul."

"He chose!" She gave him an angry look. "When he slammed that mallet through your foot, he damned himself to hell, and he knew it."

Adam winced. "Yes," was all he said. He took a deep breath.

"But he was once a little lad who followed me around with adoring eyes. It is for the lad that I pray, not for the man."

Kit had no answer to that. Instead she sank to her knees and prayed that God would keep on protecting her husband as he had done so far – with a sizeable portion of help from Kit herself.

The sergeant and his men rode off, having found nothing to incriminate Adam. William, however, stayed on, and for some weeks things were like they used to be, with William holding mass, chiding Kit about her confessions and spending whatever time he had left over plotting with Adam.

It was a complicated plan, that much Kit gathered from the bits and pieces she overheard. Rope ladders had to be procured, and boats and horses, and then there was the matter of funds – which was why Adam was to ride down to Portchester in June with some of the gold and silver presently hidden in the chapel.

"Portchester?" Kit had no idea where that might be. Adam grinned when she said as much.

"Neither, we hope, does the king."

It was also a plan involving very many people – all the way from a handful of rich London merchants to several staunch Mortimer supporters, both along the escape route and on the Isle of Wight. It made Kit nervous. With so many people, how could one be sure they wouldn't speak out of turn?

William gave her an amused look. "The queen and Lord Roger choose wisely."

"Well, Despenser is no fool, is he?" she replied, annoyed by this continuous adoring admiration of Mortimer and the queen. For the past few weeks, the plan to save Lord Mortimer had been the single subject of discussion, leaving her very much on the fringes of things as the brothers spent their time honing the details of their scheme to perfection. And no matter what questions she asked, what fears she voiced, the reply was always the same, William and Adam professing blind faith in Mortimer and the queen. Fools!

"Despenser is so busy wreaking vengeance upon the

vanquished that he doesn't notice the weed growing under his feet." William tapped his nose. "I'm the weed, see?" He winked, making Kit laugh despite herself.

Kit took to spending her days away from her husband, preferring to invest her energies in her garden and in her son rather than sitting to the side as William and Adam discussed and argued their great matter. Instead, she helped John welcome a fine litter of pigs to the world, assisted Mabel with the wool dyeing and clapped enthusiastically when Tom managed to stand, a wide, drooling grin on his face.

"So when is this plan of yours supposed to take place?" she asked one evening.

"Lammas Day," Adam replied. "Assuming Lord Roger is still alive by then, that's when the queen plans to make her move." He gave her a morose look. "It's a long time from now until then."

"An excellent choice of day," William said. "The Tower guard will be so drunk they won't be able to stand."

"They will?" Kit asked.

"It's the feast of St Peter of Vincula. Tradition has it that the constable of the Tower serves his men plenty of wine that night." William leaned closer. "And this year, the wine will be drugged."

"Oh." She felt a shiver up her spine. "And what if things go wrong?"

"They won't," William replied.

"How do you know?" She turned to Adam. "I don't like it. You're risking everything – again."

"It's a good plan," he replied, keeping his eyes hidden from her.

"Plans can go wrong. And then what?"

"You're being fanciful." William sounded condescending. "We have it all under control."

She wanted to yell at them that they were being fools, because should the plan unravel, the queen would not come to their rescue – she couldn't. But they were back to discussing yet another detail, and Kit decided to leave them to it.

She was still awake when Adam came up the stairs to the solar, listening to his slow, steady treads. Stairs were an issue – especially going down – but these days Adam preferred not to talk about his foot, unless he needed her help in soothing a sudden flare of pain. He opened the door and slid inside, moving as soundlessly as possible.

She had left the shutters open, and he moved over to close them.

"No, leave them open," she said. "It's too beautiful outside to close them." The air was fragrant with the scents of growing grass and honeysuckle, and a pale summer moon washed the room with silver. She reclined against the pillows and watched him as he undressed, lifting the quilts to invite him into her side of the bed. He laughed softly, sliding in beside her. She smoothed at his hair, kissed his neck, his chest, working upwards to his mouth. Adam made a pleased sound, but didn't do more than kiss her back. No roving hands, no mouth devouring her.

"What do you think Lord Roger might be doing right now?" he asked, moving away so that they were some inches apart. Always Lord Roger, always this overriding concern for Roger Mortimer. Without a word, Kit turned her back on him. "What is it?" He sounded aggrieved, strong hands forcing her round to face him.

She sat up. "What, you ask? I try to seduce you and you talk of your lord – you always talk of him, and sometimes I think you love him much more than you love me."

He followed suit and sat up. "How can you say thus?"

"How?" She waved her hand at the open shutters. "Moonlit nights, remember? You promised me a never-ending sequence of them."

"Am I to take it that you have complaints?" he asked coldly.

"Not as such. But lately—"

"I have other matters on my mind," he interrupted. "Matters of more importance than our bouts in bed."

"I'm not asking for all of your time. I'm asking for some of it." She met his eyes, hoping that he would at least smile at her, kiss her. Instead, he turned round and pulled the quilt up, presenting her with his back. "I won't ask again," she told his unmoving back as she got out of bed. "Ever."

It had been well after midnight when she'd crept back up the stairs to their bed, and he had pretended to sleep, aggrieved by her accusations that he ignored her. Just to show her, he rolled towards her in the morning, only to find that she was already up, disappearing down the stairs without a word. And since then, she was like an enervating butterfly, hovering always within sight, always just out of reach.

Three days later, and yet again she rose to go to bed, leaving him and William to their conversation. She had barely exchanged a word with him throughout the evening, and it gnawed at him to have her behave thus. He supposed that when he came up to bed she would already be sleeping – or pretending to sleep – and decided that this night he would call her bluff, demanding that she love him as she should. The thought stirred him, and after some minutes of further conversation he bid William goodnight.

The solar was empty. The bed was untouched, the shutters were firmly closed and bolted, as if she had taken a decision to never again allow the light of the moon to spill into their bedchamber. Adam opened them wide. The night was surprisingly warm, and a carpet of stars danced around the half-moon. As he watched, his wife appeared from the copse, walking slowly in the direction of the stream. She seemed a fairy creature, dipped in the silver of the moon. Her long skirts dragged over the grass, and as she walked she undid her heavy braid, releasing her hair to ripple down her back. She slipped her arms round her waist in a little self-hug, and it made something twist in his belly. She was right; of late she came a distant second to Lord Roger in his thoughts, not because he loved her less, but because Lord Roger needed him more. Adam cursed and made for the door.

The grass swished as he moved towards her, making her turn. He had discarded his tunic, walking only in hose and boots, his shirt unlaced. Kit was sitting on a log, her cloak spread over her knees, her hands loosely clasped.

"Here." With a flourish, he handed her the rosebud he had picked on the way. She took it, his fingers closed on hers and he pulled her upright, close enough that he could feel the warmth radiating from her. She stepped away, shaking her head. One moment she was close enough to kiss, the other she was hastening away from him. Two – four – strides and he caught up with her. When it seemed she was about to say something, he shook his head, placing a finger over her mouth. No words, not now, not tonight when the moon bathed the meadow in light, when for once the air was warm and still.

He spread her cloak on the grass, peeled off her kirtle and added it to this makeshift bed. When he brushed his nose over her nape, her skin smelled of lavender and grass, of catmint and crushed violets. A lock of her hair tickled his face. He drew a finger along her jawline, over her mouth, and she turned her face aside, her unbound hair falling like a veil between them. She was punishing him for his recent inattentiveness, standing still and unresponsive under his hands, his mouth.

Not entirely unaffected, though. When he undid the laces of her smocked chemise, she quivered and trembled under his hands. Adam nuzzled the elegant column of her neck, whispered her name against her skin. Slowly, he shoved the chemise off her shoulders, sliding it down her arms to pool at her feet. Her breasts rose and fell, and when he set his fingers to her throat, he could feel her rapid pulse. The tip of her tongue darted out to lick her lips. He cupped her face and kissed her until she opened her mouth to his, and she tasted of salt and warmth. There, at last, came her hands, sliding up his back, his shoulders, to fist themselves in his hair.

"Open your eyes," he murmured, and she did, pools of darkness that he wanted to drown in as he kissed her until she moaned and swayed in his arms, sinking towards the ground. She tugged at his clothes, pulling at his shirt, his braies. Moments of touching, of her hands exploring him as he had just explored her, and Adam sank into a sea of sensations that left him far too short of breath. Her mouth, her fondling hands, and his blood was boiling, a wild, uncontrollable heat that surged through him, collecting in his loins. Oh, yes!

Skin against skin, his legs between her widening thighs, her arms around his back, in his hair. With one forceful thrust, he entered her, and she made a series of whimpering sounds, her hips lifting to meet him. He pounded into her, and below him she writhed, calling his name. Above him, the stars seemed to be spinning. With a groan, Adam climaxed, sinking down to lie spent in her welcoming arms.

It seemed an eternity later that she shoved at him, muttering that he was too heavy. He rolled off and smiled down at her, thinking she looked deliciously wanton, sprawled naked on the ground. She, however, did not smile back, eyes hanging off him.

"What?" He picked up her hand, kissed each of her fingers in turn.

"Nothing." Kit turned her head away, and Adam sighed. When a woman said 'nothing', only a fool of a man would believe her.

"What is it, sweeting?" He nuzzled her neck until she turned to face him. She raised her hand to his face.

"I'm frightened," she said simply.

"For me?" He leaned into her touch.

"And me." She gave him an imploring look. "Must you really do this?"

"I must." One last service for his lord, he told himself, knowing all the while that it was a lie. He was Lord Roger's man, and had no choice but to do as he asked. He rolled over on his back and pulled her close, cradling her against his chest. She toyed with his chest hair, tugging a tad too hard at times, but he didn't protest, eyes lost in the dark summer sky.

"He is my overlord, and I owe him my allegiance – you know that." He owed Lord Roger much more than that, he thought wryly, cradling her to him. He kissed the top of her head. "But it is you I love," he went on, "and it is to you I will return."

"Always?" she asked.

"Always," he promised. God willing, he added silently.

Chapter 37

Kit fell back against the pillows. "Truly?" Not that she needed Mabel's confirmation – she was well over six weeks late – but she had somehow hoped she was wrong. Tom was just over a year old, and what with her husband's determination to ride to his lord's rescue, another child felt more like a source of fear than a bundle of joy.

"Yes – but you've known about it for some weeks, haven't you?" Mabel gave her a sharp look before bustling over to open the shutters fully, thereby drowning the solar in bright July sunlight. "Have you told him?"

"No." And she had no intention of doing so – not yet. She sighed. These last few weeks had been fraught with tension. First, Adam and William had ridden off together to Portchester, carrying the equivalent of a minor fortune in various small pouches on their person. She'd gnawed her nails to the quick waiting for him to return, and when he finally did, astride a tired Goliath, she'd rushed to meet him, only to be met by a grim face and reddened eyes as he explained they'd had dire news – apparently some of Mortimer's letters had been intercepted by Despenser, so now the king and his chamberlain knew there was a plan afoot to rescue Mortimer.

"So abort it," Kit said. "It would be foolish to proceed."

Adam had given her an irritated look. "Now more than ever we have to get Lord Roger out. It is but a matter of time before they slit his throat."

So now Kit not only harboured concerns about the plan as such, she went about in a haze of fear that somehow the king and Despenser knew exactly what was being planned, and if so her husband was as dead as a cockerel on a butcher's hook. He refused to listen, telling her over and over again that things were progressing as they should, and he had no intention of staying away – no matter how much his wife begged him to.

"He's leaving on the morrow," Mabel said, recalling Kit to the present. "Doesn't he deserve to know?"

"At present, he doesn't deserve anything." Kit was so angry with him, incapable of anything but going through the motions of normal life. And tomorrow he would leave, perhaps never to return, and Kit could not bear it, didn't know what to do or what to say to make him understand that he was leaving her hollowed out inside.

"He's a man," Mabel said as if this explained everything. "A good man," she added, throwing Kit a meaningful look.

"I know." She ran a hand over his pillow. Her man, her lover, and she wished she could find the words to tell him just how much she loved him without sounding clingy and needy.

"Here, m' lady." Mabel handed her a mug of honeyed water. "I'll make you a posset later – one with plenty of eggs in it. For the babe."

"For the babe," Kit echoed, caressing her belly.

All that day, she watched Adam from a distance. Goliath was shod and groomed; his sword was cleaned and honed. He spent some time in the fields supervising the ongoing harvest, and he played with Tom, making their son laugh out loud when Adam threw him into the air. Now and then, she'd catch him looking in her direction, but just as she avoided him, so he avoided her, submerging himself in a flurry of last-minute tasks before he appeared at supper, newly bathed and shaved.

She was tongue-tied beside him. The food swelled in her mouth, the wine made her gag, and when they retired to the solar she lay still and silent under his touch, her heart breaking at the thought that this might be the last time they had together. Once he fell asleep, she sat with her legs pulled up to her chest, keeping vigil over her sleeping man.

She stood to the side and watched him pack his necessities together, making no move to help him. Adam threw her a look, wishing he knew what to say to break this impasse between them, but Kit emanated nothing but a frigid composure, even if he could see just how tightly clasped she kept her hands, a sure sign the tension within her was close to unbearable.

"What will happen to me if they catch you?" she asked, breaking the silence.

He looked up from the straps on his saddlebag. "They won't."

"But if they do?" Her eyes dug into him, insisting he tell her the truth. Adam drew in a deep breath and went back to his straps.

"Then you should flee to France," he said, looking at anything but her. He heard her inhale.

"To France? I don't want to go to France. I want to stay here, in my home." Unsaid was a loud and angry accusation that he was an uncaring husband to place her so at risk.

"I know you do. And as I said, it won't come to that."

"How do you know?" She sounded bitter. "And if I choose to stay, what will happen to me and to our children?"

Adam straightened up, astounded. "Children?"

She nodded, a hand sliding over her belly.

"Why haven't you told me?" he demanded, escaping into anger.

"Why haven't you noticed?" she retorted. "Oh, but of course you haven't, because all you ever think about is how to save your beloved baron, the single most important person in your life."

"That's not fair." He tried to embrace her, but she slithered out of his hold like a live eel, retreating well out of range. "I love you, you know that, don't you?"

She gave him a blue look, lower lip caught firmly in her teeth.

"You're making this very difficult," he said, extending his hand to her.

"It is difficult." She glared at him, eyes brimming. "It's tearing the heart out of my body."

He winced, but there was nothing he could do. He was honour-bound to do as his lord bid him, and surely she understood that too. "I have no choice."

"I know – but it doesn't help, not when my innards are infested with writhing snakes from hell, not when..." She broke off. "And what if you don't come back? What if you die because of him? How am I to exist without you? Without you, there is no air in my lungs, no colour in my world. You may die to save your lord, and in doing so you kill me too."

Her words drove nails through him. "Kit," he tried, but it was too late, she was gone, the door slamming in her wake.

He mounted Goliath with a heavy heart. He'd delayed as long as possible, hoping she'd reappear from wherever she was hiding to bid him a proper farewell, but now it seemed he would have to leave with her last bitter words ringing in his ears. The sun cleared the eastern hills, a cock crowed twice, and he knew he had to be on his way and yet he held in his horse, scanning his home and its surroundings for a glimpse of her. It made him ache inside, to leave without a final embrace, one last kiss, and he was angry with her for doing this to him – to them.

"I can't find her." Mabel patted Adam's leg. "She'll come round. She's not quite herself on account of the new babe." That, if anything, twisted the knife deeper. Mabel had known about the child, but him she hadn't told. Mabel squinted up at him. "She nearly lost you once, m' lord. I dare say it makes her less inclined to see you ride away and risk your life again – for the same man."

"Will you tell her I waited as long as I could?"

Mabel nodded.

"And that I love her?"

Mabel shook her head. "She knows you do. It's just that she feels you love Lord Mortimer more."

"I don't," he protested.

Mabel gave him a shrewd look. "Maybe not. But you're risking everything – including her safety – for him. So it is no wonder if she doesn't quite believe you when you tell her she comes first, is it?"

Adam's stomach turned. How could Kit doubt that she came first in his heart? "I have no choice," he said stonily, and for the first time ever, he resented having to set everything aside for Lord Roger.

Mabel gave him a sad little smile and stood aside when he clucked Goliath into a walk. He didn't want to leave, not like this, but time was flying, and Egard was already halfway up the lane.

"Adam! Wait, Adam, wait!"

He halted the horse. Kit was running towards him, skirts held high, hair whipping in the wind. Adam dropped off Goliath and half-ran to meet her.

She crashed into him, fists beating at his chest. "You haven't promised you'll come back, you haven't told me there will be future moonlit nights." She hit him again and again. Tears stained her cheeks, bloated her face, and he didn't think she had ever been more beautiful than she was right now, her face dissolving with fear for him. Tenderly, he wiped her eyes, her nose.

"I will come back, of course I will."

She threw her arms around his neck and clung to him, her tears dampening his skin. "I don't want you to go."

"I know." He loosened her hold. "Truth be told, I don't want to go."

"Liar." She snivelled. "Of course you want to go."

"No, not when it leaves you this distraught." He brushed her hair off her face and kissed her softly on the mouth. "I'll be back, sweeting, and I give you my word that I'll never leave you behind again."

"Never?"

"Never."

They walked back, hand in hand, to where Goliath was patiently waiting. Her fingers clung to his. Adam pulled her into a hard embrace, leaning his cheek against the top of her head.

"I love you." He let her go and turned to the horse. "Much, much more than I love Lord Roger," he said as he mounted.

She smiled at him, a wobbly smile that contrasted with the tears that once again were running down her cheeks. "I know – most of the time. But sometimes I forget."

"Well, it isn't Lord Roger I promise moonlit nights, is it?" he said.

"No, that would be rather odd," she laughed. That was his last image of her as he galloped up the lane: barefoot and with her hair undone, crying and laughing at the same time.

Adam was not fond of London. The buildings seemed to tower over him, the sky was visible in patches, and there were far too many people on the streets, forcing him to halt and sidestep constantly. He walked with caution down Cheapside, one hand on his pouch, the other on the hilt of his dagger. The streets were filthy, and urchins of all sizes and ages clustered around him whenever he stopped, begging him for a coin, a crust of bread. It made him distinctly aware of just how vulnerable he was, despite his fighting skills. What good a sword when a child of six could slide up between your legs and skewer you from below? He increased his pace, trying to force his way through the throng of people.

To top it all, London was a noisy place, making it hard to hear himself think. Women screamed, vendors called out their wares, men argued, now and then groups of knights rode by, horseshoes ringing on the cobbles, and over it all were the bells, ringing out the various hours of the day. Adam longed for home, promising himself to steer well clear of London in the future. For now, there was no choice, and so he walked up and down the warren of streets that bordered the river, on both sides of the bridge.

Some days later, things were more or less arranged. Peter the clerk had found a boat to ferry them across to the south side, and Egard had been dispatched to the horse markets to find suitable horses. Only two days to go, and Adam spent some hours at St Paul's praying that the venture would be successful, before wandering towards the Tower, thinking it might make sense to reconnoitre the place beforehand.

The fortress was imposing, the barbican looming threateningly over the approaching visitors. Adam joined a group of apprentices and stepped into the cool darkness of the gatehouse. It made his skin crawl, to set foot inside the royal castle, but moments later he was out in the sunlight, with yet another tower looming before him. The apprentices made for the lions' pit, chattering eagerly among themselves, but Adam had no interest in the reeking, mangy beasts and instead followed the steady flow of tradesmen over yet another drawbridge, through one more gatehouse, over a causeway moat and under the impressive structure that was the Byward tower – near on unbreachable, Adam reflected, studying the circular towers, the multiple arrow loops and the double portcullis with approval.

And then he was through, standing on the cobbled Water Lane. To his left rose the inner curtain wall, to his right the outer wall, beyond which lay the Thames. Adam kept a constant lookout for any man bearing the distinctive badge of the Despensers, but so far all he had seen were tired men-at arms attired in the royal colours. Instead, he turned his attentions to the walls and the towers, eyes darting from one to the other in the ludicrous hope of catching a glimpse of Lord Roger.

Adam craned his head back and studied the inner wall. The drop was uncomfortably high, and his thighs bunched at the thought of scaling the wall with a rope ladder. And should they be trapped here, in Water Lane…He shivered and decided to cut his visit short – after all, there was nothing much to see beyond the walls, and no visitors were allowed into the inner bailey.

He was abreast of St Thomas' Tower when the water gate creaked opened, and Adam followed the curious spectators to the small, protected harbour, watching with interest as a barge nosed its way through the gate. The water was slimy and dank, and from the marks on the wall, Adam concluded the river had to be at high tide, causing the waters below to move restlessly, miniature waves slapping against the stone foundations of the water stairs.

In the centre of the barge sat a lad, and a whisper rustled through the spectators. Edward of Windsor, heir to the throne, grinned up at them and leapt to his feet, causing the barge to rock.

"My lord!" the woman beside the prince squealed, clutching at him. Instead of keeping him aboard, her action plunged the prince into the water. Adam didn't stop to think. He jumped in, sinking into water as dark as it was foul. The lad, he had to save the prince. There. He got hold of an arm and swam upwards, dragging the royal imp with him. He broke the surface, held the lad in his arms as he swam for the stairs. The prince was spitting and thrashing, yelling that he could swim, he truly could.

No sooner had they touched solid bottom than the prince tore himself free from Adam's hold, leaping up the stone treads.

"What did you do that for?" he yelled.

"My lord?" Adam asked, confused and angered by the lad's behaviour.

"I didn't need your help!" A drenched boot stamped at the ground.

"You fell overboard," Adam said. "I chose not to wait to see if you'd break the surface before I jumped in."

"Well you should! I don't need the help of a commoner like you!"

Adam heaved himself up from the water. "I am no commoner, my lord." The royal whelp needed to be taught manners.

"No?" The prince looked him up and down. "You look like one."

"Most fortunate that I wasn't wearing my velvet and ermine today," Adam snapped back.

"Well I was," the prince retorted, studying his drenched clothes. "*Maman* will be furious."

Adam grinned. "Women." The lad grinned back.

There was a flurry of movement behind them, a soft voice called the prince's name, and Adam sank to his knees.

"*Maman!*" the prince protested when the woman embraced him, pressing his wet head against her dove-grey gown. The queen ignored him, hands roving over him to ensure he was whole. Only once she was done did she straighten up and turn her attention to Adam, still on his knees.

"Thank you. It was most kind of you to save my son." The queen smiled, and it was like seeing one of heaven's angels come to earth. Dark hair peeked from below her veil to frame a face dominated by two large green eyes and a perfectly formed mouth. The faintest shade of pink tinted the otherwise flawless complexion, thick dark lashes swooped down to shade her eyes, and just off the right-hand corner of her mouth, a miniature dimple appeared when she smiled.

"My lady queen," Adam stuttered, wondering if she would recognise him. She gestured for him to get up and approach, her mouth pursing as she took in his limp. Those glorious eyes swept him up and down, the slightest of nods indicating that she knew very well who he was.

"I didn't need saving!" The lad squirmed free of his mother's hold. "I know how to swim."

"But he didn't know that you did," the queen reprimanded. "It is good manners to express gratitude when someone risks his life for you." She winked at Adam.

The prince glowered at Adam, bright eyes boring into him. "Thank you," he said grudgingly.

"It was my honour, my prince," Adam replied.

The queen bent and whispered something in Prince Edward's ear.

"But why?" the prince said, looking at Adam. "He looks scruffy."

"You never judge a man by his looks," the queen told her son. "And a future king should always be on the lookout for able men."

"Able?" The prince frowned. "He limps."

"And yet I can assure you Sir Adam can wield a sword like very few others," the queen said.

"You know him?" Edward craned his head back to look at his mother.

"Oh yes, I do." Yet again she bent down to whisper something, making the prince pale.

"Truly?" The lad's eyes locked onto Adam's right foot. "Despenser?"

"Despenser," his lady mother replied, and from the look the lad shared with her, it was obvious neither son nor mother held Despenser in any esteem. "So will you do as I ask?"

Prince Edward nodded and took a step towards Adam.

"I would have you swear fealty to me," he said, sounding surprisingly adult.

"Now?" Adam wasn't quite sure what to do. What was the queen playing at? She knew fair well Adam's allegiance was already pledged – to Lord Roger. But he was in no position to refuse, and from the amused look on the queen's face, she was fully aware of this.

"Now." A regal sweep of the arm had Adam kneeling at the prince's feet, clasped hands held before him. He was aware of the interested spectators, of the prince's retinue standing to the side, some of them looking anything but pleased, but most of all he was aware of the prince's eyes, a deep blue that seemed to burn their way into his soul. Slowly he spoke his pledge, and once he was done, the prince set a hand to his elbow and helped him stand – with substantial strength for one so young.

The queen approached, and Adam bowed.

"It is time, my lord, that you start serving a new master," she said in a low voice. "A safeguard, if you will, putting you out of reach from Despenser."

"And what will my present lord think of that, my lady?"

"He will not mind." It was said with utter finality. "My son has need of good men – men such as you, and Lord Mortimer." She kept her voice low. "And the horses?"

"All is ready, my lady. I just wish it was all over."

"Tomorrow, Sir Adam." She dipped her head. "God is with us in this. I know it." With one last smile she bid him farewell and floated off towards her son, graceful like a hind.

Chapter 38

The handcart was laden with barrels. Adam strained as he and William slowly manoeuvred the overloaded cart through the barbican, through the gate into the inner bailey and onwards to the hall. Out of the corner of his eye, Adam caught a glimpse of Peter, standing in conversation with d'Alspaye, the sub-lieutenant of the Tower and the single most important cogwheel in the complex plan.

D'Alspaye's eyes drifted over to Adam, who was hard put not to nod a greeting. He'd met the man before, years back, at the time a tenacious and enthusiastic servant of the crown. It made his belly gripe. Should d'Alspaye prove false, they were all dead men – and a terrible death it would be, of that Adam was quite sure.

"Where do you want the wine?" William asked one of the guards by the hall. He made a big show of wiping his face, before telling the men they had a generous constable, as with this much wine it should suffice for them to bathe in it.

The older of the guards laughed. "What? Ten barrels? That won't last us long."

"This is just the first load," Adam said with a grin. The vintner had prepared well over thirty barrels at the queen's request, all of them generously dosed with a mixture of milk of the poppy, hemlock, henbane and mandrake.

"Why are you bringing it in by handcart?" the other guard asked, taking a turn round the cart.

"The horse went lame," William said. "Our master, penny-pinching miser that he is, decided we could do the pulling instead." He grimaced. "Not his back, unfortunately."

The guards laughed and showed them where to store the wine.

By the time they returned with the last load, the inner ward was sunk in shadow. To the west, the August sun blazed bright, still a few hours from sunset, but here, within the looming walls, the light was all but gone.

"No clouds," Adam muttered in an undertone to William. He scratched at his bristling cheeks, for the day darkened by a generous application of wood ash. His hair had been similarly treated, and he'd blackened his teeth and rubbed his hands and forearms with mud. William was just as dirty, both of them wore extra padding round their waists to make them look fatter than they were, and William had even attached extra hair to his eyebrows, giving him a general resemblance to an owl.

"No moon," William replied just as softly. He threw Adam a concerned look. "Your foot?"

"Bad – but bearable." He made a conscious effort not to limp – at least not within sight of the guards – and needed to sit down somewhere and take the weight off it, massage some blood back into the protesting muscles and tendons before the coming exertions.

They took their time unloading, jesting with the guards who were already waiting in the hall. From the kitchen came an endless line of servers, carrying platters loaded with meat and bread. A group of jugglers appeared at the gate, accompanied by a handful of wenches. The guards cheered at the sight of the women, who waved and smiled, tossed unbound hair about and exposed swelling expanses of rosy skin. Some of the men whistled, other catcalled, and the gates were flung wide open to allow the female visitors entry. Adam suppressed a grin. Lord Roger knew what soldiers wanted, and this little addition to the entertainment had come at his express command.

A group of guards were moving from tower to tower, disappearing inside for some minutes before emerging a while later.

"They're checking the cells," William muttered, handing Adam the last of the barrels. "It is time."

Adam nodded. He knew what to do, ducking into a dark corner to pull off the dirty brown tunic he'd worn all day. When he reappeared, he was in yellow – stained with wine and meat-juices. William gave him a nod and set off towards the gate with the handcart, calling for the guards to keep it open.

One last look over his shoulder, and William was gone, the gate clanging shut behind him. Adam expelled a long breath. Now to make it to the kitchen.

It was simple to mingle with the servers, pick up platters and pitchers. Adam heaped meat and bread before the guards, he served them wine – even more wine – and noted with some relief that the officers were drinking as much as their men – with the exception of d'Alspaye, who merely toyed with his wine. In the light of the torches directly overhead, d'Alspaye looked ill, skin covered in a sheen of sweat.

The last of the guards entered the hall and told the crowd at large that the fortress was safe, locked down for the night. This was met with loud cheers, with hand-clapping and foot-stamping, and then the guards began their celebration in earnest. Adam took the opportunity to fill his arms with emptied platters and follow some of the servers back to the kitchen.

The cook threw him a look, threw him yet another look and jerked his head towards a bench. No words, no more eye contact beyond that initial look. Adam sank down to sit and slid as far into the shadows as possible. He eased off his boot and carefully worked his way over his foot, flexing his toes and his instep as well as he could to relieve the stiffness.

Time passed slowly. The cook yelled at the servers, at the kitchen maids, and set two lads to emptying and sweeping the huge hearth. Adam was served a bowl of soup and nodded his thanks. The kitchen emptied of everyone but the cook and Adam. From the hall came the sound of laughter and song, but as the evening wore on the sounds faded, the odd yell or guffaw making Adam start.

It was pitch dark when he sneaked outside for a breath of fresh air. After the stifling heat of the kitchen, the August night was fresh and damp – and silent. Step by step he approached the hall. There were men sleeping on the ground outside, men lying over the tables, on the floor. One man was lying in a puddle of vomit, two guards had fallen asleep with their arms round each other, and in the rushes just beside the door, one of the wenches was snoring, skirts hiked up, legs spread wide.

The man atop her must have fallen asleep midway in the act, his braies pulled down to reveal a hairy arse. At the high table, the lieutenant had pillowed his head on his arms, and with the exception of d'Alspaye, the other officers were arrayed around him, one of them still clutching his cup.

Adam stepped outside again. There was a faint light leaking from one of the towers, right under the roof. The door at the base stood ajar, and when he strained his ears he could make out the dull sound of iron striking rock. Someone moved down by the inner curtain wall. Adam shrank back into the shadows, eyes never leaving the guard who was approaching slowly, sword in hand. The man came to an abrupt stop at the sight of his companions, fast asleep before the entrance to the hall.

The guard crouched beside the sleeping men and shook them. One of the men burped before rolling over on his side, still fast asleep. The guard bent over him and sniffed, muttering a series of curses. Hesitantly, he approached the hall, sword at the ready. Any moment now and he would see the tableau of heavily drugged men-at-arms, and then it was but a matter of moments before he raised the alarm, of that Adam was certain. Adam drew his dagger and approached the man. A gurgle, and the man sank lifeless into Adam's arms.

"God forgive me," he whispered as he dragged the lifeless man to the side. He had never killed someone before – not like this. He wiped his blade clean and after assuring himself there were no more sentries prowling the inner ward, he returned to the kitchen to wait.

There was the muffled sound of feet on grass, the door to the kitchen was pushed open and Lord Roger stepped inside, armed with a crowbar. The cook took one look at him, bowed and disappeared.

"Adam!" Lord Roger opened his arms wide and Adam fell into them, clutching at his lord as if he never intended to let him go. Lord Roger laughed softly. "Time for this later."

Adam released him and turned to greet Richard, as red-headed as always, but now also with a thick beard that made it difficult to recognise him. Just like Mortimer, Richard had shrunk, the bones of his hand starkly visible against his skin when he clasped Adam's hand. With a start Adam recognised Lord Roger's tunic; it was the same one he had worn at Shrewsbury, close to twenty months ago.

"The ladder?" d'Alspaye asked once he had bolted the door.

"Over there." Adam pointed to a solitary barrel. He'd hidden the contraption under a layer of flour.

"We must go," said d'Alspaye. "For all that most of them lie in drunken stupor, someone will raise the alarm. It is but a matter of time." He led the way to the chimney and pointed upwards. "Up on the roof – and don't forget the ladder."

D'Alspaye went first, grunting with effort as he heaved himself upward, one foothold after the other. Lord Roger came next, with Richard at his heels, and last of all came Adam, the tightly coiled rope ladder slung over his shoulder. The walls of the chimney were uncomfortably warm to begin with, and difficult to scale. As the chute narrowed, progress could only be made by bracing your back against one side, placing your feet on the opposite side and levering yourself upwards. Halfway up, Adam's foot began to protest. Placing pressure on his damaged foot almost caused him to faint, but there was no alternative – beyond letting go and tumbling to a certain death. By the time he reached the roof, Adam was covered in sweat, the muscles in his right leg trembling uncontrollably.

"What ails you?" Lord Roger whispered, steadying Adam.

"My foot." He gritted his teeth.

"Your foot?"

"Long story," Adam said. "Best save it for later."

"Will you be able to climb over the wall?" d'Alspaye asked.

"If I don't, chances are Despenser will drive a stake through my other foot as well," Adam replied. "So yes, I will."

"A stake?" Lord Roger sounded disgusted. D'Alspaye was already on the move, balancing his way over the roofs. Richard followed suit, with Adam and Lord Roger bringing up the rear. Now and then, Lord Roger's arm would shoot out to offer support, and Adam was in far too much discomfort to pretend he didn't need it.

They reached the wall and huddled down beside it as

d'Alspaye unwound a length of rope from his middle, securing it to an iron ring before he let it drop over the edge. Still no sounds, no bells raising the alarm. From the inner ward came a female voice raised in drunken song, but it subsided into a hiccup. They remained where they were, listening intently. Nothing. D'Alspaye leaned over to look down the wall and beckoned Richard forward.

"Me?" Richard asked, sounding disenchanted.

"You're the lightest. If the rope doesn't hold for you, well then…" D'Alspaye shrugged.

Lord Roger chuckled. "He's having you on," he told his squire. "You go first because you're by far the nimblest."

Richard took hold of the rope and slid over the edge. The rope tautened. A couple of heartbeats later there was a soft call, and Lord Roger disappeared over the edge. Adam, then d'Alspaye, and moments later all four of them were crouched along the outer wall, pressing themselves into the shadow as a couple of guards walked by, discussing loudly as to the merits of the king's new greyhounds.

Once they were safely out of sight, Adam attached grapple hooks to the rope ladder, stood back and threw it upwards. The resulting rattle made him wince, hand on his dagger, but no one came running to investigate, and he relaxed. Instead, he tugged hard, several times, hearing the hooks screech as they caught in the parapet high above. This time Adam went first, and halfway up, one of the hooks came undone, leaving him dangling. There were some moments of absolute fear when it seemed the other hook would give as well, and from the ground came a series of loud hisses. Adam gulped in air. The rope ladder stopped swinging, and hand over hand he managed to pull himself up.

He secured the ladder and whistled, once. Lord Roger came up first, looking markedly affected by the time he reached the top. Richard, d'Alspaye and Adam pulled up the ladder and dropped it down the outer side. Minutes later they landed in the marshy ground on the river side of the wall. Adam sank to his knees, noting that his hands were trembling uncontrollably. The first part of the plan was concluded. The hawk had flown, and so far the master of the mews had not noticed.

The boat took a long time coming. Four men sitting as silent as statues on the muddy shore, four pairs of eyes scanning the broad expanse of the river for the promised barge, and at one point Adam suggested swimming across instead, but d'Alspaye shook his head; the current was far too strong, they'd drown like rats. Just when Adam was beginning to give up hope, the boat appeared, gliding silently towards them. He recognised the outline of his brother in the prow, and was ridiculously happy to clasp William's hand as he was helped aboard. And still, the night remained silent, the Tower sunk into a drugged sleep so deep no one had as yet discovered Mortimer was gone.

"God is with us," William murmured when Adam said as much.

"God is always with me," Lord Roger murmured back, scratching at his heavy beard.

Four men-at-arms were waiting when they reached Greenwich, one of them Egard. Lord Roger greeted the men, nodded his approval at the horses and mounted.

"No time to waste," he said, clapping his heels to his horse. His men fell in behind him, and as the August night shifted into dawn, Roger Mortimer left London behind in leaps and bounds – and still there was no sound of pursuit.

They rode until the sun stood high in the sky, and then they turned off the road and rode through the bordering woods, heading towards Portchester. Mortimer refused to stop, and all through that day and half the night they pushed on, until Adam told Lord Roger they had to rest – or kill the horses.

The men collapsed into heaps the moment they set foot on the ground. Richard could scarcely walk, so saddle-sore that he complained his inner thighs were chafed skinless. D'Alspaye insisted on taking the first watch, leaving Adam to sit with Lord Roger, who showed no inclination to sleep.

"I'll sleep once I'm in France," he said, when Adam suggested he should rest. "Until then, I stay awake." He drank deeply from the water skin and lay down, hands under his head. "Almost two years under lock and key," he said softly.

"Two years without seeing the sky or the sun." He turned his head to look at Adam. "And you? How did you fare?"

Adam shrugged. "Not as bad as some of the others. At least I kept my head."

Mortimer cursed. "So many good men dead, and all because of that accursed rabid dog the king keeps as his preferred pet." He sat up. "What exactly did he do to you?"

"The king?" Adam prevaricated, not sure he wanted to tell Lord Roger everything.

"Despenser," Lord Roger said, picking up a twig and stabbing at the ground.

Adam rested his head on his knees and regarded Lord Roger from under his hair. "He did no more to me than he does to others, my lord."

"What he did to you was what he wanted to do to me."

Adam laughed mirthlessly. "Despenser doesn't want to drive a stake through your foot, my lord. He wants to drive it through your heart."

"Probably. He's missed his chance, and next time I see him the tables will be turned." Lord Roger regarded Adam seriously. "He will pay, Adam. For everything – for your foot, for the way my wife has been treated, for my ailing uncle, still behind lock and key in the Tower."

"And the king? Shouldn't he pay as well?" Adam said in an undertone.

"The king is misguided," Lord Roger replied.

"The king is a weakling," Adam scoffed.

"He is," Lord Roger agreed. "But he is our king – for now." As he said it, he clenched his hands together, snapping the twig he'd been holding.

"And now what?" Adam asked, needing to get away from the subject of the king.

"I shall go to Picardy and visit my dear cousin, Robert de Fiennes." Lord Roger grinned. "And then I shall present myself to Charles of France, and offer him my services."

"What about Lady Joan?" Adam feared Lord Roger's wife would pay dearly for her husband's escape, and from the set expression on his face, Lord Roger shared that fear.

"I can't do otherwise," he muttered. "Sooner or later, they'd have slit my throat."

"No choice," Adam agreed quietly. "I'll do what I can for your lady."

"You? I thought you'd be coming with me."

Adam shook his head. "I'll be riding north once we've rested."

"They'll come for you," Lord Roger warned.

"Maybe – maybe not." Adam rose. "I have my instructions from the queen, and if they do, I think my new lord will come to my rescue."

"Your new lord?" Lord Roger's voice was very cold. "What nonsense is this?"

"It was the queen's idea," Adam said.

"The queen?" Lord Roger sounded confused.

"I have pledged myself to Edward of Windsor," Adam explained. Moments of silence, in which Adam counted his own heartbeats.

At long last, Lord Roger laughed. "Prince Edward, hey?" He laughed again. "That woman is wilier than her father, and that is saying much." Effortlessly he got to his feet, standing very close to Adam. "Very well. I release you from my service, Adam de Guirande. May your serve your new lord with as much loyalty and bravery as you have served me."

"My lord," Adam murmured, feeling as if he'd been pushed out into the cold. Lord Roger gave him a long, hard embrace.

"I mean it, Adam. And just because you've chosen to become a nursemaid, it doesn't mean I won't be calling on your services – with your lord's approval, of course."

"A nursemaid?" Adam laughed out loud. "That would not please Prince Edward."

"I imagine not," Lord Roger said. "And now, you'd best get going. Unless you want to test the fortitude of your new master – and his mother – I suggest you come up with a very plausible tale as to why you're far away from home."

"Oh, I already have the tale, my lord. I just need the proof to go with it." Adam suppressed a tremor and glanced at his foot. It would hurt – again.

Chapter 39

Kit had been counting days since she saw Adam ride off. Very long days – never-ending, even, and it wasn't only due to Adam's absence. The harvest was in full swing, and while no one expected Kit to do more than ensure was food and drink for the labourers, this in itself resulted in very long days and an aching back.

On Lammas Day itself, Kit was a bundle of nerves, unable to participate fully in the ceremonies. Distractedly she thanked her tenant farmers for the symbolic wheat they placed at her feet, and just as distractedly she listened when John led the household in prayers of thanks for the good Lord's generous gifts. All her attention, all her thoughts, were focused on distant London, and the entire day she spent praying that things would go well – at least in the sense that Adam should escape unscathed.

She gravitated towards the lane. Every day, she'd waste hours walking up and down the hornbeam hedge, sometimes with Tom toddling beside her, a determined look to his face that reminded her of his father, but more often alone. She'd stand at the top and stare towards the east, the wind caressing her face as she scanned the depressingly empty landscape for anything resembling her man and his horse.

One day. Two. Three, four and by the fifth day after Lammas she was cracking apart with anguish. He should have been here by now, so something must have gone terribly wrong. By now, her long vigils by the lane were accompanied by equally long hours in the chapel, hours in which she knelt and stared blankly at the wall behind the altar, willing her husband to be alive and whole.

As August progressed, the heat built. Days of unbearable heat, nights where the wide-open shutters did nothing to relieve the heavy pressure of the air. Kit took to slipping away at dawn for a refreshing dip in the stream, some minutes of coolness, of silent meditation by the still pond. She repeated the procedure at noon and at sunset, and still she walked about in a breathless, fevered state, and she had no idea if it was the weather or her husband's continued absence that so affected her.

On the seventh day after Lammas, three riders came galloping down the lane. Kit's heart lurched to a terrified stop. White surcoats came charging towards her, adorned by the distinctive red, black and gold of the Despenser arms.

"He's not with them," Mabel murmured, slipping an arm round Kit's waist.

"That doesn't mean he hasn't been taken prisoner," she whispered back, before attempting to straighten her back and blank her face into a mask of calm composure.

"Your husband?" the lead knight demanded, looking her up and down with interest.

"Not here." Kit relaxed her clasped hands. Not captured, at least.

"So where is he?" the knight asked, dismounting to stand before her. He was a broad man, an inch or so shorter than her, but solid like a boulder. His cheeks were covered by dark stubble, he smelled of sweat and unwashed skin – and ale.

"Where he is is none of your business," Kit replied. "And you are?"

"I am Godfrey – loyal servant to Lord Despenser and the king." He did a quick turn, inspecting the house, the surrounding land and the cluster of outbuildings. "Good enough."

"Mine," Kit told him.

He grinned. "For now. But your husband will soon have a price on his head – and once he is caught…" The man mimed a chop to the neck.

"A price on his head?" Kit swayed, steadying herself against Mabel. "Why?"

The knight raised thick, hairy brows. "You know, Lady Katherine."

"I have no idea!" She took hold of his arm and shook it. "What is it you say my husband has done?"

"He helped the traitor Roger Mortimer escape," the knight replied. "For that he will die." A loud murmur rippled through the collected household, and here and there Kit saw wide grins, hastily suppressed when the knight scowled.

"My husband?" Kit succeeded in laughing and took a step towards the knight, forcing him to back away. "My husband is a cripple – thanks to your serpent of a master."

"So where is he?" the knight demanded.

"I don't know. My husband does not feel obliged to keep me fully aware of his plans." Kit patted herself on her back; she sounded angered rather than concerned. The knight gave her an appraising look. Kit crossed her arms over her chest and stared him down. At last, the man gave up and swung himself astride his horse.

"We'll find him."

She stood straight and silent until the horsemen dipped out of sight, and then she wheeled and ran, making for the protective shade that surrounded the little pond.

She was sitting on the ground, sorting through a basket of damsons, when Mabel joined her, sinking down slowly to sit beside her.

"At least he isn't dead," Mabel tried.

"We don't know that, do we?" Kit gave Mabel a tremulous smile. "You think he's all right?"

"I think the fact that they came here means they have no idea where Adam is – or our baron." Mabel took Kit's hand. "He might have chosen to go to France with Lord Mortimer."

"And leave me behind?" Kit couldn't keep her voice steady.

"Not out of choice, m' lady, never out of choice." Mabel squeezed her hand. Kit looked away. That wasn't much of a comfort, not at present.

That same afternoon, Adam came home. Surrounded by a group of riders, his hands tied to the pommel of his saddle, he came trotting down the lane, looking dishevelled and tired. Kit gasped, seeing at first only the Despenser arms on the surcoats of the two men riding closest to him, but her shoulders sank somewhat when she recognised the bright red martlets on the other surcoats and the lead rider. The Earl of Pembroke looked as tired as Adam did, his cheeks covered in an unkempt, grey bristle, heavy pouches under his eyes.

"What is the meaning of this?" Kit asked once the troop had drawn to a halt before her. "Why is my husband tied to his saddle like a common criminal?" She focused her attention on the earl, but out of the corner of her eye she studied Adam, noting with a lurch that his right foot was unbooted and covered in a grimy, bleeding bandage.

"He's a traitor," one of the Despenser men said. Kit glanced at him, relieved to see it wasn't that obnoxious Godfrey.

"Based on what?" She scowled at the earl.

"Mortimer has escaped—" Earl Aymer began.

"Yes, yes, we know that." Kit made a dismissive gesture. "But what does that have to do with my husband? And why does he look as if he's been beaten?"

"Not my doing," the earl assured her. "It was his two captors who did that to him." He frowned at the Despenser men.

"He tried to get away," one of the Despenser men muttered, shifting under Pembroke's hard eyes.

"Well, he would, wouldn't he?" Pembroke snarled. "You'd have strung him up by the road had I not come along."

"No we wouldn't, we were just having some sport with him. Our master wants Adam de Guirande delivered to him alive," the younger of the knights muttered. "He said he'd deal himself with Adam de Guirande, outlaw that he is." Even at this distance, Kit saw the tremor that ran through Adam at the knight's words.

"Outlaw? So today you have the writ to prove it? You didn't yesterday." Pembroke eyeballed the knight, and from the way the two Despenser men shifted in their saddles, Kit suspected they'd had their ears chewed off over the last few days.

"Are you all right?" Kit asked, turning to face her husband fully. He just nodded.

"He may not speak," Pembroke explained. "Not until we have verified his story with you."

Kit's guts tightened. His story? Her heartbeat picked up uncomfortably.

"We found him on the road from London," the older of the Despenser men said.

"Ah," Kit said.

"Why was he there?" Lord Pembroke demanded. "I know for a fact he was at the Tower the day before Mortimer escaped. So what was he doing there?"

"I don't know why he was at the Tower." She gnawed at her lip. "Maybe the queen had sent for him? After all, since his pardon, it is to her he owes his allegiance."

Pembroke gave her a slight smile. "Not anymore. These days he is pledged to Edward of Windsor."

The Despenser men exchanged wary looks. "He is?" one of them asked.

"Most certainly. Saved his life." Pembroke swayed in his saddle.

"He saved Edward of Windsor's life?" Kit's eyes found her husband's. He made a depreciating move with his head.

Pembroke nodded. "He leapt into the water after the prince and saved him from drowning." The people in the yard threw Adam admiring looks, a soft, approving murmur rustling through them. Earl Aymer frowned, stilling the assembled people into silence. "Infernal heat," he muttered, wiping at his face.

"You're welcome to enter my hall," Kit told him.

"Not yet." Pembroke shook himself. "We sort this matter first. So why was he in London to begin with?" His eyes slid towards Adam, returned to her and slid in Adam's direction again. Adam moved his injured foot, flexing it up and down.

"His foot," Kit replied, seeing a ghost of a smile on Adam's face. "He went there on account of his foot." Clearly the correct answer, at least to judge from how pleased the earl looked.

"Why?" The Despenser man sounded angry.

"Why?" Kit stalled for time. "What do you think? To chop it off?"

"So where did he go?"

"Well apparently to the Tower," Kit snapped, "but there he seems to have played the hero rather than having his foot seen to."

"So he was visiting a healer?" Pembroke asked. "Not that demented French monk at St Giles, I hope."

Kit grasped at the thrown lifeline. "How demented? He came very highly recommended, that's why Adam set off to see him. Are you saying the monk is a fraud?" She stalked towards Adam. "What did he do to your foot?" Roughly, she gripped the bloodied bandage and squeezed, hard.

Adam gasped.

"Dear Lord, he has hurt you, not healed you," Kit continued, looking down at the grimy bands of linen that were wrapped around his foot.

"It could be self-inflicted," one of the Despenser men said.

"Self-inflicted?" Pembroke laughed. "I think not. A man to cut himself wide open and sew it together on his own?" He shook his head. "It's not pretty, not at all."

"It isn't?" Kit cradled his foot in her hands.

"Well, I haven't seen it, have I?" the taller of the Despenser men said. "My master will flay me to the bone if I don't verify this story with my own eyes."

"Are you questioning my word?" Pembroke asked, riding his horse close enough to loom over the Despenser men-at-arms.

"No, my lord, of course not," the man muttered, "but our master might."

"Good." Pembroke dismounted and handed his reins to one of the stable boys "I think the matter is thereby closed. Sir Adam's tale has been corroborated by his wife."

The Despenser man closest to Adam snorted. "What is to stop him from having helped in the escape and then having his foot seen to – or sliced it up himself to make it bleed?"

"What sort of fool do you think my husband is?" Kit said. "Had he been involved in the escape, he'd have been with Lord Mortimer – or am I to take it you've captured him too?"

"No," the man retorted in a surly voice. "Mortimer has as yet not been found – but that doesn't mean your husband didn't help him, does it?"

"Have you any proof Sir Adam was involved?" Pembroke asked.

"There is no proof! Mortimer escaped across the roofs, aided by d'Alspaye and several other men, him among them!" The Despenser man pointed at Adam.

"Adam? On a roof?" Kit made a derisive sound. "Your Lord Despenser has made sure he can't do that. Have you seen him try to walk? Run?"

"Even a limping man can move at speed."

"On a steep roof? Climbing walls?" Pembroke snorted. "I think not. Did you see him?"

"No, but—"

"Did anyone see him?" Pembroke interrupted.

"No." The Despenser man sounded sullen.

"Proof, man!" Pembroke roared. "And as to his foot, what kind of a fool do you think does this to himself?" He strode over to Adam, yanking roughly at the bloodied bandage. Adam muffled an exclamation, tilting forward in the saddle. The bared foot was bruised and swollen around the original injury, and there was neat incision along one side, very crudely stitched together. To further add to the damage, the skin was badly singed and blistered, as if someone had held a heated knife blade to it. Kit pushed Pembroke to the side.

"I'm going to castrate that damned monk!" Superficial damage, she concluded, the bruising rather the result of having pummelled the foot with a large stone, and as to the cut, it had bled a lot and needed to be cleansed, but it was shallow, the stitches for show, no more. The burns, however…Honey, Kit decided, and comfrey and peppermint oil.

The Despenser men stared at Adam's foot. The younger looked quite uncomfortable. "How can you even walk on that?" he said, eyeing Adam with some admiration.

"He can't," Kit lied. "That's why your dear lord staked it to begin with – to cripple him for life."

Adam scowled at her, clearly not pleased at being labelled a cripple.

"He staked it?" The older Despenser man swallowed, his Adam's apple bobbing up and down.

"You said he was a traitor," his young companion said, "but he told us he was serving the prince, and you just wouldn't listen. Edward of Windsor won't be pleased to hear this."

"Edward of Windsor? He's but a lad!" the other Despenser man hissed.

"For now," Pembroke voiced coldly. "But one day he will be your king." He jerked his head in the direction of the lane. "Your business here is done. I suggest you focus your effort on finding the true traitors instead of badgering an ailing man." When the Despenser men made no move to depart, Earl Aymer approached them. "Didn't you hear me? Off with you!"

"He's our prisoner," the elder protested. "Our lord will expect us to bring him back." He shifted in his saddle. "He'll have our hides if we return without him."

Pembroke clicked his fingers, and six swords were pulled, all of them pointing at the encircled Despenser men. "Leave," Pembroke said. "Now. I vouch for Adam de Guirande – on my honour as a knight."

"It was fortunate we came upon you," Pembroke said much later, reclining in his chair. He chuckled and winked. "Most propitious, that we should find you just where the queen thought you might be." He was in clean clothes, as was Adam, who was back to wearing boots on both feet. The foot had been cleaned and re-bandaged, with Adam admitting to Kit that the damage was most definitely self-inflicted.

"Very." Adam smiled at Kit, who was sitting as close to him as she could. "I still don't understand why they set upon me." He rested his hand on her shoulder, fingers caressing her bared nape.

"Don't give me that!" Pembroke drained his goblet and set it down with a thud on the table. "I'm not going to ask, but we both know you were involved." When Adam made as if to say something, Earl Aymer held up his hand. "Don't. I know nothing more beyond seeing a knight I trust –and in the service of our prince – being harassed by men-at-arms, this despite his ailing state." A smile flickered over his heavy features. "See it as a final repayment of the debt of honour I owe Roger Mortimer. I hope he is safe away, and by God do I hope he stays away – at least until I am dead and at rest in my grave." He gnawed his lip. "Because the day he returns, this poor realm of ours will yet again be torn asunder by war and strife."

"If he returns," Kit said. If she were Mortimer, she'd stay well away.

"If?" Adam raised his brows. "There is no if."

"No if," Pembroke echoed, sounding sad.

Pembroke stayed the night, this time commandeering the solar for his use. Kit couldn't very well protest, not when the earl had brought her husband home, and so she spent the night on a pallet on the women's side of the hall, while Adam bedded down with the men. They'd had little opportunity to talk, with far too many people hovering around them, and besides, Adam was so tired he blinked his way through supper – him and the earl both. But from what Kit gathered, it had been the queen who had ordered the earl to ride out and find Adam, explaining that she feared for his life at the hands of Despenser, and so the man had spent as many days as Adam in the saddle, stopping only to snatch a couple of hours of rest.

"Why does the queen care?" Kit asked Mabel as she punched her thin pillow into shape. Adam had explained that nothing had been left to chance: there'd been a carefully planned route, along which he knew Pembroke would come riding, following the queen's instruction. Fortunately, Pembroke had come in time to stop those two Despenser men from dragging Adam off, something which Kit intended to thank God for, over and over again.

"Why shouldn't she care?" Mabel threw Kit a distracted look, before reverting to crooning Tom to sleep. Kit brushed at her son's heavy fair hair, so like his father's. All evening, Tom had clung to Adam's leg – or sat in his lap – as reluctant as Kit to let him go.

"He's just a knight," Kit replied.

"Just a knight?" Mabel chortled. "Look at him, m' lady. A woman would have to be made of marble to dismiss Lord Adam as being just a knight."

"Hmm." That didn't make Kit any more inclined to like the queen. She regarded her husband, fast asleep on his back with his mouth slightly open. In only his shirt, one bare leg pulled up, the other entangled in his blanket, he looked vulnerable – and desirable, the golden hair on his limbs shimmering in the light of the fire. Mabel chuckled and elbowed Kit a tad too hard.

"A handsome man, your husband. And precious to Lord Mortimer – which was why the queen sent the earl off after him."

"Hmm." Kit mulled this over.

"The queen is building a following of her own," Mabel said in a very low voice, keeping an eye on the Pembroke knights, sleeping some yards away. "And first among her loyal barons is Lord Mortimer." She patted Kit on her rump. "Sleep, m' lady. By tomorrow, that man of yours will be demanding your full attention."

"I hope so," Kit muttered, hiding her smile in her pillow.

Chapter 40

She woke at first light and rose from her pallet bed, gliding noiselessly among the sleeping shapes. The sentry gave her a sleepy nod and helped her push the heavy oak door open. Kit slid outside, standing for some moments in the silence of the yard. It was not, as yet, day, but the night had been hot and the air was heavy with heat. No wind, and when she looked at the sky it was as unclouded as it had been for weeks. She wandered over the yard, detoured to pat Goliath and feed him a crust of bread, before making her way over the meadows towards the glittering stream. No dew, and her skirts swished through dried grasses, picking up burrs and leaves. She was barefoot and as she walked she undid her braid, allowing her hair to billow around her.

She reached the large alder, dragged a hand along its bark as she ducked below its branches and stepped into the protected little hollow that bordered the stream, just where it widened into a pool. Kit sank down to sit, relishing the quiet. In the shrubs, the birds were already stirring, and as the sun rose above the eastern horizon, it set the landscape before her alight, while the birds broke out in concert. She slipped off her kirtle and sat in only her shift. Still too hot, and soon the shift was lying discarded on the ground while Kit piled her hair atop her head and walked slowly into the water.

The pool was too shallow for any swimming, but it was heaven to sink into the relative coolness of the water. Moments later, and she was sitting on the bank, water droplets covering her skin. The pool was a flat surface before her, dragonflies darted back and forth over the water, and now and then concentric rings signalled the presence of a fish.

Kit slid a hand down her belly, cupping the slight roundness that contained her future child. A child…She smiled, a burst of happiness rushing through her. Until now, she had not allowed herself to feel anything at all for this new life, all her emotional energy directed at maintaining some sort of normality when inside she'd been consumed by fear for her husband. But he was back, safe and sound, and he had promised he would never leave her again, and soon there'd be another child.

She yawned and stretched out on her back, her gaze lost in the dull blue of the August sky. She pillowed her head on her arms and closed her eyes, thinking she'd just lie like this for some seconds. Her breathing deepened, her lids grew heavy and with a little sound she rolled over on her side, already half-asleep.

When Adam woke, the first thing he saw was Kit's empty pallet. Mabel was already up and about, most of the pallet beds were being folded away, and from the kitchen came the smell of baking bread – for the midday meal, no doubt.

"Kit?" he asked, rubbing the sleep out of his eyes. He had slept like the dead, he reflected, and from the way the door to the solar remained firmly shut, he supposed Earl Aymer was sleeping still. The man had looked quite haggard towards the end of yesterday, those pouches under his eyes growing darker and heavier as the evening progressed.

"Out somewhere," Mabel replied.

"Out?" He decided to do without his tunic – too hot – and belted his shirt into place instead.

"Down by the stream somewhere." Mabel waved her hand vaguely. "That woman of yours has an exaggerated fondness for water." She tilted her head at him. "Did she ever tell you what she did to get access to the constable of Shrewsbury Castle?"

Adam shook his head, intrigued. Mabel made a series of disapproving sounds. "I don't think you'll like it m' lord – but you best ask her to tell you."

That increased his curiosity, and with a nod at Mabel he set out to find his wife, water creature that she apparently was.

He was stopped repeatedly on his way across the bailey, people welcoming him home with shy smiles and bows. Now and then, there was a comment as to the gladdening news that Lord Mortimer had escaped, but it sufficed that Adam set a finger to his mouth for those comments to be swallowed back.

As of now, the household of Tresaints had only one allegiance: that to Edward of Windsor, future king of England.

He strolled through the closest meadows, hailed some of the men who were busy with the sheep, and made his way towards the little stand of trees that bordered the stream a fair distance from the house. Halfway there, he was startled when old John stood up from behind a stand of wilting gorse, crossbow in hand.

"John?"

"M' lord." John sketched him a bow. "I don't like it when our lady goes down here alone, all unguarded like."

"Ah." Adam grinned at him. "Does she know you're here?"

"Her?" John chuckled. "Your wife wouldn't hear a herd of fleeing boars until they came upon her." He lowered his voice. "Any news about Egard?"

"In France, I believe," Adam replied. "Visiting family." He moved past John, frowned and did a half-turn. "You're not ogling my wife on the sly, are you?"

John's eyes sparkled. "Had I been younger I most certainly would. As it is, I am fully capable of imagining that which I can't see."

"How fortunate," Adam said drily. "I catch any man spying on my lady wife in a state of undress, and I'd be right tempted to poke their eyes out."

"Why do you think I'm standing where I am, m' lord? There's not a lad on the manor that hasn't had that selfsame warning from me."

He found her in the little glade, fast asleep in the sun. As naked as the day she was born, she lay on her side, one arm under her head, the other lying loosely along her body. He knelt beside her and kissed her shoulder, and her lips twitched into a smile. He repeated the gesture, and she stretched languidly, rolling over towards him. Her eyes were soft with sleep, and on her cheek he could see the imprint of the grasses beneath her.

"Tired?" He lay down beside her, and his arms were full of her, all warm, naked flesh.

"A bit." She kissed his throat. "I haven't been sleeping well lately."

"Nor me." He ran a light hand up and down her back. "So what is this I hear about how you gained entrance to Shrewsbury Castle?"

"Oh, that," she mumbled. She appeared disinclined to say anything more.

"Tell me." He yanked at her hair – not too hard.

"I jumped into the river," she muttered.

Adam sat up, spilling her onto the grass. "You did what?"

She gave him an annoyed look. "Not out of choice." Briefly she told him an incredible tale about William and the constable's lad, and how they'd staged her rescue of the boy. Adam stared at her. She'd risked her life! He gripped her hand, and she winced at his pressure.

"You could have died!"

"You were about to die – and they wouldn't let me see you. So I did what I had to do."

"For me." He released her hand somewhat and braided his fingers through hers, pulling her closer.

"And for me." Eyes the colour of harebells met his. He brushed her hair back and kissed her softly on the mouth.

"For us, then."

"For us." She settled her head on his chest, hair spilled out across it. The sun blazed down on them, grasshoppers chirped, birds hopped and sang in the nearby bramble. He held her close, not needing more than her proximity – at least not yet. Kit tugged at the neckline of his shirt.

"Swim?"

"What? In the stream?" Adam chuckled. "More of a wade." But he released her, and started undressing. She wandered over to the water, sinking down to sit just beside it. The water lay like an expanse of glass, not even a ripple moving across it. When Adam stood, he could see her reflection in the glittering surface, in stark relief against the dark of the water.

Kit leaned towards her reflection, smiling down at herself. Adam stooped and picked up a pebble, flinging it to land in the centre of the pool. Concentric ripples rushed across the surface, and she turned to look at him, brows raised.

"Beware that you don't end up as Narcissus." He gave her

a small smile and stepped into the water, holding out his hand to her. She splashed him and threw herself backwards into the water, squealing like a small girl when he came after her. Cool, slippery skin, wet hair that stuck to her face and her neck. She resembled a mermaid – until she stood, revealing her bottom and long, shapely legs. Adam pounced, swept her up into his arms and carried her back to the grassy, sun-drenched glade.

"We've never bedded with each other like this," she said breathlessly. Her hands rested on his head, back arched as she raised her hips towards him. Adam rubbed his cheeks against the silken skin of her inner thigh.

"Yes we have," he replied, between kissing her in a way that made her squirm, her fingers tightening their hold on his hair. "In the moonlight. Some months back."

"But never in the sunlight." She sounded distracted.

"No, never in the sun – about time, don't you think?" He kissed his way up her front, her neck, all the way to her mouth.

"Won't they see?" she asked, half-rising on an elbow.

"They'll guess. Do you care?" He pushed her back down, his mouth covering hers. She opened to him, all of her she offered him, legs wide, mouth welcoming.

"Care?" Her arms tightened round his back, a leg hooked over his, and she exhaled, lifting her hips to meet his. "No..." Her voice drifted off, and she clung to him, eyes open windows to her soul as he loved her until she cried out, her body quivering in his arms.

Once his pulse had quieted, he pulled out and lay beside her, enveloping as much of her as he could with his legs and arms while he told her just how much he loved her. It made her laugh; it made her cry. It made her touch him and caress him; it made her kiss him until everything came together into a roaring river of heat. He took her again, this wild and voracious woman of his.

They walked back through the orchard, holding hands.

"And now what?" she asked, breaking the silence.

"Hmm?" he prevaricated, although he knew well enough what she was referring to.

"What happens next? Mortimer is safe in France but what about us, you?" She shivered despite the heat. "If Despenser—"

"He won't." Adam inspected one of the apple trees. "I am Edward of Windsor's man now."

"And what exactly does that mean?"

"For now, nothing. But the queen will call on me on behalf of her son – soon. That is the price for her protection." He fixed his gaze to the south, thinking that Lord Roger had no intention of remaining forever in exile. A formidable coalition, the queen and Lord Roger, and from what he had gathered from Lord Roger, the queen was tired of being relegated to the background by Despenser.

"Oh." Kit sounded displeased – and afraid.

"Edward of Windsor is destined to be a great king." He slipped an arm round her waist and drew her close, adjusting his stride to hers. "It will not hurt to be one of his men."

"You said you'd never leave me again."

"I won't. When the queen demands my presence, she gets yours as well." He smiled down at her. "We will grace Edward's household together – or not at all."

On the morning of her second wedding anniversary, Kit woke to the demanding sounds of shutters being thrown open. With a groan she turned on her side, regarding Mabel who was bustling about. Adam's half of the bed was empty, and Tom's pallet was a mess of rumpled bedding. From outside came the sound of her son, his high, fluting voice carrying over his father's low laughter.

She yawned and stretched, one hand bumping against the closest of the bedposts. She found her shift, a crumpled thing at the foot of the bed, and drew it over her head, struggling for some moments before she found the right openings. She stretched again and smiled. Two years since she'd wed Adam de Guirande, two years she'd never have experienced if it hadn't been for the machinations of Lady Cecily. The thought brought her up short. She hadn't thought about her purported mother in months, and doing so was the equivalent of stepping into a cold and brooding shadow. Kit crossed herself and muttered a prayer.

"What was that for?" Mabel asked, dark eyes studying her intently.

"Warding off evil spirits," she replied, trying to laugh.

"Ah, Lady Cecily." Mabel grimaced. "Well, she is far away in Bordeaux, and I dare say she has other things to concern herself with, primarily how to celebrate the return of her eldest son."

"For now."

"For now." Mabel briefly touched Kit's cheek. "I did not want her dead, but you make a better Katherine de Monmouth than our Kate ever did, misguided imp that she was." She grinned. "I dare say your lord husband agrees." With that she was off, arms laden with linen. Kit smiled after her, thinking that was the highest praise she would ever get from Mabel.

Kit rose and wandered over to the window. On the sloping meadow before her, Adam was playing with their son, two fair heads close together. He saw her, and lifted Tom into the air.

"Look, Tom, there's Mama."

Kit leaned as far out as she could, waving. Tom beamed, raised a podgy little hand, but was distracted by the sudden appearance of one of the cats. Adam set him down.

"That's how interesting I am," Kit laughed.

Adam took a step closer. "To him, not to me."

"Why thank you. I do hope you find me more interesting than the cat!"

"Much more." He grinned up at her.

I love you, she mouthed, extending her hand with her fingers splayed towards him.

In reply, he set his hand to his heart and bowed.

Adam went back to their son, from the nearby meadows came the bleating of a sheep, and in the orchard Mall was overseeing the picking of the apples. Someone was singing, a dog barked, and Kit leaned her chin on her hands and smiled. Her little corner of the world – a placid place, humming with peace and contentment.

Kit lifted her eyes to the horizon. The hitherto blue sky to the west was fast disappearing in a bank of storm clouds, almost black with contained energy. She shivered, struck by premonition. Peace would not last, she thought – it was not over yet. Her gaze flew to her husband, and her stomach knotted in fear. Roger Mortimer would be back to reclaim what was rightfully his, and with him would come the full force of an unleashed storm – and a call to arms Adam could not ignore.

God help them then, Kit thought, God help the entire realm when Roger Mortimer and the king clashed next. She clasped her hands together in fervent prayer. Not yet. Dearest Father in Heaven, not yet.

Historical Note

While Adam de Guirande and his wife Kit are fictional beings, the political events depicted in this novel are not. Roger Mortimer did rise in rebellion late in 1321, he was forced to a humiliating submission in January of 1322, and yes, he did escape from the Tower on the 1 of August 1323. He also had a squire called Richard de Monmouth, a man I have taken the liberty of giving quite the colourful (and entirely invented) family.

To fully understand Mortimer's motivations, one must take a step back and study the somewhat chaotic situation in England at the time. Edward II may have been a good man, but he was a catastrophe as a king, with a tendency to rely heavily on favourites rather than on his council – or his barons. At the time of Mortimer's rebellion, the favourite in question was Hugh Despenser, married to the king's niece and an avowed enemy of the Mortimer family.

Despenser was a greedy man – for wealth, for power. In this, he did not differ much from Roger Mortimer, but in his position as the king's favourite, Hugh could help himself to what he wanted, certain the king would always side with him. England's barons grew increasingly unhappy. In the north, the king's first cousin, Thomas of Lancaster, smouldered. In the southwest, the Marcher lords grew restless.

By early 1321 the situation had become untenable. Mortimer and Lancaster formed an alliance, and over a couple of weeks they rode roughshod over Despenser land, finally coercing the king into exiling his favourite and his father, yet another Hugh Despenser.

The king, needless to say, was not happy. In what was a most uncharacteristic bout of determined leadership, Edward turned the tables on his rebellious barons, and when Lancaster retreated to the safety of the north, Mortimer was left to face the king alone, the previously so vociferous barons melting away like snow on a sunny spring day.

Mortimer had no reason to trust the king. The treatment of the garrison at Leeds Castle, coupled with how easily the king broke his given oaths did not inspire any admiration. But as 1321 came to an end, it was apparent Mortimer could not win, and so the Earl of Pembroke was dispatched to attempt to broker some sort of truce.

Whether or not Aymer de Valence, Earl of Pembroke, did pledge his word to Mortimer, promising him that his life would be spared, is open to debate. Personally, I don't believe Mortimer would have gone anywhere near Shrewsbury on that fateful January day unless he had some guarantees as to his own safety. Guarantees, as it turned out, that were totally worthless.

And as to Mortimer and Queen Isabella – well, this will be the subject of the coming books in the series. Were they already a couple in 1321? I don't think so. Were they attracted to each other? Most definitely – an attraction that was to blossom into one of the more remarkable love stories of their time. But that, as they say, is a story for another day – or rather for the next book in the series, *Days of Sun and Glory.*

For a somewhat more extensive Historical Note, please visit www.annabelfrage.com. For those of you that want to know more – much more – about Sir Roger Mortimer, I warmly recommend *The Greatest Traitor* by Ian Mortimer, the book that to a very large extent has inspired my story.

And for those of you curious enough to want to read an excerpt from the next book – turn the page!

The King's Greatest Enemy continues in

Days of Sun and Glory

God forgive her, but Kit de Guirande had every intention of disliking Queen Isabella on sight. After months of listening to her husband's voice growing warm with adoration whenever he spoke of the queen, Kit felt entitled to hate this woman, who, apparently, was the equivalent of a heavenly angel come to earth.

She hurried after her limping husband as best as she could, too tired and confused to do more than glance at the magnificence of the royal Palace of Westminster – not that much of its splendour was visible in the flaring light of the few torches still burning in the sconces. If anything, this hasty trot in the early hours of the morning increased her resentment towards the unknown queen. Why send for them at this Godforsaken hour, why did the queen require that Sir Adam and his wife attend on her before dawn had properly broken? Kit said as much to Adam, but all she got for her trouble was a reproving look and an exasperated shake of his head.

"Better she sees us now, before anyone else is up and about," he said.

Kit rolled her eyes – discreetly. Of course, the queen had summoned Adam this early to discuss their favourite subject, that of Lord Roger Mortimer, at present in exile in France. If Kit was tired of listening to descriptions of Queen Isabella, that was nothing compared to the mental exhaustion she experienced whenever Adam spoke of his beloved Lord Mortimer.

Four months and counting since Lord Mortimer's spectacular escape from the Tower, four months in which Adam had been hounded by Lord Despenser, the only thing keeping Kit's husband safe from Mortimer's mortal enemy being the fact that Adam had pledged himself to Prince Edward of Windsor, heir to the throne. Kit glanced at her man, sending a fervent prayer to God that He would continue protecting him, keeping him far away from Despenser's grasping hands. She repeated this prayer on a daily basis, and had done so ever since Lord Mortimer fled for France.

As per Lord Despenser, royal chancellor and de facto ruler of England – what with King Edward giving his favourite anything his favourite desired – Adam was a traitor. Despenser insisted that Adam had helped Lord Mortimer escape, which was true, but fortunately there was no proof, and Despenser's attempts to have Adam arrested and turned over into his own tender care for further interrogation had been foiled, twice by the Earl of Pembroke and once by the queen herself. And thank the Lord for that: Kit had no illusions as to how her husband would fare in Despenser's hands.

Ever since Roger Mortimer's escape, the kingdom of England had sunk into a state of terror. The king – and Lord Despenser – lashed out viciously against anyone potentially involved in Mortimer's escape, and over the last few months countless men had been dragged before assizes, attainted and gruesomely executed, based on the fact that they had once served Roger Mortimer. Rotting corpses adorned gibbets all over the southwest of the country, and destitute widows and orphans were evicted from their homes, left to starve and die during the approaching winter.

The king's rage spilled over onto others as well: London merchants known to be Mortimer supporters had been severely punished, and recently the Bishops of Hereford and Lincoln had been accused and found guilty of helping Mortimer. Kit shook her head: so many men whose lives were permanently impaired on behalf of Roger Mortimer. And Hugh Despenser was not done – he intended to use Mortimer's escape to rid himself of every enemy he had in England.

Kit suppressed a little shiver and threw a hasty look over her shoulder. Lord Despenser was here, in residence with the king, and even if she had so far not encountered him, she knew it was but a matter of time before she'd be confronted by his dark eyes, his wet mouth and his wandering hands. Kit clasped her hands together, remembering all too well just how violent Lord Despenser could become should he be sufficiently riled.

"Watch out!"

Kit stumbled; Adam's hand flew out, gripping her by the elbow and thereby stopping her from overbalancing down the short flight of stairs.

"Use your eyes, sweeting," he said with a little smile, sliding his hold down from her elbow to clasp her hand instead. She pressed herself against him, an affectionate gesture that had him tightening his hold on her hand, his lips brushing briefly at her brow.

They hastened on. Kit had a stitch up her side, and at one point she had to stop, clutching at her rounded belly. Her hand smoothed the cloth that covered their growing child – an inactive babe that gave her very little trouble beyond the odd pang of pain in her lower back. Adam gave her a concerned look.

"You should not have come," he said. "A woman great with child does best staying at home."

She gave him a level look. "I wanted to." Kit straightened up and hurried on.

Twice this autumn, Adam had been called to court at the behest of his lord, the young Edward of Windsor. Twice, Kit had spent her days in constant anxiety, fearing the summons was only intended to lure Adam into Despenser's waiting hands. So when the royal messenger had come riding down their lane some weeks back, demanding that Adam de Guirande attend his lord over Christmastide, Kit had insisted on coming along, no matter how great with child she might be. After all, she'd told him, he had promised her that he would never leave her behind again – a futile promise, she knew, as Adam had little say in how his life was ordered, but he had promised.

At present, she harboured certain regrets: she would have preferred spending the middle of winter at Tresaints, in the comfort of their own manor and surrounded by their loyal household. But Adam had no choice, so here they were.

"Here." The pageboy leading the way came to a halt, gesturing at a small door set discreetly into the wall.

"Very much subterfuge," Kit murmured.

"It is best that way," Adam replied, just as low, before stepping aside to allow her to enter first.

After the dark of the passage, the room Kit entered was surprisingly bright. The windows that gave to the east were unshuttered and set with precious glass, allowing the soft light of the impending dawn to spill into the room. There were lit candles everywhere, the fire in the hearth had recently been rekindled into crackling life, and standing in the centre of the room was the queen herself.

She was just as beautiful as people said she was. A spurt of dark green jealousy surged through Kit as she took in the elegant figure of the queen, dressed in silk that shimmered somewhere in between lavender and pink. In the privacy of her chambers, the queen's hair had been left to float loose around her head, soft, dark curls caressing the white skin of her neck. A veil so sheer it was ludicrous was held in place by a circlet of sweet water pearls, and beneath elegant brows eyes as green as emeralds regarded Kit with mild curiosity, a smile tugging at her perfect mouth.

The queen moved towards them, all elegant, willowy grace – a far cry from Kit's rounded state. Kit placed a hand on her belly and dipped into a reverence, dropping her eyes to the floor.

"Rise," the queen said. Even her voice was perfect, melodious and low. With Adam's support, Kit straightened up. "Here." The queen gestured at the window seat. "Please sit, Lady de Guirande. That child of yours seems heavy." She smiled at Adam. "Big men make big children, do they not?"

To Kit's annoyance, Adam gave the queen a brilliant smile, for all the world looking like a lovesick whelp, before raising her hand to his mouth and placing a reverential kiss on it. Kit frowned and concentrated her attention on her girdle. The queen laughed.

"Contrary to what people may say, I am not in the habit of consuming handsome men for breakfast."

Kit cheeks heated with a mortified blush.

"In fact," the queen continued, "I stay clear of all men, so your husband's virtue is safe with me, Lady de Guirande."

"My lady," Adam said, shaking his head. "My wife would never—"

"Wouldn't she?" the queen interrupted.

Adam turned to look at Kit, who did her best to avoid his eyes.

"Kit," he groaned, "how can you think—"

"Think what? That you hold our queen in much affection?" Kit almost bit her tongue off. Now why would she be so foolish as to say that out loud? Adam gave her a mortified look.

The queen laughed again. "You are quite the dim-witted creature, aren't you?"

Queen or not, that remark had Kit considering raking her nails over Queen Isabella's complacent face.

"I am not...my lady," Kit replied.

"No? And yet you don't see what I see? It has been made abundantly clear to me, Lady Katherine, that as far as your husband is concerned there is only one sun in his sky, and that sun is his beloved wife."

Kit looked at her husband, who had gone an interesting hue of bright pink. "He said that?"

"More or less," the queen said. "Maybe not quite as poetically, but I am right, am I not, Sir Adam?"

In reply, Adam set his hand to Kit's face, his thumb stroking gently over the ugly scar that marred her left cheek, courtesy of a far-too-close encounter with Lord Despenser some eighteen months ago. "Yes, my lady queen. This is my sun, my moon – my everything."

Kit's vision blurred. She leaned into his touch, covering his hand with her own. He had never said anything like that in front of other people before. Her Adam preferred his declarations of love to be in private – and in bed. Kit drew in a shaky breath and decided that Queen Isabella deserved a second chance.

"And now to the matters at hand," the queen said, her voice brisk. She clapped her hands, and a maid brought in spiced wine, lacing the air with the distinctive scents of nutmeg and cloves. More clapped hands, and a page appeared with miniature wafers, bread and cheese, before scurrying off to leave them alone.

Kit settled back in the window seat, a goblet of wine in her hand, and took in her surroundings. The room was not only bathed in light, it was also ablaze with brilliant colour, from the royal blue walls with miniature fleur-de-lis strewn over them, to the bedstead painted white and red, with gold inlays. The floorboards were covered by Turkish carpets, little squares of crimson and blue that Kit would never dream setting a foot upon, so beautiful were they. Adam came to sit beside her, while the queen paced like a caged leopard as she spoke.

"I'm under constant surveillance," she said. "Despenser weaves his web of whispered half-truths tighter round my husband's head and heart, and with every day, my lord king distances himself from me, regarding me as a roe deer would a wolf." She laughed harshly. "Despenser insists I was involved in Lord Mortimer's escape, and I dare say my husband is inclined to believe him."

Given that the queen *had* been involved – albeit indirectly – Kit could not dredge up much indignation on her behalf. But as Queen Isabella went on with her descriptions of how her life was being curtailed, Kit felt a twinge of pity – and fear – on behalf of this magnificent woman who was more or less held a prisoner in her own court.

"And this situation in Gascony doesn't help," the queen finished. "I dare say the king holds me personally responsible for every reprehensible act a Frenchman may commit, starting with the actions of my dear, royal brother." She grimaced. "Charles will never back down regarding Gascony, and Edward is as stubborn as my brother, so God alone knows how this will end." She broke off, muttered a prayer, and crossed herself.

"But my lady, this may work in your favour," Adam said, leaping to his feet to replenish the queen's empty goblet. Kit gave her husband an annoyed look. Did he need to be quite so attentive?

"How?" Queen Isabella sank down on the window seat beside Kit.

"Who is better placed than you to negotiate a truce?" Adam said.

The queen sipped at her wine. "Maybe you're right," she said after some moments of silence. "I could write to Charles and—"

The door banged open and the room was filled with ladies in wimples and veils, surcoats of embroidered silk and velvet, and girdles that glittered with jewels and gold thread. Kit retreated into her corner and fiddled with the sheer length of silk that covered her head, fully aware of just how visible her braided hair was.

"What is the meaning of this?" The tallest of the ladies addressed the queen sharply. A sequence of unicorns embroidered in gold and silver pranced along the hem of her light-blue surcoat, her kirtle a darker shade of blue.

"The meaning of what?" Queen Isabella rose, her chin lifted demandingly as she stared down the ladies, standing as immobile as a statue until they all sank down into deep reverences.

"My queen," the first lady mumbled.

"And good morning to you too, Lady Eleanor," the queen replied.

Kit studied the lady with increased curiosity. So this was the famous Eleanor de Clare, niece to the king and Hugh Despenser's wife. Eleanor straightened up and glanced at Kit. Sharp blue eyes assessed and discarded her as uninteresting before darting over to Adam, where they lingered for substantially longer.

Adam bowed, and Lady Eleanor inclined her head and rounded on the queen.

"This is not seemly, my lady," she scolded. "A man in your chambers!" From under Lady Eleanor's loosely draped veil peeked a strand of red-gold hair, and for all that she had given that serpent Despenser numerous children, she still retained a slim figure, adequately curved over her hips and bosom. All in all, Eleanor de Clare was an attractive woman – maybe not as beautiful as the queen, but still.

"With his wife," the queen retorted. "And what is it to you, Lady Eleanor? Are you perchance my gaoler, put in place to restrict access to my person?"

The lady flushed. "Your gaoler? Of course not, my lady. But I am—"

"My chief lady-in-waiting," the queen interrupted. "Chosen for me by my husband, not by me." Yet again, she gave Eleanor a mild smile, while her eyes shot darts. "And as my lady-in-waiting, you should do precisely that: wait on me. Not interrupt my discussions with my visitors, nor eavesdrop outside my door, or attempt to coerce my pages and maids to spy on me."

Lady Eleanor looked as if she wanted the floor to swallow her whole.

"So," the queen continued, "as I do not require your services at present, I suggest that you retire to my solar and wait for me. I am sure there is some sewing you can do to keep yourself occupied."

She raised her brows, crossed her arms over her chest and waited until the women had left the room before sweeping her arm over the table, sending the pitcher and the goblets to fly through the air, landing with loud clatters on the floor. "She used to be my friend and now she is my guard dog. I hate that woman!"

"As I hate her husband," Adam muttered.

Amen to that, Kit thought, suppressing yet another shiver.

About the Author

When Anna is not stuck in the 14th century, chances are she'll be visiting in the 17th century, more specifically with Alex and Matthew Graham, the protagonists of the best-selling, multiple award winning, series The Graham Saga. This series is the story of two people who should never have met – not when she was born three centuries after him. A fast-paced blend of love, drama and adventure, The Graham Saga will carry you from Scotland to the New World and back again.

For more information about Anna and her books, please visit www.annabelfrage.com or pop by her blog https://annabelfrage.wordpress.com

CPSIA information can be obtained
at www.ICGtesting.com
Printed in the USA
LVHW041246090522
718253LV00002B/322